BALAM, SPRING

travis m. riddle

Publisher's Note: This is a work of fiction. Names, characters, places, and incidents are a product of the author's imagination. Locales and public names are sometimes used for atmospheric purposes. Any resemblance to actual people, living or dead, or to businesses, companies, events, institutions, or locales is completely coincidental.

Cover illustration by Amir Zand – amirzandartist.com
Author photo by Jawn Rocha – jawnrocha.com
Book Layout © 2014 BookDesignTemplates.com

Balam, Spring/Travis M. Riddle. -- 1st ed.
ISBN: 978-1984949806

balam, spring

also by travis m. riddle

Wondrous

For _____
(n*am*e [*y*ours])

Now that the treatment and antidepressants
And seven months sober have built me a bed
In the back of your brain where the memories flicker
And I paw at the synapses, bright bits of string
You should know I am with you, know I forgive you
Know I am proud of the steps that you've made
Know it will never be easy or simple
Know I will dig in my claws when you stray
So let us rest here like we used to
In a line of late afternoon sun
Let it rest, all you can't change
Let it rest and be done

John K. Samson, *Virtute at Rest*

TABLE OF CONTENTS

CHAPTER I

NIGHT AIR

Theodore Saen sat in his empty classroom, staring at the pile of ungraded tests that plagued his desk. At the top of the stack was Harley Sheere's test—which he highly suspected she had failed, despite having tutored her for the past two weeks. Hers being the first test he saw didn't fill him with much confidence or motivation, so instead of grading, he stood up and left.

Yesterday had been the last day of school. Final tests had been taken, spring had now arrived, and the students were out enjoying the light breeze and fresh air. Theo would be too, soon enough, once he pushed through what was always the worst night of the year. Anxiety bubbled beneath the surface of his skin, squirming around like termites in a log.

Outside, sitting cross-legged in the grass with his back against a tree about ten feet from the entrance of the school, Theo found Alfred Opping smoking from a thick, curved pipe. It looked to be made of some type of iridescent gemstone— amber, maybe. Or perhaps it was keena, a specialty of the nearby city of Brigher. Though "nearby" was a relative term, considering the city was at least two full days' travel from Balam.

"Hey there," Al greeted Theo as he approached. "How goes the grading?"

Al Opping was one of the few bachelors left in a town full of families, and it was hard to deny how handsome he was. He always wore freshly-pressed suits and somehow had the perfect amount of stubble every single day, without fail. His hair was short, but it was thick and neatly coifed. His green eyes made the girls at school swoon, as well as the few single women that lived in Brigher, where he often made weekend trips.

Theo returned the greeting and said, "About as well as yours seems to be going. What kind of pipe is that, by the way?"

Al grinned. He loved being asked about his pipe. About all of his trinkets, really. He took great pride in his possessions. "Only the finest keena, straight from Brigher," he said, blowing out a few mildly impressive smoke rings. "Well, probably not the *finest*. The finest available, salary permitting." He chuckled, as did Theo.

As Al put the pipe to his lips again, Theo asked, "You doing anything tonight?"

"Trying to drink away my memories of Lukas Vere. Kid's a nightmare. You got off lucky this year, man."

Theo had to agree. While he'd had his share of students like Harley Sheere who couldn't write a rhetorical essay to save her life, he'd also had the pleasure of teaching Olivia Nells, possibly the smartest kid he'd encountered during his four years as a teacher. Olivia had aced every test she faced this year, and Theo was sure she'd done the same in all of her other classes. Some kids were just smart, and Olivia was one of those kids.

"But nah, not anything special," Al went on. "Just a little trip to the pub. I think Serys is gonna come too. You can join, if you want."

Theo shook his head. "Thanks, but no. I'm gonna be spending the night at home," he said. "Lyrra is cooking my favorite tonight. She'll want to just spend the evening together, I imagine."

While what he said was partially true, Theo's wife probably would not have cared if he'd gone out to get drinks with his co-workers after dinner. But the truth was that Theo did not care for Serys White in the least. Serys was what one would describe as a truly large man in every sense, one who walked with a lot of heft in his step and spoke in a booming voice that sounded more akin to a cannon being fired than a schoolteacher speaking. His round face was adorned with a bushy blonde mustache to contrast his bald, flat head. He always spoke to Theo in a patronizing tone, likely because he had been working at the school for nearly thirty years more. But even with four years of experience under Theo's belt, Serys still saw him as a newcomer and treated him as such.

In short, Theo had no intention of seeing the man for the duration of the off-season. It would be close to impossible in such a small town as Balam, but he would damn well try.

And besides, he had other plans that night. Something written in the agenda long ago. Immovable.

"That's a shame," Al sighed, letting out more smoke. "Woulda been fun. We'll have to do it soon, though."

"Agreed," Theo said, and he meant it. He detested Serys White, but Al had been a good friend to him since he'd moved to Balam, and if nothing else, the man was always good for a laugh.

"Anyway," Al grunted, pushing himself up off the ground, "I'd better get back to it. Gotta get all this shit taken care of if I wanna go out tonight." He held his pipe upside down and tapped its underside, knocking loose any remnants that might still be within, before stuffing it into his coat pocket. "You comin' in?" Al gestured toward the front doors of the school.

"Not yet," Theo said. "I think I'll go for a walk first. Get the joints loosened up, really get my fingers ready to hold that pen." The two shared a laugh then said their goodbyes.

Theo walked eastward, toward the center of town as well as the direction of his home. He wasn't planning on going back already—he'd only left not even an hour before, and Lyrra was probably still asleep anyway—but he always enjoyed taking a walk on the first morning of spring after he got his things settled.

He decided it would be a good idea to grab a cup of coffee to help him power through the grading. He needed a boost if he was going to tackle Harley Sheere's disappointment of a test. A small part of him clung to some shred of hope that the tutoring had done its duty and gotten through her head, but at a certain point, there was only so much he could do.

He took a right at the first intersection and continued down the stone pathway that connected the entire town. There were no street signs to indicate what little avenue one was on; it was such a small village, Main Street could be seen from practically anywhere (though there was no sign officially naming it Main Street, that was how everybody thought of it), and it was impossible to be lost for too long.

At the next intersection, if he turned left, he would pass the white mage's hut. Balam's white mage was a kind jeornish woman named Freya. Theo had met her a few times at town social events, but he rarely got sick, so he never had any occasion to visit her in the domed hut that doubled as her home and office.

But he continued on down the road and soon came to yet another intersection. This time he did turn left, and shortly he reached his destination: the Sonata Diner.

According to other townsfolk, the diner was one of Balam's defining establishments, dating back as far as the town's inception. It was founded by a husband and wife named Ellis and Marjorie Vere, who also helped build the town as well as the farmland on its western side. The farm grew the crops and livestock that were then used to feed hungry denizens at the diner, and it was a pretty good situation for the Vere family. Eventually, one lazy ancestor, a man named Freddie Vere who spent his nights drinking and scolding his wife, sold off the farmland after growing tired of tending to it for so long; but he had kept the diner, and generations of Veres kept it running in memory of Ellis and Marjorie. Nowadays its owner was Walton Vere, grandson of Freddie and father of Al's unfortunate student Lukas.

Theo entered the Sonata Diner and was greeted with a cheery "Hullo, Mr. Saen!" by Missy Reen, a former student of his. She had graduated the year before and was working at the diner now, saving her money until she could afford to attend school in Din's Keep. Even a year after graduating, she had not quite dropped the habit of addressing Theo as Mr. Saen.

Theo returned her hello and seated himself at the counter. The diner was none too lively at this time of day; some were still in bed, but many were working their own jobs. He felt lucky having the time to come relax and have a cup of coffee before having to delve into any real work for the day.

"Walton in yet?" he asked Missy, watching her fill an elderly woman's coffee cup. The woman thanked her before returning her attention to the book she was reading.

"Not yet," Missy answered, coming to the counter. "Just me and the cooks for now."

"That's too bad," said Theo. "His coffee's way better than yours," he teased.

Missy's jaw dropped in faux shock. "Rude!" she exclaimed. "My coffee's the best this diner has ever seen! Let me pour you a cup and you'll be a convert."

"Fine, fine," Theo conceded, feigning reluctance. "I'll take it. Any sweet-rolls this morning?"

"Yup," Missy said, straining to reach behind the counter and grabbing a chipped, light blue mug. She poured the steaming hot liquid into it and pushed it toward him. "Taste that first, then I'll tell you if we've got any blueberry or not."

Theo did as he was told, but not before adding a touch of cream and sugar. He had never developed the taste for black coffee, which would have disappointed his father, were he around. Now that it was ready, he took a long sip from the mug then set it back down on the table. He gulped it down theatrically and wiped his lips with the back of his hand. "Not *bad*," he shrugged.

"Best this diner's ever seen!" Missy grinned. "We've got a couple blueberry sweet-rolls. I'll grab you one."

He thanked her, and as she went back into the kitchen to grab his food and fill up the coffee pot, he took another sip of his drink—which was admittedly pretty good, though not better than Walton's—and scanned the menu absentmindedly. By now he knew every item on there, but sometimes it was nice to just read something.

A few moments later, Missy returned with his blueberry sweet-roll resting serenely atop a small, square ceramic plate. The roll was round and only slightly browned on top, with the blueberry drizzle zig-zagging along its surface.

"Looks great," Theo said as Missy placed it on the countertop in front of him.

He picked up the sweet-roll and bit into it. It was fluffy and delicious, the perfect complement to his coffee. It was exactly what he needed before a full day of grading exams and evaluating final grades for multiple classes.

"I need this recipe," Theo smiled. "I think waking up to the smell of these baking in the kitchen might be the key to a perfect life."

"As if Walton would ever give it to you," Missy laughed. "He won't even tell me what spices he adds to the coffee grounds."

"So *that's* why yours is lacking."

"Oh, hush."

"I guess I'll just have to bribe the cooks instead. I'm sure Ben wouldn't mind slipping me the secret."

They went on talking for another half hour, pausing every couple minutes so that Missy could assist other customers who ambled in. Theo was draining the last of his second cup when he declared that he had to be going.

"Tell Walton I said hello, will you?" he asked.

"Sure thing, Mr. Saen," Missy nodded. "Wait, today's your grading day, right?" After an affirmation, she said, "Good luck with that. Don't be as hard on them as you were on me!"

Theo laughed and told her he wouldn't. He left her a nice tip and exited the Sonata Diner, taken aback by how much brighter the sun had gotten since he'd went inside just a short while ago.

It was such a beautiful day. It really was lucky that spring was their off-season, because the weather in Balam was absolutely amazing during the spring. Perfect for long walks and finding a nice spot outside to read and take in some sun.

But his mood was darkened by the memories he'd inevitably be revisiting later in the evening. He tried to brush them off, keep them at bay for a few more hours.

Well, he thought, *it wouldn't hurt to take another walk around the block first.*

- -

When he was a pup, mornings never suited Ryckert Ji'ca. He would always have to be yanked out of bed by his ra. Usually by the ankle, and usually with a harsh word or two.

But years had passed and things changed. Now Ryckert was long past being a pup and was entering what his people, the rocyans, considered old age, though in actuality he was only forty-three years old.

He certainly looked aged, though. What used to be thick, dark brown fur was now beginning to fade to gray. His eyes were sunken. Belly more plump than lean. He wasn't in bad shape, per se, but not as fit as he was in his younger years, before retirement. Before Balam.

Prior to retirement, working as a mercenary, was when Ryckert had grown accustomed to mornings. Oftentimes he had to be up before dawn, and it was hard at first, but it was part of the job. Being a mercenary meant there were times when he had to travel unseen, before anyone else had a chance to wake up and get their bearings. The job was important, so Ryckert had adjusted.

And he never grew out of it. Nowadays, he had all the time in the world to sleep in, living in his little shack on the Balam beach. But it was hardwired into him after years and years of forcing himself out of bed.

Ryckert spent his early mornings alone on the beach right outside his shack. He had a sturdy wooden chair set up beside a fire pit, which he sat in and drank coffee, watching the sun rise over the ocean's horizon. It calmed him. Centered him.

He didn't really talk to many people in town. It got lonely sometimes, but Ryckert told himself he preferred it. Which he believed, most of the time.

Being the only rocyan in town, he was easy to pick out of a crowd. Not many rocyans lived in the eastern regions of Atlua. Despite the ragged fur covering their bodies, they generally preferred the heat of the south. The coast wasn't made for them; they hated the wet. But Ryckert didn't mind it. He liked the sounds of the waves, the way the water's surface shimmered when sunlight hit. He had seen a lot of ugly things in his life, so he appreciated some prettiness in these final years.

After finishing his cup of coffee he'd go back inside, rinse it out, put it in the sink, then return outside. Go for a walk. Get a feel of the sand while it was still cool from the night, hardly yet touched by the sun.

Next was hunting. Ryckert mostly caught his meals, either in the sea or the woods. He didn't like to eat in town too often.

His ra had taught him to hunt when he was just a pup. He had learned how to use several types of weapons: spears, daggers, swords, firearms. Whatever it took to get the job done. It didn't take long for Ryckert to become proficient with all of them. By the time he was twelve, he was nearly as skilled at tracking and killing animals as his ra.

On one particularly memorable hunt, Jin De'ca led his son into the forest, armed with a single dagger, and told him not to return until he obtained dinner for the family. It was Ryckert's eleventh birthday, and not exactly how he'd planned to spend the day. It was his first solo hunt.

"What should I bring?" he'd asked.

"Up to you," said his ra. "Lots of animals in these woods. Lots for you to kill, but also lots that can kill *you*. Be sharp as your blade."

"Yes, ra."

"Now hunt."

Young Ryckert shot off like a dart. Twigs snapped beneath his feet. Wind whipped his face. Thoughts flooded his mind. He sniffed at the air, caught a whiff of something. A poros, he suspected. They were plentiful where he grew up, in the village of Uruh. But not enough to feed the whole family, unless he caught and killed at least a dozen of the creatures. Would that impress his ra? He thought not.

Not a poros, then. Something bigger. Meaner. More dangerous. *More dangerous the better*, he thought. Something meaty. Fierce.

A ziolo.

It was perfect. Ziolos were enormous beasts, half as tall as a full-grown rocyan but three times as wide. Their bodies were thick, with sharp spikes jutting out at every angle, and curved tusks flanking a droopy but effective snout. They were harder to track than a poros, though. There weren't as many of them around, so there weren't droppings covering almost every inch of the forest floor. He would have to rely on something else, some other marking that hinted at where a ziolo might be lurking.

It came to him in an instant: tree trunks. A ziolo's spikes would scrape against the tree trunks, tearing off the bark. That would probably be his best bet. And a pretty good one, at that. He was feeling good about his prospects.

Ryckert began examining every last trunk, as well as looking for stripped bark on the ground. He was starting to grow somewhat discouraged after an hour of searching before he finally spotted something.

He had almost missed it, too. It wasn't exactly what he'd been looking for, but he was confident it was the sign of a nearby ziolo. It was a skinny tree, a real wimp, which had been snapped in two. It looked innocuous enough, but Ryckert knew a ziolo's spike had hooked on the trunk while it trudged through the forest, and with its sheer force, it had easily broken the tree in half. The trunk now lay rotting amongst fallen leaves.

From there, it wasn't hard to spot the animal's tracks after brushing aside some leaves. Hooves had sunk into the dirt, deeper than Ryckert had anticipated. It had to be an especially heavy one. Male, no doubt. Which meant more aggressive.

Ryckert followed the hoofprints. Winding through the forest, he noted the scraped-up tree trunks he'd originally been searching for. He was definitely on the right path.

The afternoon sun hung high above his head by the time he had finally reached the clearing where the ziolo slept. Ryckert approached with caution, careful with his foot placement so as to not break any branches or crumple too many dead leaves and awaken the animal.

It was curled up by a small pond. The beast had likely filled its belly up with water, gotten too full, and plopped itself down to take a nap, which suited Ryckert just fine. Sleeping prey was easier to kill.

Ryckert crept slowly toward the ziolo. Its chest heaved with strained breaths. The thing was overweight, and every breath was a struggle. That, or it was pregnant. He was doubtful now in regards to whether it was male or female. Either way, the deep imprints made sense.

He hadn't made a peep. He was sure of that. But something about Ryckert's mere presence had alerted the beast. Its eyelids fluttered open, revealing muddled brown eyes. It stood with great effort, a few stray leaves floating off of its coarse white back.

But Ryckert was already in motion.

Dagger in hand, he was in the air. He landed with his crotch in the ziolo's face and his feet on its tusks, which he used to propel himself upward, onto its back. With his free hand, he grabbed hold of a crooked spike that stuck straight into the air to help pull himself forward. He then pierced the beast's back with his dagger. Its skin was soft and easy to penetrate. The scream it emitted was chilling.

The ziolo shook him off. Ryckert tumbled to the ground, cut by several of the animal's spikes on his way down. None of the cuts felt deep, for which he was grateful. He stood shakily.

The ziolo turned to face him, fury in its eyes and a dagger in its back. Ryckert would need to retrieve that. Quickly.

He rolled out of the way as the ziolo headbutted the ground where he'd been standing. Its long, whip-like tail lashed through the air, searching for the rocyan's neck.

It almost had him, but at the last second, he grabbed the tail and bit into it. Another screech from the ziolo. It retracted its tail, instinctively dipping it into the nearby pond to soothe its wounds. But Ryckert would give it no reprieve. He lurched forward and grabbed the tail again, pulling it from the water. He tugged, trying with all his might to overturn the beast, to get it on its back and expose its vulnerable belly, but it was too large and he was too young, not yet strong enough. A horrid miscalculation.

The ziolo used this second chance to wrap the end of its tail around Ryckert's neck. He held on to the tail while it lifted him into the air. Breath was being choked out of him, but he dug his claws into the ziolo's tail. Finally, it yelped in agony and let go, sending him crashing down onto the grass. He landed directly on the cut the ziolo had given him a minute before and pain shot through his arm.

Ryckert stood. The ziolo was retreating now. His ra would not have let it get away, so he couldn't either. He raced forward and latched onto the beast's side, clinging to the spikes that protruded from its torso. He climbed them onto its back and gripped the handle of his dagger, slicing it down along the ziolo's spine. The animal let loose its final agonizing bellows and stumbled, smashing into the ground, sending the young rocyan flying over its front, dagger in hand.

He knew the beast was dead. There was no rush now. Ryckert allowed himself to lay on the forest floor for several minutes, possibly even an hour. He let his muscles rest. When he was finally feeling recharged, he got up and looked at the carcass of the ziolo.

It was only then that he considered the fact he had no idea how to get it back home.

- -

Today's hunt wouldn't be nearly as strenuous as that ziolo hunt had been. For one, his ra had been dead for thirty years now, so he had nobody to impress. The stakes were much lower. There wasn't an entire family to feed, just himself.

He was in the mood for fish today. He hadn't had fish for a couple weeks. Ryckert returned indoors to fetch his rod and creel, then walked a couple minutes down the beach to the base of the waterfall located to the east of his shack, dragging his outdoor chair behind him. The water cascaded down the cliffside that his home was also nestled against. Up on the cliff was the actual town of Balam. He lived on a lower level, on the beach, accessible only by descending a long staircase etched into the cliffside. Just another way in which he was isolated from the townsfolk.

The river snaked through town, cascading down two separate waterfalls, and made its way here, into the ocean. One could generally find a variety of fish at this waterfall's base, so that was where he'd try first.

He set up his chair, letting it sink into the sand, and cast his line. Ryckert watched the lure bob lazily on the water's surface. The sound of water crashing into water pleased him. It canceled out every other noise around it. Helped him focus on the job at hand.

Nevertheless, his mind began to drift, thinking back to that ziolo hunt thirty-two years prior. How he'd cut the animal into individual pieces to carry it back to town. How his ra had said nothing, done nothing more than placed a firm hand on his son's shoulder.

Ryckert watched the lure and waited.

- -

Three failing grades. All that tutoring, two straight weeks, and she had still failed the final exam. Coupled with the two previous tests she had failed, it assured that Harley Sheere would not be passing Theo's class.

He scanned the test again, his eyes darting back and forth between Harley's ink-blotted handwriting and his answer key, hoping he had somehow messed up the first time and that she'd actually passed. It would make the past couple weeks feel like less of a waste, but to no avail. She had truly floundered.

Theo shuffled the papers on his desk, placing Harley's pitiful offering—a grade of 37, not even almost not-failing—beside the stack of ungraded tests, creating a new pile, and got to work on the next.

Jeremy Lyons. Theo sped through the answer key, marking Jeremy's answers with a checkmark or an X, and covered Harley's 37 with his 75.

It had grown unusually chilly outside and Theo desperately wanted to get home, but he needed to deal with these exams and he knew that once he arrived home he would start a fire, grab a plate full of Lyrra's cooking, and sit cozily by the warmth with a profound lack of motivation to get anything done. The cold pressed him onward. Al had stopped by his room a while before to say his goodbyes and offer him a spot at the bar one last time, which Theo had again declined.

It took another twenty minutes to finish up the rest of the class, and then over an hour to get through his other classes. When he finally finished, he stood and let out a weary yawn. The wooden chair scraped harshly against the floor as he pushed it away from his desk.

He left his assorted teaching materials on the desk and marched down the deserted hallways into the open evening air, turning to lock the front doors behind him. The school looked small and quaint, nestled against the rocky cliffside.

Balam was a simple village from a simple time, and its architecture reflected that. Its buildings were made of unremarkable but sturdy wood, cut from the Cerene Forest that surrounded it. It was not unlike the village Theo had grown up in, which he had been all too eager to get away from in his youth. Once he'd graduated high school, he gathered his belongings and took the first wagon out of town to study at the university in Bral Han, where he spent the next several years and met the woman he would eventually marry.

Once he and Lyrra had completed their studies, they moved to Balam in a desire to root their lives in a quiet, peaceful town after so many years in a bustling city like Bral Han. Theo's father had suggested—practically begged—for them to move back to his hometown of Padstow, a notion that Theo did not even momentarily consider. Not even his father's worsening illness could convince him.

Since leaving his home eight years prior, Theo had only visited Padstow twice before his father's death, and once more after to take care of the funeral and his possessions. Theo had inherited the house, but sold it later that week.

Now that grading was complete, it was officially the first night of spring vacation. The students had gotten to revel in this feeling the night before, but now it was the teachers' turn, and it felt divine.

It was barely past six o'clock and children were still running around outside, playing in the last of their sunlight. Harley Sheere's brother, a young scamp named Cid, darted past and bumped into Theo's dangling hand. "Sorry!" he yelped, his pace not slowing one bit.

Theo walked down the street, past the intersection he'd traveled down to reach the diner that morning. His route home took him by the cliffside that the local inn sat atop of, overlooking eastern Balam's streets and Freya the white mage's clinic. Carved into the cliffside below the inn was a small area with benches and a cooking pit for folk to gather and grill up some grub when the weather permitted. Two men sat on the benches, watching a fire crackle in the pit, sipping bottles of beer.

"I'm headin' to Din's Keep soon's the sun's up," Theo heard one of them say. It was Vince Brine, the owner of the local pub, a stocky man with a thick beard and bald head that glistened in the lamplight. "Gonna see what sorts o' new blades they've got. Hunt'll be on us soon."

His companion, a doughy fellow with bright red hair named Harold, shook his head adamantly. "You're still planning on running around with a blade?"

"You got a better idea?"

"A *gun*, you fool!"

"Nah," Vince groaned, waving his hand dismissively, spilling his beer onto the dirt.

"Say again: you're a fool. A gun is the most effective weapon out there. The Atluan Guard's been using them for years for a reason."

"I'm huntin' a bear, fer godsake! I wanna get in the nitty gritty of it. I wanna grab that bastard's hair and yank his head around while I cut into 'im. That's the fun of it!"

"You are truly barbaric."

Vince grinned as if it were a compliment.

Theo was repulsed by the whole exchange, gun or no. He felt ashamed that anyone in Balam would celebrate the Spring Hunt, given the horrific event that always preceded it. One of the main selling points for moving to Balam had been that it, like all central and eastern Atluan villages, was one that did not celebrate The Offering. Thankfully, Vince was the only resident who participated in the kingdom-wide Hunt afterwards.

Theo crossed Main Street, where he spotted Harley Sheere laying on a bench with her head in her girlfriend's lap. The streetlight overhead cast them in a romantic glow.

"Hey, Mr. Saen!" Harley called, waving to him. She sat up and jogged over, Izzy trailing behind.

"Hi, Harley," Theo said. "Hey, Izzy."

Harley looked somewhat nervous. "I, uh…" she started.

"You wanted to ask about your grades?" It wasn't much of a guess. There was always at least one student each year who stopped him to inquire.

"Yes," Harley said sheepishly, hands behind her back.

Theo's eyes shifted to Izzy, then back to Harley. "You sure you want to discuss it right now?" he asked.

Harley nodded. "Don't matter," she said. "She'll know eventually either way. It's fine."

"Okay," Theo said. "You failed the last test." In his mind, he added, *Did none of my tutoring sink in?* but he didn't want to further embarrass her in front of her girlfriend.

Harley's expression sunk.

"It's alright," Theo assured her. "It's not the end of the world. Don't let it get to you." He smiled. "We can do better next semester."

She smiled back. It was faint, but it was a smile. "Thanks," she said.

"Enjoy your vacation, girls," he said. "I've gotta get home and get some dinner in me."

The two waved goodbye and returned to the bench, resuming their previous positions.

Theo continued down the road and could see the front of his house around the curve of the cliffside, tucked neatly between it and the river. He had picked the spot because it reminded him of his childhood home near the creek in Padstow, where he'd often spent hot summer days as a child splashing about with his older sister Gwen. There were moments when he yearned for those days, back when he understood little and his dim ideas of the world had made everything seem much brighter.

- -

The bounty wasn't particularly on the heavy side, but it would be enough for a good dinner. Ryckert had caught two fish, both no more than a foot long. Their scales were a crimson red, speckled with green.

It took an hour to gut and clean them. The process was mechanical, but soothing. He carried it out on his front porch, casting the unwanted entrails and scales into a garbage bin he kept outside for occasions such as these.

When he was finished, he washed up inside, then went back out to start a fire. Fire-roasted fish was always better than anything cooked in a skillet, in Ryckert's opinion. Once the flames were high, licking the air, he speared one of the fish with a metal rod and held it over the fire. No seasoning. He preferred the natural taste of the meat.

Ryckert closed his eyes and listened to the crackling of the flames and the soft roar of the ocean waves. Outdoor noises were a comfort. They kept him sane.

He opened his eyes and rotated the rod to let the fish's underside experience the flames as well. Embers floated upward into the darkening sky.

A light char was what he was aiming for. Once he achieved that, Ryckert removed the fish from the fire and took an impatient bite into it. The heat burned his tongue, but he didn't mind. He gnashed the meat with his fangs and swallowed. It tasted great. Tasted like the sea.

Ryckert consumed the first fish in less than a minute. He was surprised by how hungry he suddenly was. Cleaning the fish must have worked up his appetite. He wasted no time spearing the second and holding it out over the flame.

A while later, both fish eaten and his belly full, Ryckert sat in the sand and watched the sun start to set. Grains of sand were caught in his matted fur.

The fire was dying down behind him, but it wasn't out just yet. He'd let it go for as long as it could muster. There was nothing but sand and water all around, nothing to catch a blaze. Nothing except for his cabin, but it was far enough away from the pit that Ryckert didn't feel it was in any danger.

He stood and brushed away the sand from his clothes, hoping he got all of it off him. He swiped at the backside of his pants, rubbed away at his arms. But he still felt itchy and uncomfortable. He needed a bath.

But right now, he was thirsty.

He gathered his wallet from inside the shack and took one last look at the meager fire before he set off for the stairway to the upper levels of Balam.

He wanted some whiskey.

- -

The door was unlocked. Lyrra always unlocked it right before he arrived home. Theo entered and locked up, sniffing the air for a hint of the night's meal.

"Hello!" he called.

"Hello!" said Lyrra from around the corner, in the kitchen.

Theo sniffed again. "Meat?"

"Meat!"

"Chicken?"

"Chicken!"

"And potatoes too. Must be the lemon chicken!" Of course, he'd already known it would be lemon chicken for dinner. It was always lemon chicken on the first day of spring.

"Lemon chicken!" Lyrra beamed, rounding the corner. She greeted him with a kiss and a hug. "How was grading?"

"As dull as ever," he replied. "But at least it's over for a couple months. I'm gonna go check on Vir."

Lyrra nodded and returned her attention to the food. "It'll be done in less than five minutes," she said, "so don't be too long."

Theo grabbed a coat from the hallway closet and wrapped himself in it before heading out the back door. In their small stretch of fenced-in yard, Vir dozed lazily in the corner by the neighboring waterfall.

It was one of two waterfalls in Balam; being three distinct layers, the town was divided by cliffs with stairways that one had to ascend or descend to reach each level. The river ran through all three tiers, dropping off each cliff until it finally wound its way into the ocean.

"Vir!" he shouted the seroko's name.

Vir jolted upright, craning her head in Theo's direction. She was tiny now, just a piglet, but in a few months' time she would be fully-grown and not much shorter than Theo. She galloped over to him and he kneeled to meet her. She nuzzled against his leg as he stroked the fuzzy, milk-white hair on her back.

He grinned and picked her up; she weighed hardly more than a textbook. He peered inside her mouth and asked, "Are your tusks comin' in yet? Huh, girl?" She squealed with delight.

Theo placed her back on the ground and took her bowl inside to fill with water.

"How's your little girl doing?" Lyrra asked him mockingly, stirring the potatoes and butter in the skillet.

"She is the most adorable thing in the world, as you're well aware," he said, turning off the faucet. Water sloshed around in the ceramic bowl. "We should let her live inside while she's still small. She'd love it."

"Absolutely not."

"*You'd* love it."

"Absolutely not. And then what happens when she's fully-grown and tries stampeding through the house, breaking everything, just so she can hop up on your chair? Which she would also break, by the way."

"You're no fun," Theo teased. "But I *do* love that chair…"

Back outside, Vir anxiously awaited his return, wagging her stubby tail. She lapped up the water with gusto.

Theo gave her one last rub on the head before returning indoors to wash his hands and eat. The scent of lemon and herbs drifted through the house as Lyrra placed the hot baking dish on top of a piece of cloth on the kitchen table. Theo dried his hands, grabbed two plates from the cabinet, and joined his wife.

"Fire tonight?" he asked, serving the food.

"Sounds like a swell idea to me. It's cold out there."

"Yeah, it's strange. Usually not this cold in the spring, even at night."

Dinner was quiet but pleasant. Nothing more than idle chatter about how good the food was, what they'd do the next day. Dancing around the subject. Finally, Lyrra asked, "So, you're alright?"

Theo nodded, but it was mostly a lie. This would be the sixteenth anniversary of his sister's death. He thought of it more as a murder, but there were those who disagreed, his father included. With each passing year it got a little easier, though it still pained him.

Lyrra smiled weakly and extended her hand for him to hold. He took it and squeezed. He always dreaded this weekend for months ahead of time.

"It's just stupid," he muttered. "The Offering's stupid, the Hunt's stupid, all of it. And everyone will pat themselves on the back as if they did some great deed."

They left it at that. The remainder of the meal was eaten in silence. Theo cleaned the dishes since Lyrra had cooked, and while he did so, she brewed a pot of coffee and got some logs burning in the fireplace. When the coffee was ready, she poured two mugs and they sat down cross-legged on the rug in front of the fire.

He sipped his coffee and smiled at Lyrra. She smiled at him too.

"Want me to go get Vir?" she asked. "She'd enjoy a couple minutes in front of a toasty fire."

"Nah," Theo said, appreciating the gesture. "She needs to get used to the cold so that she's ready for winter. She'll be fine."

They talked for an hour before winding down for the night. They washed up and read in bed by lamplight, though Theo couldn't concentrate on a single sentence in his book. Before they went to sleep, they made love; it was quiet, soft, and nice.

\- -

The pub was dirty. A scent of burnt meat and stale alcohol filled the air. It was a thick stench, which made breathing unpleasant. But it was the only bar the town had. Ryckert's ears flicked with every miserable creak of the door opening.

He heard the barkeep approaching before she ever entered his line of sight. "Need anything else? Some food, another drink?" she asked him. She looked pleasant, fairly pretty. Too pretty for a dump like this, but everyone did what they had to in order to earn some crescents. Ryckert knew that well enough.

The young woman was familiar to him, but he'd never learned her name. It was nothing personal against her. It had just always been hard for him to learn names in the first place, let alone remember them.

"No," Ryckert replied, scratching at the bump on his snout. "Thanks." After a pause, he said, "Can I ask your name?"

"Ann Marie," she answered with a warm smile. She left to tend to another customer while Ryckert took a swig of his whiskey.

It was a slow night despite being the end of the week. School had ended the day before, so most must have been spending time with their families. With their children. But Ryckert appreciated the slowness, the quiet.

He had moved to Balam two years before, when he'd turned forty-one. Older than his ra ever got to be. When that realization struck, he'd retired from his days as a mercenary and moved to a coastal town away from his old life, where he could live out the rest of his days relaxing. He had made plenty of money in his time—nothing extravagant, but enough to retire on and live comfortably in a tiny village like Balam.

Ryckert's ears flicked again as the door whined open. Heavy footsteps. Boots. They grew louder, louder, and then a skinny man with a pathetic white beard sat down beside Ryckert at the bar. A knapsack was slung over his shoulder before he shrugged it off onto the floor.

The man waved, dark gloves covering his hands. Ryckert nodded in greeting. He had never seen him around town before.

The bartender returned with a wide smile. "Hey there," she said to the newcomer. "What can I get ya?"

The young man held up his index finger, indicating to wait a second. He then leaned over into his knapsack and pulled out a pad of paper and a pencil. He wrote the words *whiskey, double*, and showed it to her.

She poured the drink and slid it over to the man, which he grabbed and kicked back with vigor. Ryckert raised his own glass and sloshed the liquid around a bit. "Kindred spirits," he said. The man grinned, remaining silent, and they clinked glasses. "Can't speak?"

The man shook his head. Despite the whiteness of his hair, he looked young, no older than his mid-twenties, though Ryckert would have guessed younger than that. Based on his hair and his tan skin, he had to be jeornish.

"Can you hear?" Another shake. "But you read lips?"

A nod.

"Name's Ryckert." The rocyan extended a hand. They shook.

The guy wrote on his notepad.

~ *Michio* ~

"Nice to meet ya, Michio."

The two shared their drinks in silence while the few other patrons began to mill out of the bar. It was getting late. Soon Ryckert would need to leave and go back home as well. It was a bit of a walk if one had an uneven step, and after another drink, he would.

Ann Marie brought one over, as well as another for Michio.

"What brings you here?" Ryckert asked the man, whose shock-white bangs covered his eyes.

~ *just traveling. seeing sights the east has to offer* ~

"Not from here?"

~ *no, from Dearmont on the west coast. went east for university, got kicked out, decided to explore before I go home* ~

"What'd you study?"

Michio grinned and held up his right hand, his five digits spread apart. Flames began to dance between his fingers, running down along his palm, illuminating the dark fabric of his glove, but not scorching it at all. The flames died down and he clasped his cold glass. Steam rose.

"Black magic. Pretty tough skill to learn. Any magic, I mean."

~ *probably why I didn't do so well* ~ He gave a silent chuckle.

Ryckert grunted in amusement. "Never understood the fascination with magic. Enjoy working with my hands."

They conversed that way for a long time, with Michio writing down his responses and Ryckert reading them. He learned that the young man was only twenty years old. Ryckert's twenties felt like a lifetime ago.

Michio was reluctant to show off any more of his magic, which Ryckert understood. From what little he knew, it was a shameful thing to be kicked out of a jeornish mage academy. Come to think of it, Ryckert had no idea where the nearest mage academy even was. Certainly nowhere near Balam, though he was no expert on the matter.

"Where was your school?" he asked.

Michio pondered the question. Finally, he wrote, ~ *few weeks' travel north from here, outside Kyring.* ~

Ryckert had heard of Kyring before, but had never visited. It was primarily a jeornish city. Other races lived there, of course, but it had been built by the jeornish centuries ago. It made sense that there would be a magic academy on the outskirts.

"Traveled a long way, then," said Ryckert.

Michio nodded and looked into his empty glass. Ryckert ordered him another, which elicited a sly smirk.

"Don't mention it," Ryckert said. "Been a while since I've had someone to drink with and talk to. Enjoyin' the company."

Even as he said it aloud, it came as a surprise to him.

Ann Marie poured both men another glass of whiskey, and Ryckert had a momentary surge of regret. He wasn't in his twenties anymore. He was going to be feeling it in the morning.

But what the hell. Like he said, he was enjoying the company.

- -

It didn't take long for Lyrra to fall asleep. Theo lay beside her, staring at the curve of her neck, scanning his eyes over her bare shoulder. She was beautiful, and he wished he could fall asleep, burrowing into the pillow and nudging against her back, but Gwen wouldn't let him.

As delicately as possible, he got out of bed and soundlessly got dressed. He went out the front door and circled around to the back, where he found Vir sleeping against the wooden fence, sung to sleep by the comforting sounds of the river.

"Hey, girl," he whispered. The seroko woke up with a start and glanced up at him, then grumbled in a mixture of happiness and annoyance. "Wanna go for a walk?" he asked. He leaned over the fencing and picked up the plump animal and set her down at his feet on the other side. "Let's go," he said.

By now the village's streets were completely empty. Theo and Vir wandered down the road, turning right at Main Street to mount the stairs carved into the cliff. As they ascended to the upper level of eastern Balam, Theo thought back to his sister telling him about all the places she'd wanted to see in Atlua. The towering university in Bral Han, the qarmish theatre in Ebonpass, the sprawling streets of Din's Keep...

At the top of the stairs, Theo turned right and Vir trailed a good distance behind, her sleepiness getting the best of her. But she soldiered on.

Grass crunched underneath his shoes as he approached the looming yunesca tree that served as the icon of Balam, with its stunning blue leaves and vibrant pink flowers that were always in bloom. Its gray trunk was streaked with spindly lines of red that split apart and criss-crossed like spider webs. It proudly pierced the sky right above Theo and Lyrra's home, and they were oftentimes treated to dry blue leaves or pink flower petals dancing through the wind in their backyard.

Theo sat on the bench in front of the tree, overlooking the town as well as the beach on its lowest level. The top level contained the entrance to Balam, as well as its pub, inn, town square, and the yunesca tree. Much of the top layer was still wooded, being on the edge of the Cerene Forest.

The middle level held most of the town's shops and residences. This included Theo and Lyrra's home, as well as the school, clinic, restaurants, blacksmith, and other such places on the east side. The western side of this level was mostly dedicated to the farmland formerly owned by the Veres, now overseen by the Reede family, which really only consisted of Rufus Reede.

The lowest level of Balam was entirely sandy beach. Not much was located there except for the docks and a cabin where an old Rocyan named Ryckert lived. He mostly kept to himself and could be found either in his home or at the pub. From this vantage point, Theo could just barely make out the rocyan's modest shack.

Vir loved this area when Theo brought her here during town gatherings. She loved rolling around the tufts of grass and eating the occasional flower, but it was late and she was exhausted, so Theo lifted her into his lap, where she quickly curled into a ball and went back to sleep. He petted her soft fur and gazed out at the town, faintly lit up by the moonlight.

This was his fourth year living in Balam, and Theo always spent this night, the anniversary of Gwen's death, walking around outside. Somehow this was the first time he'd spent the evening sitting by the yunesca tree, and he thought he might make it his new tradition. The tree was breathtaking, as was this view of the village.

"Oh," came a voice from behind him. Theo turned and saw Freya, the white mage, stepping closer. "Sorry," she apologized, "I didn't mean to disturb you."

"No disturbance at all," Theo smiled, scooting over. Vir grumbled in objection. "Feel free to take a seat."

She did so and offered thanks. "This is where I come each night after I close up the clinic," she explained. "The night air helps clear my head."

Freya was jeornish, which was obvious by looking at her. Like every jeorn, she had radiant olive skin that was only somewhat wrinkled with age. Her white hair—a characteristic of the jeornish, not of her age, which was nearly sixty—reached past the bench as she sat with her hands in her lap.

"Well, then I should be the one apologizing for intruding," Theo said. "Vir and I were just feeling a little restless tonight."

Freya eyed the seroko. "She looks more rest*ful* than rest*less*," she chuckled.

"That's true," Theo grinned. "Guess I should just speak for myself."

"I have a spell that can help with sleep," Freya said after a moment of shared silence. "It is fairly simple. I wouldn't mind performing it. I wouldn't even charge you," she joked, coughing lightly.

But Theo rebuked her offer. "It's okay, but thank you."

The two sat in silence for several more minutes, but it was not an uncomfortable or awkward silence. It was simply two individuals watching the ocean, feeling contented.

The peace was shattered by Freya's hacking cough. "Excuse me," she sputtered between coughs. "I've been sick for the past few days. Don't worry, it doesn't seem to be contagious," she added when she saw the look on his face. She crossed her arms, warming herself up. "I should get back home," she said. "And you should too, I think. It's very chilly out here."

"Yeah," Theo agreed. "You're probably right."

He stood, carrying Vir in his arms, and they began to walk back toward the stairway to the middle level, but Freya halted to cough some more.

The woman then dropped to her knees, grasping at her throat. Coughs turned to wheezes. Theo set Vir down, then rushed to the mage's side.

"What's wrong?" he asked, kneeling beside her. He placed a hand on her back, trying to comfort her.

But Freya couldn't push any words out. Her eyes bulged in her head and she was practically choking herself. Theo grabbed her wrists and removed her hands from her throat with great difficulty—her grip was tighter than he'd expected for an older woman.

She began muttering syllables that didn't form any words Theo could recognize. She fell backward, out of Theo's hands, still wheezing. She clutched her throat again and blinked rapidly.

"What in the hell?" Theo sputtered, panicking. Vir was now wide awake and pacing nearby, obviously worried.

Freya's blinking began to slow, as did her breathing. Her hands fell from her throat and came to rest on her stomach. The breeze blew her loose white robe, ruffling it against the grass.

As her breathing calmed, so did Theo's. "Are you alright?" he asked, hoping she could hear and understand him. "What do I do? What do I need to do?" He held her hand and asked, "Is there something in the clinic I can go grab?"

She lazily turned her head and looked at him with tired eyes. And then her breathing stopped.

"Shit," Theo whispered. The harshness of the word cut through the quiet night. "Shit," he repeated, putting an ear to her breast. He couldn't hear or feel a heartbeat.

He stood and backed away from the body. Vir whined a couple feet behind him. He turned and scooped her up, then looked back at Freya. What used to be Freya.

"Shit," he said again.

- -

Ryckert paid out his tab and paid for Michio's drinks as well, which he was thanked for with a hearty clap on the back.

They parted ways outside, and Ryckert watched as the young man traipsed westward in the direction of the inn, clutching his jacket to his slender frame. The night had indeed turned cold. He wouldn't mind sitting by the fire a while before going to bed. If there was any life left in it, anyway.

He made his way back to Main Street, groaning at the thought of having to travel down two huge flights of stairs to reach the beach level and his cabin. Too many drinks, too many stairs.

But he hadn't even reached the first staircase before coming upon a commotion in the town square, next to the yunesca tree. There was a small crowd of people gathered, circled around what appeared to be a motionless body lying on the ground. Men and women spoke in hushed tones, presumably trying to figure out what should be done.

Ryckert was intrigued, but too drunk to do anything about it. Nothing he said or did in this state would be useful or welcomed, so he continued on toward home. Toward much-needed sleep.

He looked back up as he lethargically made his way down the stone steps. What he saw was a young man with a baby seroko sitting on the bench underneath the yunesca tree, staring out at the black horizon ahead.

CHAPTER II

TUFTS OF DULL GRASS

Ryckert awoke the next morning with, as expected, a pounding headache. It rivaled the one he'd had after getting into a particularly memorable bar fight with a fellow mercenary named Leif over some unmemorable matter. That night, he'd gotten his head slammed into a stone countertop, so the amount of whiskey he'd consumed must have been impressive.

He sat up and groaned at the head rush. Too fast. This would be a slow morning.

With great care, he got himself out of bed, tossing the sheets aside—no use making the bed every day—and zoned in on the coffee pot. He was starting to run low on beans, but that could always be remedied later in the day, when he didn't feel like dropping dead.

The sun was already burning bright and high in the sky by the time he poured himself a cup and went outside. Coffee and fresh air would do him good. He had slept in way longer than intended, but wasn't that what retirement was for?

The coffee was extremely bitter, just the way Ryckert preferred it. Growing up deep in the southern woods of Atlua as part of the Caer clan, they did not have access to things like cream or sugar or other non-essential food items, so he had grown up drinking his coffee black, just like his ra and his ra's ra before him. The taste had taken a while to grow on him, but after gulping it down every morning before a big hunt, he started to enjoy it. It put him on edge, made him feel ready. Eager.

After getting through his morning routine (coffee, cleaning up, his walk), he opted to go into town for a meal instead of hunting. His head still wasn't cooperating, and he knew it would be no easy feat trying to concentrate.

The walk to Balam's middle tier was excruciating, given how many steps he had to trudge up, but the sun felt good on his fur. He could admit he was starting to feel a little better.

Balam was aflutter. Children and teenagers who were now finished with school for the next couple months milled about, playing games or chatting with each other. Going shopping, getting something to eat, reading a book. Enjoying themselves. The men and women who had to work for a living must have surely been envious.

The thought tickled Ryckert as he made his way to the Sonata Diner. The only other places in town to grab a cooked meal were the pub and the inn, but both were on the town's upper level and Ryckert had absolutely no intention of traveling that distance right now.

The Sonata was brimming with guests. Almost every table was full, but there was plenty of room at the counter for a lone patron such as Ryckert. He took a seat and said hello to the man standing across from him, the diner's owner, Walton Vere.

"Hullo. What can I get ya today? Bit o' coffee to start?"

"No, thanks. Already had my fill," Ryckert replied. He didn't need to look at a menu to know what he wanted. "Plate of eggs and some toast'll do me just fine."

"You got it." The plump man gave him a thumbs up and scurried into the kitchen to alert the cook.

The room was positively buzzing, and when Ryckert reached deep into his mind, he suspected he knew what the chatter was about.

He'd almost forgotten, but he was able to conjure a memory of stumbling through town late last night and seeing a mob of people gathered around a corpse. Well, maybe it was premature to call it a corpse. Maybe it was just a *body*.

Ryckert's ears twitched as he listened closer. There was a couple sitting at the table by the door, probably in their mid-thirties, taking a break to get some lunch. The man's voice was low, husky, but enthusiastic. This hot piece of gossip was the most intriguing thing that had happened in Balam in years.

"—says she just dropped. Just like that. Just *dropped*."

"Well, I mean, there must be more to it than *that*," the woman said.

"I dunno. That's all I've heard. Theo was standing around talking to her and she just dropped dead the next second."

"What were they even doing up there together?"

"Dunno. But no one's even sure what she died of yet, since she's the town's white mage."

Ryckert had heard enough to get the gist of the situation. The town's white mage had apparently dropped dead and the only witness appeared to be a man named Theo. He thought back to the night before, an image of a young man sitting alone on the bench underneath the yunesca tree. That had to be the guy.

It was at that moment Walton returned with a plate of fresh eggs and toast. The eggs had already been liberally salted and peppered, and they smelled delicious. He set the plate down in front of Ryckert and said with a smile, "Dig in."

So Ryckert dug in. As he chewed, he looked back at the couple on whom he'd been eavesdropping. Upon a closer listen, they had changed the subject and were now talking about their trip to Din's Keep next weekend, once the Spring Hunt festivities had died down. He turned his attention back to Walton.

"You heard what happened last night?" he asked.

"Sure," Walton shrugged. "Bits 'n' pieces, more'n anything, but sure."

"They say a guy named Theo saw the whole thing."

"Yar, Theo Saen. He's a teacher over at the high school. His wife Lyrra works at the inn. You never heard of the Saens?"

Ryckert shook his head. "Names don't really stick with me," he explained.

Walton gave another shrug. "Fair enough. Anyways, Theo's the one who was with Freya when it happened. Up at the square."

The town square, by the yunesca tree. "No one knows what the cause of death was?" Ryckert asked.

"Nope. Far's anyone can tell, it was a heart attack er somethin'. Some folks said Theo said she was grabbin' at her neck 'n' couldn't breathe."

"You think he's telling the truth?"

"Why wouldn't he be?" Walton looked taken aback, like this was the most outlandish thing he had ever heard.

Ryckert gave an innocent shrug. "Might be he had something to do with the death. Got caught near the body, so he had to make something up."

But *that* was truly the most outlandish thing Walton Vere had ever heard. "If you knew Theo Saen at all, you'd know how crazy you sound right now," the man muttered. "He wouldn't hurt nobody. And 'sides, he's the one who ran 'n' got help! What kind o' murderer would kill somebody then go get help?"

It was a fair point. Maybe the woman really did just drop dead.

"Where's the body?" Ryckert asked.

Walton blinked in surprise before answering. "How'm I supposed to know?" he said. "Prob'ly in the clinic, I'd wager. That's where they usually go. But with no white mage to examine it, I guess I ain't sure."

That was enough to go on for now. Once he finished eating his meal, Ryckert planned to head over to the clinic—it was only a few minutes' walk from the Sonata—to see if someone might let him examine the body. His natural curiosity was getting the better of him, and he wanted to know what had happened.

He piled the rest of his eggs onto the piece of toast and scarfed it all down. He left the three crescents he owed Walton and scooted off of his stool, heading back outside, bee lining for the clinic.

– –

Ryckert entered the clinic portion of the building. The setup of the white mage's hut—what was her name? Freya?—was that it had two sections, both domed huts, connected by a short hallway. The larger dome was the town clinic. Every village in Atlua had at least one resident white mage to handle any medical issues. Bigger cities had several, but for a small town like Balam, just one sufficed (except for unforeseen situations such as this). The other, smaller dome, connected by the hallway, was where the mage lived. It was beneficial being close to her clinic in case anyone came in the night with an emergency.

The rocyan cautiously pushed the door open with a creak and peered inside.

What he saw wasn't anything remarkable. Given his previous line of work, Ryckert had visited many a white mage clinic, and this one looked largely the same as all the others.

In the center of the room was an examination table for a patient to sit or lay on, with a chair beside for the mage to occupy. There were shelves and cabinets lining the walls with ingredients to craft potions, and Ryckert could spy a sword and shield hanging on the back wall. Peculiar.

He entered and closed the door quietly behind him. But not quiet enough, apparently, because a man appeared in the doorway to Ryckert's left that led to the connecting hallway.

"What do you need?" the man asked. Ryckert recognized him as the town's butcher, a tall man built to fight, named Bernard Tilling. Behind him stood his wife.

"Hello, Bernard," Ryckert greeted the man. He was one of the few residents Ryckert knew; on occasion, they would talk meat at Bernard's shop when the stillness of his cabin made him restless. "I was lookin' for the mage."

Bernard's face sunk. "Sorry to say, but she passed last night. Mr. Reede is working on getting a replacement soon as he can, if you're able to wait. Dunno how long it'll take, though, unfortunately." His wife retreated further down the hallway, leaving her husband to speak with Ryckert.

"I'm aware," Ryckert said. "Don't need medical help, thankfully. Just wanted to see if the body was here."

Bernard cocked an eyebrow. "What for?"

"Curious, mainly," Ryckert replied. "Heard a little about how she died and it sounded suspicious. Also heard there's no one in town to examine the body. Thought I might could help with that. It's good a new mage is on the way, but by the time they get here it could be too late to find out what killed her. The evidence don't always last."

After taking a second to digest it, this explanation seemed to satisfy the butcher. "Body's back in the house," he said, pointing a thumb in that direction. "Lisa and I are here to guard the door. Not that we think anything dubious is gonna happen; just better safe than sorry, y'know?"

Ryckert nodded. He then followed Bernard through the hallway past Lisa, who he gave a reassuring nod to, and unlocked the plain red door at the end.

"Just takin' a look," Bernard explained to his wife as he extracted the key and turned the knob. "How long are you gonna be?" he asked Ryckert.

"Not sure," he shrugged. "Long as it takes."

Bernard nodded and stood aside.

The room on the other side was small, but cozy rather than cramped. It included two offshoots on the right-hand side, one being a tiny kitchen and the other a closed door that Ryckert could only assume led to a bathroom.

Freya's bedroom was sparsely decorated. She was evidently a woman of plain tastes. Ryckert could relate.

Her bed was in the center of the room, flanked by bedside tables. On the one closest to the bathroom was a lamp and clock, nothing else. On the other sat a framed photograph of a young male jeorn, somewhere in his thirties, who Ryckert assumed must be her son. He briefly wondered how long it would be before the jeorn received news of his mother's death.

Around the walls hung banners of red and white, which Ryckert surprisingly recognized as the colors of the mage academy in Bral Han. There was also a dining table near the entryway of the kitchen, sized for only two people. Besides that, the room held no other furniture or decorations except for the everyday essentials: a wardrobe, one bookshelf lined with tomes, a dresser.

But on the bed in the center of the room was the mage's body. A slight sulfuric odor drifted from it, the sign of a poorly-cast Preservation spell. There must have been a black mage living in town or staying at the inn (*Michio?* Ryckert thought for a moment, but decided the mute probably wouldn't get himself involved in the town's affairs) who had cast the spell in order to delay the body's decomposition. The black mage was either still relatively unskilled or was simply not trained in Preservation, hence the smelly side effect.

But as Ryckert grew nearer and gave the body a once-over, he saw the spell was doing its job, at least. There were no early signs of decay. She merely looked as if she were in a deep sleep.

What was nice about Preservation was that it kept the body in whatever state it was in at the time of casting, so Ryckert would still be able to do an examination and try to determine what had befallen the unfortunate mage. Medicine had never been his strongest subject, but Ryckert figured he stood a better chance of finding a cause than somebody like Bernard Tilling or Walton Vere. In his previous line of work, he had witnessed a lot of people—friends and enemies alike—die different kinds of deaths. It was possible he might be able to identify a detail that had escaped others thus far, which could be helpful if the symptoms wore off before the new white mage's arrival.

He started by gently turning her head to the side to better inspect her neck. There were poisonous bats in these woods, and she could have been bitten while out on a walk. It wasn't very likely, seeing as there would be no reason for her not to simply heal herself immediately if such an event occurred, but it didn't hurt to check.

As expected, no bite marks on either side. So that was out. Ryckert racked his brain for any other poisonous critters that called the Cerene Forest their home. There was only one that came to mind, a slimy no-limbed creature that slithered along the forest floor with a stinger on its end. He checked the woman's ankles for any signs of a bor piercing, but found nothing. Again, it had been unlikely, but it was worth a look.

Next, he checked the woman's face for any swollen veins. He hadn't seen any on her neck while checking for bat bites, so he didn't think asphyxiation was the cause either, but he checked regardless. He found nothing. No signs of cyanosis either, but that probably would've worn off by the time the Preservation spell had been cast anyway.

Which led him to the part he had hoped he could avoid. He needed to check if her tongue or throat had swollen in an allergic reaction and caused blockage to her breathing that way. It would explain what Walton had told him the witness had said about her grabbing at her neck before she died.

With his two furry index fingers he delicately pried open the woman's lips. He felt deeply uncomfortable and suddenly questioned why he was doing this at all. What stake did he have in this mystery? He was just some rocyan who lived on the beach in a shitty shack that nobody cared about. Why was he going through all this effort?

But he proceeded.

He propped her mouth open with one index finger and thumb, then reached carefully inside with the other hand and pinched her tongue between two fingers. He tugged, pulling it out into the open, and took a close look.

Nothing seemed out of the ordinary. No redness or inflammation. Looked healthier than his own tongue, if he was being honest. He let go and closed the woman's mouth, taking a step back. He was running out of theories.

Then one last idea popped into his head. But it was an unpleasant thought, and once again he was asking himself: *Michio?*

He knew of one black magic spell that could potentially kill its target with few indicators. It was referred to as *Splice* and acted much like a poison dart, or a bullet. A nearly invisible orb of energy shoots through the air at the mage's target, piercing their body and emanating outward from its point of entry, basically poisoning them. It was an extremely difficult spell to master, so Ryckert doubted a man as young as Michio who claimed to have been kicked out of the mage academy could have learned such a thing, but how well did he really know the man? It was possible that Michio could have cast Splice then sauntered into the pub for a drink and a bite to eat while the spell worked its way through the rest of her body.

Ryckert turned the body over, lifted her arms, legs, whatever he needed to do to examine every inch of clothing. Assuming these were the clothes Freya had been wearing the night she died (why would anyone have changed her?) and Splice had indeed been cast on her, there would be a hole where the orb penetrated her. Finding nothing, he then began to look over every bit of exposed skin.

But the woman had no wounds. It wasn't Splice.

There was some relief knowing that his companion from the night before probably hadn't been involved. Though now that the idea had entered his mind, he couldn't help but feel somewhat suspicious.

Ryckert's expertise extended only to the external, and he was now completely out of ideas that fit the symptoms the witness had described. If the cause of death had been something like a heart attack, he would have no way of telling. That was work for a white mage. And if Freya's replacement didn't arrive soon, he thought the villagers might start to worry, probably incite a small surge of hypochondria. Every little symptom would seem so much worse if there was nobody around to fix it.

He gave Freya one last look then exited the room. Bernard and Lisa cut off their conversation and turned to face him as he entered the hallway.

"Figure it out?" Bernard asked.

Ryckert shook his head. He felt frustrated, but he had to ask himself again: why did it matter?

Why had he even come here in the first place? In a few days' time, at most, a new white mage would arrive in Balam and check out the body and determine a cause of death and then there would be a funeral and then life would go on. No reason to go all detective like he was. He'd gone into town today to get a meal. That was it.

So why had he come here?

"That's too bad," Lisa said with a sigh.

Ryckert nodded in agreement. It *was* too bad. Because he had wanted to be the one to solve the mystery. To prove that he still had what it took. Just prove it to himself.

Because, he realized, he had grown bored.

- -

Theo was not feeling particularly good the day after seeing a fellow townsperson sputter to death.

He slept in until noon and was still exhausted when he finally awoke. He discovered Lyrra had taken the day off work to tend to him, and he assured her he'd be fine on his own, but she insisted.

"And besides," she said, "who doesn't want a day off work?"

The night before, after Freya stopped breathing and Theo stopped swearing, he attempted mouth-to-mouth resuscitation. He wasn't exactly sure what it entailed, but he thought he had the general idea down. First he tilted her head back. Then, one hand over the other, he began chest compressions. His fingertips grazed one of her breasts and he felt like he was violating her, but he pushed the thought away and pressed down on her chest. After thirty or so compressions he opened her mouth, pinched her nostrils, and breathed into her. Her lips tasted of salt.

After several repetitions of this, he decided it was of no use. Nothing was happening. He checked her heartbeat one more time, just to be sure, and felt nothing. Freya was dead.

Something had to be done. He couldn't just sit there with a dead body and he couldn't just leave Freya there in the cold all night. The closest buildings were the bar, the Vere household, and the Tilling household. If he knew anything about Walton Vere and his son, he knew they'd be of little help. The Tillings might know what to do, but he didn't want to disturb them. He also couldn't trust anyone in the bar to be sober enough to assist.

The inn was a little further away, but it was his best bet. He raced over there, nearly tumbling over a bench in his delirium, and burst into the inn gasping for help.

He returned to the scene with a handful of individuals—one of the night shift managers, a man named Gregory Van re Von whom Lyrra was not a huge fan of; a guest all the way from Gillus named Mhar Cown who had been checking in and claimed his brother was a white mage (as if this implied he himself would be helpful); and Hilli White, one of the two receptionists on duty, who happened to be his colleague Serys's daughter.

"So what happened?" Mhar asked as soon as they arrived, kneeling down beside Freya's body. He brushed aside his flowing white jeornish hair.

Theo explained in as much detail as he could manage, but he was flustered and sure he'd left something out. He mentioned how Freya had been coughing beforehand, how she dropped in front of him, clutching her throat.

Gregory stood with his hands on his hips, overseeing everyone. There wasn't much else for him to contribute, until the drunks from the bar began to shuffle by on their way home and wanted to see what the fuss was about. It was then that Gregory's expertise as a manager came in handy as he wrangled the growing crowd and kept them a good distance from the body.

Hilli, ever the doting assistant (she had been harboring a crush on her boss for a couple weeks now), helped him with this task.

Mhar's brother was a white mage, but he himself had studied black magic at the academy. "Not much use here, I suppose," the man said, "but I think there's one thing I can do. Take a step back, friend."

Theo did as he was told. Mhar began to gesture over Freya's body, creating a light fog that seemed to rise from his fingers and encase her.

Theo decided he didn't want to see any more and turned to walk away. It felt wrong somehow to just leave and go back home, climb into bed with his wife, and try to forget what had happened. It would be disrespectful.

Instead, he took a seat on the bench where he and Freya had been sitting less than twenty minutes before. Vir sat on the ground at his feet, gazing at the crowd of people. She may have been sleepy before, but she was now deeply invested in what everyone else was doing.

By now, Walton Vere and Bernard Tilling had emerged from their homes and joined the crowd outside. Both men wore their pajamas unashamedly as they surveyed the scene. With Mhar's work finished, Bernard offered to transport the body back to Freya's clinic for the time being. Once everything was settled and the group dispersed, Theo finally felt like it was okay for him and Vir to go back home.

Lyrra was awake in bed when he entered the bedroom. Her first question was why he was back so late—she knew about his annual late-night walks, try as he might to keep quiet, but being gone for so long this time had worried her. When she saw how shaken he was, she went to him and wrapped him in a tight hug.

They sat in bed for half an hour as Theo told her what he'd witnessed. She refrained from looking shocked or confused or asking any questions and just let her husband speak freely. When he finished, she gave him a kiss and said they should get some sleep. She said he would feel better in the morning, and they could discuss it further if he wanted to.

It took a long time to fall asleep. He shivered with the thought of Vir out in the cold.

\- -

After he finished going over the story with Lyrra again that morning, he forced himself out of bed so he could feed Vir.

"I already took care of her," Lyrra said. "You can stay in bed. Let me cook you something."

Theo refused. "I don't want you to have to wait on me," he said. "Besides, maybe cooking will get my mind off it. Help me relax."

She conceded and let him prepare their lunch. It was nothing fancy or complicated, just a couple of grilled meat sandwiches with a side of pickles. They ate side-by-side on the couch with her leaning against him, warming him. It felt good. The warmth of his food and his wife's touch were putting him at ease. He didn't plan on leaving the house all day, if he could help it.

They returned to bed without cleaning the dishes and began to read their respective books. Theo was able to focus on his better than he had the night before, but not by much. He still had to read some lines two or three times before fully absorbing them. His mind flashed the image of Freya's choking face over and over. He shuddered.

Time crawled by.

The two spent a majority of the afternoon reading, but some time was also allotted for a quick doze and playtime with Vir. She was groggy from their late night as well, but still had enough liveliness pent up for a few races around the yard. It cheered Theo up to see the tiny seroko so full of energy and joy.

While he played with Vir, Lyrra left the house to go speak with Gregory (who had agreed to cover her shift, despite having been up all night, which gained him some points in her book) about what was going on with Freya.

She returned a while later with the news that Mr. Reede, who was for all intents and purposes the mayor of Balam although there was really no such official title, was already in communication with Allinor University, a mage academy located further north in the Cerene Forest, in hopes that they had a freshly-graduated student ready to take on a clinic. Or at least someone still in training that could take over temporarily while a more permanent replacement was sorted out.

It was definitely good news, but Theo didn't want to talk about Freya anymore today. That night was already bad enough for him, and now this incident would probably plague him each year as well. He wanted to push it aside as much as possible. Perhaps he could just deal with it next year.

Lyrra understood his reluctance to talk, so she went back inside and left him to play with Vir. The sweet, round-faced little animal looked up at him with her bright green eyes and let out a soft purr. He rubbed her head, flapping her pointy ears.

"Sorry you had to see all that last night," he whispered to her. "I guess I should've just left you alone here to sleep, huh?"

Vir gawked at him, wide-eyed. As he smiled at her, she began to wag her thin tail.

"Bet you were having some good dreams, too," he said, lifting her and placing her in his lap. He stroked her back and she nestled into him, nuzzling his stomach with her eyes shut.

He looked over at the waterfall, then to the left where the yunesca tree blotted out the sun high above their home.

A lone blue leaf broke free of the tree's branches and floated down, drifting back and forth in a lazy arc, and landed only two feet away from where Theo sat.

- -

Ryckert stood on the cliffside in front of the inn, wrestling with himself. There was no real reason to be here, and if he really got to the core of things, he should just go back home to sit on the beach and stare at the ocean.

What he should certainly *not* do was go inside, find Michio's room, and question the man on why he had come to their town. What was the point? What was the likelihood he had anything at all to do with the white mage's death?

But it kept gnawing at him. Ryckert knew it would turn into an uncontrollable itch if he just went back to the beach and let things lie, no matter if that was the smarter move or not.

He looked out over Balam. From here he had a view of the clinic, the Sonata Diner, and almost every building on this side of the village. The river ran far to his left, out of sight on this level of the town but perfectly visible on the lower tiers as it made its way to the beach.

Whatever. He had already made his choice. He was going to see this through. Nothing would come of it, just like nothing had come from his inspection of the corpse, and then he would buy a cut of meat from the butcher and cook it on his fire pit and fall asleep drunk.

Better get a move on.

He entered the inn. It was a building he had not stepped foot in since he moved to Balam two years prior. He had lodged there while he built his cabin during the day, which had only taken around a week and a half.

The receptionist smiled as he approached the front counter. "Hello!" she said warmly. "How can I help you today?"

Ryckert glanced down at the woman's nametag. "Hello, Reyna. I'd like to get some information on one of your guests," he said, hoping the use of her name would help him come across as friendly and personable and make his request seem less intrusive. "I believe he checked in yesterday."

The woman frowned. "I'm afraid I can't divulge any guest information," Reyna told him.

He'd expect such a policy in a large city like Bral Han or Din's Keep, but for some reason Ryckert had hoped they would be more lax here. His nametag gambit had failed. He had a simple lie prepared, though, which he hoped would be sufficient.

"Right. The man's an old friend of mine, though. Expecting me. Just not right now. He came to visit for his birthday, arrived last night, and I wanted to surprise him early today, take him out to lunch."

It worked. "That sounds like a nice afternoon. I think we can make an exception for you, Mister…?"

"Ji'ca," he finished for her.

"Mr. Ji'ca. What is the guest's name, please?" She opened up her room ledger to search for the name.

"Michio."

She ran a long fingernail down the edge of the page, scanning the list of names. "I don't see anyone here with the last name Michio," she said.

"Apologies. That's his first name."

Reyna ran through the list one more time but only offered an apologetic look. "No one with that name has checked in. Maybe he didn't arrive last night after all? The Hunt is starting this weekend, so the roads are probably a bit clogged. He might have been delayed."

Ryckert nodded. "Probably so," he said. "Thanks for your assistance."

Her face lit up. "You're welcome," she said. "Feel free to come back later to see if he has checked in."

He returned to the cliff's edge and looked out at the clinic once more. The night before, he had seen Michio leave the pub and head toward the inn. If he wasn't staying here, where was he staying? Why wouldn't he just stay there, unless he was hiding from people? Didn't want them to know where he was?

More unanswered questions. Ryckert was going to drive himself crazy with all of this. Could be Michio knew somebody who lived on the upper level of town and was staying with them. There were only a few houses up there, but it was plausible. Balam would be a strange choice of town to travel to if one didn't already know somebody living there, after all. That was probably what Michio was doing.

Since it had already been close to noon by the time he finally woke up, the afternoon was beginning to wind down and it would soon be time for dinner. The wise, healthy choice would be to head down the stone steps and go to the butcher to buy a nice rack of ribs or a thick cut of steak. The unwise move would be to head to the pub, which was much less of a trek, and get some food there. It would be much greasier and make him feel a lot shittier than he already felt after such a weird, long afternoon. But that was what he wanted: something greasy and shitty. And something alcoholic.

To the pub.

- -

Theo's plan to not leave the house was a resounding success. Lyrra had suggested they grab dinner at the Sonata, but Theo politely declined, saying he wasn't feeling up to it. So Lyrra, being a better wife than Theo knew he ever deserved, offered to head over there and pick up something to bring back home.

Unlike lunch, they ate their dinner at the kitchen table. She had gotten Theo the diner's signature dish, which was dubbed the Moonlight Sonata. It was a flattened mound of rice topped with a black bean puree that only covered a portion of the rice, leaving a crescent shape to look like the moon. Surrounding this were assorted lightly fried vegetables and grilled chicken seasoned with herbs and drizzled with honey.

It was delicious, and it brought Theo one step closer to feeling normal again. If that was possible.

"So, what do you wanna do?" Lyrra asked as she threw away the disposable plates that had come with their meal. "Back in bed for some reading?"

"Nah," Theo answered. He knew he wouldn't have enough focus to read and he didn't want to irritate himself by trying and failing. "Maybe some coffee out on the porch?"

That sounded like a splendid idea to Lyrra. She changed into warmer clothes while Theo prepared a pot of coffee. As he filled his cup and added cream and sugar, he made a mental note that they were almost out of the latter.

He carried both mugs outside and Lyrra shut the door behind them. They sat in adjacent chairs on the porch, resting their steaming mugs on top of their laps. To their left was the river, and a ways ahead of them was the stone bridge that went across it, granting access to the butcher's shop and several homes.

Theo took a long, hot sip of his coffee that burned his tongue, but he didn't really care. He asked Lyrra, "Did I ever tell you about my dad's spot?"

She told him no. He hadn't figured he'd told her; his father wasn't a subject he ever brought up. There was a lot of lingering resentment. There had never been any forgiveness before the man's death.

"My dad was a woodsman," he started. This much Lyrra already knew, but she didn't want to interrupt. "He'd chop down trees whenever more land was needed in Padstow, which would also provide the wood for building the buildings." He suddenly felt embarrassed, like he was giving his wife a school lesson. "Well, at some point, he decided he wanted a place where he could go to get away from everything for a while. Away from us kids, away from my mom.

"It was just outside of town, probably a good twenty-minute walk from our house. You followed the path into the forest at first, but then veered off at this one big boulder—it was very distinct, if you knew what you were looking for—and walked for about five minutes past it. There was a small clearing there, with one tree in the middle. My dad cut down the tree and just left the stump behind. So he'd sit at that stump and relax. I don't really know what he'd do there. He wasn't much of a reader, so

I doubt it was that. Maybe he brought his harmonica and played some of his shitty music, I don't know.

"But he also planted flowers there, in that clearing. A little patch by the stump. These ice-blue flowers with a hundred tiny petals on each of 'em. By far the best thing he did in his whole miserable life."

Lyrra watched him, not saying a word. Not even drinking her coffee. Theo took another sip before he continued.

"He never showed that place to us. Never told anyone about it. I only know about it because I followed him there once, without him knowing. Then I went there myself, every once in a while. Those flowers were really beautiful. I have no idea what kind they were."

Theo sighed. He didn't know why he was telling this story. There was no real point to it. It had nothing to do with what happened to Freya, or what happened to him. But for some reason the blue leaf from the yunesca tree that he watched fall earlier that afternoon had reminded him.

"I went there when I had to go back to Padstow after my dad died. I figured I'd get one last look at those flowers, since I wasn't planning on ever going back to that fucking place.

"I followed the path, looking for that big stupid rock. When I reached the clearing, though, I thought for sure I must have gone the wrong way somehow, because it wasn't the same. The tree stump was still there, but all the flowers were gone. There weren't even that many of them to start with, but their absence just completely changed how the place looked, to the point where I thought *surely this can't be it*."

He remembered entering that clearing, his eyes automatically trained on the area where the flowers had bloomed so many years before, and saw nothing but tufts of dull grass. The disappointment that had flooded him was nearly overpowering. He'd had to take a seat on that stump, staring blankly down at the grass where the flowers were supposed to be.

"I guess what happened was that the flowers died. I don't know why, or how. Maybe they'd needed some special fertilizer. I've never seen those flowers before or since; maybe they needed something special to grow. And so I think my dad hadn't been there since my mom killed herself. So the flowers died and I'll probably never see them again."

He didn't turn to look at Lyrra, but if he had he would've seen tears welling in her eyes. One dropped into her cup of coffee, the saltiness mingling with the sweetness of the cream. She wiped away the rest of her tears and reached for his hand.

They gripped each other firmly. He looked down at the top of her hand, at the light hairs and shallow wrinkles of her skin.

"I dunno," he finally sighed after a long silence. "It just pisses me off, how he let those flowers die too."

Lyrra brought his hand to her lips and planted a soft kiss on his skin. It gave him goosebumps. He drained the rest of his coffee and looked at her, giving her a meek smile.

"I love you," she told him.

"I love you too."

They sat outside for a while, until the sun had completely set and the village was draped in darkness. Then they went inside, changed into their pajamas, and got in bed. Lyrra held him close to her and kissed him on the neck. He could finally feel his breathing slow for the first time since he'd seen Freya.

- -

It was looking to be another drunken night with another morning spent hung over. Ryckert mentally kicked himself. This wasn't how he usually behaved, and he was aware he would regret it the next day, but he was committed to the cause.

He chalked it up to feeling foolish about how he'd spent his day. Playing detective like some idiot kid. There was never a chance he was going to discover the cause of Freya's death. He realized that now. Yet in the moment, it had felt like the right thing to do. The natural thing.

With a glass of whiskey in hand, Ryckert sat at a table in the back of the pub, watching the rest of its customers mosey about, playing bar games, chatting amongst themselves. In front of him was a mostly clean bowl that had previously housed a thick, meaty stew filled with soft potatoes and carrots. Now all that remained were tiny scraps of onion, residue from the liquid, and his spoon.

The pub was busier than usual. People were worried about the white mage being dead, and even more so because they didn't know what had done her in. It was an understandable fear, and it was leading some men and women to drink.

The corner Ryckert occupied was dark. He was too embarrassed to sit at the bar, though it wasn't as if anyone here had any idea that he'd visited the clinic earlier. Or that he'd uncovered absolutely nothing there.

Back in his prime, Ryckert had been fairly good at investigative work. Far from an expert, he admitted, but passable.

One time, he'd tracked the whereabouts of a woman's missing daughter. This was on the western coast, in a town called Colkirk. Probably the dingiest town Ryckert had ever set foot in, but a different job had landed him there and while he waited a week for the airship he was intending to ride out of town, he'd decided to take on another job for some extra crescents to line his pocket.

The woman suspected her ex-husband, the girl's father, had been the one to steal her away. According to her, the man—whose name was Frederick Feiri, but whom the locals had dubbed The Flame—was a gangster who specialized in drug trafficking but rumor had it was looking to expand into the sex trade. Selina, of course, hadn't a clue about the extent of this man's dark side when she'd met him and gotten pregnant with his baby. They were still technically married, but once she realized what terrible business he was getting himself into, she left him and took Maritza with her.

Selina's theory was that this hadn't set right with The Flame, and he had taken matters into his own hands by having one of his goons abduct Maritza. Selina feared her daughter's fate would be at the hands of perverted old men who wanted a taste of young flesh.

This job had gotten under Ryckert's skin and he'd promised to find Maritza. He even told the mother he wouldn't accept any payment for the work, despite that being the sole reason he'd decided to look for a quick job.

He had started by following Maritza's route from her school back home, inspecting the pathways and alleys for any signs of distress. During the first walkthrough, he'd found nothing, but he didn't trust that. He searched again, and upon a second pass he found what he had been looking for: an insignificant scratch on the wooden docks Maritza passed every day on her way home.

There was a clear view of a nearby island from that dock. Maritza must have stopped that afternoon to take a seat and watch the island, watch ships sailing by, listening to the waves and tasting the salty sea air on her lips. And then some dirtbag The Flame hired grabbed her by the back of the neck and dragged her to her feet, but Maritza had resisted, attempting to latch onto the dock but instead only leaving a few scratch marks behind, which Ryckert had found.

Now that he had a starting point, things would be easier.

While examining the various bootprints sunken into the dirt near the dock, Ryckert noticed that one pair had a much larger stride than the others—obviously, most men working on the docks or just passing by would be walking at a normal, perhaps even languid, pace. A stride this long implied the owner had been running; damn near leaping, from the look of it.

It seemed like messy work. Even at that moment, Ryckert had the thought, and it felt off to him. Someone like The Flame wouldn't hire someone so stupid as to snatch a little girl off the docks in broad daylight.

Ryckert followed the suspicious footsteps through some back alleys, finally leading out of Colkirk and into the woods, where he'd come upon an old, dilapidated shack hidden away from the rest of the world. There had been no doubt in his mind that Maritza was tied up inside.

As Ryckert got closer to the shack, a rank odor assaulted his nostrils and he momentarily cursed his heightened sense of smell. It was a familiar scent: the smell of rotting flesh. Not a good sign, by any stretch.

No more time to dawdle. He'd raced forward and rammed his left shoulder against the doorway, crashing through in an explosion of splinters as it collapsed to the floor. He'd looked back and forth, all over the room, and almost didn't see Maritza right before his eyes.

In front of him, laying underneath the window so that sunlight spilled onto it, warming it up, had been the corpse of an older man somewhere in his forties. Well, most of a corpse. The man's legs were nowhere to be found, and one arm lay severed and bloody, no more than a stump, a few feet away. Chunks of meat had been carved out of the man's torso and now lay scattered on the wooden floor, caked in sunlight and a layer of squirming maggots.

Maritza lay asleep amongst the flesh.

Ryckert had dropped to her side and yanked her out of the carnage. He was dismayed to find her right leg had been lopped off at the knee. He didn't see it anywhere in the room. Without it, the girl was out of luck. If Ryckert had been able to recover it, Colkirk's white mage might've had a chance at reattaching it. White magic was powerful.

He'd lightly slapped the girl's face to wake her up, and when she had snapped out of her daze, she shrieked at the sight of the rocyan holding her to his chest.

"Don't shout," he'd whispered to the child. "Here to help. Name's Ryckert."

"…Maritza," the girl sighed. That one word had almost been too much for her to push out.

Ryckert carried her out of the shack and all the way back to Colkirk. First, he'd stopped by the clinic to get her cleaned up and presentable; he didn't want to alarm Selina more than he had to. It was going to be hard enough for her to process the fact that her daughter was now missing a leg. The white mage, a fresh-faced young man just out of school but with the knowledge of someone at least triple his age, had concocted a potion that helped Maritza to be more awake, more focused. He'd also done something, of course, to dull the pain.

Selina's theory about her daughter being abducted had been correct, though not by The Flame and his men. It had actually been a crazed man, someone nobody in Colkirk knew, who had wandered into town and snatched her. He'd taken her back to the timeworn cabin he'd found, with the intention of devouring her. A dock worker had seen the incident and given chase, but as Ryckert saw, it hadn't ended well for him. The cannibal had slain the man and enjoyed his meat before turning to Maritza.

Ryckert had spent the next evening staking out the shack, and when the cannibal returned—regrettably, the man in question turned out to be a fellow rocyan—Ryckert sprung from the corner and slit his throat. When the night grew late and the moon hung high in the sky, Ryckert carried the monster's corpse out to a tall cliff on the northern end of town and cast it into the rocky sea below.

That had been the most satisfying job Ryckert had ever taken on. When he left on the airship a few days later, he'd made a mental note to return to Colkirk in order to check up on Maritza, see how she was faring. But that was seven years ago, and he'd never gone back. The girl would be nineteen years old now, already an adult.

He hoped she was doing okay.

- -

Not drunk yet. But he'd be there soon.

Ryckert rose from his reminiscence to order another drink at the bar, inviting the hangover. It raised his spirits, thinking back on a time when he had done some good. As he ordered, Michio waltzed through the door.

He began to wave exaggeratedly at the deaf-mute man, and when he finally caught his attention, Michio smiled and waved back before heading over to the table.

Once he was settled in, the mage extracted his notepad and pencil.

~ hello ~

"Hello," Ryckert growled back. He was glad the man couldn't hear his tone. He wanted to pile on the accusations, but a part of him knew that it was just drunken aggression, and he could not let that side of him steer the conversation. He thought he'd missed his chance to speak to Michio before at the inn, and he couldn't blow it now that he was here. Drunk or not.

~ gonna order a drink ~

With that, Michio stood and ambled over to the bar. He gave a charming grin to the bartender as he sidled up to the counter. Ryckert struggled to remember her name. Something with an A. Anna? Annabelle? It would come to him. Maybe.

Michio returned a minute later with a whiskey sour and a smile. *~ Ann Marie is a sweet girl. ~*

Ann Marie. That was it. Ryckert nodded in agreement. She was definitely his favorite of the waitresses here. He really needed to start doing better with names.

"Tried finding you at the inn earlier," Ryckert said, rotating his empty glass. The half-melted ice cubes clinked against the glass walls and each other. "Receptionist said you weren't on the list. Using a different name?"

Michio mimed a laugh, then wrote, *~ no fake names. not staying at inn. ~*

"Staying with a friend?"

~ no friends here. can't afford inn. staying in woods ~

Ryckert cocked an eyebrow. "Can't afford a night at the inn, but you've got enough for drinks at the pub every night?"

The man gave that charming jeornish grin. ~ *Priorities.* ~

That answer wasn't good enough for Ryckert, though. He leaned forward and said, "Seems to me it's less about priorities and more about not wanting to be seen. With a woman mysteriously dying last night, a stranger living in the woods won't look too great to the townsfolk."

At first Michio looked stunned, then his face contorted into hurt. He hurriedly scribbled on his paper:

~ *didnt kill anyone* ~

Ryckert eyed him, trying to see if there was anything in Michio's expression to give away that he was being deceitful. But the young man appeared genuinely hurt by Ryckert's implication. He leaned back, crossing his arms on his chest.

"Didn't say you did," Ryckert then said. "Just said it seems suspicious. If you've got crescents, why not stay in a warm bed? It's been unusually cold. Sleepin' in the woods can't be too pleasant."

Michio nodded. ~ *It's not. But too expensive. Drinks cheaper.* ~ His handwriting was less messy and he'd gone back to taking his time, apostrophes and all, now that Ryckert seemed to be cooling off.

Ryckert tapped his long, sharp fingernails on the tabletop and glared at Michio. He wanted to ask more questions, such as how he came to be in Balam at all, why he'd been kicked out of the academy. But he was already feeling too woozy to want to read what would surely be a long explanation, and he doubted Michio wanted to write it all out. He watched as Michio sipped innocently from his whiskey sour. The yellow liquid wetted his upper lip, which he licked away.

~ how did the woman die? ~

A pause before he answered. "Don't know," Ryckert said. "That's the big mystery. Something respiratory, maybe." Michio gave him a confused look, then twirled his finger in a gesture urging Ryckert to repeat himself. *"Respiratory,"* he said again, slower, so that Michio could take in all the syllables. It was probably not a word he encountered often, so he hadn't immediately grasped it.

~ sorry to hear it ~

"Mhm."

That was how they left the subject. Michio was visibly uncomfortable, and Ryckert could tell the mage wanted to leave. Ryckert felt bad for being so severe toward the young man, but he couldn't help himself. He'd said what needed to be said. Gotten it out of the way as quickly as possible. Now they could move on.

"If you need a place to stay, you can stay with me," Ryckert said. The words fell out of his mouth before he really comprehended what he was offering. He was less sure today than yesterday that he trusted Michio, but maybe keeping him close would be the right call. Easier to keep an eye on him, see what he was up to.

~ Don't have to do that. Too generous. Fine in woods. ~

Ryckert waved him off. "Not any trouble. I'd be glad to have the company."

He found that the words weren't entirely false. In addition to the boredom, he'd been feeling much lonelier lately. The isolation was starting to get to him. When he felt this way, he missed Fenn's companionship more than usual.

Michio pondered the proposal, taking curt sips of his drink. But in the end, he shook his head.

~ I'm okay. But thanks for the offer ~

And with those words, Ryckert was positive the mage had something to hide.

CHAPTER III

ARRIVAL

The following two days were easier for Theo. Not by much, but still, they were easier. The shock was starting to wear off and his appetite was returning. Soon, he hoped, he would be able to enjoy his spring vacation.

Ryckert, meanwhile, had dropped the subjects of Freya's death and Michio's arrival. A nagging part of him still suspected they might be connected, but it did not take long to convince himself that he had simply lost his edge during these quiet years in this small coastal village. He was being paranoid. Just thirsting for some thrills.

On the third day after Freya's death, a wagon rolled into Balam with its new white mage. Her name was Aava Yren.

- -

Aava's journey through the Cerene Forest had been dull. The town's mayor (or who she assumed to be the mayor; in retrospect, he'd never stated that was his title), a man named Rufus Reede, had contacted the headmaster at Allinor University, claiming the nearby town of Balam was in desperate need of a white mage, even if it was only temporary.

Aava had graduated from Allinor mere weeks before the university received Mr. Reede's urgent letter. Her brother, Svend, was two years younger and still in training, so she had opted to continue living there with him until he graduated. Dormitories were plentiful on the campus and the library was bursting with reading material she could sink her teeth into for years.

She had been looking forward to a relaxing spring, one spent reading by the central fountain, taking walks through the woods, and experimenting with new spells. But the headmaster had come to her with Mr. Reede's request and asked if she would be willing to take on the task, being one of the graduating class's top students—and, most likely, the only one who still remained on the grounds.

It made her nervous. There was no denying that. She was only eighteen years old, and she had finished school only fifteen days prior. But this was what she had been studying for over the past four years; the opportunity had simply presented itself far sooner than anticipated. And besides, it would only be temporary. Once a suitable permanent replacement was found, she could shuffle on home and spend the next two years further mastering her craft before she sought a real job.

She informed the headmaster of her decision, broke the news to Svend, and then began packing. She would depart the next morning.

"Are you sure you even wanna do this?" Svend had asked her.

He was sitting at a desk in the common room of their dormitory, which was divided into two bedrooms, a common room (with a small kitchen), and a bathroom. In front of him was a textbook flipped open to a section detailing Sleep spells. It was a fairly low-level spell, one that Aava had to learn as well, but it was certainly useful. There were two levels to the spell; Svend had already gotten the basic method down and had successfully put a few of his classmates to sleep, but the higher-level method was giving him trouble. He was only half-paying attention to the text while he spoke to his sister.

"I think so," she answered, the uncertainty apparent even in her tone of voice. "It's a unique opportunity, that's for sure. It's like an internship. Go for a couple weeks, help people out there, then head back home after. It's kind of ideal, if you think about it."

"You've already done internships, though," Svend pointed out as he reread the same sentence over and over. "And those weren't in some no-name town in the middle of nowhere."

"It *has* a name, which is *Balam*, by the way," she'd told him with a smirk. "And it's not in the middle of nowhere. It's southeast of here. Only a couple days away by wagon, actually."

"Well, my point still stands," Svend grumbled. "It's nothing like when you went to Bral Han for a summer semester, where there were tons of people every day who needed help. How many people do you think you're *actually* gonna see each day there?"

"I don't know."

"I bet the whole town's population is less than the amount of patients you had per day in Bral Han!"

Aava had laughed at this. "Well, then it sounds a lot less stressful!" She continued folding her shirts and stuffing them into her modestly sized suitcase. She worried she wouldn't be able to fit enough clothes for the trip; the last time she'd been away for so long was the aforementioned internship in Bral Han, and Svend had unfortunately torched the suitcase she'd used for that trip while practicing his upper-level Fire techniques.

By the time she was set to leave the next morning, Svend seemed to have come around to the idea. Or at least he was pretending to, which was good enough for Aava. She knew he was only being stubborn because he would miss her, and she would miss him too.

She'd placed her bag inside the wagon Mr. Reede had arranged for her, then turned and gave her brother a tight hug.

"I won't be gone long," she had said, not knowing whether it was true or not. "You should come visit. You're not going to be doing anything here anyway!" she grinned.

"Yeah, right!" He pushed away, giving her a mockingly stern look. "I'm gonna be here training to be the best black mage this dumb place has ever seen."

"By putting serokos and hollions to sleep?"

"Hey, they're good practice," he shot back.

"I'm not sure they are," Aava said with a chuckle. "They sleep through most of the day anyway. How would you know it's your spell that did it?"

"Whatever, get outta here," Svend grumbled. He smiled and gave her another hug. "I'll write to you soon. We can plan a visit."

"Sounds great," she'd said.

They broke off and she stepped into the back of the carriage. She waved again through the window.

"All ready?" the driver called from the front of the wagon. He gripped the leather reins, which wrapped around the horns of a male bulloko. Its blue fur bristled in the chilly breeze.

"Yep!" Aava replied. Her words were tinged with eagerness and energy.

She couldn't wait to find out what Balam had in store.

- -

The uneventful trip through the forest had dampened Aava's enthusiasm somewhat. Having nobody to talk to except the driver, a man named Wendell Grote who had proven to be a bit airheaded and unexpectedly sexist, she had grown exceptionally bored and spent most of her time staring at the trees passing by or lying on the carriage bench, trying to nap. Most of her conversations with Wendell involved him expressing his disbelief that such a young jeornish woman would be assigned as a town's sole white mage, or him regaling all the times he'd been the driver for traveling qarmish theatre troupes. He was a huge fan of the qarmish, she had learned.

During the one night they'd had to camp together (Aava planning to sleep inside the locked carriage, he in a cramped tent pitched a few feet away), Wendell had gathered a bundle of sticks for a fire to heat up some beans for dinner. He'd grown agitated when Aava continually assured him she had no idea how to cast Fire, so he had to resort to the old-fashioned way of lighting a spark.

The beans tasted okay. They weren't bad, but a touch salty, in Aava's opinion. After they'd finished eating, a chance to show Wendell that she was in fact a capable young woman presented itself.

Wendell had wandered off the road into the woods to relieve himself after a day of chugging water from his canteen, and when he returned to their makeshift campsite, he'd tripped over himself and fell forward. He'd managed to extend his arms to break his fall, but his right hand had plunged into the hot ashes at the base of the still-burning fire.

He yelped and pushed himself backward, clutching his injured hand to his chest. "Fuck me!" he cursed, then began to blow cool air onto his burn. The bulloko, which was grazing serenely nearby, paused to observe what was going on.

Aava rushed to his side and extended a hand. "May I look?" she asked.

Wendell reluctantly exposed his palm to her. The skin was red and bumpy. It didn't look like too bad a burn, given he had only touched the ashes and not the flames, but she knew it still had to hurt quite a bit.

She knew a spell called VoidBurn, which would allay the pain he was feeling, and then she could use a simple Cure spell to heal the skin.

Aava released his arm and held her hands flat over Wendell's. She looked him in the eye and said, "I can heal this. It's easy. Would you like me to?"

Wendell shrugged. "Sure."

Don't be too grateful, Aava thought irritably. He had made it abundantly clear he didn't think a woman so young would be of any use to a whole village, but maybe she could show him that she knew what she was doing. She was young, but she was no novice. Not as if she needed to prove anything to this man, but she had to confess it would feel kind of nice to be vindicated.

She concentrated on the burn and visualized the spell in her mind. She then began to gesture with her fingers—every spell looked ridiculous, and when she had first started classes at Allinor she had felt supremely embarrassed every time she'd had to cast a spell, though now she had grown accustomed to the gestures.

For VoidBurn, the motions were simple: she crossed her middle fingers under her index fingers, then ring fingers under her middle fingers, repeated three times. A light red glow then shone from her fingertips, which she used to rub the surface of Wendell's skin where he had been hurt.

From the look on his face, she could tell the burning sensation was fading. He was astonished; not because he didn't think white magic worked, because of course it did, but because *her* white magic worked.

Once she had covered the entire area with the spell, she drew her hands back and the glow disappeared.

"Thanks," he said in a low voice. "Feels a lot better, actually."

Aava ignored his "actually" and set to work casting Cure. The skin healed instantly and looked good as new. It was as if the incident had never occurred at all.

He offered another meek showing of gratitude as he examined his palm. "Looks pretty good." He then went to take a sip of water from his canteen, which he had left with its cap undone, but immediately spit the liquid out onto the ground.

Aava gave him a quizzical look.

"Must've knocked ashes into it when I fell," he said, wiping his lips with the back of his forearm. "Dammit."

Aava held her hand out, inviting Wendell to give her the canteen. He did so, and she placed it in her lap, holding both her hands out above the opening, with all of her fingers outstretched and her thumbs resting with one on top of the other. She then curled the four fingers on each hand and separated her thumbs. After this display, she handed the canteen back to Wendell and said, "Good as new."

The man took a cautious sip, then, realizing it was fine, gulped it down and nodded his approval. "What'd you do to it?" he asked, clear water dribbling down his chin.

"Just a simple cleansing spell called Purify," she said.

"Thanks."

"You're welcome," Aava said, rising. She was on her way back to the carriage to perhaps read for a little while before going to sleep when Wendell spoke up again.

"Hey, why don't you stay out here by the fire a little longer? Get to know each other?"

She could already tell where this was going, and she was not the least bit interested. But Wendell Grote did not seem like the type of man who would take kindly to resistance. She had helped him out, so now he was being nice to her, and since he was being nice to her didn't that mean she should…?

"No, I'm fine," she said in return, facing him with her hands behind her back. Not all men were like Wendell Grote, but she'd encountered a couple of them in her time spent in Bral Han and she had grown weary of them.

Wendell let out a sizeable yawn. "Okay," he groaned. His eyelids fluttered and he began to drift back and forth woozily. He then curled up on the ground a few feet away from the fire and began to snore.

Aava grinned with satisfaction and got back into the carriage, locking up behind her. Maybe she would give Svend some lessons on that spell when she returned.

- -

Luckily, Wendell being a bit too full of himself was the only problem they encountered on their trip. No bandits, no wolves, no goblins, nothing. A peaceful journey, by all accounts.

As the sun set on that second day and dusk began to envelope the woods, Wendell yelled back to her.

"You up?"

"Yes," she responded, leaning out the window.

"Gather up your stuff if you need to," he said. "We're just about there."

A knot tied in Aava's belly. Soon she'd be meeting Mr. Reede, and settling into the town's clinic, and seeing patients to help with their ailments. All at once she felt woefully unprepared.

That's foolishness, she told herself. *You're ready. You were one of the top in your class. You know what you're doing.*

But simply convincing herself was much different than actually demonstrating her worth in a clear, identifiable way. It still made her anxious, and she hoped she could live up to the patients' expectations as well as her own.

As they rounded a curve in the road, a wooden sign came into view that read BALAM. The town was just ahead. She could see a tall, storied building in the distance. Probably the inn.

The wagon came to a stop at the edge of a stone staircase etched into a short cliff, roughly twenty feet high.

"And this is where I leave you," Wendell said loudly, hopping off the wagon to stretch his legs. "Enjoy your stay."

Aava exited the wagon, suitcase in hand, feeling more nervous than ever. She felt out of place and suddenly very lonely, having to enter the town all on her own with nothing but a single bag. She wished Svend was there with her.

She bade Wendell farewell and descended the steps, not looking back to see what he was doing. She walked down the winding pathway, flanked by tall trees with vibrant green leaves. The moon was starting to share its light, but was tucked behind unmoving clouds.

The first building she passed, on her right side, was the inn she'd seen from the road. The windows were lit up and she could hear piano music coming from inside, as well as the din of chatter. It was two stories tall and looked cozy, even from the outside. She thought she would've enjoyed staying there, if white mage clinics didn't already come with their own lodging.

Up ahead was what appeared to be an even wider walkway, paved with stone, which cut through the center of the village. She now had a better view of the town and could see it was multilayered. An interesting layout, one she hadn't seen before.

What she also saw was an enormous crowd of people gathered on the other side of the stone street. They were milling about what must be the town square, grabbing plates of food from tables that had been set up on the square's perimeter. Children played underneath a looming, blue-leafed tree to the right of the square.

"She has arrived!" a short, skinny man squawked at the sight of her.

The group immediately ceased their conversations and turned to face Aava. Every eye was awkwardly boring into her as she completed the easily forty-foot walk that remained.

When she was finally almost to the town square, the thin man skipped forward and clapped a hand on her shoulder.

"Welcome!" he beamed. "I'm Rufus Reede. You read my letter?"

"Yes. My name is Aava Yren," she said with a nod, and they shook hands.

"Ahh, good. Pleasure to meet you, Aava! So you know our situation, then. Would you like to come with me to see the body?"

The body?

Aava had known the town's previous white mage, a woman named Freya, had passed away recently and so they were in need of a new mage to manage the clinic. But why was the body still here? The letter hadn't mentioned that.

"I…" Aava started, before deciding it didn't matter. "Okay."

But Mr. Reede himself waved the idea away. "What am I doing?" he asked. "Answer: getting ahead of myself, as always. Apologies!" He gestured toward the gazing crowd that stood behind him. "Let me introduce you to some folks here."

The first person Mr. Reede brought forward was a round man with an impressively thick brown mustache and close to no hair on his pate. "Hullo, dear," the man greeted her, offering his hand to shake. She took it and learned his name was Walton Vere.

"Walton Vere here's the—" Mr. Reede stopped himself to laugh at his own rhyme. When he recovered, he continued, "—he's the owner of our lovely Sonata Diner. Best steak you'll ever eat! You like steak?"

"On occasion," Aava smiled. "Nice to meet you, Mr. Vere."

"Call me Walton," he mumbled with a warm grin. "Ever'one else does."

Walton took a step back and a breathtaking woman with cropped, shimmering blonde hair took his place. Aava was sure she'd never seen anyone prettier.

"This here's Vanessa Dower," Mr. Reede introduced her. "She's our head blacksmith. Runs the shop with her husband, Bromley. Isn't that right?"

"That's right," Vanessa said with a charming smile. "We're glad to have you here." Her voice was as silky and smooth as her hair.

Next she met the town butcher, then the owner of the general store, then an older man who taught at the local school. She was surprised by the types of people she was meeting. No town officials, no officers of the law; just everyday townsfolk. Balam was shaping up to be quite a change from Bral Han after all.

"And this is Theodore Saen," Mr. Reede said, pulling forward a young man who had to be somewhere in his twenties. "He's a literature professor here at our school. He's also the man who was with Freya when she passed, rest her soul."

Theo was handsome in a boyish way, with short red hair and arresting green eyes that were noticeable even in the growing dark. Aava smiled wide as she shook his hand, but he looked less enthused by their meeting.

"Theodore here can walk you through what happened that night whenever you're ready. That'd be tomorrow, I presume. You'll want to get settled tonight, I'm sure! No time for work, no ma'am." Words spilled out of Mr. Reede's mouth like slippery slugs. "Shall I show you to the clinic?"

"That sounds fine," she said.

She followed Mr. Reede down to the middle level of the town. No one from the gathering followed, instead staying behind to continue eating the food that had been laid out for her arrival. Her stomach growled and she regretted missing the chance to grab a plate.

No use keeping quiet about it, she thought. "Would it be alright if we went back to the square for some food afterwards?" she asked. "I actually haven't had any dinner."

"Oh! Strike me down!" Mr. Reede gasped. It was an overly dramatic phrase and gesture (smacking his hand to his heart), but somehow it seemed genuine, rather than sarcastic, coming from this odd man. "Of course, of course! We'll make it a quick tour. My apologies."

Thankfully, it was a short walk to the clinic, which was only two blocks down on their right, just off Main Street. Neatly trimmed bushes surrounded the domed hut, which appeared to be connected to another, smaller dome on the building's left side. That had to be where she'd be living for the next undetermined number of weeks.

"And here is the clinic," Mr. Reede said, gesturing flamboyantly toward the dome. "Pretty nice, is it not? Allow me to show you around inside." He skipped ahead and unlocked the front door, then handed her the key. "Don't worry," he said, pushing the door open. "I had Bernard move the body out of here already."

Aava blinked in confusion.

- -

Theo walked over to Lyrra, who had stayed back by the salad bowl, filling up her plate and munching on lettuce and tomatoes while Mr. Reede had made the town introductions.

"She looks young," was Lyrra's first comment.

Theo nodded. "Yep. I assume she's good, though, otherwise the academy wouldn't have sent her."

That had been his first thought too. He had been taken aback by how young the jeornish mage appeared. Not that it was necessarily a bad thing; he had just expected somebody older. He felt guilty and hypocritical about the assumption, considering how much grief he always got at work from Serys White for his own age.

"How much longer do you wanna stay?" he asked, picking a piece of lettuce off Lyrra's plate and popping it into his mouth. There was a wet, satisfying crunch as he chewed it.

She shrugged and gave him a joking glare for stealing her food. "Not too much longer, I guess. I wanted to chat with Vanessa a bit, though."

"Alright. Maybe you can ask her if Bromley is ever gonna shave that little baby mustache he's got growing," he teased.

Lyrra laughed and spooned a few pieces of grilled meat onto her plate before sauntering off to the yunesca tree, where Vanessa was sitting on the bench watching her two sons play. Theo watched as the women said their hellos and Lyrra took a seat beside her.

"How you holdin' up?"

The voice came from behind Theo and startled him. He turned and found Al Opping grinning like a fool with a shank of meat in hand, his fingers wrapped around the bone and slicked with grease.

It took a second for Theo to really hear the question. "What do you mean?" he asked.

"I heard you were having a rough time the past few days," Al said before tearing off a chunk of meat. He smacked his lips as he chewed the fatty piece he'd bitten off. Theo resisted grimacing.

"Where'd you hear that?" he wanted to know. Were people talking about him? Was there gossip floating around Balam about Theodore Saen's mental state? Surely not.

"Dunno," Al shrugged. "I think Serys might've mentioned it."

"You're spending an awful lot of time with Serys."

"Guess so. He likes to drink, and I like to drink."

"Point taken. What did Serys say about me?" He felt dirty knowing that Serys White was blathering about him behind his back.

Al tore off another piece of meat and began to speak with his mouth full. "Not much, really. His wife's the one who told him. Said Lyrra had to take off work to stay home with you. Do you need some help, man? You know I'm here if you need anything."

It made sense. Theo had forgotten Elena White, along with her daughter Hilli, worked at the inn with Lyrra. Of course she'd know if Lyrra didn't come in to work. At least he could assume now that there wasn't news spreading all over town about how he didn't have the energy or motivation to get out of bed.

"Yeah, I know," Theo said. "Thanks. I'm alright, though, really. It just…surprised me, is all," he muttered. "It took a couple days to process what happened, you know? I'm fine now." He thought it sounded convincing.

"Alrighty," said Al. "If you say so. But come get me if you ever need to, you hear me?"

Theo gave him a smile. "I hear you."

Al grinned back. "Me and Serys are gonna hit the pub again tonight. You in this time?" Theo was starting to decline when Al interjected. "Nope! Not gonna let you say no! C'mon, it'll be fun. Let's celebrate the new mage comin' to town, whattaya say? And besides, Serys has been wanting to see you. He's been asking after you, tellin' me to invite you out with us."

In no world would Theo ever have guessed Serys White wanted to spend time with him. He knew Al was making stuff up to convince him to go get a drink, but he let up and agreed.

"Fine," he conceded. "Let me go tell Lyrra."

He briefly interrupted her conversation with Vanessa, who was glad to see Theo out and about ("We have to have you two over for dinner soon!" she exclaimed), and let her know he was going out with Al. Lyrra seemed pleased to hear he was going to be spending time with some friends rather than going back to the house. He gave her a peck on the cheek and said he'd see her in a while.

"Ready?" Al asked, tossing his meat bone into a garbage can a couple feet away.

"Ready."

- -

The bar was nearly empty; most people were out at the gathering that had been organized for Aava's welcoming. But there were a few choice residents scattered about, including the rocyan who lived down on the beach. He sat at the counter, eating a sandwich and drinking from a stout glass filled almost to the brim with an amber liquid.

Serys awaited them at a table to the right of the entryway, behind the volleywag table. He waved them over and indicated "two more" to a waitress by wiggling two meaty fingers at her.

Al sat across from Serys, and Theo sat at Al's side. "Hello, boys," the older man greeted them. "How's the night treating you?"

"Pretty well," Theo answered cordially.

"Glad to hear it. Ordered you fellows some beers. Next round's on you," he said, nodding toward Al.

Al found this to be more than fair, and downed half his beer as soon as it was handed to him. He wiped wetness from his lips and told Serys, "The new white mage is here, by the way. Her name's Aava."

"Pretty name," said Serys. "The jeornish always have such pretty names."

"You certainly have a thing for them," Al grinned. "That why you married one?"

"Of course, of course!"

The two had practically forgotten Theo was even present, which suited him just fine. The less he had to interact with Serys outside of work, the better. A drink with Al would've been one thing, but with Serys there, Theo wished he had gone home to Vir instead. But he knew this would get Al off his back about going out drinking for a while, so he had obliged.

They carried on that way for almost an hour, with Serys and Al talking about trivial things while Theo chimed in with a sentence or two whenever he could edge a word in. He kept it to the bare minimum to still technically count as being part of the conversation.

A few rounds later, though, Theo was starting to give in to the effects of the alcohol. It had been a long time since he'd gone out drinking with Al, or anybody at all—aside from the occasional glass of wine with dinner, he tried to abstain from drinking too much during the school semesters—and the beers were hitting him harder than he thought they would. As a result, he was laughing at Serys's shitty jokes more, which stroked the man's ego despite the fact the laughs were more *at* than *with*. Being drunk himself, Serys couldn't tell the difference.

"I really should go home," Theo mumbled, noticing the time. It was only nearing ten o'clock, but that was later than he usually stayed out. He was a man who enjoyed getting comfortable in bed and reading a while before going to sleep. He had to unwind somehow; he wasn't the type of person to just get home, get in bed, and fall asleep. Alfred Opping could not relate.

"No way!" Al objected. "It's barely dark outside! You can stay up a little later!"

"It got dark, like, two hours ago…" Theo pointed out, stumbling over the words. His tongue felt like it weighed a pound.

Al had no retort for this. He looked to Serys for help, but he was all dried up as well.

Theo's eyes wandered over to the counter, where Ann Marie stood idly by herself, polishing a glass.

"Look," he said, pointing. "Not even the rocyan's here anymore. If he's gone, you know it's closing time."

"No, you know it's closing time when the bar closes."

"Well, I'm leaving anyway," Theo said. He pushed himself up out of his chair and immediately became lightheaded. He grabbed the table to steady himself before attempting to walk.

Serys hopped up and scurried to his side. "Let me give you a hand, there, bud," he said, wrapping an arm around Theo.

He helped Theo over to the entrance. Theo reached into his pocket to hand Serys a couple crescents, to cover his last drink, but the man told him not to worry about it.

"Listen," Serys then said in a hushed voice. "I wanted to ask you something."

"What?" Theo asked. The sheer surprise of Serys having anything to say or ask him was sobering.

Serys shot a quick glance over his shoulder to see if Al was watching or listening. He wasn't, instead focused on trying to balance a crescent on the neck of his beer bottle. He scanned the rest of the bar, which was basically empty except for one patron in the back corner, far away from them, and Ann Marie at the counter. Satisfied, he turned back to Theo and, with great intensity, asked, "Did she say anything before it happened?"

Theo blinked. "What?"

"Freya," the man said, even softer. "Did she say anything before she died? Anything meaningful? Noteworthy?"

Drunken Serys sure was curious about strange things.

"No," Theo answered. "She didn't say anything. Just choked on nothin' and dropped dead."

Serys took in a fast inhalation through his nose and breathed it out after a moment. His eyes darted to the ground, then back up to Theo.

"Okay," he said. "Thank you."

With that, he reclaimed his seat across from Al and gave Theo one last glare.

Theo left the bar, thoroughly weirded out. His steps were uneven and unpredictable. He might have to get home and go straight to sleep after all; there was no way he would be able to read words on a page, no matter how hard he squinted. He headed toward home and comfort, welcoming the cool air on his face.

- -

Aava had eaten a quick, conversation-filled meal with Mr. Reede at the town square, where she had met a few more friendly people, and she was now back home at the clinic, getting ready for bed.

Calling the clinic her home felt unnatural on her tongue. She'd only known two homes before: the dormitory she and Svend shared at Allinor, and their childhood home back in Oxhollow. But she supposed this was her home now, however fleeting it might be.

All of Freya's possessions still filled the room. Her mementos, her family photographs, her decorations. The framed photos made Aava feel slightly uncomfortable, so she moved those onto a table in the clinic. She would start packing away Freya's things tomorrow (with the help of a woman named Lisa Tilling, Mr. Reede informed her) so that her son could pick them up sometime next week. She would then be able to unpack her own belongings and decorate the abode as she saw fit.

Dressed in her voluminous pink pajamas, Aava got herself snug in bed and pulled the sheets up to her chin. It was cold outside, and being in a warm bed after a night spent on a wooden bench was most welcome.

Overall, it hadn't been a bad first night in Balam. Sure, the man who acted as its leader was a bit peculiar, and the layout of the town would take some getting used to, but it seemed like a perfectly lovely place to live.

She closed her eyes and hoped for pleasant dreams and pleasant days to come.

CHAPTER IV

THE BODY

Ryckert had once again awoken with a headache, which was becoming far too commonplace for his liking. He told himself he needed to get a grip, to stop wallowing. This was the life he had chosen. Either accept it or pick a new one, if it was so terrible.

He was now propped up in his chair, fishing line bobbing lackadaisically in the water near the waterfall's base. The fish he'd caught there a few days prior had been fairly tasty and he was craving more.

Last night, he had purposefully not attended the welcoming party for the new white mage. The crowd had dispersed by the time he left the pub and the mage was nowhere to be seen, so he still didn't know anything about the person. All he knew about them was that they had come from Allinor University, which he had gained from overhearing a conversation in the Sonata.

He'd known that if he met the mage, the temptation would be too great. For some reason he *needed* to know how Freya had died. He absolutely thirsted for it.

Even though all signs were pointing toward a natural death, something felt off about it. It was nothing more than Ryckert's gut that told him this, but his intuition had gotten him out of some tight spots in his day.

That was in the past, though. He kept telling himself that, and yet still he thirsted. This was the white mage's business now, not his. He would need to somehow be content sitting here on the beach, fishing and watching the waves.

The same could be said of Michio. There was something off about the man, something suspicious, but Ryckert didn't know what. Why else would a man so poor he had to sleep on the cold dirt in the woods turn down a night indoors unless he had something to hide?

None of your business, Ryckert thought. An increasingly familiar phrase.

A tug at the line snapped his focus back to the real world, away from thoughts and theories about the young black mage or the white mage's mysterious—*but* was *it mysterious?*—death.

Ryckert felt the fish pulling to the left, so he carefully yet firmly veered the rod in the opposite direction and began to slowly reel it in. He then gave the fish some slack, let it think it was in control, then started to pull it in once more. He fought with his catch like this for a minute or two before giving it one final yank, sending the fish flying out onto dry land. It flopped pathetically on the soft ground, kicking up sand like a child at play.

It was the same type of fish he'd caught before, as he'd expected. About a foot long, scales a deep red. But this time there was more than a dash of green amongst the red. At least half the scales were tinted green on the fish. It looked more like a discoloration than just its natural hue.

Ryckert gave it a swift whack on the head to kill it. With the floundering ceased, he picked it up by the tail and rotated it in the air. Sunlight glinted off its strange scales.

He gave it a sniff with his long, powerful snout. There was no foul odor, nothing to suggest the fish was sick or spoiled. Perhaps this one merely had different scales than the others. An outcast, maybe. The idea that it might be an entirely different breed of fish crossed Ryckert's mind, but it was just as quickly cast aside. It definitely looked like the fish he had eaten before. Same length, body curvature, eye placement, mouth shape. It was the same. Just different.

Neither his head nor stomach were agreeing with him this morning, but Ryckert possessed enough self-awareness to know that if he ate only one fish for lunch he would be hungry again soon after. So he set back to work, and twenty minutes later (twenty long, daydream-filled minutes wondering about the town's new mages), he caught another fish. This one's scales were more in line with what he'd caught before. He grinned at the dead outlier that lay beside his chair. He'd found himself a rarity. It would cook up nicely, too.

Two would be enough. He left the chair behind and gathered up the rest of his belongings and moseyed back over to the cabin. By the time he finished cleaning his bounty, it'd be around lunchtime.

And, on the bright side, maybe working with his hands would distract him from those pestering thoughts. Maybe he'd let it all go and just enjoy the day.

But probably not.

--

Aava awoke that day feeling wildly disoriented. When her eyes first opened, she'd momentarily forgotten where she was. She took in the unfamiliar sights—the bright red door directly across from the bed where she slept, the bookshelves crammed with books on her right, the slightly ajar door to her left leading to the bathroom. The only thing she recognized in the room were the red and white banners hanging from the walls. These were the Ballastia Academy school colors, the mage academy located in Bral Han. These were what brought her back up to speed. She was in Freya's home.

Ballastia's school colors made her yearn for Allinor. A clock on the bedside table informed her that it was nearly nine o'clock, much later than she usually slept. If she were still back home, at the university, she would probably be eating breakfast outside in the courtyard right about now. A light breakfast, so as to not fill herself up too much and have to skip lunch. Usually a piece of toast with honey and some berries. That sounded great to her. Maybe the diner owned by that man she'd met last night would have some.

She was starting to get out of bed with the aim of getting dressed and going out when she realized she had no clue where the diner was, or if it was even open at this time of day. She sat back down on the bed, deflated.

No matter; a walk would do her good, she decided. It was the start to her day that she required if she was going to be performing an autopsy. While she wandered the town she could learn where places were located, and hopefully see the diner's business hours.

She got dressed in something light yet resilient, since the sun was blaring but there would be cold winds. She wore a thin white t-shirt with a maroon corduroy jacket and tight-fitting, light brown pants. She brushed her teeth and checked herself out in the bathroom mirror to ensure her hair was presentable.

Miraculously, it was almost perfectly straight today even after what must have been a restless night, if the bags under her eyes were any indication. The tips of her shimmery, white hair brushed against her shoulders. Not long ago, her hair had reached midway down her back; she had never gotten it cut before. One of her friends at the academy, Jasmiin Vira, had encouraged her to give short hair a try.

Jasmiin had grown up in Bral Han, where the fashion among young jeornish women was what she referred to as a pixie cut. Aava had of course seen women with this hair style before, but she'd never heard it given a name. Jasmiin fawned over Aava's hair, but always said that she would look amazing with a pixie cut.

"Guys would practically be tripping over themselves, trying to push past each other to talk to you," Jasmiin had said. She was constantly complimenting Aava's looks, and as a result, Aava had harbored a small crush when they had first met, but that had long since passed and been replaced by other crushes, both male and female alike.

Suitors were not really Aava's priority at Allinor, though she admitted it would be a pretty nice bonus. But she hadn't felt comfortable chopping off all of her hair, and compromised by getting it cut just above her shoulders.

It had now grown out an inch or so, and she quite liked how it looked. She smiled at herself, running her fingers through her hair.

Now ready to go, Aava clambered through the hallway connecting the "home" dome to the "clinic" dome. This was how all white mage clinics were built—not always as domes, but always two buildings connected by a hallway. For cities with more than one white mage on duty, it was the head white mage that lived at the clinic while the others rented apartments or bought homes. It had seemed weird to Aava when she started her studies and held her first internship, but now she found the practice cozy and comfortable.

Not to mention useful. There had been more than one instance during her second internship, in a village called Ebonpass, when a small epidemic had broken out amongst some of the town's hunters and they all came rushing back early from their expedition at two in the morning, banging on the clinic's front door. As it turned out, the group had been assaulted in their sleep by a horde of five or six vissians, wolf-sized insectoids with a poisonous bite. If Aava and Fahleran, her mentor, hadn't been present to provide aid, all of them would have undoubtedly perished.

That night had been quite a learning experience for her. She'd read about the process in school, but that night she had been required to craft an antidote to the vissian poison, an antivenom made from its own poison. It was a lengthy process, which Fahleran had already gone through so he had some antivenom on hand, but he walked her through each step to craft more after it had been safely administered to each man.

Aava cast no more than a sideways glance at the ingredients and tools stocked in Freya's clinic. There would be time later to make note of where everything was and rearrange it how she saw fit, because it wasn't Freya's clinic anymore. It was *her* clinic. That fact would take some getting used to.

The weather was the mix of warmth and briskness that Aava had been anticipating. She appreciated the chance to wear her favorite jacket.

Balam was bustling with activity today, even so early in the morning. Perhaps nine-thirty wasn't very early for these folk. She was too accustomed to university life, where if you had to wake up at eight to attend class an hour later, it was the worst thing imaginable.

But here, everyone was out and about. She was greeted with smiles by men and women as she passed them on the street, heading out to run errands or visit friends or maybe even grab a bite to eat.

She had taken a left outside the clinic and navigated toward Main Street, since that was what she was most familiar with at this point. She looked up and down the road and saw teenagers sitting on benches, deep in conversation. A father and his son nearby were walking their dog, which stopped to urinate on a bush and accidentally sprayed a bit onto the street, garnering a soft scolding from the father. As Aava turned to face the direction of the ocean, a familiar face popped into view.

"Hello!" Mr. Reede beamed, waving madly as if trying to get a blind man to see him. "I hope you slept well! How are you liking Balam?"

It might not be early for everybody else, but it was far too early for Aava to handle Rufus Reede's unbridled enthusiasm.

"I slept just fine," she answered politely. "And Balam seems to be a very nice town indeed. I think I'll settle in nicely here."

This pleased Mr. Reede a great deal. Aava was worried his smile was going to grow so wide he'd tear his cheeks and she would have to operate on him right there in the middle of the street. "Wonderful!" he exhaled. "Wonderful, wonderful!"

If she was going to be forced to speak with this man, she figured she might as well glean some useful information from him. "Mr. Reede, I have a question for you."

"Of course! Fire away. Ha-*ha!*" Mr. Reede found this phrasing to be humorous despite there being no apparent pun or joke. "*Fire*, even though you're a white mage, not a black mage. Ha! Anyway, go on, go on."

It took all of Aava's willpower not to groan. She succeeded and asked, "Where can I find the diner owned by…?"

"Walton Vere," Mr. Reede finished for her, with a look of satisfaction on his thin, wormy face. "You can find the Sonata that way—" he turned and pointed in the direction of the beach, but just to the right "—on the next street over. If you drop into the ocean, you've gone too far!" He laughed heartily at this joke. "You'll see the blacksmith first, and the Sonata is just a little farther down, on the opposite side of the street."

Aava gave the man a sweet smile and thanked him for his directions. "I must be going," she then said. "I need to get some food in me."

"Of course!" Mr. Reede exclaimed once again. The man was exhausting. "Would you like me to accompany you?"

"That won't be necessary," Aava blurted out. "I like a bit of time to myself before I start the day, you see."

"Right, right. I understand completely. I enjoy having a bit of quiet time myself, you know!"

Aava severely doubted that, but she did not contradict him. They said their goodbyes and she pressed onward toward the diner. She was anxious to begin her autopsy, but knew it would be hard to focus with a growling stomach.

She passed the blacksmith's shop, where she was sure Vanessa Dower was getting ready to open up (the sign out front claimed they opened at ten o'clock), and easily spotted the diner a little ways down the road. Across from the establishment was an exquisite view of the sea, which glimmered brilliantly in the spring sun. Aava soaked in the sight for a moment before entering.

Walton Vere fulfilled her request for toast and berries, bringing out a beautiful, colorful plate with a piece of honeyed toast in its center. It was delicious and much-needed on a morning such as this.

It was time to get to work.

- -

Aava had been told by Mr. Reede during his brief tour of the clinic that the butcher she had met, a man named Bernard Tilling, had transported Freya's body to a storage shed behind his home on the upper level of town. The news had made Aava cringe, as it sounded crude and disrespectful, but Mr. Reede had assured her it was actually a pretty nice shed, and that the measures they'd taken were necessary; they needed to delay burying the body so that they could figure out the cause of death. The body was periodically having a Preservation spell cast on it by a mage named Mhar who was currently staying at the inn.

So when she finished her meal, Aava found her way to Bernard Tilling's house just north of the town square, based on the directions Mr. Reede had given her at dinner. As she neared Bernard's house, Aava realized she had no idea where Mr.

Reede lived, and hoped she'd never find out. She rapped her knuckles on the front door and took a step back.

It was opened by a woman with flowing black hair that contrasted against her light yellow dress. "Hello," the woman said. "You must be Aava. I'm Lisa, Bernard's wife. He's at the shop already, but I can show you back to the shed."

Aava thanked the woman and followed her around the house, into the backyard. There stood a massive shed, almost the size of a second house. It was set against a backdrop of trees, which extended back to the twenty-foot high cliffside. Lisa explained this shed was where Bernard did a lot of his work cutting the meat before bringing it to the shop to be sold. This knowledge made Aava even more uncomfortable with the body's storage.

Inside, the aroma of raw meat permeated the shed. A metallic odor struck Aava's nostrils. However, it was cleaner than she would ever have thought a butcher's workspace could be. Bernard must have hosed the place down before bringing Freya over. Perhaps it wasn't such a disrespectful situation after all. Everybody was showing great care for this woman. Hooks hung from the ceiling, their sharp tips reddened by dried blood. On a steel countertop in the middle of the room was the body.

"I'll leave you to it," Lisa said solemnly before stepping out.

Aava slowly approached, pausing after every couple steps. She didn't know why she was so stricken by this woman's corpse. It was far from the first time she had seen a dead body in person, but none of them had been fellow white mages. Maybe that was the distinction.

Freya was a pretty woman. Or *had been* a pretty woman.

Aava wasn't sure whether to think of her in present or past tense. The latter felt wrong, brushing the woman aside as nothing more than a memory.

A small smile sneaked its way onto her face at the sight of Freya's exceptionally long hair. She had a feeling they would've gotten along very well.

She started by stripping the body (which took a not-inconsiderable amount of effort on her own, trying to lift limbs full of dead weight while simultaneously pulling off clothing) and inspecting every inch of skin for any animal or insect bites. There was some discoloration on the woman's stomach, a large red blotch, likely due to her advanced age. Aava also checked for any signs of black magic, though she thought this to be unlikely and indeed found no traces of any spells. Having discovered nothing of note, it was time to delve deeper. Inward.

This next part was tricky. It had taken Aava a long time to get the hang of, but after many failed attempts, she had eventually passed her exams on the subject.

What she needed to do was extract a sample of Freya's blood. The process was very involving and somewhat gruesome, as it entailed using magic to manipulate the idle blood resting in the body's veins, pushing it through the bloodstream until it could literally be pulled out of the body—usually through the mouth or nostrils. Luckily for her, Preservation had been cast on the body after death so it wasn't stiff, and blood manipulation would not be too strenuous.

An area in the upper arm would be easiest to manipulate, given it had the least amount of tissue between the outer layer of skin and the blood vessels she needed to reach, while still being relatively close to the mouth. Of course, the cheek or neck would have the least amount of resistance and were much closer to the mouth, but from the arm one could obtain a thicker, more useable sample.

Her index and middle fingers on her left hand hovered over Freya's left shoulder. She then stroked downward, not touching the skin, all the way to the elbow. She was searching for the blood, trying to make a connection to it. When she did, she would feel it—it would latch on to her, an invisible connection linking from her mind to her fingers to the blood.

She caught it mid-stroke and immediately stopped. Now she had to move in the opposite direction. Concentrating on her two fingers, Aava began to move them back up the arm toward the shoulder, curving around to the collarbone. This was the part where she had messed up so often in school, having her focus broken by some distraction or other and losing the connection. Right now, though, it was going swimmingly. The spell's symbol—written in the ancient Ustrel language—began to etch itself into the top of her hand, and she smiled with satisfaction at the light burning sensation. The symbol would fade away a few minutes after she completed the spell, unlike black magic users, whose symbols generally cut deeper into the skin and took a few days to heal.

Next, she led the blood up through Freya's frail neck, pushing it up to the woman's face. It was a slow, deliberate process, and took several minutes while the blood snaked its way through her bloodstream. Now Aava's fingers hung in the air above Freya's open mouth. She turned her hand over and began to coax the blood out, slowly hooking her fingers in a beckoning gesture.

A long, thin, viscous string of blood emerged from the back of the throat.

It was nasty business, but Aava brought the string of blood out, sneaking it past Freya's rows of teeth. It floated in mid-air above the body until Aava took a couple steps back, the blood following her movements, beginning to spool into a small blob.

The blood formed into a perfectly smooth sphere once it was out in the open. The ball was the size of an acorn and appeared to be congealed, but Aava knew better. She would be able to tear it apart and reshape it without any trouble.

Now that it was in the light and out of the shadows of Freya's mouth, Aava could see that the blood was not the shade it should have been. There was a tinge of brown to it, almost like diarrhea. Aava's face twisted in disgust as she stepped closer.

There was undeniably something wrong with this woman's blood.

Aava rotated the ball of brownish blood in mid-air, examining it from every side, and knew she had seen symptoms similar to this before, though not exactly. This was different, but Aava did not yet know what precisely made it different. There was one thing she could conclude without any doubt, however.

Freya had been poisoned.

- -

Aava had cast Preservation on the blood sample she'd collected and stored it in a container she brought from—the word still sounded weird, in regards to Freya's dome—*home*.

After conducting a few more tests, which did not turn up anything conclusive, she had left the shed and returned to the Tillings' front door to inform Lisa she had completed her task.

Lisa left behind a note for her husband telling him they were done and a funeral could now be arranged, and then together they had walked down to the middle level of Balam, back to the clinic, in order to box up Freya's belongings.

Conversation along the way was stuttered, but not unpleasant. Aava was torn between wanting to keep her distance from everyone (since she did not intend to stay for an extended period) and wanting to get on good terms with them. Lisa was proving to be a friendly woman, and Aava found herself looking forward to getting to know the woman more as they packed.

When they arrived at Aava's doorstep, what they found was a hastily scrawled note pinned to the thick red door.

Aava was puzzled, then immediately felt a pit in her stomach. It was probably Mr. Reede, looking to take her to lunch or something similarly trivial. Who else would it be?

Lisa remained a few respectful steps back as Aava tore the note from the door and read it.

Mage,

I would like to speak with you. Please meet me at my home on the beach if you are available before nine o'clock. If you are not available before then, I will stop by the clinic on my way to the pub. If you are not there, please meet me in the pub.

Ryckert Ji'ca

Aava turned to Lisa. "Who's Ryckert Ji'ca?" she asked, recognizing the surname as a rocyan convention. The first two letters of your father's name, an apostrophe, and then the first couple letters of your clan's name. She couldn't tell what clan this Ryckert belonged to; there were countless rocyan clans across not only Atlua, but the other kingdoms as well.

Lisa let out a soft chortle. "He's an old rocyan who moved here a few years ago. He lives in a cabin he built himself down on the beach. He mostly keeps to himself, but he gets along with my husband pretty well. The note is from him?" Aava nodded and showed Lisa the note. She read it over quickly and shrugged. "Pretty odd," she said.

"Mhm," Aava agreed. She folded the note and pocketed it. "Do you mind if we do this later?" she then asked. "I feel I should go talk to him. The note seemed kind of pressing, in a sort of roundabout way." She felt guilty about Lisa walking all the way here then having to walk all the way back home.

"Not a problem," Lisa smiled. "I can stop by tomorrow sometime, if that works for you." Aava told her that'd be fine, and they planned to meet shortly after noon, once they had both eaten lunch.

It wasn't a very long walk to the beach, and Aava was delighted to have discovered there was a beach at all, since she hadn't had a chance to explore this part of the town yet. As she descended the stone steps to the lowest tier of the village, the rocyan's shack came into view on her left, as did a breathtaking waterfall that splashed into the sparkling ocean. It was quite a place to set up one's home.

A fire pit sat before the cabin, still burning low. Ryckert had been using it recently. She walked past it and up the rickety steps onto his porch. Her plan had been to knock on his front door, but it was already standing open, granting her a clear view inside.

Ryckert was several feet away, his back turned to her as he washed some dishes in the sink.

"Mr. Ji'ca?"

He turned to face her. He stood nearly six and a half feet, a solid foot taller than Aava. His muscles bulged from his ill-fitting tan shirt, though Aava could guess from the rips and stains on his clothing that this was less a method of showing off and more a mere lack of clothing options. He had brown, coarse fur and on top of his long, dog-like snout was a noticeable bump. All in all, Ryckert Ji'ca looked like he had had a rough go of things.

"Call me Ryckert," he said, his voice a low growl. He took a couple long strides forward and presented his hand for her to shake.

"As you wish. You wanted to speak with me about something?"

"Yes. Let's sit outside. Cramped in here."

Back on the sandy beach, Ryckert gestured toward the one chair he had sitting beside the fire. Aava took a seat while Ryckert paced back and forth. The fire crackled, sprinkling their conversation.

"Dumb," Ryckert mumbled. Aava wasn't sure what was dumb, so she waited for him to continue. "Shouldn't have invited you, but oh well. What's done is done. Got a question about the mage that died."

"Okay," Aava said, uneasy. Ryckert's pacing was making her anxious.

"Wanna know what killed her."

"Why do you want to know that?" Aava asked. She shifted uncomfortably in her seat. It was a combination of the rocyan making her edgy and the chair itself being of poor craftsmanship. She wondered if he had built the chair, just as he had his cabin.

Ryckert stopped pacing and glared at her. She suspected there was no ill intent behind the glare; that was just his face.

"Because, I…" He trailed off. This was obviously hard for him to get out. He almost seemed ashamed. "I tried figuring it out myself, and I couldn't. Just curious, is all."

That wasn't enough of an explanation for Aava. "Why are you curious?"

Ryckert groaned. "Don't know," he said. "That's the truth of it. Don't know why, but I need to know."

He stared at her, waiting. Aava stared back. He stuffed his hands in the pockets of his tattered pants, embarrassed.

He seems innocent enough, she thought. *He really does just seem curious. That's not a crime.*

"She was poisoned."

Ryckert's expression was unmoving. He processed her words for a moment, then said, "You're sure?"

"Yes."

A nod. "Think it was a potion? Or quillis? Or could it have been black magic?" He was curious indeed.

Aava shrugged. "It's too soon for me to tell," she answered. "I have a blood sample that I was going to analyze further tonight. Right now, it could go either way." She then tacked on, "I trust you won't speak of this to anybody else? I believe it's premature to let the word out that I know she was poisoned. Whoever did this might get spooked, and…" She finished the thought internally: *kill me*.

It suddenly seemed very stupid to have told this man, this stranger, anything at all. Why had she done that?

Because he seems trustworthy, was her answer, though it was based on almost nothing. The reality was she had slipped up. Nothing to be done about it now except hope Ryckert Ji'ca was as trustworthy as he appeared.

"Course not," he said. "I wanna get whoever did this too. Not gonna jeopardize the investigation."

"Thank you."

"Think I can help, matter of fact," he said.

"How is that?"

Ryckert shot a glance at the staircase leading back up to the village. He then grew closer and knelt by her side, leaning a furry arm on the armrest.

"Got a suspect in mind," he said.

This was intriguing.

"Who?" Aava asked. She had not anticipated the conversation going in this direction at all. Her heart was racing.

"Guy rolled into town a few days ago, right around the time Freya died. Black mage. Keeping a low profile. Not staying in the inn, refused an offer to stay with me even though we were becoming friendly. Decided to keep sleeping in the woods instead."

"He's just sleeping in the forest?"

"Yep."

"That's strange."

"Yep."

"How sure are you he's the culprit?"

"Not very," said Ryckert. "But he's my best guess. Stranger shows up in town the same night someone drops dead, and then avoids contact with everyone in town? Mighty suspicious."

"Pretty suspicious," Aava agreed. "Though if he's avoiding everybody, how do you know him?"

Ryckert pushed himself up and resumed pacing. "Stops by the pub every couple nights. I've been spending time there myself lately. Met there, had a few drinks together. Young guy. Told me he was kicked out of his academy, somewhere over near Kyring."

"That could be either Asal University or Veler University. Both are in the vicinity of Kyring. But either way, that's a long distance for someone to travel without a destination in mind."

"Yep," Ryckert said again. "And Balam's a pretty odd place to stop, if you don't know no one."

Aava could agree with that, based on her short time in the town so far. "Well, as far as black magic goes, what I saw doesn't fit the symptoms of the base Poison spell, which is pretty simple itself. It could be something more complex, though, something more uncommon. Like Bio, perhaps. That's used more so in hunting or warfare, so I haven't encountered it in any patients. I'd need to read and refresh my memory on how it presents itself in the body."

"Alright," Ryckert said. "Though I wouldn't rule out a regular poisoning, either. Potion or powder mixed in a drink. Not sure what this guy's resources are. Or his motive."

"Of course," Aava nodded. "I'll get started on it tonight."

It would be a long night of analysis, but Ryckert's information about their secretive guest had exhilarated her, while simultaneously filling her with dread. She had come to Balam with the understanding that she would be filling in for a white mage while Mr. Reede sought a replacement, not solving a murder case.

"Good. I'll try tracking the mage down, see if he's got anything stored at his campsite. Any ingredients, or something similarly incriminating."

Aava smirked. "Why are you so invested in this?" she had to ask. She appreciated the helpful hand, but she was surprised that a random citizen—especially one who appeared to have removed himself from public affairs as much as possible, given where and how he lived—would care about this woman's death.

Ryckert shrugged. "Curiosity's just piqued, I guess. Wanna see it through."

"I suspect there's more to it than that," she egged him on.

Ryckert sighed and rubbed the bump on his nose before replying. "Used to be a mercenary," he said. "Retired a while back. Got the itch again, I s'pose you could say."

She waited, still smirking.

"No more to it than that."

"Okay," she said, believing him. Aava rose and held out her hand to shake Ryckert's again. "It was nice meeting you. I can't say I expected this in the least, but I believe it was a good conversation to have."

"Agreed," Ryckert said, firmly gripping her hand. His nails gently dug into her forearm as they shook.

As they separated, she said, "Would you be free to meet again tomorrow? To discuss what we both find?"

"Sounds fine," said Ryckert. "What time do you wake up?"

"Uh…" Aava muttered. "Just whenever I wake up, I guess. Let's call it eight. Is that too early?"

"Not at all. I'll be avoidin' the pub tonight, so that'll help."

Aava grinned. "Should we meet here again? Or at the diner?"

"Not the diner," he said, shaking his head curtly. "People present. Wanna keep this between us, right?"

"Right." She felt foolish for not thinking about that. Of course people would be at the diner, all within earshot. And to think she had been the one chastising Ryckert about keeping this matter quiet just a few minutes before.

"Can meet here again, if you prefer. Can make us some breakfast. Not the best cook in the world, but I'm passable, at least."

"How about I pick us up something from the diner?" Aava offered. "My treat. To say thank you for coming to me with your information."

"No thanks needed, but thanks to you all the same," Ryckert told her. "Sounds like a fine idea to me. Partial to most things on the menu, so anything's fine."

As she walked away, Aava's own curiosity got the best of her. She stopped and turned back to face Ryckert, who was standing still, observing the low fire burning.

"Can I ask you something? And if it's too personal, feel free to not answer," she said.

Ryckert only nodded.

"What's the bump on your nose from?" she asked, stupidly pointing at her own nose, as if Ryckert wouldn't be able to pinpoint the body part otherwise.

To her surprise, he let out a small laugh, almost a growl. "Been a long time since anyone's asked me about that," he said. "Long time since I've thought about it, too. Just a snake bite that never fully healed. Nasty thing, four feet long, thick. Some piece of shit swamp in Gillus. Fell from a tree, bit into my snout on its way down. Bastard held on tight while I swung it around, tryin' to yank it off. Finally did, and killed it quick." After he wrapped up his story, Ryckert let out another chuckle. "Guess you could say I've got some poison in me, too."

CHAPTER V

SUN TO MOON

The inn was nameless.

When its founder, a man named Halloran Remli, began construction on the establishment, he had wanted to call it Hal's Place. His wife had strongly urged against this idea, as it sounded more like a bar than an inn and, regardless, was a fairly poor name. So Hal refrained. By the time the inn was ready for its grand opening, Hal had still not figured out what to call it, but since Balam was such a small town and there were no competing inns, he decided a name wasn't really necessary. Plus, he never found a name that, in his humble opinion, beat "Hal's Place." A couple years after the inn had taken off, Hal was making enough profit to open a restaurant inside the inn, and for this, his wife granted him permission to name it Hal's Place. The Remli family had long since moved out of Balam and the inn was under new management. Most recently, it had been bought by Vilisi Lyons, the adoptive mother of Theo's pupil Jeremy.

Theo was sitting alone at a table in Hal's Place, waiting for Lyrra to finish her shift so they could eat dinner together. One perk of being an inn employee was half off meals at the restaurant, which the Saens took advantage of at least once a week. Theo was partial to their buttered pasta with breaded vissian.

He had ordered a beer and nearly drained the glass while waiting. Lyrra wasn't running late; all he had been doing was sitting around the house, so he thought it'd be nice to get out a little early.

Their waitress was taking his order for one more beer when Lyrra sat down across from him. Theo thanked the waitress then greeted his wife. "How was work?" he asked her.

"Not bad," Lyrra replied. "That man, Mhar, is being touted as a hero. He posts up in the lobby, drinking drinks and regaling the story of how he handled the incident the other night."

"What did he handle? He did almost nothing! He cast a spell that basically equates to 'keep a person dead for longer.' What is there to regale?"

"No idea," Lyrra laughed. "But he's really soaking it up, and so are the other guests. The staff is unimpressed, if that's any consolation."

"Kind of," Theo chuckled. "Stories of such bland heroics sound right up Hilli's alley, though, so I have to say I'm shocked."

Lyrra waved this away. "Nah, Hilli is still infatuated with Gregory. He could take a shit in the middle of the lobby and she'd fawn over it, saying it was a beautiful expression of his inner being."

"Well, given what I know about the guy, a piece of shit in the middle of the floor might actually be an expression of his inner being."

At this, Lyrra laughed so hard it turned into a cough. She gulped down her water to clear her throat, then looked at Theo with a grin once she had recovered. "You might be right," she said. "But keep your voice down, he might be around the corner!"

She looked exceptionally cute in her work clothes; she usually favored jeans and tanktops, nothing fancy, but for work she dressed in a sheer, white button-up shirt tucked into tight-fitting light-brown pants. Her olive jeornish skin lit up her bright yellow eyes.

They spent a few minutes perusing the menu and placed their orders once the waitress had come back around. Theo stuck to his tried and true vissian pasta dish, while Lyrra had opted for something new, a seasonal dish that consisted of baked chicken, roasted vegetables, and a spicy pepper sauce made from derilus peppers that only grew in the spring.

While they awaited their food, conversation turned to the subject of their impending vacation. During most springs, Lyrra would take a week off work and they'd make the trek to her hometown of Bral Han to visit her parents, Daere and Calyssa Fiss.

Lyrra had always maintained a very close relationship with her father. He was the person who had taught her how to cook, which Theo greatly appreciated, considering how useless he himself was in the kitchen, aside from a few choice dishes that his mother had taught him before her passing. Daere owned his own modest restaurant in the theatre district, and whenever they visited, on their first night in town he always prepared a lavish meal in their honor.

This year was to be no different. All that needed deciding was which week to go, and who would watch over Vir while they were away.

Their options boiled down to either Al or the Dowers, and Theo was worried Al had grown too unreliable in recent days, spending all his evenings at the bar with Serys. Vanessa and Bromley Dower were the safer bets, and their children would love playing with Vir. The little seroko would be delighted to entertain children for a week.

"Well, that settles that," Lyrra said, taking a sip of her own beer. "So when do you wanna go?"

Theo shrugged. He had all the time in the world. "It doesn't matter much," he answered. "Whenever you can get the time off is fine. Just give me the word and I'll book the carriage."

"Alright. How about in…two weeks?"

"Two weeks from today?"

"From…" Lyrra tallied up the days in her head. "…two days. Two weeks from two days from now."

"Sounds good to me," Theo said.

"Great! I'll give Gregory some warning and ask Vilisi if it'll be alright. I should probably know sometime tomorrow."

"You're working? I thought you had the day off."

"I did, but that was Gregory's condition for switching with me the other day. I'm taking over his shift tomorrow so that he can have a beach day or something, I don't know."

Now that she mentioned it, it sounded familiar. She had already told him, but the information had gotten lost in the haze of the past few days. He grinned and said, "Better let Hilli know he'll be in the buff so she can race down there tomorrow and scope it out."

They were giggling at this when their food arrived.

- -

Ryckert's meeting with the new white mage earlier in the day had reinvigorated him. He still felt ashamed for being so caught up in this debacle, but now he was feeling at least somewhat justified. Freya had been poisoned. Foul play was involved, and he intended to be the one to solve this little mystery.

Night had fallen over the quiet coastal town, and Ryckert was hiding out in the densely wooded area across the street from the pub. His brown fur helped him blend in with the tree trunks, especially in the darkness. Chances of being spotted were slim to none.

The plan was to wait and watch.

Michio had spent most of his nights in town getting drunk at the pub, despite claiming he didn't have enough money to afford even the most rudimentary room at the inn. Tonight should be no different. Once Ryckert saw the man enter, he would trace Michio's footsteps—literally—back into the forest, all the way to his campsite, and search it for any evidence that would point to his poisoning of Freya.

Ryckert's fur protected him from the frigid night air. It wasn't a terribly cold night, but after sitting in one place for so long with a breeze constantly blowing, any human, jeorn, or qarm was sure to get chilled. It was a good night to get a drink and a warm bite to eat at the bar, especially if you lived out in the woods. Any doubts he'd had about Michio showing up were starting to recede.

Close to an hour after settling into his lookout spot, Ryckert spied Michio approaching. The mage sorely stuck out, as he had circled from around the back of the building rather than coming down the road.

This told Ryckert that Michio was sleeping in the wooded area on this upper level of Balam. A vast majority of the Cerene

Forest was technically located above town and one was required to travel up a flight of stone stairs to reach it, but the pub was backed up almost to a cliff face. A fairly high one, at that; no way Michio had hopped down off of it. He would have broken an ankle. If he had come from behind the building, that meant Michio had walked through the trees from the eastern side of town, closer to where Bernard Tilling lived, somewhere behind the man's shed. Ryckert had visited Bernard there a handful of times.

Michio slipped into the bar, and Ryckert was on his feet in an instant.

Being a rocyan, Ryckert was faster than most. He was out of the trees, across the road, and behind the pub within less than ten seconds. And, being a rocyan, his eyesight was none too shabby in the dark.

He took a knee, squinting down at the dirt, searching for Michio's footprints, however faint. The grass was short, but Ryckert could still make out the blades that had been marginally pressed down by the mage's steps. Ryckert's eyes looked up, tracing along what he believed to be the trail, and when he felt he was correct, he stood and began to follow it.

Just as he had predicted, Michio's trail led east, through the woods behind the pub, along the cliff. The tracks became easier to follow the further Ryckert traveled, now that they were crumbling dead leaves and snapping fallen branches. Michio had been careless, but Ryckert couldn't blame the kid. He'd had no reason to think anyone was investigating him. Hell, Ryckert might have been the only person in town who was actually aware of him.

The tracks led to a denser pack of trees huddled together in a cul-de-sac of cliffside, roughly eighty feet back from Bernard's shed. The greenery here was lush, filled with thick bushes, vibrant flowers, and massive trees. Nobody in Balam ever had any reason to go back here, and therefore it was mostly untouched, aside from the occasional kids running through to play or teenagers sneaking away to fool around.

What Ryckert found up against the cliff was a makeshift tent constructed out of long, sturdy tree branches. Green but dying leaves had been gathered, wrapped together with thin twine, and placed on top of the wooden structure to act as a roof in case of rain. Several feet away from the opening was what Ryckert presumed to be the remains of a fire, which seemed pretty stupid to light surrounded by such dense forestry. Perhaps the black mage had a method of containing the flames he conjured and it wasn't an issue. Scattered all over the ground were discarded wrappers, empty cans, and assorted kitchen utensils. From the smell still hanging in the air, Ryckert guessed the cans had contained beans, perhaps with chunks of meat mixed in. Michio might have been buying dinners at the pub, but he was still eating a few meals out here on his own, and he had no qualms about littering. Ryckert noticed a symbol painted on one of the branches that comprised the entrance of Michio's dwellings, but he didn't recognize it or understand its meaning. It looked like a square with two lines drawn diagonally across through its center, extending beyond the perimeter of the box. The interior of the branch structure was around six square feet. Not nearly enough room for Ryckert to sleep comfortably, but he supposed it would do for someone of Michio's size, though not by much. Especially with the man's leather pack taking up extra space, like it was right now. Ryckert grinned and hunched over, reaching toward the sack.

He pulled it out and stood upright, holding the bag from the bottom while he rummaged through its contents.

What he found was less exciting than he had been counting on.

There was a ratty notebook, clasped shut and locked. Its cover was a faded green, stained with scratches and dirt. It bore no title.

A journal? Spellbook, maybe?

Ryckert pushed the book aside and checked out the rest of the items. Nothing of value or note was inside: a hairbrush, a hand-drawn map of the region, a couple crescents (which, if this was all Michio had, he wasn't lying about being broke).

Nothing. Nothing to link him to the crime.

Unless there's something written in the journal.

He cast aside the thought. Busting open the tiny lock would be no problem, but then he'd have no way of fixing it. The mage would know someone was on to him.

He began feeling around the lining of the bag. Oftentimes these things came with—

—and then he found it. A secret compartment, hidden in the side of the bag. He gently unzipped it and reached two fingers inside the small pocket, extracting a nearly weightless pouch.

Ryckert smiled. This looked promising.

He untied the bag and peered inside. It held a silvery powder, almost translucent. There was a faint glow to it, reminiscent of moonlight.

Surely this must be it. Michio had slipped some of this powder into Freya's drink, or her food, and later that night her functions began to shut down and she had collapsed in the middle of town square. But it still begged the question: why?

Question that's better asked later, Ryckert thought to himself. *Should get moving. Get back to Aava.*

Ryckert had used many a poison in his mercenary days, but none like this. He didn't recognize it at all. Most poisons he had encountered were darker, earthier, no matter whether they were powders or liquids.

The most common among his profession was a powder called *quillis*. It was the ground-up root of a vegetable found in Herrilock, the country east of Gillus and far from Atlua. Herrilock was mostly desert, with some pockets of savannah, and in the savannah was where quillis grew. Importing quillis all the way from Herrilock was not cheap, considering how few grew each year to begin with, but just one root could last you a few years and it was extremely effective, so it was worth the cost and trouble.

But an old acquaintance of Ryckert's, a man named Leif (who he spent most of the time trying to forget about these days), preferred a different type of poison.

Leif's signature move was using a poison colloquially dubbed "the shitter." It was not a fanciful or imaginative name, but then again it was named by mercenaries, a traditionally uncreative bunch. It was a brown, murky liquid that was ironically similar in appearance to the most terrible, fiery diarrhea. When a man or woman was unfortunate enough to receive the shitter (which, somehow, had no taste, so it was never detected), they spent the last few hours of their lives constantly running to the bathroom, shitting their brains out until there were no brains left. It was an extraordinarily unsophisticated and embarrassing way to die. Leif liked to reserve it for aristocrats, town officials, and other such individuals with large reputations that he could make look like buffoons in their final moments.

This silvery powder was positively not quillis. What it most resembled was barnas, but that was more white than silver, and its effects were nothing like what had happened to Freya. He just had to hope that Aava would have some answers.

Ryckert was in the process of arranging everything the way he'd found it when he heard the unmistakable sound of someone approaching. His ears flicked wildly, homing in on the person's location. They weren't far.

"Shit," he growled. He left the sack where it lay and ducked out of the raggedy tent, darting through the trees.

The smart thing to do would have been to keep running, to head back to the main part of town and go home. Or he could ignore their plan to meet tomorrow and go straight to Aava's clinic to tell her what he had found. But Ryckert had not been feeling particularly smart as of late, and so he stopped when he deemed himself sufficiently far away and hidden by the night, then turned to watch the camp.

Michio appeared a moment later, stumbling through the brush with an irritable scowl.

The mage looked to his right, then his left—right where Ryckert was crouched down, hopefully cloaked by nightfall and bushes—and groaned. Michio pulled off the glove on his left hand, peering at something on his palm that Ryckert couldn't make out. He put the glove back on and stepped forward into the tent.

He was looking at a spell, Ryckert realized.

It hadn't occurred to him that first night when he met Michio in the pub and he had performed his Fire spell, but his gloves were covering up the magic symbols on his hands that appeared when mages cast spells.

The symbol above the entryway.

Some kind of security alarm, Ryckert thought with a grunt. *Probably felt an itch on his hand so he ran home. Smart. Almost had me.* If Ryckert's hearing weren't so good, he likely would have been found out.

He was standing up to finally leave (thankful that he didn't have to keep quiet in addition to out of sight) when something caught his eye. A glint in the distance, low to the ground, around the back of Michio's tent.

A dark, formless blob was coming forward, shaping into something humanoid. It was short, around four feet tall, but hunched over so that it was almost dragging its knuckles in the grass.

As it came into view, Ryckert could see that it was a goblin. Its skin hung loose from its face, its saggy jowls swinging with each step. The nose was bulbous and crooked, like it had been broken and never set. Thin, greasy hair hung in patches and brushed against the creature's pallid green flesh. In its hand, the glint that Ryckert had spied, was a dagger.

It was ambling toward the opening of Michio's tent, and the mage couldn't hear it. He didn't have the faintest clue.

- -

Aava's meeting with Ryckert was the first time she had felt truly welcomed in Balam, despite Mr. Reede's brash eagerness to ensure she was comfortable.

Something about the rocyan had made her feel like she was part of something. In a very literal sense, she *was* part of something; she was reluctantly embroiled in this mystery surrounding Freya's death. But speaking with Ryckert had made her feel like she wasn't alone.

She missed Svend. To his credit, he annoyed her a lot of the time, but she loved her brother and wished he was here. He would've found Ryckert to be a pretty interesting character. Something told her Svend might also be able to help with the investigation. Not that he had any real experience dealing with such matters, but maybe he would have a theory to offer, or an idea to follow up on. His mind had always been much more creative than hers. This was only her first full day in Balam, but she made a mental note to write a letter to Svend in the morning. Even if he didn't have any advice, it would be nice to hear from him.

Aava had spent the past half hour at the Sonata Diner again, eating her dinner. She hadn't made a trip to the general store yet, and she was in no mood to cook anyway. During her meal, the townsfolk had been much chattier than they were in the morning. Several people interrupted her mid-chew to ask what their symptoms indicated or what exactly had happened to Freya.

Her stock answers were "I can make a diagnosis if you schedule an appointment at the clinic" and "I cannot say at this time."

"Please, I might not have *time* for an appointment," begged a mousy fellow named Benedict Crogley (*What an unfortunate name*, Aava thought) who was staying at the inn.

"Mr. Crogley, I'm sure you're well enough to wait until tomorrow," Aava assured the man, but he was having none of it.

"I've been coughing. Coughing a *lot*."

"I haven't heard you cough once."

"Well I'm not doin' it *now*, but I've been coughing. I swear it. Just like that lady who died! She was coughing too, I heard! Everyone's talking about it! And there's an itch in the back of my throat. Woke up with it the morning after I went outside and saw that dead lady layin' dead in the street, dead as dirt. *Cripes*, I'd never seen someone *dead* before!" The man was practically hyperventilating. "I know I got what she got. Has to be somethin' in the air, right? I've been coughing non-stop."

Aava wanted to point out that he couldn't possibly be coughing non-stop if she hadn't heard a single cough since entering the diner, but she let it slide. She wanted to put him at ease, but it wouldn't be wise to divulge the fact that Freya had been poisoned, rather than succumbing to a contagious sickness. So for now, all she could do was resort to the stock answer.

"I can only make a proper diagnosis if you schedule an appointment at the clinic. We can even schedule it right here, if that would make you feel better. How does ten o'clock sound to you?" That would still give her ample time to meet with Ryckert.

Benedict Crogley did not believe he would last until morning, but he conceded. "Fine," he sighed, returning to his own table. "I'll see you tomorrow." He added a harsh cough as punctuation.

In total, she had scheduled three appointments for the next day, all from people blowing the white mage's death out of proportion. A batch of hypochondriacs, most likely, who were resolute in their belief that they were going to die in the same fashion as Freya. Aava would check them out and probably issue a clean bill of health then send them on their merry way.

But still, it was mildly exciting to have patients. Her first real patients, all her own! It made her giddy.

The feeling hadn't lasted once she returned home, though. She wasn't looking forward to examining the blood sample she had extracted that afternoon, scared of what it might reveal.

As it turned out, there wasn't actually a whole lot to be revealed. Answers were elusive as she conducted all the obligatory tests on the sample, as well as a few extras that later came to mind.

The blood's brown hue was the most obvious red flag, and so she tried to pinpoint what element was giving it that unnatural color.

There were several potions she needed to make in order to run these tests, and it took her close to an hour to get them all boiling and mixed correctly. She had then extracted small droplets from the sample, three in total, and plopped each one into a separate potion. The two leftmost liquids had remained unchanged, while the third had begun to produce billows of steam.

The first vial ruled out quillis and mirelight, the two most frequently used poisons that she had learned about in school.

The second told her that whatever it was that had worked its way into Freya's bloodstream, its source wasn't a liquid. Some sort of powder was her first guess, and in a distant second was magic, though it was still too soon to rule that out, especially depending on what Ryckert uncovered about the black mage sequestered in the woods.

The steam from the third vial spoke to her as well. Whatever had mixed with Freya's blood was acidic. It might have pained her while coursing through her body, but that wasn't necessarily the case. She probably would have died much sooner if so, or been rendered immobile from the agony. In all likelihood, this acidity was a latent symptom, something that had not occurred until post-mortem. Which, while it was good to know, did not really help Aava deduce what type of poison had killed Freya. This was unfamiliar.

This was something new.

- -

The goblin must have scaled the cliffside, then snuck its way around to the back of Michio's tent. The creatures were highly unintelligent, and they mostly kept to themselves deeper in the Cerene Forest. It was strange that this one was this far out, and on its own, no less.

Ryckert's claws dug into the side of the tree trunk, weighing his options. Michio could defend himself, he was sure—if he got the chance to do so. The goblin might just stab the dagger into Michio's back or jab it into his side and that would be the end of it. Or Ryckert could leap forward, kill the goblin himself, and make his presence known. Not the best idea.

Might solve all our problems, Ryckert pondered, imagining the goblin killing Michio. *But not if he ain't the guilty one.*

Michio was still tucked away inside his pathetic structure, presumably kneeled down, facing away from the entrance. Ryckert stepped out of the shadows and barked, *"Hey!"*

His plan was to lure the goblin far from the tent and kill it out of Michio's sight. Making a ruckus was not of any consideration. The kill didn't have to be swift or clean.

The goblin halted and looked toward Ryckert. That was all it took to distract such a stupid creature. Its mouth crept open in a sharp, ugly grin, exposing yellow fangs. Without another wasted second, it raced forward, dagger raised.

It had been a long time since Ryckert was engaged in a real fight, but he was ready. A goblin was nothing; child's play to a rocyan. Literally, in Ryckert's case. One of the first kills with his ra he could remember was a goblin camp on the outskirts of their clan's village. It had been easy then, when he was hardly more than a pup.

So he wasn't worried now.

They were off to a good start: the goblin tripped over a tree root poking out of the ground and tumbled forward, smacking its head on the ground with a hard *thunk!* that was so loud, Ryckert swore it could alert even Michio.

The goblin rolled on the uneven ground and came to a stop a few feet away from Ryckert. He swiftly circled around to the goblin's backside and planted his boot in the middle of its spine.

It yelped in pain like a cat with its tail trod on. Its tongue lashed out in the dirt. The shoddy dagger was still gripped tightly in its right hand, swinging aimlessly in the air, attempting to strike the rocyan.

Ryckert laughed.

And then he slammed his other foot into the goblin's wrist, pinning it to the ground. There was a wet snap as the bone broke and the muscles tore. The goblin shrieked again as its hand went limp, dropping the dagger into the dry grass. It squirmed and screamed in protest, yelling what amounted to nonsense in Ryckert's ears.

"Thanks," Ryckert whispered, snatching the dagger.

He jammed it into the goblin at the top of its spine and tore through the flimsy skin all the way down its back.

Finally, the goblin's movements stopped completely. Ryckert glanced over his shoulder and saw that Michio was inside the tent. That was good.

He lifted the corpse and threw it toward the cliff. It collided with the brown rock, shattering the goblin's skull. The body collapsed in a heap behind a berry-rich bush.

With one more glance at Michio's camp, Ryckert decided it was way past time to get moving. He ran.

- -

Dessert followed dinner, and a walk followed dessert.

On a night such as this, they would have walked from the inn across Main Street and sat below the yunesca tree, but Lyrra had enough sense to know that would be less than ideal for her husband. So they walked around town a while, gazing into the windows of the Sonata to see who was out tonight, and circled their way back around to their home. It was what Theo had needed to clear his head after a nice meal. He silently thanked whatever gods there were for placing Lyrra in his life.

She led him straight to the backyard, where Vir was rolling in the grass. The seroko sprinted over and greeted them with happy squeals and licks.

"Hey," Lyrra smiled. To Theo, she said, "I thought we could watch the waterfall a while."

Just what he needed.

They sat cross-legged in the grass, eschewing the chairs on their back porch. The grass was cold between their fingers.

"Do you remember our first date?" Lyrra asked him.

"Nah," he joked. She gave him a playful shove, followed by a kiss on the cheek.

"I always think about it when I look at the waterfall," she said.

He had met Lyrra while they both attended school in Bral Han. Their university had focused on literature, visual arts, craftsmanship, culinary arts, and other such subjects. Theo had, of course, been studying literature. Lyrra was a culinary student.

They'd met in a general instruction course and became fast friends. It had taken him over a year to muster up the courage to ask Lyrra Fiss—the most beautiful girl in the entire university, as far as he was concerned—on a date. And when he finally did, she'd said no.

The second time, though, a few weeks later, she'd agreed. Reluctantly. It wasn't that she didn't like Theo, or that she didn't have feelings for him (in fact, she had quite the crush). She feared their friendship and her own studies becoming strained by a relationship.

But on their first date, Theo had picked out a stunning spot in the woods next to a natural spring, and packed up a homemade lunch—nothing extravagant, just sandwiches topped with a coleslaw of his own invention that he prayed would not embarrass him in front of the culinary artist. He'd obtained a bottle of wine, but on their way through the woods, it had slipped from his hand and shattered, splattering red wine all over the grass and his pants. He ended up having to throw away the pants because he never could get the stains out. Lyrra had found the incident quite humorous, though.

They had gotten situated on some flat rocks that had a nice view of a short waterfall that cascaded into the spring below. Hours passed spent talking about school, their childhoods, and anything else. Day faded to night, sun to moon.

"I love it out here," she had said. "The breeze feels so nice. I used to go camping with my dad a lot, when I was a kid. There's nothing better than sleeping beneath the stars, if you ask me."

Conversation dwindled, as conversation tends to do, and they sat in contented silence, watching the moon's reflection waver on the water's surface.

Theo was taken aback when Lyrra leaned over and kissed him on the mouth, a kiss full of energy and passion and excitement.

She pulled away, blinking her bold, yellow eyes at him. Theo was rendered speechless.

He never did find a word.

They kissed again, and again, and again.

The waterfall behind their house reminded him of that date as well. It was part of the reason why this house had seemed so perfect for the two of them, the perfect place to settle down and start their lives.

"Do you want some coffee?" he asked her. They'd already had a cup with dessert, but one more wouldn't hurt.

"Tea, maybe?" she suggested.

That sounded even better, now that she mentioned it. He gave Vir a pat on the back, Lyrra a kiss on the lips, and stood to go get the water boiling.

- -

Aava had run a few more tests, all inconclusive (aside from re-affirming that the poison was indeed acidic), and now sat slumped in a chair at her bedroom desk. The clinic's lights had begun to hurt her eyes this late at night and she needed to rest.

She was already in her pajamas when there came an urgent knocking at the door, faintly heard through the connecting hall-way. She had nearly missed it. Whoever was there had evidently not spotted the button on the side of the door that would have rang emergency chimes throughout both buildings.

Without thinking to put her normal clothes back on, Aava rushed through the hallway into the clinic and swung the door open. Ryckert stood before her, panting lightly.

"Evening," he said.

"Good evening," she said to him. "What are you doing here? I thought we agreed to meet tomorrow."

"Did," he said. "Can I come in?"

She stood aside to allow him entry. He hiked himself up onto the examination table and sat looking at her.

"What happened?" Aava asked, concern on the edge of her voice. "Why couldn't this wait until tomorrow?"

"Maybe it could've," he admitted, "but I'm not sure. Guy's gotta be suspicious now. Suspicious that someone's suspicious of him, I mean. Camp had some sort of spell cast, like an alarm.

It told him I was there. He came runnin' back shortly after I'd started to snoop around. Knows somebody was in his tent."

"That's not good."

"Nope."

"But he didn't see you leaving? Or hear you?"

"Nope," Ryckert said again. "Got away clean. Had to kill a goblin in the process, but that's all. Not even worth the mention, really."

Aava ignored this, not wanting to hear the grisly details. She moved around to the side of the table and took a seat in the chair she'd be planted in tomorrow, observing patients such as Benedict Crogley.

"So, was it worthwhile?" she asked. "Did you find anything noteworthy?"

Ryckert nodded. "Think so. Wasn't much there—journal, scruffy blankets, old food—but there was a pouch in a hidden compartment of his bag. Powder inside."

Aava's heart skipped. "What did it look like?" she asked, her voice low and unsteady.

"Nothin' like I'd seen before. Silver. Luminous. Almost like barnas, but more…*otherworldly*," he said. The word was not a common part of his vocabulary.

"It doesn't sound like any poison I've ever dealt with," Aava said. "The closest thing does seem to be barnas. Could it have been that, just silvery in the moonlight?"

"Don't think it was barnas, or even some strange strain of it. This is something different. Not sure what."

It aligned with Aava's findings. She told Ryckert about the tests she conducted on the blood sample, how all she had concluded was that it contained a kind of acid and that the poison was most likely a powder. "Could be a weird variation of a Bio spell, perhaps, but I don't think so," she finished.

"Found me a powder I don't recognize, and you found a poison you don't recognize that you claim comes from a powder. Seems like—"

Aava didn't get a chance to hear what Ryckert was going to say, because in a flash he was up and at the sink, vomiting violently.

"Are you okay?" she asked, rushing to his side. Instinctively, she placed a comforting hand on his back. *To make the patient feel more at ease.* Most of her instincts these days were nothing more than tactics taught to her by mentors for *making the patient feel more at ease.*

Ryckert remained bent over the sink for five minutes, hurling every thirty seconds or so. The bile was green and hot. When he was done, he wiped his mouth on a towel she provided.

"Sorry," he apologized, looking genuinely embarrassed by the spectacle. "Think I might've eaten some bad fish earlier. Should've known better." Aava told him it was fine and urged him to continue what he was saying while she rinsed out the sink.

"Don't think I had anything else to add," he said once he had latched onto the thought again. "Just pointing out that it seems like a clear connection. One we shouldn't ignore."

"I agree," Aava said, taking the towel. She tossed it into the sink. She would deal with getting it cleaned in the morning, now that she would be free until her first appointment. "What do you propose we do?" Solving crimes was not part of her wheelhouse.

Ryckert, with a hand on his weary stomach, approached the door. He stopped and faced Aava. "My next move will be to keep an eye on the mage, make sure he don't leave Balam. Maybe get closer to him, if I run into him at the bar. Interfere as little as possible, but if he tries to split, you can be sure I'll stop him. If you're still unsure what poison he's using, maybe talk to the guy who witnessed everything go down. Don't remember his name, but he's a teacher, I think. Probably easy to track down, if you ask around. Get him to tell you every last detail. Maybe there's somethin' there you haven't heard yet that'll unlock everything else."

Aava nodded. It was a pretty good plan. The best they had, at any rate. It would have to suffice for now.

"Thank you for your help," she told him as he opened the door to depart.

"Likewise," he said. And then he was gone.

Aava returned to the other dome, crossing through the hallway's plain red doors, and settled into bed.

Attempting sleep was useless. Her mind was incapable of slowing down. Things had snowballed drastically since the previous night. Her mind and body were both exhausted. It felt more like a week since she'd rolled into town rather than a day.

She decided to scoot out of bed and sit back down at her desk. She could stand to stay up a little later now that she didn't have to wake up so early. She fished a piece of paper and a pen out of a drawer and wrote to her brother.

Dear Svend, the letter began, *Have I got some interesting news for you!*

CHAPTER VI

PAST THE CUCUMBER PATCH

The funeral service for Freya Jeyardin took place six days after her death. It was a small ceremony, despite the entire town being in attendance. Even Ryckert had shown up, finding himself a spot in the back row.

Like most other funerals in Balam, it was carried out on the farmlands located on the western side of the village, on the middle tier just past the school. There was an empty plot of land on the southern end of the farm, overlooking the ocean, which had been set aside for events such as these.

The service was put together by Barbara Vere, with assistance from Harold Hoskings and Kim Reen, who worked on the farm and were tasked with setting up funerals and weddings whenever they were held on the premises. Barbara had gotten on Harold's case over and over about the placement of the flower bouquets, but in the end he had to admit she had been correct. Dozens of vibrant, multicolored flowers flanked the podium and gave a sense of serenity and beauty to the affair.

The sun shone brightly, warming the crowd's skin while the gentle breeze cooled them off. Relaxing sounds of the ocean waves lapping against the shore could be heard from most places in Balam, and this area was no different. Birds fluttered from tree to tree, twittering amongst themselves. The wind blew against the farm's crops, rustling their healthy leaves and stalks.

In addition to setting up the event, Harold was also its musician and was behind the farthest row, plucking the strings of his guitar while everybody got situated. They took their seats at ten o'clock in the morning, chatting in hushed tones until the service began fifteen minutes later.

A stirring speech was given by Freya's son, a banker who lived in Din's Keep. His name was Artemis Jeyardin, and he had not seen his mother in over seven months, though they wrote to each other every few weeks. News of her death came as a shock to him; he'd had no idea his mother was remotely ill. He had grabbed his mail and found a letter from Rufus Reede explaining what had happened, and he immediately dropped everything and made arrangements to travel to Balam with his husband and daughter.

In his speech, Artemis spoke of his mother's courage, her intelligence, her beauty, her strength. He spoke of everything she had done for him, for her granddaughter, for everyone she had ever met. "She was the most generous woman you could know," Artemis said, his voice faltering. "That was apparent in the work she did every day as a white mage, but it was also abundantly clear in how she approached her relationships with others. She was always looking for a way to help, or a way to comfort. And she always did so with a smile on her face." His speech moved Serys White to tears.

There was then a small recitation and prayer given by the town's priest, Elder Culla, at Artemis's behest. After Elder

Culla's remarks, Mr. Reede took to the podium and invited everybody to join him in celebrating Freya's life with a reception at the town square. "And yes, there will be food provided," he added, eliciting a soft chuckle from the audience.

A majority of the attendees shuffled over to the town square together for the reception. The only exceptions were Lyrra Saen, Elena White, and Hilli White, who had been saddled with the responsibility of tending to the inn's guests, though all three of them expected everyone at the inn to make their way over to the free brunch being provided by Mr. Reede. But they needed to be at the inn "just in case," said Vilisi Lyons, who would herself be enjoying the aforementioned free food.

The reception had been entirely put together by Mr. Reede, who loved planning parties. He had coordinated with Barbara to ensure the flower colors all matched, for continuity between the two events. He would not stand for visual discord.

The brunch spread was fantastic. It had been curated by Walton Vere, of course. It consisted of scrambled eggs with spiced pork, sweet-rolls, kabobs skewered with grilled vegetables and vissian meat, fresh fruit, roasted potatoes sprinkled with salt and pepper, several types of juices, and champagne to mix with the orange juice, if one felt so inclined.

One by one people made their way down the buffet line, thanking Walton for his hard work, congratulating Mr. Reede for throwing together such a nice party, and offering Artemis and his family their condolences.

With his wife at work, Theo hung around Al and Serys, though he kept himself removed from the conversation for the most part. Aava, much to the surprise of the rest of the townsfolk, was chatting amiably with the rocyan who lived on the beach. "How did they even meet?" was the hot question on everybody's lips.

No one had anywhere else to be, and so the reception lasted two hours. Adults conversed while children played with each other and their pets. Vir chased a dog round and round the mighty yunesca, which stood tall and brilliant above the proceedings.

Hidden away, peeking out at the square from behind the Tillings' household, was Michio Loz. He observed the gathering from afar, under the assumption he would not be welcome. He rapped his gloved fingers on the thick wood that had been chopped and assembled by Bernard himself many moons ago. He hummed a tune that he had never actually heard with his own ears, but the vibrations in his throat pleased him. There was one person in particular he had locked his gaze upon, and that person was Ryckert Ji'ca.

- -

The day before the funeral, Aava and Lisa Tilling had gotten together at the clinic to gather Freya's possessions and box them up before Artemis came to town. He would look through everything, decide what he wanted to bring back with him to Din's Keep, and the rest could either stay at the clinic, be sold, or be thrown away.

Aava escorted Artemis to the clinic once the reception was winding down. The sight of his mother's space, where she had spent most of her life and made her mark on the world, had almost caused him to choke up. The walls and desks and shelves were all plain, stripped bare, but the sight still had a profound effect on him.

"I'm sorry," he said. "I'm not sure why that, uh…" He trailed off, his eyes wandering around the room, glancing over the walls, the ceiling, the floor, every inch of the building. Aava placed a comforting hand on Artemis's arm, and with the other hand (out of his view) her fingers flashed a quick gesture. The spell she had cast would soothe the man's nerves, give him a sense of harmony. "Thank you," he said, which made her feel stupid. She had intended for it to be a silent, unseen help, but she should have known the son of a white mage would be able to detect when magic had been cast on him.

A pile of boxes lined the right-hand wall. Freya had not really owned much, and all of her stuff fit snugly into four mid-sized crates. Artemis stepped toward them and lifted the lid of the nearest one.

"Clothes," Aava said, feeling stupid again as he rifled through what was obviously a box full of clothing.

"I guess I don't need any of this," Artemis said, brushing his bangs aside as he looked through the box. "This is just clothes? No jewelry or anything like that?"

"No, that stuff is in that one," she said, pointing to another box.

"Okay." He shut the lid and moved on to the next box. It was jammed with the various knickknacks and décor from the bedroom like Freya's clock, her folded-up Ballastia banners, her jewelry box, and more.

Artemis found the jewelry box near the top of the stack. It was crafted from the white wood of a birch tree, with a keena stone set on its lid. He undid the clasp and peered inside, rummaging through the various earrings and rings until he found what he was looking for.

He held up a silver ring that held a small green gemstone. "My great-grandmother's ring," he said. "I know she'd want Lily to have it."

He pocketed the ring and held the opened box toward Aava. "Is there anything here you'd like?" he asked her. "Otherwise it's just going to be sold, I suppose. With Jonathan out of work, we could always use the extra money."

She fervently waved away the suggestion. She couldn't take jewelry from a woman she hadn't even known, especially if her son could make good use of it. "No, but thank you very much for the offer."

Artemis closed the birch box, returning it to the crate. He sifted through the items a bit more and then suddenly stopped, staring at something within.

Aava couldn't see what he was looking at until he lifted it out of the crate. It was the framed photograph of him and his mother. He looked to be somewhere in his thirties in the photograph, so it had to be at least a decade old, by her estimation.

In the photograph, Artemis stood with an arm wrapped around his mother's shoulder, beaming brightly. Freya shared the same large, warm smile. They looked remarkably similar, even for a mother and son. They were standing in front of a building in what Aava assumed to be Din's Keep.

The hand in which he held the photograph began to tremble, and a wet splotch splashed on the glass. Aava glanced upward and saw Artemis was crying, on the verge of breaking into a sob. He tried, and failed, to keep his composure, and more tears rained down, obscuring the photo.

"Sorry," he apologized again, setting the frame down and wiping his eyes and cheeks. "I guess it's sorta just starting to hit me, y'know?" He blinked the remaining tears away. "It's weird that she's gone now. Really weird."

Aava nodded. "I know how you feel," she said. "Loss is very hard to grapple with sometimes."

"Have you ever lost somebody?"

It was an incredibly personal question, but she did not mind answering it. Things like this sometimes came up in her line of work.

"Yes," she answered. "I lost my mother when I was just a girl, actually. Four years old. I grew up in a quaint village called Oxhollow, far to the east. It was fairly secluded; I'm not sure it's even on most maps, but it's there, I assure you!" She smiled, thinking of her hometown. "Living deep in the woods, there were a fair number of creatures that roamed the outskirts of town. One day, while out on her usual afternoon walk, my mother encountered one such beast. It was a tantalus. Do you know what that is?" A shake of the head from Artemis. "Well, tantaluses are pretty huge. Males even more so, and this was a male. They have smooth, oval-shaped bodies and six bulky legs that jut out, three on each side. Their faces are long and reptilian, with rows of hundreds of sharp teeth and twelve white, beady eyes on the top of their heads. Big and nasty.

"My mother was no pushover; she had studied black magic for years. But the tantalus had caught her off guard, leaping down from the treetops and crushing her before she even knew it was there. Broke her legs. She tried crawling away, cast every spell she could muster—and she managed to blind the beast. But unfortunately, that just sent it into a fury. I won't get into any details, but it was over quickly, for which I am grateful.

"When she didn't return for dinner, my father and older brothers went out searching for her, given that they knew her typical route. They found her body, and shortly thereafter they returned home and tearfully tried to explain to me what had transpired. It was hard to grasp, at my age."

"That's terrible," Artemis muttered, casting another glance at the photo of him and his mother. He rubbed away the tears on the glass that had obfuscated the image. "How did you cope?"

Aava shrugged. "I just got through each day. I'm not sure how to explain it better than that…" She searched for the right words. "As I got older, and could understand what had happened, I began to process my emotions. I realized it did no good to concentrate on the fact that my mother was gone. I had good memories of her, and I loved her, and I knew she had loved me. That was a great comfort. It's hard, yes, but I found that if I focused on the day-to-day, rather than the big picture, it was easier to push through those days. Even the tough ones."

Artemis smiled. "Thanks," he said. He returned the photo to its box and closed it up.

Not a word of the story was true. Except for growing up in Oxhollow—and her description of a tantalus, she supposed. Her mother was not dead, nor was she a black mage, and Aava was in fact the oldest sibling; Svend was her only brother. At Allinor, they had been taught to lie to the patient if they asked for a personal anecdote and you either genuinely did not have one or did not feel comfortable sharing. A fabricated story was better than no story at all, to help connect to the patient and make them feel like they're not alone in their experience. Whatever it took to *make the patient feel more at ease*, naturally.

They continued on to the next box, which held an assortment of papers Freya had kept in her desk drawers, scattered across tabletops, basically anywhere she had been able to store them. These were primarily personal documents such as letters, her diploma, legal documentation, and the like. Recipes for complicated potions and spells, as well as any other mage-related notes Freya had taken over the years, had been filed away in a drawer within the clinic.

"I wasn't sure what you might need, so I just boxed it all up," Aava explained.

Artemis nodded and began to shuffle through the loose sheets of paper, setting aside the ones he'd examined on the floor in two separate piles, presumably one to keep and one to toss.

Aava watched him go through this process for several minutes. In what she assumed to be the *keep* pile, he placed his mother's birth certificate, her white mage certification, and a few letters from her closest friends.

In the other stack were old receipts from the stores around town, pamphlets advertising sales in the bigger cities, and—

She pointed at the paper Artemis had just tossed on top of the pile. "May I look at this?" she asked him.

"Sure," he shrugged. "Looks like a recipe for something."

She plucked the paper from the pile and scanned the scribbled text. It was indeed a recipe, but the type of recipe was why it had caught her eye. The ingredients she'd noticed were common in potions, usually ones that were meant to cure respiratory illnesses. She must have somehow missed this when packing everything the day before, or Lisa had been the one to stuff it away, thinking of it as nothing more than a random recipe, like Artemis had.

While some of the ingredients were familiar to Aava, the combination of them was not. Freya had not written down any regular old respiratory cure concoction; most white mages knew them by heart, especially one of Freya's age and knowledge, since they were so simple and common. And even if she happened to have forgotten how to brew them, the methods could be found in several different texts, all of which Aava herself had seen on Freya's bookshelves. There would be no reason to copy them down. This was a potion of Freya's own invention. Of that, Aava was sure.

She knew something more serious than a run-of-the-mill cold was ailing her. She was experimenting, trying to cure herself.

Aava ran through the list of ingredients and noted that everything could easily be bought in a general store. Admittedly, she had not yet visited Balam's, but the herbs and broths listed were so commonplace, she would be amazed if they weren't stocked there.

So availability had not been the issue. Had she run out of time before being able to try out her new potion? Or had it simply not worked?

"Do you mind if I keep this?" Aava asked, holding up the recipe. "It's for a potion, actually. It must have gotten put in the box by mistake."

"Of course, go ahead," Artemis said absently, tossing aside more papers. She could tell he was growing weary of this chore. He was probably far beyond ready to be back home.

Aava thanked him and walked to the countertop where Freya had housed a few pre-made potions. She read the handwritten directions once more, noting Freya's description of the potion's final form (hue, consistency, fragrance) and checked it against the five bottles resting before her.

None matched, which was a disappointment. And it still didn't answer the question of whether Freya had gotten the chance to try the potion. Aava could brew it herself, but if this illness were a one-time occurrence, there would be no one to test it on to see if it worked. She felt at a loss, but it would be beneficial to keep the recipe on hand.

She left the page on the counter and resumed her position at Artemis's side as he sorted the papers. Only one box remained, and then their sorrowful task would be complete.

- -

Ryckert didn't really think Michio would show up for the funeral, especially if he was the murderer, but he kept an eye out anyway. As expected, Michio never showed, so if Ryckert was going to get closer to attempt wringing any information out of the man, it was time to head to the tavern.

Night had fallen on Balam and many had retreated to the nearby pub once the reception was over. As a result, the place was more packed than Ryckert was accustomed to. Generally the pub was pretty empty save for a few regulars on nights like tonight, but now it was nearly full. The only available seats were at the bar, so that was where he sat.

He scanned the room, trying to spy Michio in the crowd. Not likely that he would be sitting at a table with someone, as Ryckert was sure he was the only person Michio had even interacted with in town besides the bartender, but he needed to cover his bases.

No sign of Michio.

That was fine. The night was still young, not even eight o'clock yet. Plenty of time for the black mage to show up before closing.

Ryckert had eaten dinner at home before coming to the bar, so he declined Ann Marie's offer of appetizers, but he told her he wouldn't mind a whiskey. She grinned knowingly at him and poured the glass.

"Been here a lot lately," Ryckert said to her before taking a swig of his drink. "Working extra shifts?"

"Yep," Ann Marie answered. "With Vince gone for the Hunt, I'm in charge. Gotta be here most of the time, looking out for things."

"Sounds like a drag."

"Sorta is, but it's extra money, at least. Until Vince gets back with whatever he's caught."

"He a good hunter?"

Ann Marie laughed. "You ever been here for our Hunt specials after all the festivities end?"

Ryckert shook his head. He hadn't even heard of these specials. Balam usually never spoke of the Spring Hunt. Vince, the bar's owner, had to be the only townsperson who partook in its tradition. "It's in my blood, what can I say?" Vince would tell those who questioned him.

"Well," Ann Marie said, "the specials ain't ever that good. And they don't last long, if you know what I mean."

Ryckert smirked. "A lean bounty, then."

"Lean indeed. Can I get you another?"

She pointed at his glass, which was empty. He hadn't even realized he had downed the drink already. But he told her sure, and so she poured another.

Ryckert reluctantly paced himself for the next half hour while he waited. He could have easily consumed another three or four drinks, but he held off after that second glass and told

Ann Marie he was fine for now. He listened to the conversations of those around him—not intentionally, really—and ordered himself some fried clams after all, more out of boredom than hunger. None of the conversations he picked up were anything noteworthy; couples chatting, someone saying how nice the funeral was, someone else arranging a babysitter so they could go on a business trip. The everyday talk of a bustling little village on the coast.

Finally, when the clock's wiry hands neared half past eight, the front door creaked open and Ryckert saw Michio in the corner of his eye.

He remained facing forward, chomping down on his last clam. Better to not appear as if he were waiting this whole time, as if he didn't even know Michio had shown up. Let him come to the bar. Let him initiate.

A hand clapped Ryckert's back as Michio sat down beside him on one of the pub's few empty stools. His thin beard was growing fuller, though not by much. There was a smile on the young man's face as he pulled out his trusty pen and paper.

~ hello Ryckert! ~

"Hey there, friend," Ryckert greeted him, returning the pat. "How've you been these past few days? Haven't seen you around."

~ good. just busy. ~

Ryckert nodded. "Been a long time since I've been busy," he sniggered. "Retirement's slow and easy. Just like they say it is." He looked down at his plate, empty except for the tin cup of creamy pink sauce that had accompanied the clams, and apologized. "Woulda saved you some, if I'd known."

Michio waved away his words and gestured to grab Ann Marie's attention. As she made her way over to him, he wrote his order on the crinkled paper. Ryckert didn't see what he'd requested, but when Ann Marie returned, she was carrying two tall glasses filled to the brim with golden beer, with just a thin layer of foam on top. The mage pushed one of the glasses toward Ryckert.

"Didn't have to do that," Ryckert said, "but thank you much." They clinked their glasses together and drank. The foam got caught on Ryckert's furry upper lip and he licked it away as he set his glass down. "Don't usually go for the beer here, but that's pretty good. Might have to start makin' exceptions."

Michio only nodded and took another sip of his own. He licked his lips with pleasure.

~ *I heard the funeral for the mage was today* ~

"Yup," Ryckert confirmed. "Pretty nice service. Didn't see you there, though. Or at the reception after."

~ *didnt think would be appropriate to go, didnt know her* ~

"Makes sense. Missed out on some good food, though." By now he'd drank half of his beer, and so he gulped down the rest in one go. It truly was better than he had thought it would be. He usually didn't have a taste for beer and stuck with hard liquor when he was looking to get drunk.

Michio was nursing his beverage. It might be because he could only afford two drinks that night, so his crescents were already dried up. Ryckert decided to return the favor and regain some of the trust he'd lost the other day.

"Might not be as good as Bernard's kabobs, but they've got some decent food here too. Pick whatever you want off the menu."

The young man looked genuinely shocked by this offer, but he hurriedly snatched up a menu and began to browse the entrees. Ryckert had to wonder when Michio had last eaten a real, full meal and not just a puny can of beans. He seemed ravenous just reading descriptions on the menu.

Michio pointed at an item, then slid his gloved fingertip over to its price. He gave Ryckert a questioning look.

"Sure," the rocyan said. "Whatever you want, it's no problem. Eat and enjoy."

Michio smiled wide as Ryckert called Ann Marie back to them.

"What can I get ya?" she asked with a smile. "Another whiskey?"

"Not right now," he said. "Right now all we need is some vissian stew in one of your bread bowls for my friend here."

Ann Marie shifted her gaze to Michio. "Want an apple with that?"

Michio nodded enthusiastically.

Probably been a long time since he's had any fresh fruit too. Outskirts of Cerene are a bit bare.

"Comin' right up." Ann Marie turned on her heel and withdrew to the kitchen to place the order.

~ thank you ~

"Don't mention it," Ryckert told him. "Like I said, no trouble at all. The stew's mighty fine, but the real star of that dish is the bread bowl. Believe me."

Michio exaggeratedly licked his lips and rubbed his stomach in anticipation. They both laughed at his buffoonish miming.

Michio was being a lot more open and friendly, like he had been on the first night they met. Ryckert had soured things between them with his accusations, but with the beers and food they were getting on solid footing again. The plan was working so far.

"So, how long you plannin' to stay in town?" Ryckert asked. Maybe the mage would be willing to divulge a bit now.

Michio pondered the question a few moments before writing his reply. *~ not much longer. week or so maybe. ~*

"Where you off to next?"

~ nowhere specific. wherever I end up is where I end up ~

Ryckert nodded. "I hear good things about Brigher," he said. "Not too far, neither. Only a couple days' travel. Though that's on wagon, not sure about on foot."

~ what's in Bryer? ~

"Nothin' particularly special. Just a nice town, is all. Friendly folk, good food. Bigger than Balam, so there's more to do and see. And it's with an I-G-H, not a Y. In case that trips you up trying to find it on a map or somethin'."

~ Brigher ~ He looked to Ryckert for verification. The rocyan nodded. *~ maybe there, then ~*

Soon after, Ann Marie returned with a steaming bowl of vissian stew. It smelled heavenly to Ryckert's sensitive nose; the spices mixed with the long-simmering broth and the chunky vissian meat were a delicious combination. Ryckert was beginning to regret eating at home, now that he could smell Michio's food. While she was present, Ryckert asked Ann Marie for another round of beer for the both of them. One more beer wouldn't hurt. Not tonight, anyway. Tomorrow was another story, but tomorrow was tomorrow.

Michio wasted no time at all digging into his bowl. He gulped down the hot stew with vigor, scraping his spoon along the sides of the bowl to get some pieces of moist bread with each bite. He gave Ryckert a lively thumbs up in between spoonfuls.

When Ann Marie brought their beers, Ryckert proposed another small toast. "To Brigher," he said jokingly and held up his glass, almost spilling some of the liquid as it sloshed near the brim.

Michio gave a silent laugh, setting down his spoon and raising his glass as well. The two clinked them together, but upon impact, Michio's glass shattered into several large, pointed pieces, spraying beer all over the counter, the floor, and their pants.

They both hopped up and brushed bits of glass off their clothing. "Shit," Ryckert cursed. "Apologies."

Michio bent to the ground to gather the shards, but Ryckert stopped him.

"Eat," he told the mage. "Stew'll get cold. I'll get it."

Michio silently thanked him and returned to his stool while Ryckert collected the sharp glass fragments in his padded hand. He stood back up and placed them on the countertop, and seconds later Ann Marie was before them.

"You two are causin' quite a ruckus," she said in a playfully scornful voice. She eyed the damage and grabbed a rag from behind the counter to mop up the liquid that was dripping onto the floor.

"Sorry about that," Ryckert said. "I can pay for the glass."

"Don't worry about that," Ann Marie told him. "Drunker idiots break more shit than this and Vince never gives 'em any grief. Are you alright?" she asked Michio.

He held up his hands, showing her the gloves he always wore. No cuts.

"Good. I'll grab you another beer."

Michio shook his head and waved his hands. He then hastily grabbed the pen and paper. ~ *maybe sign I had too much to drink already* ~

"Allow me to still pay for that drink, then," Ryckert said to Ann Marie. "Least I can do for the trouble."

She smiled. "Alright, then. If you insist." She slipped away to deal with her other patrons.

Ryckert wiped any excess beer off his stool with a napkin and took his seat once more. Michio had wolfed down half the stew in only a few minutes' time.

"Can see you like it," Ryckert said, nodding at the bowl. Michio nodded and gave another thumbs up.

The crowd was thinning as people finished their dinners and had their fill of alcohol. Ryckert drank his beer while Michio silently ate by his side. He observed the men and women as they talked, ate, drank, laughed. His vision began to blur, to grow hazy. He felt his body wobbling side to side. Maybe this beer had been the *one too many*.

Nausea hit him in an instant. He blinked rapidly, looking down at his beer, not wanting to puke in public, especially not after causing such a commotion with the broken glass.

Swirling in the liquid, he saw what he thought to be a silvery shimmer.

Ryckert looked to Michio, who had stopped eating, his spoon raised in mid-air as he stared at the rocyan. A grin broke out across his face.

"You fuh…"

The rest of the syllables were swallowed back down as Ryckert lost consciousness and collapsed to the floor, his shirt soaking up even more of the lost beer as well as his own beer that now exploded apart, crushed between his body and the wood floor. Bits of jagged glass pierced his skin and got tangled in his brown fur.

The light of the pub grew dark. Everything was black.

- -

Michio looked down at the unconscious rocyan, stupidly heaped on the bar floor like a dead animal. He would've laughed if it wouldn't have given him away. The bartender raced over and knelt beside Ryckert's crumpled body.

"Dammit," she sighed, placing two fingers underneath his nostrils to ensure he was still breathing. "What the hell happened? You two really *are* causing a ruckus tonight."

By now, everyone in the establishment had quieted and turned to stare at the three of them.

Michio shrugged then grabbed his paper.

~ *too much to drink I guess. I'll take him home* ~

"Alright, thank you," Ann Marie said with a sigh of relief. "Good thing Vince is gone, or else he'd be real pissed right now. He's got a low tolerance for people who've got a low tolerance and don't limit themselves. Finish up your food if you can do it fast, and then get him outta here, okay?"

Michio nodded and pushed his tray away. He was sad about not being able to eat the entire bread bowl, but he had other things to tend to. He hopped down off his stool and wrapped his arms around Ryckert's body, lifting the rocyan up with a great deal of effort.

"You need help there, son?" asked an older man who sat at a table a few feet away.

Michio shook his head, though he wished he could have accepted. The motherfucker weighed a ton, and it was going to be hell getting him back to the campsite. But it had to be done.

No use complaining.

- -

Nobody in the pub questioned Michio dragging the unconscious rocyan out of the bar. The man had simply gotten too drunk, passed out, and needed assistance getting home. It happened to the best of them. No harm, no foul.

And nobody saw Michio drag the body around the back of the pub, into the secluded wooded area behind the Tilling and Vere households. Most everyone was either still in the pub or tucked away in their warm homes.

If Aava had witnessed the event, she surely would have gone to Ryckert's aid, despite not having much experience dealing with conflict. But she would try because, against all odds, Ryckert Ji'ca was her first and only friend in Balam.

If Theo had witnessed the event, he probably would not have thought much of it beyond "That's weird." Maybe he would have said something to Al, or to Lyrra, but then it would have been forgotten while he slept in fits and starts, plagued by troubled visions of Freya Jeyardin collapsing in the soft grass underneath the yunesca tree.

The only person who was out and about to potentially witness what Michio Loz was up to was Harold Hoskings, but he was unfortunately nowhere near the pub, and regardless, he had other business.

- -

So Michio carried Ryckert through the woods, scraping the rocyan's heels along the dirt, bumping his elbows into tree trunks and bushes. After several minutes, he finally came to a stop in front of his lodgings, which even he had to admit were less than ideal.

He dropped Ryckert's heavy body with a *thud* on the forest floor, glad to be rid of the immense dead weight. The rocyan looked lean, but there was considerable muscle under that fur, and Michio had absolutely felt its heft.

There were a few minutes for him to catch his breath before Ryckert would wake up. He hadn't given the rocyan too big a dose, so he knew he shouldn't dally, but there was time at least for a cigarette. He grabbed one from his pack in the tent and lit it with the snap of his fingers, grinning to himself. That trick always amused him, even if everyone else found it to be trite.

Heat filled his chest and he was consumed by its comfort.

Michio sat cross-legged in the entryway of his bundle of sticks, smoking his cigarette and watching the mechanical heave of Ryckert's chest. It was still slow and steady, which was good. If it started to pick up before he did what needed to be done, there'd be trouble. No doubt Ryckert could easily overpower him. The rocyan had him beat on speed, and in close proximity, that mattered a great deal.

What the fuck is your deal? Michio wondered to himself as he stared at Ryckert. Maybe that would be the first thing he asked. Nice and simple, straight to the point.

All Michio had wanted to do since coming to town was lay low and keep to himself, but this jackass kept poking and prodding. And for what? What was there to gain?

A groan escaped Ryckert's lips as he shifted in place, and the movement startled Michio out of his thoughts. He snubbed the end of the cigarette and scurried on hands and knees over to Ryckert. He then propped up the rocyan's body, scooting it toward the cliffside to the left of the tent so that Ryckert was leaning against the rocky wall. Michio clasped the rocyan's hands together, interlocking the fingers, and gestured with his own hand on top of Ryckert's. A feeble yellow light flowed from Michio's fingertips and enveloped Ryckert's hands, creating an invisible vice grip that would keep his hands held together no matter how much force was enacted upon them.

He then pushed Ryckert's legs together in a straight line in front of his body and cast the same spell, locking the legs into place so that Ryckert could not run either. Michio wanted to keep him right here for now.

Ryckert stirred.

- -

When Ryckert's eyes fluttered open, he was staring into Michio's smirking face as the young man sat on a fallen, moss-covered log, smoking a cigarette and looking quite pleased with himself.

Michio gave a tiny wave.

Ryckert glanced to his left and saw Michio's campsite. That was good; he was at least cognizant of where he was. That was a start.

He tried to bend his legs, but his muscles were frozen stiff. He could still feel the ground beneath them, still felt chilled by the night breeze slapping against them, but their motor functions had completely shut down. He found the same to be true when he attempted to unclench his hands from each other. His long nails dug into the tops of his hands, but he was unable to retract them.

"What'd you do to me?" Ryckert snarled. Before even waiting for an answer, he asked, "You slip me that poison, you piece of shit?"

The mage feigned offense, placing a dainty hand to his chest as if to say, *Me? Poison you? What ever do you mean?* He sucked the end of his cigarette with a grin, dropping his hand back down to his side. He ran his gloved fingertips over the dull green moss, picking at it, tearing pieces off.

"What're you gettin' at here?" Ryckert demanded. "You gonna kill me for sniffin' around? That it?"

Now Michio looked irritated. He had already grown tired of the game. He pulled out his pad and wrote two letters, then held it up for Ryckert to read.

~ *No* ~

"What, then?"

Another frustrated sigh. Holding the skinny cigarette between his thin lips, he scribbled hurriedly on the paper.

~ *I'm the one with questions here* ~

"Well ask 'em, then," Ryckert spat. "No sense wastin' time. Go on."

Michio nodded. Ryckert was glad to see they agreed.

~ *Why did you break into my home? What were you looking for?* ~

Ryckert remained silent.

Michio, impatience growing more and more severe on his face, underlined the two sentences.

But still Ryckert said nothing.

Michio sighed. He set the pad of paper down on the log and held his newly free hand up, palm facing Ryckert. The glove's fabric was worn and faded, almost a dark gray rather than black. Michio curled his fingers, bending them at the knuckles, then crossed the thumb over the palm. One by one in quick succession, pinky to index, Michio touched each finger to his thumb then returned it to its previous position. He did this twice, then immediately unfurled all of his fingers and pushed his open palm toward Ryckert.

A burning sensation lit up Ryckert's chest. He squirmed where he sat, instinctively trying to pat away the invisible burns but unable to move his hands. He doubled over and gritted his teeth, wanting to roar out in pain but not wanting to give the brat the satisfaction. After half a minute, the sensation subsided and Ryckert leaned back against the cliffside with relief, his eyes closed.

He breathed in and out, slowly, trying to calculate his next move. Some kind of attack or escape plan. But without the use of his legs, practically everything would be impossible. He was stuck.

Ryckert opened his eyes to the sight of Michio holding up the pad again, displaying the two underlined sentences. Ryckert scoffed.

"That wasn't so bad," he said. "I've felt worse. You ever have a dagger in your knee?"

Michio drew a second underline.

When Ryckert refused to break his silence, Michio tore off the piece of paper, crumpled it up, and tossed it among the rest of his trash that littered the area. He then wrote something else.

~ *asked if I poisoned you. looking for poison?* ~

"Found poison," Ryckert said.

Michio blinked with confusion, then wrote:

~ *no poison* ~

"Alright," Ryckert grunted. There was nothing else to say. He knew what he saw.

~ *why do you think I have poison?* ~ Something then clicked in his head and he rolled his eyes. ~ *still think I had to do with that woman dying? are you crazy?* ~

"Been called crazy before," Ryckert shrugged.

~ *why would I kill that woman?* ~

"You tell me."

~ *I wouldnt. That's my point* ~

"Poisoning and kidnapping me seems like awfully shady behavior for someone who's got nothin' to hide. Coulda talked this out at the pub."

~ *tried that already. and then you still rummaged through my shit like an animal* ~

Ryckert's eyes narrowed in a sharp glare. He learned from his ra not to take talk like that from anybody.

"Better watch what you fuckin' write next," he growled.

Michio rolled his eyes again.

~ *didnt mean it like that. calm down.* ~

Ryckert wasn't entirely convinced, but he dropped the subject for now. Once his hands were free, things could come to blows if he still deemed it necessary.

"Unbind me," Ryckert said. "We're not gonna get anywhere with this. You can keep burnin' me and I'll keep sittin' here like a jackass, not able to move my feet, and we'll go on and on until the sun's high in the sky and Walton's coffee's in the pot. Let's not waste each other's time. Sound good to you?"

There was a momentary pause, and then Michio looked like he was about to laugh. He stood and walked toward the tent, bending down to pick up the crumpled piece of paper he had thrown a minute before. He straightened out the page, smoothing it on his knee, and took a few steps closer to Ryckert, pointing at the one word he'd written near the top of the page.

~ *No* ~

He then tossed it aside once more.

"Well, you ain't gonna get the info you want, and it seems like I got the info I need. So I guess we can either sit here in silence, you can kill me, or you can let me go."

~ *are you gonna keep giving me grief if I let you go?* ~

"Looks that way."

Michio flew into a rage, throwing his pad at the shelter he'd built. It collided with the branch that held the magic Ustrel symbol, which lit up with faint orange sparks. The mage then ducked into the tent, digging through his belongings, and emerged with the vial of silver powder in hand. It glimmered in the dim light.

Ryckert began to internally panic at the sight of it. He maintained his composure on the outside, not letting Michio see how worried he truly was.

The young man popped the top off and stood before Ryckert, who remained immobile. He gestured forward, inviting Ryckert to open his mouth and willingly ingest the powder.

Ryckert resolutely shook his head.

Another roll of the eyes. Michio had grown tired of the rocyan's attitude. He gestured with his free hand and suddenly Ryckert's maw shot open, his tongue lolling to the side.

He tried to clasp his jaw shut, but it was no use. Michio was in control of him.

Michio kneeled down and tapped a few drops of the powder into the back of Ryckert's throat, then used his hand to snap Ryckert's mouth closed.

Soon after, the world was snuffed out of sight.

- -

The night was cold, as they had all been this past week. It didn't bother Harold Hoskings any; he was a thick man, and a brisk breeze never did him any harm.

He had worked hard to set up the chairs and flowers and whatever else Barbara Vere asked him to for the funeral, and now he was working hard to get it all put away in storage. There was a large shed beside the cemetery, on the western edge of the farmland, where chairs, tables, the podium, and other items were kept for various events. Thankfully, someone else had been recruited to break down the reception, so Harold didn't have to carry those tables all the way back to the farm. He just had to deal with some chairs.

There had been time to relax once the reception wound down, and Harold had taken the opportunity to do so at home. He figured the chairs would still be sitting there waiting for him, and he didn't mind staying up a little later. Better to rest his feet. He was nearly fifty now, not as spry as he used to be. It was dismaying how often he felt the need to rest these days.

As a child, he had always teased his father for napping the afternoons away when there were better things to do, like explore the woods or play fetch with the serokos. Nowadays, he understood.

So he'd taken a nap in his oversized, comfy armchair in the middle of the living room. Izzy was out somewhere, probably with Harley, so he had the house to himself. Peace and quiet. Years ago, when he would try taking naps in his chair, he was frequently woken up by his wife Meredith messing around in the kitchen, or telling him a story about her day. The interruptions had annoyed him then, but now that it had been three years since her passing, he found himself missing the banging of those pots and the sharp inhale before she dove into a tale.

Izzy had returned home for dinner, which Harold had ready for consumption by the time she arrived. Pasta with white sauce, one of their favorites, especially on such a chilly night. They ate together and talked in spurts, mostly trivial subjects like what she'd done that day, how the farm was, and other boring things that Harold imagined all fathers spoke to their daughters about. The deeper talk was for the mother, he thought. Not because he didn't want to have those types of conversations with Izzy, but because he assumed she did not want to have them with him. And even if he attempted to strike up conversation like that, he wouldn't know where to start. Harold Hoskings was a simple man, and he liked that about himself, but sometimes it left him longing for a stronger connection with his daughter.

Harold had the foresight to bundle up before leaving his home. He wore a long-sleeved white shirt, a puffy green vest, and a blue cap that covered his fiery red hair. The hair on his head was thinning now, but when he was younger he wore it spiked up (which he had thought was exceptionally cool), and Meredith would come to him saying, "Are you feeling okay? You look like you're burning up," and then she would put a hand on his forehead to jokingly take his temperature.

He shuffled out the door, leaving Izzy to her books, and trudged through the cold back toward the farmland. He let out a deep sigh as the rows of chairs came into view, and an even bigger one when he eyed the podium. The podium had somehow slipped his mind. It would be a chore dragging it through the dirt paths back to the storage shed.

There was a figure, draped in shadow.

Harold hadn't noticed the silhouette at first, but as he grew closer, he spotted the person standing behind the podium, staring out at the ocean. Moonlight gleamed on its surface. With each step, the figure came into sharper view, and Harold was able to recognize his visitor.

"Hullo there, Serys," he said with a chatter in his teeth.

The man turned around, startled, and breathed with relief when he saw who had snuck up on him. "Hey there," he said. "Sorry to bother you. I didn't realize anyone would be taking this stuff down today."

"Not a bother at all, friend," said Harold. He could not recall an instance when he had heard Serys speak in such a soft voice. "Just surprised to see you, is all. What brings you out here?"

Serys returned his gaze to the sea. "Just thinking," he shrugged. "Freya's death has been weighing on me," he said. Then, quickly, "Because it's reminding me of my own age. And Elena's."

"I know exactly what you mean." For a moment, Harold returned to that terrible day when he'd had to tell Izzy her mother was gone. The heartbreak on that little girl's face. He couldn't bear the thought of her losing a father too.

"Elena and I are even older than Freya was. I'm almost sixty! When the hell did *that* happen?"

Harold said nothing.

"Oh well. I should return home, I suppose. Elena and Hilli are probably wondering where this old geezer wandered off to. It's too cold for me, anyways. Unless you would like some help with these chairs? Pardon me for taking so long to offer!"

Harold shook his head. "Nah, I'll be fine. You're right, it's a cold one tonight. You should get back inside, get home to your family. I won't be out here too long."

"Are you quite sure?"

"Yeah, I'm sure," Harold chuckled. "Don't worry 'bout me, old man."

"That was rude," Serys said with a laugh. "But fine. Don't work yourself too hard." He came down from the overlook and rested a hand on Harold's shoulder, which Harold reciprocated.

"You too, bud. Take it easy."

Serys smiled, though it was feeble and pained. He gave Harold a quick pat, then departed, heading east toward his house on the edge of the cliff. Somehow Harold felt confident that the man would be spending a few solitary minutes looking out his window at the ocean again when he got home. Seeing Serys White in such a melancholy mood was putting Harold in one as well. The man was usually boisterous and, subsequently, a tad obnoxious.

But no matter. There was a job to do, and Harold wanted to get it over with so he could get back home. Izzy had the right idea, curling up in her warm bed with a book to read. He might have to follow her lead. He was near the end of his mystery novel, and he was dying to know how Balthaz He'ra, the rocyan soldier-turned-guardsman, was going to escape the sticky situation he'd found himself in.

Harold kept thoughts of Balthaz He'ra at the forefront of his mind. Theorizing about the novel's outcome would be good motivation to finish sooner rather than later. He worked swiftly, managing to put away the front two rows of chairs within little more than ten minutes, and when he returned from the shed to commence row three, he decided to get the podium out of the way instead.

"Chunky old bastard," he mumbled as he wrapped his arms around the chilled rectangular hunk of wood. It was light enough that he didn't have to resort to dragging it along the ground, but he could not lift it more than a few inches off the ground. Maybe in his younger days it would have been easier, but not at the ripe age of forty-seven.

He carried the podium past the remaining rows of seats, waddling as he tried to maintain his grip on the slippery wood. He shambled past the cornstalks, past the cucumber patch, down the short pathway flanked by trees, until he reached the town's modest-sized cemetery. It wasn't an enormous plot of land, but it seemed to be enough to fit the town's population, although it would likely need to be expanded in the near future. Since she had spent most of her days in Balam, Freya had written in her will that she wanted to be buried there, and Harold could spot the fresh dirt piled on her plot. Her tombstone was a stout square, adorned with a stone star on its top.

The storage shed was on the back left-hand side of the cemetery, on the outside of the short metal fence that surrounded the cemetery grounds. Harold dragged the podium around, his breathing getting heavier with each tiny step, until finally he felt the sweet reprieve of setting it down in front of the rusty door.

He leaned against the door for a moment, catching his breath. He regretted eating so much pasta, now that it was sitting like a brick in his stomach. Once sufficiently restored, he pushed open the door and dragged the podium inside.

As he positioned the podium in a back corner of the shed, he heard a harsh sound outside. The shattering of stone, the scuffling of feet. Harold waited a moment, cupping his ear to listen, and seconds later there was a shrill shriek. Someone was in the cemetery. Or some*thing*.

Harold gulped. He was not generally a violent man, though he had participated in the occasional hunt with Bernard and he enjoyed the fight scenes in his mystery novels. But he did not have much experience in combat, and worry began to twist into a tight knot in his chest.

Not a heart attack, don't have a heart attack, he begged himself. *The town already had to bury Freya this week, don't add yourself to the list. Can't do that to Izzy. Don't have a heart attack, you stupid old bastard.*

The sounds of scraping and the gargled cries of whatever was out there continued. Harold almost called out, but quickly realized that would be foolish. Right now he had the advantage of being unknown. He could land a sneak attack, if it came to violence.

He edged out of the shed, maneuvering his protruding belly around the door so as to not push it on its creaky hinges and give himself away. He fit through and peered around the corner of the building, out into the graveyard.

What he saw filled him with dread.

A creature was in the cemetery. It was medium-sized, about the same height as the fence that enclosed the plot, which came up to Harold's waist. At first he thought it might be a vissian, but while it was definitely insectoid, it was not anything he had ever seen before. Its thorax was two feet long and oval-shaped, with a murky green carapace. The abdomen was short and curved in on itself, the end almost coming around to pierce its underside. The head was rounded and held two rows of three eyes each that all blinked in unison. Feelers jutted from its forehead, patting against the ground while it dug in the dirt with its two front legs that ended in large, scooping claws. It stood on four hind legs, the middle of which had similar claws but the back two of which were clubbed feet. It appeared to be oozing a thick, green liquid from the joints in its body as it examined the earth at its feet.

It was standing in a large hole where Freya had been buried. There was another, smaller hole beside the one in which it stood.

"What the fuck?" Harold muttered.

His words had been no louder than a whisper, but either they had carried in the silence or the beast had outstanding hearing, because it immediately turned its head and spotted him standing by the shed, mouth agape. Harold fumbled through another curse word as the insect sprang forward, almost halving the distance between them in one leap.

Harold scrambled backwards, nearly tripping over his own clumsy feet, as he tried to get away from whatever the thing was.

It jumped again, flying over the fence with ease, and landed just a few short steps away from Harold, who was now embroiled in a full panic.

The creature chirped and took a few cautious steps forward, which Harold matched going backward. But his trembling legs got the best of him and he fell over, crashing with a hard thump on his ass.

"Shit!" Harold cried, kicking at the insect as it took another step toward him. His boot connected with its face, smashing two of its eyes, and it let out an anguished shriek. Blood and black pus squirted from the two ruined eye sockets as the green liquid continued flowing down its spindly legs.

The monster stepped back, fumbling around partially blind, and Harold took this opening to push up off the ground with some great effort. He mentally scolded himself for the weight he'd gained over the past couple years and scorned the pasta he'd cooked tonight.

He raced into the shed and momentarily considered slamming the door shut, locking himself away inside until the creature fled or the sun rose, whichever came first. But then he regained rational thought and remembered there were a handful of shovels stowed away inside for digging graves.

Harold ran back to where he had placed the podium and grabbed the handle of a shovel that lay dirty and dusty on the hard floor. "That'll do," he said with a nervous grin.

He darted back outside, shivering uncontrollably (though he did not know if it was from the cold or the immense fear he felt), and found the insectoid beast scurrying slowly along the side of the fence, back toward the farm and Balam.

"No you don't!" Harold roared, racing toward it, shovel raised high in the air like a mighty sword. "This is the end for you, and I feel no shame!" he added, stealing a line from Balthaz He'ra.

The shovel came down with one swift swing on the creature's abdomen, sending it crashing to the ground, slamming its face into the dirt.

Harold stood at its side and raised the shovel once more, then brought it down hard and fast, spearing the beast's midsection.

It squirmed and screamed with terror, trying to crawl away but unable, pinned to the forest floor by Harold's makeshift blade. After a couple moments of struggle and some horrid, piercing sounds, the thing's body slowed and came to a stop.

Harold took in a deep breath and plopped down next to the creature with the exhale. He blinked in astonishment, his eyes moving up and down the shovel that still stuck straight up out of the ground and through the monster's body.

Did I really just kill this thing?

He had, and he was amazed. He didn't know he had it in him. During his hunting expeditions with Bernard, he was mostly just company for the butcher and never really killed anything besides maybe one or two vissians, but those were mostly pure luck. He was a farmer at heart, not a hunter.

It took a couple minutes for Harold to regain his composure. Once he had, he stood and removed the shovel from the monster's thorax and lopped its head off, just to be safe.

He left the corpse where it was and stumbled back down the pathway in a daze, past the cucumber patch, past the cornstalks, and stared at the buildings of Balam standing before him, trying to choose which one to go to. His mind raced with thoughts of who he needed to tell about this first.

Barbara is gonna be pretty peeved when she sees I didn't finish with the chairs, he found himself thinking. He let out a barking laugh.

CHAPTER VII

OLD FRIENDS

Walton Vere was the first person Harold told about the previous night's incident; not out of any sense of duty or obligation, but because Harold went directly from the graveyard to the Sonata to grab a cup of coffee, thinking it would calm his nerves.

News spread throughout town the next day, and Rufus Reede sent out a notice that there would be a town meeting at the square around ten o'clock. Food was unable to be provided on such short notice.

While Mr. Reede arranged the meeting, Harold and Bernard were tasked with handling the monster's body. The men decided to store it in Bernard's freezer in his shed (wrapped up securely, so as to not allow any of the creature's viscous ooze to drip onto any other meat and infect it). As Bernard stuffed the insectoid corpse into the freezer, having moved as much meat into the auxiliary freezer as possible, he thought it extremely likely he would end up disposing what was left inside anyway, despite the precautions they had taken. Better safe than sorry. He couldn't let his reputation suffer due to poor sanitation.

The reason for keeping the monster's body rather than immediately disposing of it was because Bernard, the town's most seasoned hunter, had never seen anything like it. The only other resident who regularly hunted monsters was Vince Brine, but he was presently out of town for that precise purpose.

Bernard had stated—and Mr. Reede had agreed—that they needed to more closely examine the beast. In addition, he knew a world traveler who might be able to grant them more insight into the monster.

The problem was that he could not find Ryckert Ji'ca anywhere.

- -

A raucous banging on their front door woke Theo from a pleasant dream wherein he was visiting his mother and sister in the flower-filled clearing his father had created. His sister Gwendolyn was sitting in the middle of the ice-blue flowers, delicately running her fingertips along their fragile petals, while his mother leaned in close to whisper something in his ear.

And then he was back in his bed, bundled up with Lyrra's back pressed to the curve of his body, while someone slammed their fist repeatedly on the door.

"What…" Theo sputtered, too groggy to even complete a sentence. With a huge amount of willpower, he cast the blanket aside and pushed himself out of bed.

In the living room, Theo walked past their messy plates on the table, left behind and forgotten in lieu of a passionate night in the bedroom. They would be much harder to clean today, but the trade-off had been worth it. He pulled open the door just enough to peer through the crack and see who was there. It was Al, whose expression and body language were lackadaisical and completely in contrast to the urgency with which he had been knocking.

Theo opened the door the rest of the way and Al grinned at the sight of his white and green-striped pajamas, which Theo had owned since he was a teenager and remarkably still fit his thin frame. "What?" Theo asked. "You do realize you're knocking like a madman, right? I half-expected to find someone dying at my doorstep, the way you sounded."

"Did I wake you?" Al asked sarcastically.

"Why are *you* up so early?"

"Can I come in a minute?"

Theo stood aside and Al sauntered in, heading right for the sofa. He took a seat and stretched his arms, letting out a loud sigh.

"Lyrra's still sleeping," Theo told him. "Try to keep it down."

Al apologized and let out a yawn. "I'm awake for the same reason you are."

"Someone banging at your door like a lunatic?"

"Yes. But in my case, it was Gillian."

Gillian Markby was another teacher at the school, a woman that Al had had his sights on before learning she was happily married with two daughters. She and Al were neighbors, with their houses positioned right across the river from Theo and Lyrra's.

"What'd she want?" Theo asked. "Why is everyone being so neighborly this morning? And so *early*?" he added, looking at the clock. It was barely past nine.

"Somethin' big went down," Al told him. "I don't know the details, because Gillian didn't know 'em, and I came straight here after she told me. And after I got dressed, of course," he said, chuckling at Theo's outfit.

"They're pajamas. People sleep in pajamas. You woke me up from sleeping. Why is this amusing?"

"Sorry, sorry. Anyway, she told me Rufus is holding an emergency town meeting at ten and that I should let people know. So here I am, letting you know."

Theo wondered what could have happened. Was another person sick like Freya? Had there been another death? It didn't take much for Mr. Reede to call for a town meeting in general, but an *emergency* meeting was almost unprecedented. He could only recall one other time it had happened in the years he had lived in Balam, and that was when a fierce storm had sacked the town for over twenty-four hours, flooding the farm and destroying the Reen household. The meeting had been called for Mr. Reede to request donations to help fund the rebuilding of the house (which Theo had found peculiar, considering how wealthy Mr. Reede was and most of the Reens were his employees, but Theo had contributed anyway).

"Ten o'clock?" Theo verified.

"Yep. See you then," Al said, standing. He contorted his body in another wild stretch, this time keeping quiet while he did so. "I would ask that you get the word out, but I'll do it for you since you seem a bit *indisposed* at the moment," he said with a smirk.

"They're *pajamas*. I'm not *indisposed*," Theo laughed. "Do you not wear pajamas to bed? Do you hop in wearing whatever you had on all day?"

"Nah," Al said, heading for the door. He swung it open and took a step out into the brisk morning air. "I don't wear *nothin'* to bed." He gave Theo a wink, and then he was off.

Theo chuckled and closed the door, then returned to the bedroom. He slipped back under the sheets and nuzzled up next to Lyrra, kissing her lightly on the back of her neck. He breathed in her scent and let out a relaxed sigh.

"Was that Al?" she asked quietly, pushing through her sleepiness. Her eyes remained shut.

"Yeah," Theo answered. "Sorry. I told him to be quiet, but you know…"

"Loud by nature."

"Loud by nature," Theo said with a smile. It was their personal slogan for him.

"What'd he want?" Lyrra slurred. It came out more like *whuddy wuhn?*

"He said there's an emergency town meeting in an hour."

This perked Lyrra up. She turned her heard toward Theo, her eyes now open and alert.

"Emergency meeting? Why?"

"Don't know," Theo said.

"He didn't think to tell you what happened?"

"He didn't know either. Gillian told him, and she didn't know. I'm not sure if anyone does, besides Mr. Reede."

"If it's an emergency meeting, it must be for something serious," Lyrra said.

"We'll find out in an hour, I guess. Are you gonna go? I can just tell you what he says, if you'd rather stay here. Get some more sleep, make yourself a nice cup of coffee when you get up."

"No," Lyrra replied, removing the blanket. She stood, stretching with much more grace and elegance than Al could ever hope to achieve, and marched to the bathroom. "I wanna go. I wanna hear what's going on." She closed the door behind her, and a few seconds later, Theo heard the shower faucet running.

He placed his head back on the down pillow and sunk in, the sides of the pillow rising up to cup his head as it caved in the center. It only took a minute before his eyelids fluttered shut again.

It would not take him long to get ready. He could sleep a while longer. If he was lucky, he might find himself transported back to that flowery field so that he might hear his mother's words, her voice lifted on the breeze.

- -

Most everyone was in attendance at the town square. Mr. Reede had situated the small, oval wooden stage he procured for such events on the northern side, resting on the cobblestone with its edge grazing the grass. The stage had been handcrafted by Mr. Reede's father before he passed away, specifically for his son to stand on and make pronouncements.

The sun hung high in the sky and cast a warm glow on the proceedings. The wind was pleasantly chilly, not harsh enough to require a coat, especially with the sunlight bearing down. The blue leaves of the yunesca tree rustled in the breeze overhead.

Al found the Saens in the crowd and stood next to Theo. "Hey," he said to Lyrra, and she returned the greeting. To Theo, he said, "I liked your outfit this morning more."

"Good one, very humorous," Theo said.

Theo saw the new white mage, Aava, standing on the opposite side of the square with her arms crossed, tapping her foot. He followed her line of sight and saw she was eyeing Harold Hoskings, who stood beside the oval stage and looked even more anxious than her.

Harold was watching Mr. Reede, who stood on the stage and waited until he deemed the crowd size to be sufficient. When people finally stopped milling in, he boomed, "Hello, all!"

A murmur of hellos in response. As Theo looked over his fellow townspeople, he saw that it was not just Aava and Harold who were nervous. Everyone seemed to be on edge, unsure of the reason for this gathering. It was then that Theo began to hope that the absences he had noted were just that—absences, and not deaths.

"I know you are all wondering why I called this meeting," Mr. Reede began, an expression of joviality on his reedy face. "I did not mean to alarm you all so much, and for that I apologize deeply! I truly believe the issue we are gathered to discuss is already behind us and that there is no need to worry, but I thought it best we get together and discuss it anyway. I'm sure you are all thinking to yourselves: get to the point, Rufus! Why are we here? Answer: there has been an incident with Freya Jeyardin's body."

The crowd broke into hushed whispers that pulsed and grew into a roar. When Mr. Reede regained control of his audience, he continued.

"Our very own Mr. Hoskings bore witness to this event, and so he will be the one to describe it to you all. I have already heard the tale, and it filled me with terror and sorrow. I now leave you all to Mr. Hoskings. Harold?" He took a step down from the stage and gestured toward Harold to take his spot.

Harold appeared as if he was about to puke right there in front of everyone. He had heavy bags under his eyes, like he hadn't gotten any sleep the night before. He cleared his throat and waved meekly to the crowd.

"Hi, everybody," he muttered.

Mr. Reede leaned forward with a showman's grin on his face. "You're going to have to speak up, my friend," he said. "We can't have those in the back left wanting, can we?"

Harold nodded, then repeated himself in a louder, more confident voice. "How are y'all doin'?"

There were impatient mumbles from the audience, and Harold knew he had to quit stalling.

"As y'all know, I'm in charge of dressing up and down the services at the farmstead," Harold started. "Well, I went there last night to fold up and put away the chairs, carry the podium back to the storage shed, all that. Just like I always do. For those of you who don't have any reason to visit the farm regularly, or the graveyard either—and if that's the case, then you're lucky—you might not know that they're pretty close together, and the shed where we keep all the supplies for Mr. Reede's events is propped up right beside the cemetery. Not even a stone's throw away, more like a pebble's toss. Right by the fence, y'see." Harold wiped a bead of sweat from his brow. He was rambling, but Theo could see he was nearing the point of all this. "So I was near the cemetery last night, is what I'm gettin' at. Real close. And while I was puttin' away the podium, I heard a strange sound coming from there, so I went outside to take a look at what was goin' on."

Harold looked out at the crowd, then down to his feet, and exhaled a deep sigh.

Theo surveyed the crowd as well and spotted who he surmised Harold had been searching for: Artemis Jeyardin. Whatever had transpired, Harold certainly wished Freya's son was not present to hear it. But alas.

"There was a beast," Harold said bluntly. "It had snuck in, I guess, and dug a hole straight through to Freya's casket. Broke right through the wood. Seemed to be no issue, really. And then it..." he trailed off, casting a quick glance at Artemis, who stood stoically watching as the story was told. "...it tore into the body, too."

Gasps. People began to whisper to each other before Mr. Reede hushed them all again with a few curt claps.

Theo and Lyrra exchanged confused, worried looks. He then saw that the mage Aava had brought a hand to her mouth, her eyes widened with disbelief. Artemis appeared unmoved by this revelation.

"It weren't huge, but it weren't small, neither," Harold went on. "About the size of a healthy wolf, I'd say. Looked kinda like a vissian, but a little off. Big-ass bug, in other words."

"Language, please, Harold. There are children present," Mr. Reede interjected.

"Sorry. Anyways, it was a big bug. Green body, lots of eyes. Big claws that it was usin' to dig and rip. And it was leaking a thick, green liquid from its joints or somethin'. I'm not sure what was going on exactly, since it was so dark, but the thing definitely weren't right. I managed to kill the thing"— relieved sighs from everyone present—"pretty easily, so the bastard weren't that tough. Sorry again for saying 'bastard.' But the thing's dead now."

"What about Freya's body?" someone called out. It sounded like it might have been Cilia Nells.

"Please, no questions yet," Mr. Reede said from behind Harold. "Go on, Mr. Hoskings."

"S'alright, Mr. Reede. The cemetery's being guarded right now by Walton Vere and Dennis Reen. They'll make sure no more critters come by, and if any do, they'll take care of 'em. We did plan on asking our new white mage here if she'd take a look at the body after the meeting, though," he said, looking down at Aava. She nodded ardently, her silky white hair bobbing up and down.

"Excellent," said Mr. Reede, stepping back up onto the stage. He placed a hand on Harold's back. "Thank you, Mr. Hoskings." That was Harold's cue to vacate the stage. He returned to the crowd, taking an open spot next to Aava.

Mr. Reede clapped his hands together and held them clasped, rotating his head back and forth, inspecting everyone like livestock.

"So," he said, "the theory we have constructed is that the creature, whatever it may be, was attracted to some scent from our dearly departed Freya's body, which we presume had something to do with her illness. Since nobody else is sick, I do not anticipate any further trouble from these pesky beasts! But I thought it prudent for you all to be informed of what took place so that you may exercise due caution when out at night, just in case. It's like I always say: better safe than sorry! Are there any questions?"

There were indeed some questions.

Mostly, people insisted on knowing what exactly the creature was, but Mr. Reede did not have an answer. "We are going to be investigating the matter," he assured them. "Bernard is going to be taking a closer look this afternoon, with the assistance of our rocyan friend Ryckert Ji'ca. Once they have determined what the beast is, I will surely let everybody know."

Theo didn't have any questions, and he didn't figure any that were asked would be answered satisfyingly, so he and Lyrra elected to leave the square. Many followed suit, but Mr. Reede and Harold stayed behind to attempt answering any questions they could from those who stayed.

"Pretty wild," Al said as the three of them walked down Main Street, toward the middle tier and the Sonata Diner. Theo and Lyrra were starving, having not had time to cook any breakfast before the meeting. Only Vir had gotten a good meal in their household.

"Yeah," Lyrra concurred. "I'm not sure what good having the mage look at Freya's body will do, though. What are they hoping to glean from that?"

Theo had nothing to offer.

"I dunno," said Al, "but I hope Serys ain't around to see it. Was he at that meeting? Did you see him?"

"I don't think he was," Lyrra replied. "I saw Elena and Hilli, but not Serys."

"Guess he figured it might've had something to do with Freya," Al shrugged. "Can't blame him."

Theo looked at Al as they descended the stone steps. "What do you mean?" he asked. "Why would that make him not go?"

Al returned the look, and when he saw that Theo wasn't joking, he had to laugh. "You serious?" he asked.

Theo nodded.

Al leaned to look at Lyrra. "Do you not know either?"

"Know what?"

As they reached the bottom of the staircase, Al jumped ahead of the couple and grew close to whisper to them.

"Serys and Freya were having an affair," he said. "Guess I thought that little tidbit was more widespread than it actually is. I thought at least *you'd* know, you dolt."

"How would *I* know?" Theo asked. "How do *you* know?"

"Because he told me!" Al exclaimed. "We're buds. We tell each other shit."

Theo then thought back to that night he spent in the pub with Al and Serys, and Al's comment: *You certainly have a thing for the jeornish. That why you married one?*

He then involuntarily imagined Serys sauntering into the clinic, sidling up next to Aava, and laying out some tired pick-up line. Theo shuddered at the prospect.

"Does Elena have even the faintest clue about this?" Lyrra asked, resuming their walk to the diner.

"No, hell no," Al said. "Of course not. Well, *I* don't believe so, anyway. Serys had gotten sorta paranoid lately, though. Thought they weren't covering their tracks well enough, or something. Suspected the beans might spill soon, intentionally or otherwise."

"He thought Freya might tell Elena?" Theo asked. "Why would she? What in the world would she gain from that?"

"Who knows, man," Al said. "He was just getting spooked, I guess. Or his conscience was finally eating at him, I don't know."

"What an idiot," Lyrra muttered. "Elena is such a lovely woman. And they have such a beautiful daughter together."

Theo had always felt like Serys was kind of a sleaze, and this only strengthened his stance. He was also surprised that Freya had gone for such a repugnant man.

"I dunno what to tell you," Al said.

They were halfway to their destination. Theo and Lyrra held hands as they walked down Main Street with Al at Theo's side. Theo looked to his right as they passed the street housing the white mage clinic, and his wily mind once again conjured the image of Serys leaning against the countertop, rapidly raising his eyebrows up and down like a caricature while trying to seduce the youthful Aava.

He shook the thought away and said, "I need some food."

- -

Ryckert awoke feeling groggy and gripped by hunger. Hours later, he had still only eaten a handful of berries picked by Michio.

He remained immobilized, sitting on the forest floor with his back scraping against the rocky cliffside. He watched bugs crawl up and over his legs, unable to swipe them away.

Humiliation and anger filled him in equal measure. He had taken on this investigation of his own volition because he had grown tired of doing nothing day in and day out. Looking back, he was unable to pinpoint what made him think he'd enjoy such a quiet life. Maybe after all the drama with Fenn, he'd thought it'd be preferable.

But now he had tried to fill the void with this murder mystery and found himself tied up and in over his head. How had his skills been so dulled in the passing years? Was he ever all that skilled to begin with? He thought perhaps not, if he had been so easily overtaken by the arrogant young man before him.

He had also ingested a lot of Michio's silver powder. It might not have been quillis or barnas (or even Leif's infamous shitter), but it was surely nothing to scoff at. It had taken Freya's life, and Ryckert began to wonder how soon he would start feeling its effects.

"Why you doin' any of this?" he asked again, not expecting a clear answer. "What'd you have against Freya?"

Michio rolled his eyes. It was becoming a habit. A reflex.

~ *didn't do anything to her* ~

The mage was certainly sticking to his story. Ryckert was starting to feel like maybe he'd pegged the wrong guy, and that made him feel even stupider than he already did. But that begged the question: why restrain him if there was nothing to hide?

"What're you hidin', then?" Ryckert growled. "Why all the goddamn secrecy? And why're you keepin' me here?"

While Ryckert was leaned against the cliff (at one point earlier that morning, to his sheer embarrassment, he had fallen on his side and had to be propped up again), Michio was sitting in the entryway of his meager hut. A cigarette dangled limply from his lips as he knocked the tips of his shoes together. He inhaled and began to write on his pad of paper. The pencil he used was short and stubby, nearing the end of its lifespan. When he showed Ryckert the writing, there were two lines.

~ *not your bizness* ~

~ *cause you won't agree to let me be* ~

"Think it *is* my business now," Ryckert said. "Soon as you slipped me that poison, it became my business."

Michio cocked an eyebrow. He reached back into the hut and pulled out the pouch of powder that Ryckert had previously found. He shook it, indicating as if to ask, *You mean this?*

Ryckert nodded and felt a growl rising in his throat. He suppressed it, though, not wanting to give weight to the man's "animal" comment from the night before.

More mimed laughter. Ryckert was getting sick of watching this guy. He wanted to pounce, wanted to tear at him. He felt patronized.

~ told you already no poison ~

"What is it, then?" Ryckert asked.

At that moment, he wished for another goblin to hop down from above and land directly on Michio's smug face. Rip into it, tug at his ears, bite into his neck. But it was the middle of the day, so any nearby goblins would be tucked away in their dwellings until the sun disappeared and the moon took its place.

Another eye-roll, and then Michio pierced the top of a can of beans with a knife, circling around the lid. He popped it off and stabbed the blade into the dirt, leaving it standing upright. After a moment of searching through his tent, he emerged with a spoon and dug in, scooping a mountain of mushy brown beans into his mouth. Juice dribbled down his chin into his white beard.

On any other day, Ryckert would have found the display wholly unappetizing—disgusting, even—but today, he was hungry. Very hungry. And so that soft, brown mush looked pretty tasty.

"Chance you might spare some of that?" Ryckert asked. His stomach growled with desire.

Michio shook his head.

Ryckert sighed and furrowed his brow. "Just gonna sit here, then? Smackin' on beans and watchin' the mangy rocyan try to squirm his way outta here? Just gonna watch me til I starve?"

Michio once again shook his head.

"What, then?"

Michio took another bite, then set the can down with his spoon submerged in the dense mixture of beans and sauce.

~ just agree to leave me alone ~

"Can't," said Ryckert. "Something ain't right about you."

The mage wrote nothing else and resumed eating his paltry lunch. Ryckert hoped that Michio didn't catch him licking his lips.

The last time Ryckert had found such terrible food to be so appealing, he had been on an assignment with Leif, the assignment that had changed everything for him. The two of them had been stationed in the city of Lors, far east of the town Ryckert had called home at the time. They had been there for months, holed up in a shitty, run-down motel in the middle of downtown. The type of motel that only makes any money because it's at the heart of where tourists want to visit, and the owner rakes in a large profit because he overcharges for the rooms and never upgrades or fixes any of the accommodations. The food served at the motel had been no better than old, nasty shit like beans and soup and the occasional canned meat (all of which, Ryckert suspected, might have been long expired, given the digestive troubles he had faced), but he and Leif needed to stay put while they observed their mark. After living in the motel for so long, something strange had happened in the wiring of Ryckert's brain, and he didn't find the food to be so bad anymore, and he ate it merrily, despite dearly paying for it later once he found himself on the toilet.

As he sat there watching Michio eat, he thought about the dreadful food he'd consumed at that motel in Lors, which led him to thoughts of Leif and, inevitably, Fenn. His mind jumped from Leif to Fenn, back and forth, as it often did over the years. He then saw Fenn's weary expression in the doorway of what was once their home. That drained look on his face that Ryckert had been unable to mend.

"Y'know, people are gonna be lookin' for me," Ryckert said softly to Michio.

Mimed laughter and a shake of the head.

~ *watched you. no friends. no one but me* ~

Ryckert grinned. When he'd said it, it had somewhat tasted like a lie, but he realized there was a dash of truth to it. "Must not've been watching all that close. You woulda seen me with the new white mage. She knows I've been lookin' into you. If I'm gone too long, she'll let someone know. There'll be a hunt for the mysterious mage who lives in the woods. And we ain't all that deep in the woods, kid."

~ *ok* ~

"Don't believe me?" Ryckert asked. "Aava's resourceful. Wouldn't underestimate her, if I were you."

Michio perked up at this. He scrambled forward, knocking his can of beans aside, and came to a stop at Ryckert's side. He scribbled furiously on his notepad, almost snapping the lead of his pencil.

~ *take me to her* ~ he wrote, the letters wavy and almost unreadable. ~ *take me to see Aava & then our bizness done* ~

It sounded like a fair trade to Ryckert.

"Let me up," he said irritably. "Let's go."

- -

Her examination of Freya's desiccated body had yielded nothing conclusive or particularly useful, and so Aava had returned home that afternoon feeling downtrodden and more confused than ever.

It was obvious that the monster, whatever it may be, had been specifically attracted to Freya. No other grave had been touched, and it had torn into her stomach with ferocity and purpose. What it had hoped to find within, Aava was unsure. Not even a guess.

Fearing more of the insectoid creatures might lurk within Cerene Forest and make their way to the cemetery, Mr. Reede requested that Aava cleanly dispose of the body. Seeing his mother's mangled corpse had chilled Artemis, though he had showed no signs of breaking in front of company, and he had agreed that getting rid of the body would be for the best. Someone suggested Artemis might transport it back home with him to Din's Keep, but Mr. Reede rightly pointed out that, given the creature's unknown origins, transporting the body might put Artemis at risk during his journey home through the woods, not to mention once he was back home. Who knew how far the beasts might travel, or how many there were in the world?

So it had fallen on Aava to cast a spell that was rarely used by white mages, though it was fairly uncomplicated. Generally, when planning for a funeral, the deceased's kin would choose whether they wanted a burial, a cremation, or what was called (insensitively, she thought) a cessation.

Cessation was a spell that, as one would expect, caused the body to cease existing, for lack of better phrasing. It only worked on the dead, thankfully, and therefore could not effectively be used by those with more sinister intentions.

Aava had cast the spell on Freya, and the small gathering (which included Aava, Artemis, Mr. Reede, Bernard, and Harold) observed in solemn silence as the vandalized body rose a few inches into the air, hovering for a moment before pointilizing. Each tiny dot that now comprised Freya's body shimmered in the sunlight for a moment, rotating on its axis, growing fainter and fainter with each rotation. After four or five, they were gone, leaving the group staring at nothing but dirt and grass.

The three Balam townsmen stared slack-jawed, having never seen such magic in their lives. Aava and Artemis were less in awe. To Aava, this was simply part of her job; to Artemis, it was yet another goodbye to his mother. The man showed no sign that any of this was affecting him, but having witnessed his tears the night before, Aava still felt a pang of sadness for him.

They all parted ways shortly after. Harold went home to finally attempt getting some good rest; Bernard wandered off with Mr. Reede; and Artemis left to finish packing his belongings at the inn in preparation for his carriage's departure that evening. He and Aava were the last two remaining in the quiet cemetery, and he thanked her profusely for all her help, giving her a tight hug before making his way down the dirt path through the farm and back to town.

She was now in the clinic, reading over Freya's notes for the antidote that had either been unfinished or unsuccessful. The woman's recipe had been clever, incorporating ingredients Aava would never have thought to include in a poison antidote (mir root, powdered sage), which only lent credibility to the idea that this illness was something Aava was entirely unfamiliar with. But Freya had been onto something.

Although it all seemed like a moot point now. Freya had died, and that was that. No need for a cure anymore.

But Aava kept reading and rereading the recipe, searching the depths of her mind for any idea as to why it might have failed or how she could improve upon it. The mir root was such an unexpected addition, it made it seem irreplaceable. Something must have led Freya to believe it needed to be there, so Aava kept it. The rest of the list was more expendable, though it was an intriguing mix.

There was a jar of mir root on the shelf above Aava's head, which she took down and opened up. It was filled halfway, with specks of dirt stuck to the glass near the jar's top. A sign that it must have been full at one point in time. Aava was suddenly confident that Freya had tried making her potion and it had not worked. There would be no other reason to just have mir root on hand, if not for this potion, and clearly some had already been used.

Cerene Forest has a lot of mirwood trees, Aava thought. *There are a few scattered about town, too. Or at least I think I saw some during my tour with Mr. Reede.*

Her stomach grumbled in discontent. She realized she hadn't eaten anything besides a small bowl of fruit before the town meeting. From there, she had gone straight to the cemetery for the Cessation, and then directly back home to look over Freya's notes. She could continue hypothesizing about the mir root later. Right now, it was time for a much-needed and -deserved lunch. Much to her own annoyance, she still had not made time for a trip to the store to buy food to keep in her own pantry and cook, and she admittedly did not feel up to the task at the moment.

Guess it's back to the Sonata.

She could do with a thick, juicy burger. One with extra pickles and a lot of mustard. All that vinegar would make Svend grimace with revulsion, and the thought made her chuckle.

Just as she was putting her bright red coat on, there came a frantic knock on the door. The last thing she wanted to do was see a patient. That vinegar-topped burger was calling to her. She could practically hear it yelling out her name!

But she had a duty, so she opened the front door to assist whoever was there and instead found a surprising sight.

Ryckert stood before her with his arms stiff, hands behind his back. A look of extreme frustration melted into relief as he laid eyes on her. Behind him was Michio Loz, whose face lit up as they locked eyes.

"Michio?" she muttered.

Ryckert's eyes widened, an expression of shock that she had never seen on the rocyan. "You know this guy?" he said, his voice scratchy and tired.

"Yes," she said, ushering them in. The next thing she blurted out was, "What are you doing here?"

His back had been turned, so he had no idea she had said anything at all. When he took a seat in the chair next to the examination table, Aava shut the door and repeated her question.

He took out a notepad and began to write. It was different than the one he had used at school when they had met and started dating. It was a little bigger, more surface area to write on. She waited for his reply while Ryckert stared quizzically at the two of them.

~ *just passing thru* ~ was all he wrote.

"How do you know him?" Ryckert asked, nodding his head toward Michio. His hands were still clasped behind his back.

"Why are you standing like that?" Aava asked, ignoring his question. When he looked at her with confusion, she pointed at his hands.

"Tied me up," Ryckert explained. "Some spell. Won't undo it."

Aava gave Michio a stern look. That was all it took to convince him to remove the spell. Ryckert shook his hands free, wringing his fingers to crack his stiff joints with a satisfying *pop*.

"How do you know this fuck?" Ryckert asked again as he stretched and scratched an itch behind his left ear.

"We both went to Allinor," she said.

Ryckert laughed and looked at Michio, then back to Aava. "Allinor?" he scoffed. "Told me he went to…what was it?" He thought it over for a few seconds, then said, "Actually, never said the name. Said it was outside Kyring, though, and Allinor ain't near Kyring, is it? Unless I'm forgettin' my geography."

But Aava shook her head. "No, it's not near Kyring at all."

"Interesting." He turned to look at Michio again. The mage was unfazed.

She was just as intrigued as Ryckert, but a new thought occurred to her. "Wait," she said, "is this the mage you were talking about? The one you think poisoned Freya?"

Ryckert nodded, and Michio gave her a companionable look.

"Sorry, but no," Aava said with a slight grin. "There's no way he had anything to do with Freya."

The rocyan's face sunk. "Sure about that?"

"Positive," she said. "I know him, Ryckert. We dated for a while."

Ryckert barked out a laugh. "Well I'll be damned," he sighed. "What're the chances of this?"

"Allinor isn't too far away," Aava shrugged. "I guess it's not so wild for him to wind up here. But why did you leave?" she asked Michio. He shrugged, but began to write.

~ *kicked out* ~

"That much he told me," Ryckert said. "Said he got booted from school and decided to see the sights before he went back west. Said he's from Dearmont."

Another peculiarity. "He's not from Dearmont," Aava said. "He grew up in Bral Han. More western than Allinor, yes, but not as far west as Dearmont. Why are you lying? What's with the secrets?"

Michio was starting to get angry. His face was not saying so, not yet, but Aava noticed the slight twitch of his upper lip that always happened when he began to lose his temper. His hotheadedness was what had eventually led her to break things off.

~ *maybe I dont want everyone I meet to know my bizness* ~

As she read his reply, she couldn't help smiling at his short-hand for "business." Some things never changed.

"Coulda just said so," Ryckert mumbled. "Didn't have to lie about it."

Ryckert was right, but agreeing with him wouldn't help ease the tension. She asked, "When did you leave Allinor?"

~ *few weeks ago* ~

That checked out. They had not seen much of each other since breaking up, but she had at least seen Michio in passing every once in a while when she was wandering the halls or reading outside. He was a year younger than her, and therefore still embroiled in his studies. Until being kicked out, anyway.

"Why did they expel you?"

Michio just stared at her, not writing anything on his paper.

"Fine," she said, dropping it. She intended to prod more later, but for now she needed to defuse whatever situation had arisen between the two men. "So what's going on here, Ryckert?"

"Went to get close to him, like we talked about." As he spoke, Ryckert paced throughout the clinic, stretching his legs, edging nearer to the back wall where there were shelves lined with jarred ingredients. "Passed out at the pub. Dragged me back to his campsite. Force-fed me that silver powder." With this last sentence, he shot a nasty glare at Michio.

When Aava looked to Michio for an explanation, she saw he was mid-eyeroll. He reached into his jacket pocket and extracted a small pouch, tossing it over to Aava. She caught it and pulled open the lip of the pouch, peering inside. Just as Ryckert described, it was filled with a silvery powder. She looked back up at Michio and saw he was presenting his pad.

~ *birchrot* ~

She read the word, then looked back down at the powder. A flood of embarrassment washed over her. Of course it was birchrot. How could she have been so stupid as to not think of it before? She had been blinded, thinking only in terms of poisons, and of course birchrot was not a poison. It hadn't even occurred to her.

"This is a sleep powder," she explained to Ryckert. "It's used medicinally, to help patients fall asleep when they're experiencing pain or insomnia or even just normal restlessness. Michio uses it every night to curb his insomnia."

Now it was Ryckert's turn to roll his eyes. "A sleeping powder?" he grumbled. "Explains me passin' out, I guess."

Michio turned his head to face Ryckert and nodded his head up and down slowly, with great exaggeration. As he turned back around, he rolled his eyes again.

"So he ain't got no poison, and you vouch for his upstanding character," Ryckert said with a sigh, walking back toward the front door, where Aava still stood. "Leaves us in a bad place, I'd say."

Aava cocked her head to the side. Behind Ryckert, Michio was kicking his feet back and forth as they dangled from the chair.

"Why?" she asked.

"Because," said Ryckert, "it means we're back at the start. Means we ain't got the faintest idea how Freya got poisoned. I don't have any suspects in mind. Do you?"

She shook her head and said, "No, I don't."

Ryckert said to Michio, "Sure it wasn't you? That'd make things a whole lot easier for us."

Michio shook his head and grinned.

"So here we are," Ryckert said, crossing his arms. His eyes narrowed in a scowl and he exhaled harshly from his snout. "Nothin' pointin' us in any direction."

Aava had no words. Of course, Ryckert was right. They had nothing to go on. Practically the only thing they had was the potion recipe she'd found, but even that was near useless. If she somehow was able to reverse engineer it and come to a definitive conclusion as to what the poison was, that still wouldn't help them find the culprit. She was at a loss.

And she was hungry, too. Her stomach chose that moment to give her a gentle reminder.

"Let's get something to eat," she said. "I was heading to the Sonata when you two showed up."

"Let's do the pub," Ryckert suggested. "I'm starving too. Need to eat something big and meaty."

Michio nodded and began to write on his paper. When he presented it to them, there was only one word, written at the bottom of the page, below everything else he'd said in the clinic.

~ pub ~

\- -

That night, Theo dreamed again, but it was not a pleasant dream like the one he'd had about his mother and sister in the blue clearing. This dream was based in reality, and it was a memory that Theo was none too eager to revisit.

He was ten years old, still just a boy in the dingy little town of Padstow, where he had been born and where he assumed he would live out his life. At his age, his thoughts did not go beyond homework and games played outdoors with friends. The world—and life—beyond the town limits of Padstow never occurred to him.

His sister Gwendolyn was fourteen and had already begun her upper level of learning at school. She was a bright student, one who always aced her exams and wrote well-constructed, thought-out essays. At the time, young Theodore did not realize what such attributes entailed.

Padstow was a western coastal city, and western cities in Atlua had much different traditions than towns or cities in any other part of the country. Traditions which many called backwards or deplorable. But Padstow called them *necessary*.

Every year, these towns felt it necessary to make a sacrifice to some unnamed Other, so that they may continue living prosperous and peaceful lives. They feared that if this beast did not consume its annual sacrifice, it would reign destruction down on Atlua. This sacrifice was carried out every spring, at the end of the school year.

The sacrifice was chosen by a panel of teachers, who convened the day after school ended, each divided into groups of three or four, who then nominated one female student they taught that year and who demonstrated the highest levels of intelligence and athleticism. Theo's student Olivia Nells would have been a prime candidate, had they lived in the west. Only the absolute best for the Other, or else who knew what might be wrought?

All the teachers would then discuss the nominees, usually four in total, and then vote on the winner. The young girl, always fourteen or fifteen years old, would then be taken from her family and brought to the city of Dusceir, where the all the sacrifices from up and down the coast would be rounded up at the highest cliff overlooking the sea, in full view of hundreds of individuals who made the pilgrimage to witness the spectacle.

When their family was told Gwendolyn had been chosen to be Padstow's sacrifice that year, Theo did not understand what the news meant. They had all gathered in the living room, and their mother immediately rushed back into the bedroom, bawling. Their father remained on the couch with his children at his side, casting an uncomfortable glance at his daughter, whose lip was trembling.

"So the decision's final?" his father had asked, looking back to the person who had brought them the news.

The man, one of Gwen's teachers, nodded solemnly. "I'm afraid so," he said. "I'm sorry to be the one to inform you." He then looked at the young girl he had gotten to know over the past year, but said nothing.

"When does she leave?" was all their father asked.

"Tomorrow afternoon. The escort party will be here promptly at noon to collect Gwen."

Gwen now broke into silent tears. They streamed down her face, dripping onto the floor. Her eyes bore into her teacher's. Theo had never learned the man's name, though nowadays he harbored much hate for him.

"Okay," said their father. "Thank you." He stood and led the man to the door, where he bade him farewell then returned to his seat beside his children.

"Where's Gwen going?" Theo had asked. His grasp on the yearly tradition was tenuous at best. He knew young girls were chosen every spring for some task, but he didn't know what.

In the dream, his father's face was stern. That was how he always remembered this moment, though in the intervening sixteen years, it was hard to know if that had truly been the expression on the man's face.

"She's going away," was all he had said. "She's going to Dusceir, and we'll go too, to say our goodbyes."

He placed a rough, scabbed hand on Gwen's shoulder. She was now staring down at the ground, unable to face her own father, who had failed to come to her rescue. Had even *thanked* the man who informed him she had been hand-picked to die in the name of something without a name.

Theo watched as his father gripped her. Still, his expression was unchanged.

"It's a great honor," he had said to her. "Soon, you will understand that. It's the greatest honor that there is. You are saving countless people for generations to come. Atlua will prosper because of you."

"I don't want to," Gwen had choked out.

"It doesn't matter what you want," their father said. "What matters is that you were chosen, and soon you and the other amazing young women will shower prosperity on the land, and we'll celebrate with the Hunt."

"*I don't give a shit about the Hunt!*" Gwen snapped. Theo had never heard his sister swear before. He expected her to be scolded, or punished, but their father acted as if he hadn't even heard.

"Your mother will prepare a nice meal for you tonight and you can get an early sleep. Tomorrow's journey will be long and arduous. It's a few days' walk to Dusceir, but the roads are very beautiful. You'll enjoy it."

The dream suddenly branched away from what had happened in reality; the young Theo was suddenly filled with the knowledge and understanding he possessed in the present day, and he spit vitriol at his father. "You didn't put up a fight for *your own daughter* at all, and then you had the fucking gall to tell her she would *enjoy* her death march?"

His father looked at him with cold eyes and said, "Son, you're too young to understand. Someday you will, and you will know what a great honor this is for our entire family."

"It's not an *honor*, it's *bullshit*. This whole tradition is bull-shit, make-believe nonsense that some psycho came up with years ago and all you people are too stupid to let go of it!"

These words were drawn from a nasty argument he and his father would have six years later, long after his sister and mother were gone, having left him alone with the man he so loathed.

The dream-Theo then reared back his fist to punch his father in the face—right in his hard, unloving, hateful face—when all of the energy abruptly drained from Theo's body, and he was back to being a weak, helpless ten-year-old watching his older sister cry on their couch while their father did nothing to comfort her.

Theo could hear his mother sobbing in the other room through the closed door. Not a single tear stained his father's cheek.

And Theo would always remember that.

CHAPTER VIII

A BEAUTIFUL DAY

Theo woke from his anxious dreams the next morning to the sound of Lyrra's hacking cough. It wasn't too bad at first, but quickly grew in both volume and intensity, and she had to sit up in bed to control it and steady herself. She inhaled, and Theo could hear phlegm course down the back of her throat.

"You alright?" he asked, sitting up as well. They were both wearing long-sleeved shirts, bundled up to counteract the chilly nights. "That was a pretty bad one."

"I think so," Lyrra replied weakly, her hand covering her mouth and muffling her words.

Theo recalled she had been coughing for a few days now, and it seemed to only be getting worse. "Maybe you should go to the clinic," he suggested. "See if Aava can give you a potion or something for it."

"Maybe," she said, nodding. "I could use some coffee first, though."

He was still feeling slightly disoriented after being yanked into consciousness, and unwanted thoughts of his family swirled in his pounding head. Part of him wanted to go back to sleep, but at the same time, he knew more dreams would await him.

"Coffee sounds good," he said, pushing the words through his own grogginess. "But tea would probably be better for your throat. I can cook us something to eat and get the water boiling. Eggs and sausage?"

Lyrra shook her head at this, though she gave him a smile. "I'm feeling a little nauseous," she said. "I'm gonna pass on breakfast."

"Just the one egg and sausage for me, then," he said. "Got it." After lethargically climbing out of bed, he said, "Let me know if you change your mind and I'll heat you something up."

She graced Theo with another sweet smile and thanked him. "I would kiss you, but…"

"But I wouldn't accept," he teased.

"Rude."

First things first, he went out back to grab Vir's bowls. He said hello to the seroko, gave her a good scratching behind the ears, and returned indoors to fill her up with food and water. He could hear Lyrra coughing again in the other room, so he got a pot of water heating up before finishing with Vir's business.

He spent a few minutes outside, soaking up some sunshine, which made him feel much more awake. He left Vir grunting cheerfully as she gobbled up her breakfast and returned to the kitchen to get started on his own. He called to Lyrra, "What kind of tea do you want?"

"Mir," she called back. "I've got a hankerin' for something sweet!"

"Got it," he said. The water was nearly at a boil. He grabbed two packets of mir tea from the pantry and set them on the countertop while he prepared his food and let the water come to a boil.

His sausage link was frying in the pan with some oil and sliced onion while he poured the hot water into two mugs over the tea packets. They steeped for several minutes while he watched the meat; his next move would be to scramble some eggs in the leftover oil and sausage juices.

Once the tea had properly darkened the water, Theo blew on its surface and took a cautious sip from his mug. He winced as the liquid burned his tongue, but its taste was sweet and inviting. It was made from the crushed leaves of the mir trees that populated Balam and its surrounding forest, but Theo had no idea what other spices or additives gave it such sweetness. All he knew was that it was delicious, and it was the most popular tea available at their general store. Half the time he and Lyrra went to buy some, it was sold out.

Theo carried his wife's lavender mug into the bedroom, where she sat propped up against the headboard, reading a book. It was a novel written decades ago by a jeornish man named Killian Vearnas, and it chronicled the lifelong journey of a young woman as she traveled from Atlua to Herrilock in order to track down a fortune her ancestors were said to have hidden away somewhere centuries before. The book was called *Lyrical Tide* and it was one of Lyrra's favorites. One of the characters had a cat named Virtute, and it was where Lyrra had gotten the idea when it came time to name Vir. This was her fourth or fifth time reading the book; personally, as much as Theo enjoyed reading, he did not see much sense in reading the same story over and over. He would rather pick up a new book and experience a new tale, new characters. But Lyrra enjoyed it, and that made him happy.

He handed her the mug (the tea packet still floating happily in the murky water), and she took a long, deep sip as steam rose into her face. She closed her eyes to block it out. As she placed the mug on her bedside table, she sighed with deep satisfaction.

Theo leaned in to kiss her cheek. She reciprocated, and he couldn't help himself from smiling at the sight of her big, pretty yellow eyes. Her eyelashes were long and curled, something she got from her mother.

The first time Theo had met Lyrra's parents, he had known her for about a year and a half but they had only been dating for close to six months. The two of them were both only nineteen years old (which seemed like babies to him now, despite the fact he was now only seven years older), and he had been filled with a teenager's dread of meeting the girlfriend's parents. A fear which Lyrra had attempted to assuage, but to no avail. Her parents were going to despise him, he was sure of it. If not for something stupid he said or did, then only because he was dating their precious, beloved, only daughter.

"Just don't tell them you've defiled me," Lyrra had joked as they walked the streets of Bral Han to her childhood home. "If you avoid that, you'll probably be fine."

The last thing Theo wanted to even remotely think about at that moment was sex, as a new fear entered his mind: getting an erection while in the company of Daere and Calyssa Fiss. He instantly began to push the thought away, to beat it down, pummel it, obliterate it. He told himself over and over again: *do not think about erections.*

Having such a close relationship with her parents (something Theo could not begin to relate to), Lyrra had relished the opportunity to study in her hometown so that she could get the education she wanted while still being close to home. The university she and Theo attended, fittingly called the Bral Academy, was located in the heart of Bral Han, one of the largest, most populated cities in all of Atlua. It was a far cry from Theo's small-town upbringing in Padstow.

Lyrra's family lived on the northwestern edge of the city. Not on the city limits, but pretty close. Somehow, Theo had gotten away with dating Lyrra for six months in the same city where her parents lived without ever having to encounter them. But now they were on spring vacation, and there was no avoiding it anymore.

The streets of Bral Han were decked out with festive garlands of pink and purple flower petals hanging from streetlight to streetlight to celebrate the coming of spring. Street vendors pushed their wares on passersby, selling everything from jewelry to tunics to small-press books. Food sizzled on portable grills, coals roasting underneath and smoke rising into the sky. Theo loved vissian kabobs, and they had smelled undeniably delicious, but they were going to her parents' house for dinner. Couldn't spoil his appetite.

"Maybe we could eat here instead," he had suggested, only half-joking.

"Don't be such a baby," she said, lightly jabbing him in the side with her elbow as they walked. "It's not gonna be that bad. You're overthinking things."

"It's just nerve-wracking, meeting the father," he said, taking in the sights and smells of the food that flanked them on either side of the cobbled street, his mouth watering with the subtle hints of spices.

"Why?"

"What do you mean *why*?"

"Why is it nerve-wracking to meet the father? Why doesn't my mom intimidate you? Is this some dumb masculinity thing?"

"No! It's…well, maybe in a way, I don't know. It's just different. Guys know how other guys think. He's gonna take one look at me and think, *This idiot is the one who thinks about nothing but having sex with my daughter.* It's awkward. So awkward."

"He's not gonna think that."

"He is."

"Well, like I said, just don't talk about having sex with me. I'm sure we can probably avoid the subject altogether. Sound like a plan?"

Of course, his worries had been totally unfounded. When they had arrived at the Fiss household, Lyrra's parents greeted them at the door with warm smiles and even warmer hugs. Theo had not encountered such barefaced affection since his own mother had passed away.

Daere Fiss had wrapped his meaty arms around Theo and patted him on the back. "Good to meet you, Theodore!" he said, his scratchy beard rubbing against Theo's smooth cheek. Theo had made sure to shave before coming, in order to look as presentable as possible. Like a nice, young gentleman.

As Daere pulled away, Theo had said, "It's nice to meet you both, too! Lyrra talks about you guys all the time." To Calyssa, he said, "I hear your sweet-rolls are amazing."

Her mother blushed and waved away the compliment. "My sweet-rolls are fine, I suppose, but Daere here is the real chef. Come on in, he's already got dinner ready!"

They had spent the meal talking mainly about Lyrra's studies, but naturally conversation led to questions pertaining to

Theo's pursuits as well. Calyssa had been especially impressed with Theo's aspirations to teach. Daere, unsurprisingly, never once brought up the topic of his daughter's deflowering.

After the meal (which Theo had offered to help clean up, but Daere utterly refused), the four had played a board game out on the back patio while drinking a special hot chocolate blend, which was one of the specialties at Daere's restaurant.

A few hours later, Lyrra and Theo were in her bedroom while she got ready for bed. There was a guest room prepared for Theo, for which he was eternally grateful. He loved sleeping in the same bed as Lyrra, and it was still a miracle in his eyes that she allowed him to do so, but he would not have been able to bear the thought of her parents knowing they were sharing a bed.

As she brushed her hair, she said to him, "Tonight went really well."

"You think so?" he'd asked, still feeling uneasy about the whole thing. In that moment, he wasn't sure he would ever be able to shake off the feeling of anxiousness, though eventually he would prove himself wrong.

"Yes," Lyrra laughed, giving him an *are you serious?* look. "They loved you. Dad especially."

"Yeah, okay."

"They did!" she said, putting down the brush. She hopped onto the bed where Theo was laying and waiting for her to finish. She swung her right leg over his waist, straddling him. "They thought you were great. Stop thinking you're not."

"Fine," he had conceded, smiling.

She leaned down and kissed him, interlocking her fingers with his. She squeezed her legs, tightening her grip on his body. Their lips parted with a deep exhale. He let go of her fingers and ran his own through her long, white hair, which was silky and smooth, like running his hand through water. When he reached the ends, which hung down, nearly touching his chest, he moved his hand to the back of her neck, caressing her skin as he pulled her in for another kiss. As they parted again, she sat up straight and gave him a wide, toothy smile.

"What are you lookin' at?" she asked him with some faux sassiness, sitting in their bed in Balam with her book in hand.

"You," he answered. Then, "I take it you wanna read a bit before going to the clinic?"

She nodded. "Just a bit."

"Okay."

Just then, he heard the crackle and pop of oil in the kitchen. His sausage was likely about to burst.

"Shit!" he exclaimed, racing out of the room to salvage his meal. Lyrra laughed at him and took another sip of tea, returning to her make-believe adventure.

- -

Ryckert had spent the remainder of the previous day resting at home after he left Aava's clinic. His body was stiff and sore after his night with Michio (which was not the type of soreness he typically enjoyed after spending a night with a handsome man), and all he had wanted to do was lay in bed.

But Bernard Tilling had come by only an hour into Ryckert's nap, knocking politely but with a sense of urgency. "Ryckert, you in there?" he'd called, every other word punctuated by his fist pounding the door.

Reluctantly, Ryckert had answered, and Bernard had explained to him that they had the corpse of a strange creature stored in his freezer that no one could identify, and if you're not busy, could you come by and take a look?

Ryckert was exhausted and therefore cranky, but Bernard was one of his few acquaintances in town, so he agreed to come by the following day. Bernard had looked unhappy about having to wait, but thanked Ryckert all the same and went on his way.

So now Ryckert, feeling only mildly refreshed after a full night's sleep, was headed toward the upper level of Balam to visit Bernard's shed and try to parse out the origins of whatever monster they had stumbled upon.

When he arrived at the Tilling household, Bernard was outside, hard at work chopping wood for his fireplace. "Hullo!" Bernard waved, wiping sweat off his brow. "Give me a second."

The sound of the wood splitting was strangely calming to Ryckert. It reminded him of his nights spent on the road, traveling for jobs. He had always had a taste for camping.

It didn't take long for Bernard to finish up. "That should do it," he said, tossing his axe into the grass. "How're you doin' this fine day?"

"Just fine," Ryckert replied. "Yourself?"

"Just fine," said Bernard. "Didn't expect you so early. Not even noon yet."

"Apologies," Ryckert said, taking a step back. "Can come back later. Schedule's open all day, it's not a problem."

"No, no! Didn't mean it like that," Bernard assured him, chuckling a bit to himself. "Was just surprised, is all. You seemed pretty out of it yesterday, so I thought you might be off to a late start today."

"Not really one for late starts these days."

"Me neither," Bernard said as he pulled off his protective gloves. "Never have been. Used to piss off my ma and pop, to be honest. I don't think they got any sleep until I moved outta the house." He laughed at this, and Ryckert joined him. "Anyways," he went on, "let's get to it, I guess. The ugly bastard's back in the shed. Don't know if it oozed everywhere already. Hoping not, so I don't have to replace a bunch of equipment. That stuff costs more'n an arm and a leg."

As they approached the shed, Ryckert asked, "Where did it come from? Was somebody attacked?"

Bernard stopped and faced Ryckert, giving the rocyan a quizzical look. "You didn't hear?"

"Hear what?"

Bernard's brow furrowed in confusion. "Guess you weren't at the meeting yesterday. Well, Harold was attacked the other night, after the funeral. He was putting things away in the shed next to the cemetery, and he found this thing trying to munch on Freya's body."

Now he had Ryckert's attention. "The creature was going after the mage's corpse? Hers specifically?"

"Sure seemed like it. Already broken into the casket and torn her up a bit before Harold killed it. Lucky break, honestly. The thing looks vicious as all hell. I'm glad he came out the other side of that fight."

If Bernard had mentioned any of this at all the previous day, Ryckert would have dragged his ass out of bed and gone straight to the shed. Now he had wasted nearly twenty-four hours lazing about like a useless sack of apples.

But Ryckert did not allow his severe interest to show in his expression. All he said was, "Let's take a look."

Bernard led him into the dimly-lit shed, into the back corner where he kept his freezer, stocked with meats and ice. As of now, the only cut of meat inside was a wolf-sized insect that Ryckert had never seen before. Its rounded head had six eyes, all hanging open lifelessly. The carapace was a dull, icy green, but he couldn't be sure how much of that was natural and how much was discoloration due to the cold temperature. Two feelers protruded from the creature's forehead and were bent against the wall of the freezer. They were thin and frozen, and Ryckert could tell that if he applied any amount of pressure to them they'd snap in two. Its six legs, four of which ended in meaty claws, were curled up against the body like a sleeping cat. Ryckert didn't have the faintest clue what it was, but something about it seemed familiar.

The two men slowly lifted the monster out of the freezer, careful not to break its feelers or any other appendage, and transferred it to the large steel slab in the middle of the room where Bernard did his work. They placed it down gently, its frozen shell of a body clanging against the steel.

"So," Bernard said, "any idea what the fuck this thing is?"

Ryckert shook his head. "No," he said. "First thought was a vissian. Some alternate breed, or something. Sure you guys had the same thought."

"Sorta," Bernard confirmed. "I ain't convinced of it, to be honest with you, but Bromley took a peek at it too and is sure that it's just a regular vissian. Won't hear a word otherwise."

"Bromley's a fool," Ryckert said.

"Agreed."

"That said," Ryckert continued, "not sure it's a different breed of vissian. I know of a few variations, and they've all got one thing in common."

"The tail."

"The tail," Ryckert nodded. The man knew his stuff. That was why Ryckert had taken such a liking to Bernard when he had first moved to Balam. "Every vissian I've encountered, from here to Herrilock, had that long, tough tail with the damnable stinger on its end."

"And this ugly bastard don't have a tail."

"Nope."

"You don't think this might be one? Either the start of one, or a stump? Maybe it got lobbed off." Bernard pointed at the insect's abdomen, which arced into a steep curve and almost came to touching its underside.

Ryckert placed a hand where the abdomen came to an end, rubbing it at first with his full palm and then with just a few fingers. He shook his head and said, "Don't think so. Didn't lose a tail here; the shell is smooth, not cracked or uneven to imply that it was broken at some point. And if this is just the start of a tail, it's one hell of a design flaw, because whatever stinger grows is gonna go right into the thing's stomach."

Bernard shrugged. He had no retort, no other suggestions. He and the others had gone through their list of ideas already and came up with nothing concrete.

Ryckert wasn't confident he would be able to offer a satisfying explanation either. "Tell me more about that night," he said. "How was it acting?"

"Well, I only know the story secondhand. You'd have to ask Harold if you want the full details. But as far as I know, it was digging with those front claws, trying to get at the body for whatever reason. Uh... I'm not sure what else you wanna know."

"I'm not sure either," Ryckert confessed. He was no zoologist, so he was only kidding himself if he thought being told the creature's behavior and movements would be of any help. He was stumped.

He gave Bernard a pitiful shrug. Another failure in this investigation to add to the ever-growing list.

"Not a problem," Bernard told him. "I don't think we're gonna have any issues with whatever this is anymore. We disposed of the body, which is what it seemed to be attracted to, so if it's got any brothers or sisters, they're probably far off without any idea how to get here. I just thought you might know what it was since you've certainly traveled much more than I or any other chump in this town has. Just curious, is all."

"Be sure to properly dispose of this, too," Ryckert said, nodding toward the insect's corpse. "Might have pheromones or something its kin could sniff out. Better to avoid inviting any friends over."

"No doubt about that. That's what the firewood's for. Gonna burn this thing to a crisp, cook it 'til it ain't nothin' but ash."

"I'd suggest a cleaner method," Ryckert said. "Something fast that won't give off any scent at all. I know a black mage; could ask him if he knows Demi."

"Mhar Cown, over at the inn?" Bernard asked.

Whoever Mhar Cown was, he was indeed not the mage Ryckert had been referring to, but he thought it simpler to go along with it and nodded.

"Mhar's the one who helped out the night of Freya's incident, so I'm sure he'd be willing to help out again. Good idea." Bernard clapped his hands together, as if they had accomplished a great deal. "I'll head on over there and talk to him. I don't think he's leaving town for another week or so. He's the first of many tourists that I'm sure are gonna be filling our streets soon, now that spring's in bloom."

"Let's hope they're kept safe," Ryckert said, glaring at the creature on the table.

"Let's hope," Bernard agreed.

- -

The walk to Aava's clinic was a pleasant one. The sun was shining bright and the wind was blowing freely; it was, by all accounts, a beautiful day in Balam.

Theo and Lyrra held hands as they walked down the stone pathway to Main Street, which was unusually deserted considering the time of day. Usually everyone was walking to and fro, and children could be seen running around at play.

"Everyone must be nervous about that monster," Lyrra said. "Seems like they're staying home."

"Yeah," Theo said. "Can't say I blame them. Sounds like whatever it was, it was nasty."

Lyrra nodded, then coughed. Theo frowned and rubbed his thumb on her hand as he held it.

The only other person on Main Street that afternoon was Dennis Reen, Missy's father. He worked at the farm alongside his wife and Missy's mother, Kim.

Theo gave the man a polite wave, and it was reciprocated. "Howya, Mr. Saen?" he called over. He was sitting on a bench about fifteen feet down the walkway, in the direction the two were heading.

"Not bad, Mr. Reen," said Theo. "How about you?"

"Been better," said Dennis, "but none too bad, neither. Bit crazy over at the farm with all this monster business. Rufus has us workin' overtime to build a wall around the perimeter."

"Makes sense, I suppose," said Theo as they grew nearer. "Sorry he's got you all working so hard, though."

Dennis shrugged, his shoulders prodding his long hair. It hung in brown, ratty strings, framing a thin and acne-scarred face. "Work's work, I s'pose," he said. "Just glad me and the missus and my girl weren't around when that thing came."

"That was certainly lucky," said Lyrra.

"Yes ma'am, it was," Dennis nodded. "Harold gave that thing a helluva wallop, though. I oughta buy him a drink this week. You get a good look at it?" he asked.

"No," Lyrra answered, the pitch of her voice rising. She was curious.

Dennis's face lit up, eager at the opportunity to divulge the information he held.

"Ugly sucker," he began. "Big insect-lookin' thing. Lots of claws and eyes and legs. Nearly clipped off Harold's head, from what I've been told. Green, ugly shell coverin' its body. And it was leaking some gross pus, too. Just a real ugly sucker," he said again.

The predominant descriptor for this thing seemed to be "ugly," which did not surprise Theo in the least. A lot of wildlife, especially in the Cerene Forest, was not pleasant to look at, in his opinion. He was glad to come home to his adorable seroko every day.

"It sounds like a real nightmare," Lyrra said with a sympathetic frown. "You got to see it for yourself?"

"Yup. Caught a glimpse before Bernard hauled it over to his shed. I'm proud of Harold for knockin' the thing out, since he's not much of a hunter. But it's easy to see why Rufus wants better defenses."

"Well, we've got to be getting somewhere," Theo said, recognizing that the conversation was probably about to begin looping in circles.

"Where you headed?" Dennis asked. He was always one to ask questions, whether the answers were of any relevance to him or not.

"The clinic," Lyrra responded. "I've got a bit of a cough."

Dennis scratched his chin and looked at her with his bugged-out eyes. "Ahh," he groaned, "I hear there's somethin' goin' around. I think most of the Dowers have it. And John, too."

Theo knew he was referring to John Nells. In a small town like Balam, it was easy to know everyone by name.

"That's unfortunate," Lyrra said. "I hope our new mage has a cure all ready to go, then. It was nice seeing you, Mr. Reen. Tell Kim and Missy we say hello."

Dennis nodded again, still seated on the bench with one leg crossed over the other. "Will do," he said. "Take it easy, you two."

They continued down Main Street and turned right at the next street, where they could see the clinic dome protruding from the earth like a bubble about to pop. Aava was outside, checking her mailbox.

"Hello, Aava!" Lyrra called. She then coughed into her hand, her throat strained by the shout.

The young woman turned her head, whipping her hair across her face. She smiled as the couple approached.

"Good afternoon," she greeted them, offering a small wave. "You'll have to forgive me, but I'm afraid I'm still learning names around here."

"Lyrra and Theo Saen," Lyrra said, shaking the woman's hand.

Aava's face lit up in recognition. "Right!" she exclaimed. "Theo Saen," she said, pointing at him as she spoke. "I was going to go find you this evening, actually. I have something I hoped to discuss with you."

Theo blinked. He had no idea what Aava could possibly want to talk to him about. They hadn't even spoken since the night of her arrival. Lyrra appeared similarly perplexed.

"Oh," was all Theo managed to blurt out. "Okay. Good thing we came, then."

"Yes, indeed," Aava said, flashing him a half-smile. "But first, why *did* you stop by? Let's take care of that before we get to my business. Please, come inside." She led them into the clinic, clutching a few pieces of mail in her hand. She placed the envelopes on a countertop at the back of the room, then gestured toward one of them to take a seat on the examination table. "Who is the patient today?" she asked.

"That'd be me," said Lyrra, taking a seat. Theo stood a few feet away with his arms crossed.

"What is ailing you?" Aava asked, moving around to the front of the table to face Lyrra. She clasped her hands together, hanging down past her waist. She wore a pleasant smile.

Lyrra shifted on the table, rubbing her throat slightly, and said, "I've had a cough for the past couple days, and it doesn't seem to be getting any better. I'm not sure if there's anything that can really be done about that, but…"

"Have you run a fever?"

"No, not as far as I know."

"Any congestion or other symptoms besides the cough?"

"Nope."

Aava nodded. "It sounds pretty run-of-the-mill," she said, "and it should clear up on its own pretty soon. Several people have come to me with this same exact thing. There must be a bug going around. But I have a tea that can aid the process, perhaps get it moving quicker. How does that sound?"

"Sounds great," Lyrra said with a smile.

Aava returned to the back counter, where she rummaged through a purple wooden box filled with tea bags. She picked out six and brought them over to Lyrra.

"Brew this twice a day for three days, and your cough should clear right up. If not, just come by again and we can get you a stronger brew."

"That's all?"

"That's all," Aava said warmly. "We may be trained in a lot of different magic, but sometimes the simplest solution is the best one."

Lyrra stood and said, "Thank you." She took the tea bags from Aava, and both women turned to smile at Theo. "*Ha*-ha, I get to drink fancy, tasty tea," she teased.

"Damn me! If only I were gross and sick too," he said with a smirk.

Lyrra chuckled and came to his side. Aava stood before them, her kind expression gone and replaced with something more uneasy. She looked stressed about whatever was coming next.

"So," she began.

There were several moments of silence. She looked from Theo's eyes to the floor, then back up to his eyes. Hers were a bright, piercing yellow, just like Lyrra's.

"So," she said again. "What I wanted to talk to you about is Freya."

Of course. What else could it have been? Theo's body seemed to deflate, his chest caving in on itself. He felt a foot shorter. How many times was he going to have to relive this?

"What do you want to know?" he asked with reluctance. Lyrra grasped his arm, trying to offer some amount of comfort.

"Well," Aava said, once again injecting filler words in a futile effort to delay the conversation. "It's a delicate situation. What, uh…" she glanced over at Lyrra, perhaps evaluating whether or not it would be okay for her to hear this, and seemingly decided it was. "What we suspect is that Freya was poisoned. Her cause of death does not seem natural, as far as I've been able to tell. Her symptoms showed signs of poison."

Theo was suddenly woozy. Everyone in Balam knew everyone else. He couldn't wrap his mind around one of their neighbors deliberately poisoning Freya.

But there was one word he honed in on. "'We'?"

Aava nodded. "I have been working with Ryckert Ji'ca on an investigation into the matter. Do you know him?"

The rocyan who lived on the beach. Everybody knew him, but few *knew* him. "I'm aware of him," was Theo's answer.

"Well, he has been assisting me. He's a very smart man. Very kind. In any case, I wanted to ask for your telling of the night's events. So far, I have only heard from people who weren't present. I would like to hear it straight from you, so that I may see if there are any other indicators to help point me in the right direction and figure out exactly what type of poison was used. Even the smallest, most seemingly insignificant detail could be helpful. Would that be alright?" A smile returned to her face, to goad him into telling the story.

Theo nodded. "Of course," he said. "Well, uh…I was sitting under the yunesca tree when she showed up."

He told her everything he could recall about that night, underneath the yunesca tree. About Freya's cough shifting into chokes. Her sputtering on the ground, clutching at her throat. Her eyes bulging out of their sockets. Anything at all he could conjure from his memory. The retelling only took a minute or two, but he felt like he was reliving the incident in real time. Clear visuals danced through his head and he wanted to sit down. To relax his body and clear his mind. When he finished his story, Aava's smile had disappeared and been replaced by a thoughtful frown.

"I see," was all she said.

And then something else occurred to him. Something Al had told them the other day.

"So you think someone intentionally poisoned her?" he asked, already knowing the answer but wanting to clarify. Dancing around the topic, just like Aava had a few minutes prior.

"Yes, as unfortunate as it may be."

Theo almost didn't want to say it, but he had to. It might be helpful to the investigation. It might be the key.

"Serys White was having an affair with Freya," he said. Aava did not seem surprised by this, probably because she had little to no idea who Serys White was or the fact that he was married. So Theo said, "Serys is married. And, uh…apparently, he thought the word might be getting back to his wife some-how. My friend says he's been paranoid about it for a while now." Lyrra's grip on his arm tightened.

"That is very interesting," said Aava. "Who is Serys White, and how did he think his wife would find out about this?"

"He's a teacher. He lives on the south side of town, not very far from here," Theo said. "Right on the cliff's edge. And I'm not sure how he thought Elena would find out, but maybe he thought Freya would be the one to tell, for whatever reason."

Aava nodded. "Do you believe he would be capable of kill-ing her?"

The pit in Theo's stomach deepened. His heart was racing.

"I…" he started. "I don't know," he said. "Don't get me wrong, I don't like the guy at all—but would he kill someone?" He looked to Lyrra, who seemed as lost as he was. "I don't know. I can't say for sure one way or the other." He felt guilty for saying this.

Aava nodded once more. "Okay," she said. "Thank you for all your information. Truly. I think it will be a big help. I'll inform Ryckert as soon as I see him again."

"Is there anything else you needed?" Theo asked, hoping the answer was no.

"No, that was it. But thank you again." Then that smile re-turned to her face.

As they moved toward the door, Lyrra said, "So, two of these each day?" She held up the tea packets. Theo knew she was only asking so that they could end the conversation on a different, lighter note. He appreciated the gesture.

"Yes," said Aava. "That should do it."

Outside, with her hand in his, Lyrra asked, "Do you really think Serys could've had something to do with this?"

Theo worked with Serys, but Lyrra worked with his wife and daughter, so he imagined she too was filled with as much dread as he was right now. But all he could do was shrug, and all he could say was "I don't know."

- -

The sky bloomed pink as the sun began its slow descent toward the horizon to be swallowed up behind the sea.

Aava had offered her old flame Michio a chance to stay with her in the modest dome (despite there being no guest room and probably not enough spare pillows or blankets to construct a makeshift pallet), but he had declined. He had written on his pad of paper that he enjoyed the outdoors, and it would help him keep a low profile. She still wasn't sure why that was necessary, but she did not want to push him just yet.

She had met Michio through Svend, as the two were both black mages in training and shared some classes. He had come along shortly after Aava's crush on her roommate Jasmiin had subsided, and she had been enraptured by the young man from the first minute they'd met.

The two started dating a few weeks later, much to Svend's chagrin ("It's weird! You dating my friend is weird! And him choosing to date my sister is probably even weirder!"), and the honeymoon phase had been quite magical. Michio ended up being the only person Aava had dated long-term at Allinor. But after eight months that eventually gave way to disagreements which then gave way to too many arguments, she had broken things off with him and subsequently had not seen much of him in her remaining time there.

Needless to say, him showing up in Balam had been more than a shock to her.

But a pleasant shock. She was surrounded by unfamiliar locales and unfamiliar people, and finding a familiar face in the crowd had admittedly perked her up. She had learned where he was living from Ryckert while the three ate at the pub, and she planned to visit whenever possible. Michio had objected to this, underlining the word "no" a record five times, but she didn't care. Messiness didn't bother her, so he had nothing to be embarrassed about. It would be fine.

Ryckert had also detailed Michio's treatment of him, which had appalled but not totally surprised Aava, considering the mage's past outbursts. He had never been violent with her, and she knew that he would never do such a thing, but some of his words had stung. His turns of phrase had some bite to them. She had also seen how fierce he could become during training bouts with his classmates. Fire was always his specialty. But he never got the hang of Blizzard, as far as she knew.

The two men were beginning to warm up to each other, though, now that suspicions had been put to rest. Ryckert seemed to trust her judgment, and Michio had no qualms with Ryckert if the rocyan was going to be leaving him alone. So that made Aava happy.

After the Saens left the clinic, she got to work crafting more tea bags. She still had plenty of ingredients, but she was running low on bags, with so many people coming to her with the same illness. She had done a thorough diagnosis on her first patient, a fifty-year-old man named Tarr Sheere, who had come by a day or two before. She had come to a conclusion and prescribed him the tea, and since then, several more people had come by with the exact same symptoms, including the entire

Dower family (save for Bromley), Barbara Vere, and, unfortunately, the hypochondriac (or was he?) Benedict Crogley. It had been easy to pin the same sickness on Lyrra after seeing the signs so many times over the past couple days.

She was crushing sun-dried leaves with her mortar and pestle when there came a knock at the door. There was a soft clang as she placed the clay pestle on the countertop and went to answer. She opened the red door and smiled at her visitor.

"Good afternoon," she said to Ryckert.

"Hey," he greeted her. He stood motionless with his arms dangling awkwardly at his sides.

"Oh, come in," she said, moving out of the way. "I was just breaking down tea leaves. There's a bug going around town, it seems. You haven't been feeling sick, have you?" As she spoke, she returned to her workstation to complete her task while they conversed.

"Nope," Ryckert replied. "Feeling fine. Don't really get sick that often. Immune system is pretty good in rocyans. Helps us fare out in the wilderness."

Aava chuckled. "You make it sound like rocyans are savages," she said. "I know your clans don't live out in the middle of nowhere."

"Got towns and cities, sure. But nothing on the same scale as Bral Han or Din's Keep. Like to keep to ourselves, keep quiet. Most rocyan villages are even smaller than Balam."

"Where did you grow up?" Aava asked. "What was your clan called? I know your name is *Ji'ca*, but I'm afraid I'm not too familiar with the various rocyan clans." *Ca* was not much to go on to determine the name, considering the vast number of rocyan clans scattered throughout the three kingdoms.

"Caer was my clan. My ra was Jin De'ca. Grew up in the south, near the Gillusian border. Small village called Uruh. There were three clans that claimed Uruh as their home: Caer, Marash, and Rein."

"So your father was born among the Caer," Aava said, making an assumption based on the fact Ryckert's ra's surname was *De'ca*. "Was your mother, as well?"

Ryckert nodded. "My la was Belliivi Maas'ca. She and my ra grew up together in Uruh. Never left the village, except for hunts. Think I might've been a disappointment, leaving home."

Aava did not want to make presumptions about his family, nor did she want to come off as patronizing by saying she was sure his parents still loved him in spite of his choices. It was what she believed, but truth be told she did not know Ryckert that well, and she was not rocyan, so she did not know how highly rocyans might value something of that nature. Better to play it safe and keep her mouth shut.

Instead, she said, "So I take it you were not lucky enough to find the love of your life in Uruh, like them?" She had a pressing matter to discuss with Ryckert, but she had become enthralled with his history. She had not anticipated him opening up like this, and she wanted to dig as deep as she could before he snapped shut like a clamshell.

"Nope," said Ryckert. "Found him elsewhere. In a town northwest, far from Uruh, called Trael. I'd been workin' as a mercenary for about ten years by that point and I was there for a job. Typical assignment, just tracking down some scumbag and killing him to get the client's stolen goods back. Was staying at an inn, got to chatting up a man who worked there. Fellow rocyan, kindred spirit, all that."

"What was his name?" Even as the words spilled out, Aava felt weird about using the past tense. Obviously something had happened to this man, since she knew Ryckert lived here alone.

"Fenn," Ryckert said. As Aava ground up the dry leaves, she could hear Ryckert taking a seat behind her. "One thing led to another. Started out as nothin' more than a fling while I was stationed there for the job, but it grew to be more serious. Decided to call Trael home."

She thought she might have heard his voice waver. Whatever had happened between Ryckert and Fenn, she decided to drop it for now. It had to be either a break-up or a death, and either way, she was sure Ryckert would prefer to keep the matter private.

"Did you like it there more than here?" she asked.

"More'n Balam? Not really," Ryckert said. "About the same, I suppose. Nothing special about the place, but nothing bad, neither. But it was home, for a while."

Aava set down the pestle once again and turned in her chair to face Ryckert. She saw he hadn't been looking at her while he spoke, and in fact the chair he sat in was still facing the examination table. He was staring down at his hands, his fingers laced together.

"I had something I wanted to tell you," she said, breaking the momentary silence. "I have some new information about the Freya case."

The Freya Case. In her head, the last word was capitalized. She felt like the star of some cheap pulp novel. Who was she kidding?

Ryckert looked to her, his ears perked up in anticipation. They flicked in her direction.

"I talked to the man who witnessed everything, like you suggested. Theo Saen. Based on how he described the event, it does indeed sound like a poison. I confidently believe it was not an illness that killed Freya."

"Doesn't sound like new info to me," said Ryckert.

"I haven't gotten to the new part yet. But while I think it was a poison, it doesn't really explain why Freya was attempting to concoct a cure for it. She must have been feeling the symptoms for several days, at least, which obviously indicates it was a slow-acting poison, whatever it was."

"Still not hearin' anything new."

"Okay, well here it is. You're just the pillar of patience, aren't you?"

Ryckert grinned at this.

She went on. "Something else Mr. Saen mentioned was that a man named Serys White was having an affair with Freya. And it's worth noting that Serys White is married and might not appreciate this sordid secret getting back to his wife, if you catch my meaning." She was leaning into the pulp novel starlet role. She had to admit, it was somewhat thrilling.

"Caught," Ryckert nodded, scratching his furry chin. "So you think Serys White was the one who poisoned her. Thought she might tell his wife, ruin his marriage, ruin his reputation. Does he have a reputation to ruin?"

"I don't know, you tell me," Aava laughed. "You're the one who's lived here for two years."

"Fair point. But you think he's our guy?"

"I think he's worth looking into," Aava said. "He sounds awfully suspicious to me, don't you agree?"

"I do," Ryckert said, rising. "Pretty sure I know which house is his. Recognize the name. Think he's one of the guys who's been puttin' in a lot of time at the pub recently. Makes sense why, if he's mourning a death. Or trying to soothe his conscience after committing a murder."

Aava nodded. "You're going to look into him?"

"I'll see what I can find," Ryckert said, moving to the door. "Can stop by his place tonight, see what I see. Stake it out to make sure it's empty, then break in and look for any evidence of a poison among his belongings. Said it was a powder, right?"

"Most likely," Aava confirmed.

It was possible they had cracked the case and were nearing its resolution. She wasn't sure if she should feel bad about how excited it made her.

"Alright. I'll check and get back to you tomorrow."

He was just about to leave, his hand turning the doorknob, when Aava called out to stop him.

"Wait!" she said. "You went and looked at the creature, right?" Ryckert removed his hand from the knob and faced her. It was then she noticed a feature she hadn't seen before, when she had asked about the bump on his snout: there was also a small chunk of his left ear missing. Another story for another time.

His reply was nothing more than a curt nod.

"Any idea what it was?"

"Nope."

And then he left.

Alone again, Aava returned to her bowl of dark brown leaf bits. She sighed and grabbed a bag of another type of leaf, these brighter and sweeter, and dumped a handful into the bowl as well. She began to grind them down.

- -

Ryckert didn't know what had gotten into him back there. He hadn't been able to stop himself from talking about Fenn, the man who he tried more than anything else to forget. But Aava had somehow coerced it out of him.

Maybe he had wanted to talk about it, deep down. He had never really talked to anyone about what transpired between Fenn and himself all those years ago, so he was long overdue for a conversation about it. But all the same, he appreciated the fact that she had changed the subject before things got too serious.

Sitting on the bench outside the Sonata Diner, he had a clear line of sight down the road on his left. On the same road, but across Main Street, was the home of Serys White. Ryckert sat while the sky grew progressively darker, waiting for his opportunity to present itself. So far, the mother and daughter had left the house, but a light still shone in one of the windows with its curtains drawn. Serys was still home.

While he waited, Ryckert's thoughts involuntarily wandered to Fenn and Leif, his old mercenary friend. Serys White's infidelity unavoidably reminded Ryckert of his own, and all the painful memories associated with it.

When it had happened, he and Fenn had been together for five years. Ryckert was thirty-two years old, still taking mercenary jobs that carried him across Atlua and back, sometimes even down south into Gillus, but he always returned to the home he and Fenn shared in Trael. The worst part of it was that there had been absolutely no problems between the two, nothing Ryckert could blame his stupid, rash decision on. Nothing but himself.

He had been out on a months-long assignment in central Atlua, scoping out a gang's operations. The contract was through the Atluan Guard, who felt they needed some hired hands to assist with the investigation. It was one of the biggest cases Ryckert had worked on up until that point, and the pay was nothing to scoff at. He had accepted with no hesitation, and had been glad to find several of his friends had been recruited as well, including Leif.

There was not much to the story. Nothing to distinguish it from thousands and thousands of other stories about infidelity told throughout the ages. All it boiled down to was two people fucking.

Ryckert had known Leif for years, long before he had ever met Fenn, and so they were close pals. Never anything more than that, though Ryckert had felt a mild attraction to the man when they had first met, back when they were both in their early twenties.

But as a result, they were incredibly comfortable around each other, and it was a relief to have someone to talk to since the job could take anywhere from three weeks to three months, and letters to and from Trael could only travel so fast.

Much to everybody's disappointment, the assignment had taken much more than three months. They were gearing up for month six when things finally boiled over.

Loneliness had long since gripped Ryckert, and he desperately wanted to feel Fenn's strong, warm embrace. The dingy motel he was staying in was nothing compared to the inn where Fenn worked, yet everything about it reminded him of home. Of his man. Of their first meeting. He wanted this job to be over, crescents be damned. It wasn't like they were getting paid any more for the job extension anyway.

Ryckert was frustrated, both sexually and with the job at hand. Everybody was, mercenaries and soldiers alike. While some men and women partook in the local brothel, Ryckert was cooped up in his room, writing letters or carving wooden totems to give to Fenn as a gift upon his return.

But one night, it had all been too much for Ryckert to handle, so he had gone to the bar and gotten as drunk as possible. Whatever it took to get his mind off of Fenn. He had asked Leif if he wanted to join, and the man had said yes.

One thing led to another. Nothing to distinguish it from all the other tales everyone has heard before.

The next morning, Ryckert awoke in Leif's bed with a raging hangover as well as a cocktail of confusion and regret. But when Leif had smiled at him and trailed his hand down Ryckert's chest to his groin, Ryckert had not stopped him.

The two rocyans continued their affair through the remainder of the assignment, which lasted another two months. They amicably parted ways once everything was said and done, neither harboring any delusions that they were now a "couple." Ryckert had Fenn, and Leif did not want any commitments.

When Ryckert returned to Trael, the guilt overwhelmed him and he immediately revealed his transgressions. Fenn was surprisingly calm while he digested the news, and he had simply told Ryckert to leave. Ryckert felt he had no right to argue or defend his actions, so he obeyed Fenn's wishes and left Trael. Not quite the homecoming either of them had wanted.

Ten years had passed since, and not once had Ryckert spoken to Fenn in person. Three years after the confession, he had finally garnered the courage to pen a lengthy letter to his former mate, but it had gone unanswered. Ryckert had taken a handful of lovers in those ten years, but none since settling down in Balam, and none had ever compared to Fenn Ver'nek.

Ryckert impatiently tapped his foot on the ground as the streetlamps flickered on, lighting up the darkened streets. It was harder to see Serys's house now, but Ryckert's rocyan eyesight was keen. He wouldn't miss anything.

An hour passed, and the smells drifting from the Sonata were enticing. More than once, Ryckert almost went inside to grab a burger or a bowl of soup, but he could not take his eye off the house. Serys might leave at any minute.

Or he might stay home all night, and this would prove to be an enormous waste of time. But still, Ryckert waited.

Another half hour passed, and it was getting close to eight o'clock. He would have to eat soon, as his rumbling stomach continually reminded him. The operation might be a lost cause tonight. There was always tomorrow, or the next day. He would keep trying until he was successful. After so many missteps thus far in the investigation, he needed a win. He needed to pin this guy for what he had done.

Ryckert's ears flicked in the opposite direction of Serys's house. There was a noise coming from the house down the street to his right, not quite but almost next door to the Sonata.

It was a woman's scream.

It was muffled through the house's walls, but Ryckert was sure she was screaming for help.

Without a moment of hesitation, Ryckert leapt up and darted toward the house. It was a pleasant home, one story tall but wide and long. This was surely no farmer's house; a lot of money had built this house.

Light leaked through all the front windows. Ryckert jiggled the handle of the front door, but it was locked. He took a step back, then kicked the wooden door off its hinges.

In the back of the room, near a doorway that seemed to lead to a kitchen, kneeled a thin woman with cropped blonde hair. Even though her back was to him, Ryckert could recognize her as the head blacksmith. He did not know her first name, but the name of the store was Dower's Weaponry.

The woman was sobbing and shrieking, her hands clutched to her chest. She screamed for help, anybody, please, hurry. In front of her were two small bodies, convulsing and gasping on the floor.

Ryckert ran to her side and placed a reassuring hand on her shoulder. She jumped at his touch, but at the same time looked relieved to no longer be alone.

"Please," the woman begged. She sounded desperate. Hopeless.

The figures on the floor were her sons. Neither of them could be any older than ten, by Ryckert's estimation. Both of their faces had turned a shade of blue, and their eyes seemed fit to burst out of their sockets. Fear drew harsh expressions on their faces as they clutched at their own throats, choking out short gasps and unintelligible syllables.

Ryckert didn't know what to do.

The boys kicked at the floor, flailing their legs wildly, trying to force out words, but unable. They were blinking rapidly, but the pace began to slow, and their bodies moved more lethargically. Whatever was going on, it was ending. It would be over in a few short moments.

The first to stop moving was the younger-looking boy, a kid with long brown hair and vivid green eyes. His grip on his own throat loosened and his arms fell to the floor.

"Vickery!" the woman screamed, grabbing the boy by the shoulders. She shook him frantically, trying in vain to wake him up, but Ryckert could see that the boy was dead.

The other followed soon after, and he earned his own scream from his mother (*"Bartleby!"*) as well as some shakes, as if this would shake free something in the boys' brains or hearts that would allow them to start pumping blood again.

With nothing left to do, the woman wrapped her arms around Ryckert and bawled. Warm, salty tears dropped onto the rocyan's plain tan shirt, leaving behind dark blotches. She muttered her sons' names over and over, her voice strained and scratchy. She yelled until the sound turned into coughs, and then she said their names again, as if to summon them back to the world.

But still, they lay motionless on the floor, and Ryckert did not know what to do.

CHAPTER IX

FALTERED, DIMMED

The morning was chaos for Aava. She had actually only slept for a couple hours in the middle of the night. Shortly after she ate dinner, read a bit, and tucked into bed, a barrage of urgent knocks assaulted her door and she was bombarded by several people rushing inside, which included Ryckert and Harold Hoskings, carrying two tiny bodies, trailed by the grieving Vanessa and Bromley Dower.

When she was finally able to calm the parents down (not without the help of some white magic), she was told what had happened, and it was not at all hard to see the similarities to Freya. She cast a knowing glance at Ryckert, and he nodded in silent agreement.

So it wasn't poison after all.

Serys White was off their suspect list, and there was probably no list at all anymore. The man might be a scumbag, but even he had seemingly no motive to murder two prepubescent children.

Which left her in an equally dire situation: there was a sickness going around that she had never encountered before. And it was fatal.

Bromley and Vanessa had both fully thrown themselves into their grief. The four (Harold had left shortly after delivering the bodies) sat around Aava's clinic as one day became the next. She continually cast soothing spells on the Dowers to keep them calm and present so that Vanessa could give an account of the incident. When Aava found the information at her disposal sufficient, she told the two they could return home and that she would speak with them at another time if needed. Bromley thanked her profusely for her help, and with that, they had left.

But Ryckert remained, looking grim with his arms crossed and his eyes glaring down at the floor while he thought.

"Ain't good," he started by saying.

"One good thing," Aava said, "is that we can rule out poison. Or any ill intent, I suppose. Unless there's someone you're aware of who had it out for both the town's white mage and two small boys."

"Nope."

"Then we're dealing with a sickness. Plain and simple."

Except that nothing about the situation was plain or simple. Aava had never seen anything like this in her months of training, nor had she learned about it at the university. She was at a loss, and her head hurt, and she was tired.

She asked, "How did you, of all people, end up with these bodies?" She glanced at the two corpses resting on her examination table and shuddered.

"Was watching Serys White's house. Happened to be sitting right in the middle of his house and theirs. Heard the mother scream. Figured White could wait another day. Went to help."

"Did you see it happen?" she asked.

Ryckert nodded. "Got there right at the end." He then explained what he saw, which matched up with Vanessa's description, as well as Theo's, which she had heard earlier that day. Or yesterday. Whenever it was, now. She needed sleep.

Then something else dawned on her. "I saw these boys the other day," she said, bringing a shaky hand to her mouth. Her eyes widened. "They were sick, and their mother brought them to me. I gave them a full check-up and determined they were experiencing nothing out of the ordinary. I prescribed them *tea*. For *this*." She looked to their bodies once again and felt like crying at the sight of their small, limp limbs. Their eyelids shut, never to open again, never to see the world. But she got ahold of herself and went on, looking back to Ryckert. "Vanessa Dower was showing early symptoms as well. I told them to come back to me if they persisted and I would give them more tea bags. Ryckert, I've seen *several* patients this week, all with the same symptoms. And all I've given them is *tea*!" Each time she said the word, it sounded stupider and stupider. Like she was a child playing dress-up. Giving tea to her sick dolls, as if it were a catch-all solution. She wanted to pound her fists on the table. She almost did, and would have if not for the bodies. An uncomfortable tingle danced down her spine.

The rocyan remained stationary, no longer looking at the floor. He bore into her with his dark, fierce eyes. But his words were unexpectedly gentle.

"Not something to blame yourself for," he said. "We were lookin' in the wrong direction. It led to this, which ain't good; no denying that. But it's not somethin' you should start kickin' yourself over. You made a mistake. I did too. Time to move on and try to figure out a new way to handle things. Right?"

"Right," she nodded, barely able to choke the word out. She wanted to cry again, but not over sadness about the boys. She wanted to cry because she had not realized precisely how lonely she had felt here in Balam, in over her head and surrounded by strangers who likely thought of her as nothing more than a solution to their problems (those who did not think of her as too young to actually solve any problems, that is). She missed Svend, and she missed her friends, and she missed Allinor. But she had found a companion here, unlikely as he may be. She had found someone to call a friend. And they were in this together.

Regrettably, Ryckert had noticed the tears welling in her eyes, which she tried to subtly wipe away, to no avail. He smiled at her.

"It's alright," he told her. "Gotta let it out sometimes. Don't deny yourself that. But we gotta be strong, too."

She nodded. She was strong. Stronger than anyone in this town knew.

"Now that we know it weren't a man-made poison," Ryckert said, "we can start looking in the right direction. Got any theories?"

"Not right now," she said. "I'm too tired, honestly. I can't think straight. Maybe something will come to me tomorrow."

Ryckert nodded. "Reasonable. Get some rest. Can come by in the morning, if you'd like. Or afternoon, if that suits you better."

"We can get lunch," Aava told him. "How's that?"

"Sounds fine," Ryckert said. They bade each other farewell, and he left.

So Aava had cast Preservation on the two bodies and crawled back into bed, but sleep had not come easy. What little she got was restless, kicking at the covers, jumping back and forth between too cold and too hot, while images of the boys flashed in her mind. Mere days ago, they had been smiling and laughing in the streets. Now they were dead and laying on her table.

She had no idea what time it was when she pulled herself out of bed again. All she knew was that it was still dark outside, the only light coming from the moon and the streetlamps. Everyone was tucked tightly in bed. Everyone but Aava. She wandered down the connecting hallway and entered the clinic.

The bodies on the table looked peaceful.

Her head was clearer now, so she figured she might as well attempt to get some work done. She had already wasted enough precious time chasing a false lead. How many days had been spent following Michio and Serys and whoever else they suspected might have poisoned Freya? Trying to find a culprit rather than an antidote, working under the assumption that it was a one-time occurrence. Never anticipating that others might be afflicted.

She stripped the boys naked and examined their bodies like she had Freya's. There was an overwhelming sense of shame and guilt tightening its grip on her body like a snake. She felt nauseous. If she had been smarter, more adept, these boys would not be dead on a table. Maybe if a different mage had been sent to replace Freya, everything would have worked out better.

They came to me, they trusted me to make them better, and I let them down.

They too shared the large, red splotches on their stomachs. So it had not been a sign of old age, like she had first thought. Theirs was a fainter red than Freya's had been, likely because their deaths were fresher. Still, she did not know the cause of the markings. They were inconsistent with what seemed to be some sort of respiratory failure.

What followed were the same tests and procedures she had enacted on Freya's body, and all the results were the same. The brown blood still confused and disgusted her. She slipped the samples into vials and marked them "B. Dower" and "V. Dower" respectively.

After filing away the samples, she redressed the boys and cast another Preservation spell on them. The sun was starting to make its first appearances on the horizon, and she decided she should try to get another hour or two of sleep before things—she assumed—got out of hand, once word got out that there were new deaths. And children, at that.

But she never got the chance. A knock at the door startled her out of her thoughts, and she found Rufus Reede at her doorstep.

"Good morning, Aava," he greeted her with a bow. He was dressed quite presentably for so early in the day, with a purple pinstriped suit and a red bowtie.

"Hello, Mr. Reede," she said, ushering him inside.

His face fell at the sight of the two Dower boys. He inhaled deeply and turned around, facing his back to the table.

"This is precisely why I am visiting you so early this morning," he said, a deep frown etched into his face. "I heard about what happened to the Dowers. Terrible, terrible thing. Just *terrible*. From who did I hear, I'm sure you're wondering? Answer: Mr. Hoskings. Harold is a supremely loyal employee of mine, and when he reported to work at the farm bright and early today, he could not help himself from tap-tap-tapping away at my door until I answered—quite groggily, and in my pajamas to boot—and informed me of the terrible news. Just *terrible*," he said again.

Given how much importance the man seemed to heap on his appearance, Aava could only imagine how mortified he must have been, forced to answer the door in his pajamas.

"Yes," Aava said, "Harold was here last night. He and Ryckert helped the Dowers carry their boys here."

"Ryckert?" Mr. Reede asked, as if he had misheard.

"Yes," Aava said again. "He has been extremely helpful to me over the past few days."

This appeared to be a shock for Mr. Reede, but he quickly wiped away the expression and replaced it with a smile. "Well, splendid!" he said cheerily. "I am glad to hear he has been good to you. He tends to not interact with most people, as I am sure you've heard, but we are glad to have him nonetheless!"

Aava could not comprehend how the man was so perky so early in the day, especially after hearing that he was unexpectedly woken up with such awful tidings.

She wanted to move things along. "What can I help you with, Mr. Reede?"

"Right, right. Of course," he said, shoveling out words. "You see, Aava, this is a tragedy. I don't have to tell you that, of course. Every death is a tragedy, but especially when it befalls such young souls as these." He gestured toward the Dower boys, in case she had forgotten to whom he referred. "News about this is going to spread like wildfire throughout Balam. There is no avoiding that. I am aware of such things. That is the nature of gossip in a small town. So all I humbly ask is that you do nothing to *fuel* these discussions. Do you follow?"

"I'm not sure I do, Mr. Reede."

"Allow me to elaborate. Harold did me the courtesy of describing what happened last night. The conclusion he seemed to draw was that the children passed in the same manner as our late Ms. Jeyardin. Would you concur, based on your examinations and testimonies?"

"Yes. It appears that all three died of the same cause."

"And what would that cause be, exactly, Ms. Yren?"

There was a catch in her throat. But she managed to say, "I'm not sure yet."

"Precisely," said Mr. Reede, strutting past her, to the door. He gave it a firm shove to make sure it was closed all the way, so that their words would not travel beyond the clinic's walls. "There will be panic. You can be sure of that. I am beyond sure of that, unfortunate as it may be. So we all must do our part to ensure we do not incite *even more* panic. Do you follow?"

Aava thought she might. "You want me to keep quiet about the sickness."

"Yes," said Mr. Reede. "Continue seeing patients, of course. Continue investigating the cause and any potential cures. But do not worry our poor townsfolk. If any exhibit similar symptoms, try to treat those symptoms, but I do not believe you should tell them just how sick they may be."

"In other words, lie to them."

"No, no!" said Mr. Reede, waving his hands in alarm. "Of course you should not *lie*! I would never be so bold as to request that. No, I am simply suggesting that you omit some details. They know they're sick, you know they're sick. You have some potions or teas or spells that can help. That is all it needs to be, correct?"

"I suppose so," Aava whispered.

Mr. Reede beamed. "Excellent. I am glad to hear we're on the same page." He clapped a hand on her shoulder and gave a tight squeeze. He let go and grasped the doorknob with the same hand. As it turned, he said, "Please keep me updated on your progress. I am confident you will soon discover a cure and we can all put this nasty business behind us."

"Me too. Have a good day, Mr. Reede."

"Good day, Aava!"

Sunbeams now crashed through the windows, filling the domed hut with light. Time had passed, but she hadn't felt it. A new day had begun. She might as well get to work.

- -

Lunch with Ryckert was good. They ate at his cabin down on the beach, which was a fascinating place. Quaint, but cozy in its own way. It fit him well. She was impressed to learn he had built it himself, which he shrugged off modestly. "Nothin' to it," he had said. "Been good with my hands ever since I was a pup. My ra was a good craftsman."

He had cooked stewed vegetables sprinkled with zesty seasonings and bought a loaf of fresh bread from the market, which Aava had used to soak up broth that leaked from the wet vegetables on her plate. She still felt queasy from earlier, but she knew she needed to get some food in her, so she ate. It was a simple meal, but it was good, and it filled her with the energy she required to face the oncoming day.

After clearing away the plates, Aava told Ryckert that the bodies in her clinic would need to be moved if she were to see any patients, which she was absolutely sure she would. He agreed to help transport them to the cemetery, where a funeral service could then be prepared for by Barbara Vere. She would be glad to be rid of the bodies. She didn't need the constant reminder of her immense failure.

Once Ryckert, with Harold's help, had bagged the bodies and carried them out of the clinic, Aava hung a sign on the door stating she would be open for business starting at two o'clock, then locked it and walked to the back of the circular room to the countertop holding all of her various ingredients, as well as the potion recipe Freya had left behind.

She gathered the necessary components: the mir root, the sage, the villium stems, some water, a bit of chicken stock, and a few other sundries.

But as she had determined before, Freya had likely already concocted this potion, and it obviously had not worked. So Aava sat in front of the pile of ingredients, brainstorming a way to alter the recipe in a beneficial but not too drastic fashion.

The water and chicken stock would be the base, though maybe a different kind of stock would be better. A tougher meat, perhaps, with more natural vitamins. Something to boost the immune system.

So mir root, kaya root, water, and perhaps hollion stock. Villium stems could be kept, as they were a natural ingredient used in most potions that dealt with respiratory problems, and Freya had stocked plenty. She would add honey, for flavoring. Something sweet, a component which Freya had sorely been lacking, to help wash down the bitterness of the kaya root that surely overpowered any meager sweetness provided by the mir. Taste must not have been an important factor while Freya was experimenting.

After a few more additions, replacements, and exclusions, Aava had a revised recipe that she felt somewhat confident in.

Confident enough, at least, to brew a batch and start doling it out to patients. If not an outright cure, it might hopefully be preventative, so that she could continue striving toward a cure.

I won't let it claim more lives.

It was a promise she wanted to keep, but another part of her did not want to get her own hopes up. Freya's original potion had failed, and hers might too. That was a reality she had to come to terms with.

But I have to try.

She poured six cups of water and four cups of hollion stock into a large pot and flicked the heater on. Once the liquid came to a boil, she would add in the mir root and stir slowly, allowing it to soften and break down. She would do the same with the villium stems, and once everything was dissolved and blending together, she would add the rest of the ingredients all at once and let the mixture simmer for an hour. By then, it would be nearly two o'clock, and she would be ready to see her patients.

While she waited, she wrote Svend another letter. She had not gotten a reply from him yet, but writing to him was cathartic. She went into detail about the sickness ailing Balam, and requested that he ask for advice from a few choice professors there. The stock was coming to boil when she sealed the envelope and wrote her brother's name and address on the front.

Svend Yren, Allinor University, Apt. D-23

The words made her heart flutter. She longed to be home, but she had a duty here. There were people that needed her aid.

She grabbed a handful of mir root, caking her hand in dirt, and dropped it into the pot. The surface of the liquid bubbled and popped. An earthy fragrance wafted upward. She sat back and waited patiently.

--

As predicted, a large congregation was waiting outside the clinic once two o'clock rolled around.

By noon, practically everybody in town had heard what happened to Vanessa Dower's boys. Several men and women had stopped by the Dower household to pay their respects and drop off meals.

But now several people were lined up outside the clinic, awaiting explanations and potions and spells and whatever else Aava could offer to ease their troubled minds.

Just remain calm, Aava told herself as she opened the door. *They will not be calm, but you must be.*

"Hello, everyone," she greeted the crowd, which was already anxious and noisy. "I will now see you one at a time, so whoever was here first, please step inside."

The first person to stroll through the door was the last person Aava wanted to see, though she hadn't realized it until she saw him.

"Hi," said Benedict Crogley, looking more disheveled than usual.

"Good afternoon, Mr. Crogley," Aava said, remembering to stay calm. "I see you're still in town. Long vacations are always nice. How can I help you today?"

Crogley wasted no time leaping to accusations. "I *told* you something was wrong with me. I *told* you the cough was more than a cough. And now look! Those kids with the same thing as me are dead! Dead as dirt! What do you have to say for yourself?"

The man had overreacted before—Aava still stood by this, despite what had transpired, because Benedict Crogley's symptoms were far less severe than anybody else's in town—but now he was feeling validated. All of his fears had come to fruition. The sickness was real, and he was convinced he had it.

But Aava remained calm, because Benedict Crogley was not.

"Mr. Crogley, I assure you I am doing everything in my power to ensure no one else gets any sicker than they already are," she said.

"Well maybe that isn't *enough*," said Crogley, his words and expression dripping with venom. "Maybe what this town needs is a different white mage. Someone with more experience handling stuff like this."

Aava took a deep breath. Then she said, "Mr. Crogley, I assure you I am perfectly capable. All I can suggest is that you either accept my aid, or, if you would like to seek the professional opinion of an alternative white mage, you may book passage to Bral Han or Brigher and speak to my colleagues there."

She said this all with a smile.

Crogley groaned and pinched the bridge of his nose with his thumb and index finger. "I don't have time to go anywhere else," he muttered. "Just please tell me what you suggest we do here."

"Certainly," Aava said warmly. "I have concocted a new potion that should ward off any symptoms you are experiencing. Since it is, as I mentioned, a new potion, I cannot say with certainty how long it might take, so if you are still feeling poorly once you have depleted your supply, feel free to return and request a refill."

She presented him with a small vial of the potion, which had turned a shade of lavender as it cooked. Before opening her door to patients, she had thankfully found enough time to individually package the batch she'd cooked up.

"What's in it?" Crogley asked dubiously as he plucked the vial from her hand. "Looks odd."

"It is called miria," Aava said, blurting out the first name that sprung to mind. She hadn't even considered naming the potion before Crogley had asked. "It's got some sweetness to it, so it shouldn't go down too harshly. Just take half a spoonful with each meal until the vial is empty."

"Easy enough," Crogley said.

"Easy enough."

He looked up from the glass tube and locked eyes with her. "Thank you," he said, somehow sounding simultaneously reluctant and grateful.

"You're very welcome," Aava said. "And feel free to come by any time to let me know how the potion is working for you." She would take any feedback she could get, even from Benedict Crogley.

The man nodded and stuffed the vial into his pocket. As he left, she told him he could send in the next person waiting in line.

She took in a deep breath, then exhaled. She was feeling better now. Everything would work out. If she could handle Crogley, she could handle the rest of these people.

"Hello," she said as a tall, brown-haired woman entered the clinic. "What can I help you with today?"

\- -

The trek from Aava's clinic to the small building on the outskirts of Rufus Reede's farm did not take long, and Ryckert had stuck around because Harold Hoskings seemed like he was in need of companionship that afternoon.

They had brought the boys' bodies to the building where they would be sized for and placed in caskets for their funeral, placing the thick leather bags containing the bodies on top of two low, sturdy wooden tables near the back window. Sun shone through the rectangular piece of glass and warmed the cold bodies.

The two men exited the building and stood by the doorway, looking out at Mr. Reede's fields of crops. Ryckert noticed Harold's gaze was fixated on the graveyard far to their right. He recalled the man had a daughter of his own; poor Harold was visibly shaken by the prospect of children becoming susceptible to this strange illness.

"You alright?" Ryckert asked, knowing the answer was *no* but that Harold would say *yes*.

To his surprise, Harold mumbled, "Not really." The chubby man sat himself down on a chair a few feet away and leaned back against the building's front wall. "Worried about my daughter. Worried for this whole town, truth be told. You want a beer?" Harold asked.

Ryckert nodded and said, "Sure."

Harold sauntered over to a wooden box at the edge of the lettuce patch and extracted two bottles. He unscrewed the tops and handed one to Ryckert.

"You ever read the Balthaz He'ra books?" Harold asked him.

"Nope," Ryckert answered. "Can't say I ever got into readin' much." He had read a few books during his time on the road, especially when holed up in tiny, dingy towns with nothing better to do, but he had never made a habit of it.

"Damn," said Harold. "You oughta check 'em out. The hero reminds me a lot of you, actually. Strong, ruthless rocyan that don't take no shit from no one. Used to be a soldier in the Atluan army, served in a war, then quit and joined the Guard. The series is about all the different investigations he gets involved in. Pretty riveting stuff. The one I'm reading right now is about him taking down a drug smuggling operation in Din's Keep. Not sure if the books are based on anything real or if it's all just fictional, but it's exciting stuff either way. You can borrow some, if you want. I've got tons."

"Thanks," Ryckert said with a smile. He took another sip of his beer. Harold seemed to have already downed half his own bottle. "Might take you up on that."

Harold took another swig, then gestured toward the farm with his beer.

"All this reminds me of a song I heard as a teenager," he said.

"The farm?"

"No, just...today. All of it. Everything goin' on," Harold said. He took a deep breath, then, "I don't remember what it was called. Don't remember who originally sang it, neither. I first heard it when I was livin' in Bral Han, trying to become an Atluan Guard. Obviously that didn't pan out," he grinned. "Me and a few friends were at one of the bars in town, a place called The Roaring Canary. Not sure if it's still around, but it was popular back then. We was just drinkin' and actin' like some drunk fools, like teenagers do, when this guy got on stage with his guitar and started singin'. Pretty simple tune, but it stopped me in my tracks."

Harold cleared his throat and began to sing softly, a light melody that carried on the breeze.

"There, she sang to me
A cry of something wanted
The light through all the trees
And all the branches swayed in breeze
I thought I knew her song
But all at once, was lost to me
The light through all the trees
It faltered, dimmed,
Suspending me…"

There was more to the verse, but Harold trailed off, staring wistfully at the farmland. Ryckert had heard the song a few times before. It was an old tune, a pub classic. Sung on late, drunken nights when the moon was full and hearts were left broken.

"My wife died a few years back," Harold then said.

He and Ryckert had never shared more than a few words at a time since Ryckert had moved to Balam, so the rocyan had not been expecting Harold to be so willingly open. But Ryckert, despite his isolated nature, was an empathetic man, and so he lent an ear to Harold's woes.

"Happened three years ago," he continued, running a hand through his thin, red hair. "Before you showed up, I believe. Don't think you ever got a chance to meet her."

Ryckert shook his head.

"Her name was Meredith. Beautiful woman, both in the face and in her heart. She was a writer. She helped me out at the farm, of course, to earn us more money, but her passion was writing. Had two stories published in the paper up in Bral Han. I was so proud. So was she, but she was humble and wouldn't ever admit it. But she got sick four years ago. Real sick. Freya tried helpin' her out, o'course, and when nothing she prescribed did the trick, I got her to Bral Han to see if any of the specialists there had any bright ideas. But they didn't. She had...there was some sorta disease in her, eatin' away at her. It was in her bones, in her stomach, in her brain. Eating away at her for an entire year before it finally took her. She was withered away, no more than a husk, by the end of it. I hated seeing her like that, but thankful for every moment I got with her. My Izzy cried for days and days after her mother died. I did too, but I had to wait until she was asleep, so that she wouldn't see. Had to be strong for her, y'know? But now, seein' what happened to Freya and to these boys, it's got me feeling like I did when Meredith was looking so thin, so frail, just laying in our bed, waiting for her day to come. I felt hopeless. And I feel hopeless now. I can't get sick and leave Izzy all alone. And if Izzy gets sick, I don't know what I'll do."

Harold's voice was breaking, but his eyes were dry. He looked out at the swaying crops. Ryckert didn't know what to say. There were the usual, mundane words of comfort that everybody knew and regurgitated every time someone needed reassurance, but he was not the type of person to mince words.

"Sorry," Ryckert said. That would have to be enough, because that was all there was.

"S'alright," Harold sighed. There was nothing else to say.

The silence was broken by a screech and the shattering of glass behind the building. Harold leapt from his chair and they both raced to the door that hung open a few feet away.

The back window had been broken, and now sunlight slid through a large, jagged hole in the glass. Both leather sacks had been ripped open, and one of the insectoid creatures that had assaulted Freya now stood on top of the right-hand table, its face and claws soaked in blood as it straddled its six legs over one of the boy's bodies, which hung limply out of the bag.

Harold roared in anger and agony. Ryckert was silent, but he felt the same emotions coursing through him.

The creature's beady eyes blinked rapidly, observing the intruders. It then leapt off the table, scrambling toward the window through which it had entered.

But Ryckert was fast. He rushed forward, bumping the boy's hanging arm as he scooted past the tables, and grabbed the green beast by one of its hind legs. He yanked it down off the windowsill and slammed its head into the left-hand table with a satisfying *crack*!

The beast screeched in pain as Ryckert pinned its body to the ground with his foot. It wrapped a meaty claw around his leg and snapped shut, cutting through the pant leg and through his skin. Warm blood gushed down his leg, but Ryckert did not make a sound.

Harold still stood in the doorway, clutching his chest. He wheezed and stumbled backward until he was past the threshold and back outside, though with a clear view of the proceedings.

It didn't matter. If Harold could kill one of these things on his own, Ryckert assumed he wouldn't have trouble doing it himself, and this one was half the size of the beast Harold had slain.

Before it could sink its other claw into his leg, he grabbed it by the arm and pulled until he ripped it from the socket. Thick, green goo sputtered out of the wound. Ryckert haphazardly tossed the limb and heard it smack against a wall.

The animal unclenched its claw. Ryckert moved his leg aside, ignoring the deep burn that engulfed it, and laughed as the beast tried to crawl away.

Ryckert bent down and grabbed the insect by the neck then slammed its face into the hard floor, grinning at the immediate *snap* he heard as the thing's shell shattered, puncturing its muscles and brains and sending more green goo splattering everywhere. Ryckert smashed the creature's face down over and over until its legs ceased flailing.

He stood woozily, his left leg covered in blood. He needed to sit down. He needed Aava.

"Shit," Harold murmured. "You really *are* just like Balthaz He'ra."

Ryckert barked out a hollow laugh. "Please fetch the white mage," he said, slowly lowering to sit on the floor next to the carcass.

"Right, o'course," Harold mumbled. As he started to leave, he stopped himself and said, "You really oughta read those books."

--

The day was finally drawing to a close. It had been long and rough for everyone in Balam, though naturally it was harder for some than others.

Vanessa Dower had not gotten out of bed all day, leaving her husband Bromley responsible for making sure she got enough food and water, though she slept through most meals. While she slept, he sat in his oversized, overstuffed chair in their living room and stared at the spot where his boys had collapsed, crying to himself.

Theo Saen washed out the mug that had held the tea Lyrra drank before bed. He placed it on the countertop by the sink to dry overnight, and as he moved through the hall back to the bedroom, his wife's knackered coughs echoed through the house. He stood in the doorway of their bedroom, frowning, watching her toss and turn, trying to fall asleep.

She opened her eyes and saw him staring at her. "Are you okay?" she asked him.

"Yeah," he said, but he was scared.

CHAPTER X

IDIOTS

Healing Ryckert's leg wound had been simple. All it took was a medium-strength Cure spell; any white mage could do it, but Aava was pleased with herself nonetheless. She had finally succeeded in helping someone.

Afterwards, she had been required to travel to the farm to cast Cessation on the two Dower boys. It was a painful experience, but she felt sorry for whoever was forced to inform their mother and father there were no longer bodies to bury. But it had to be done, for the safety of everyone in Balam.

It was now only a day later, far too soon to tell whether the miria potion (the name had caught on) was effective or not. She expected people to either see results by the end of the week or get sicker. For the time being, she would continue to prescribe the medicine.

She had observed a few more patients, and it was alarming to see how many townspeople were beginning to show early signs of the illness. The population of Balam was not terribly large, and Aava estimated she had already seen close to a fourth of it. Soon, it would be an outright epidemic. She couldn't help but be thankful that she hadn't gotten sick herself. Nor had Ryckert.

It was now her lunch hour, and she had been joined by Ryckert, who brought sandwiches for the both of them with a side of pickle slices. She thanked him and dug in, relishing in the crunch of the lettuce and lightness of the bread. A simple, well-made sandwich was hard to beat.

The day before, Ryckert had filled her in on the details of the attack while she mended his leg. It sounded harrowing, and she took pity on Harold, who had been the unfortunate witness to both attacks so far. At first she had been stunned by the re-appearance of these monsters, but it had to be expected. Something about the diseased bodies was attracting them. She just hadn't realized how quickly the creatures could show up.

As Ryckert ate his sandwich, with blobs of mustard getting caught in his fur, he told her, "Gonna hunt today. Try to find the things' nest."

"Nest?"

"Mhm. Not sure if they nest together or live on their own, but they're big insects, like vissians. Easy to assume they nest just the same. Worth a look, anyhow. And they must live close, if that tiny one managed to scurry on up here so fast to eat at those boys."

The image made Aava shiver. "Do we have a name for them yet, by the way? Something besides 'the things'?"

The rocyan shook his head. His damaged ear flicked. "If anyone's named 'em, they ain't told me about it."

"Well, we should call them *something*," she said, pondering the subject. "Just for ease of conversation, you know? So that everyone is on the same page when we discuss the issue."

"Don't gotta convince me," Ryckert smirked. He took a bite of his sandwich, almost said something in between chews, but caught himself and swallowed first. "Any suggestions?"

"I'm afraid not."

"Seemed like you'd given it some thought."

"It actually just came to mind. Sorry."

Ryckert took another bite of his sandwich, gazing down at the table, lost in thought. He took a bite of his pickle as well. He looked up at her. "What's the name of your potion again?"

"Miria. Named after the mir root I use to make it."

"Let's just call 'em that," Ryckert said. "Since the disease seems to be what attracts 'em. Mirias."

"No!" Aava objected, her voice high-pitched in exaggerated outrage. "You can't call the monsters killing people the same thing as the potion that is supposed to cure them!"

Ryckert laughed. It was more like a bark: short and loud, but warm.

"Got a point," he agreed. "Fine. Association wouldn't hurt, though. How 'bout mirials?"

"An L? Adding an L is your big edit?"

He shrugged innocently.

She sighed, then let out a laugh. "Fine. Mirial will do for now. At least between the two of us." She then asked, "Are you alright to hunt? Your leg is feeling fine?"

Ryckert smiled and said, "More'n fine. Feels better than before. Spell did wonders."

"Good." She was happy to hear that. "Will you be alright on your own, though? If just one did that much damage to you, I don't even want to think about an entire swarm..." She remembered the dried blood that had caked his leg. While it had been an easy fix, it had still looked exceptionally gruesome. The mirial's pincers were not to be taken lightly.

Ryckert shrugged. "Think I can't handle myself? Too old for the job?" She started to protest, to try to explain herself, but he laughed. "Joking. Another fair point. Was caught off-guard yesterday, though. Gonna be more prepared today. Should be fine, I think."

"Still," said Aava. She wasn't sure what the second part of her thought was going to be, but then an idea came to her. "What if you brought Michio with you?"

Ryckert was unenthused. His pointy ears drooped. "Michio?"

"Yes," she smiled. "He studied to be a black mage. By my brother's account, he was fairly good, too. He could prove to be useful. It never hurts to have someone watching your back."

"True," Ryckert nodded. "Fine. Ask him. Probably more receptive to you than he is to me."

She had to laugh at this. "I think he's over whatever problems he had with you," she said. "Now that you aren't hounding him about being a murderer."

"Yeah, well…" Ryckert grumbled.

"Don't worry. I'll ask. We can go to his campsite after we finish eating. I still haven't seen it."

"Sounds like a plan. Though it don't seem like it's *you* askin' if I'm right there with you."

"Oh well!" she gave him a playful grin.

He took another bite of his pickle with a smirk. Juice dribbled down his chin, and Aava couldn't stop herself from chuckling.

- -

The campsite was in as much disarray as ever. Ryckert felt secondhand embarrassment for the unsuspecting mage, who had no idea a pretty girl from his past was about to trespass and see how much of a slob he was. Though if they had dated, perhaps she was already aware.

Michio was dismayed and bare-chested when he saw the two of them approaching. The hair on his chest was as pale and patchy as his beard. He scrambled back inside the makeshift tent and returned a moment later, pulling on a shirt and grasping his notepad.

"Hello," Aava said kindly as they came to the perimeter of the young man's campground. It was still littered with trash and wet, freshly-washed clothes drying in the sun.

He wrote greetings to them both on his pad then asked why they had come. Ryckert waited for Aava's explanation.

"Ryckert is going to go hunt for the monsters that are terrorizing Balam," she started.

Ryckert noticed she had avoided using the word *mirial*, which had been her idea to avoid wordiness in the first place; probably because Michio would not have recognized the word on her lips, he realized. She was clever. Something so trivial would not have even crossed his mind.

"He's going to try finding their nest so that he can exterminate them and hopefully rid us of the problem. I thought it made sense for you to join him. Your magic could be put to good use. And it does not seem like you're busy," she added, pointedly glancing around his campsite.

Michio shot Ryckert a leer. The rocyan had to admit he was none too fond of the black mage either, and had not been particularly eager to see him. While the meal they had shared after the hostage situation was pleasant enough, they hadn't seen each other since, and Ryckert did not regret that one bit.

~ why me? why not that mage who's staying at the inn ~

"Because I know you and trust you," Aava said with a shrug.

Michio still wore an expression of doubt. He looked from Aava to Ryckert, then back to Aava. He cracked a smile.

~ for you ~ was all he wrote.

She smiled wide and wrapped her arms around Michio, squeezing him in a tight hug. "Thank you!" she said. He hugged her back.

After parting, Michio wrote, *~ when do we go? ~*

"Soon as you're ready," Ryckert said. "Already got everything I need with me."

~ can leave now ~

"Good," Ryckert said. "Gonna start at the place where it attacked yesterday. Farm's right on the edge of the forest. Might be able to follow its trail back to wherever it came from."

Michio nodded, then stood there motionless. After a few seconds, it became apparent that there was nothing he needed to grab to take with him. He really was ready to go.

Ryckert turned, and though Michio couldn't read his lips, he still said, "Let's get to it."

- -

They walked Aava back to her clinic, seeing as her lunch break was nearing its end and it was on their way to the western side of town anyway. Ryckert and Michio then marched through Mr. Reede's farmland, observing the various workers shuffling about (Ryckert gave a polite wave to Harold, who he was genuinely surprised to see had not taken the day off) as they made their way to the building where Ryckert had his leg cut open the day before.

They circled around the building to the back window, where a jagged hole remained in its middle and looked out on the threshold of the Cerene Forest. The woods surrounded Balam on all sides except for the shoreline in the south and southeast. Woodland covered a large portion of Atlua in general, surrounding all inland cities and towns. The trees enclosed Balam on both the upper and middle tiers, while the lowest was mainly beach. All of it was considered the Cerene Forest, stretching westward across Atlua until Bral Han, where there was enough of a divide between treelines (due to the city's immense size) that the other side of it was given a different name.

Ryckert kneeled to examine the shards of glass laying in the dirt patch behind the building while Michio paced back and forth with his hands in his pockets. The two had declined to converse during their walk from Aava's to the farm, and Ryckert assumed the whole affair might be mostly wordless.

There were tracks in the dirt. And they led into the forest.

Definitely matches the mirial's claws. Tracks are messy; looks like it was scrambling. In a hurry to get snacking.

He ran his fingertips along the dirt and into the grooves of the clawmarks. The ones leading toward the forest were shallow, but some at the base of the window were relatively deep.

Must be where it poised itself to jump through the window.

Ryckert stood and faced Michio, which caused the man to stop pacing and look at his face. He pointed down at the tracks, then drew an imaginary line, leading his finger upward until he was pointing into the woods.

"Found a trail. Might fade out pretty quick—the mirial seems to not have a ton of weight, so the tracks ain't too deep. Especially in the underbrush, it might be hard to keep track of."

Michio cocked an eyebrow. He scribbled on his pad, ~ *the mural?* ~

Right. They had invented a new word. It had already slipped Ryckert's mind. He gestured for Michio to hand him the pad and pencil, a request which was obliged. Ryckert wrote the terminology he and Aava had chosen in a messy scrawl.

"It's what we're callin' the monsters," Ryckert explained after Michio read the word and looked back up at him.

~ *honestly dont even know what we're looking for* ~

"The monsters that've been attacking the bodies that had whatever disease is goin' around. We talked about it when we ate with Aava after you had me tied up." The words were tinged with malice, but Michio wouldn't know that.

~ *oh* ~

It didn't matter if Michio knew what they were looking for or if he even cared at all. As long as he didn't get in the way and helped when help was necessary, that was enough for Ryckert. They pressed onward.

Ryckert's eyesight was keen enough that he didn't need to stay low to the ground to track the mirial's clawmarks. He was able to follow them without any issue, zig-zagging past tree trunks and circling around thick, blooming bushes needed. Michio followed closely behind, lightly humming a melody Ryckert didn't recognize. They were probably still far enough away from any potential nest that he didn't need to hush Michio just yet. He'd let the kid enjoy himself a while, though Ryckert couldn't fathom what pleasure he might gain from humming a song.

The Cerene Forest was filled with mirwood and birch trees. The mirwood branches were thick with leaves, and the bushes scattered throughout the woods were blooming with bright pink and yellow flowers to celebrate springtime. It had been a long while since Ryckert had taken a walk through the woods.

He felt at peace. It felt like home.

\- -

Lyrra's health wasn't improving. She said the tea was making her throat less sore, but aside from that, it was doing nothing for her cough or body aches.

It had taken a lot of urging from Theo, who was becoming more and more concerned after the deaths of Vickery and Bartleby Dower, but Lyrra finally conceded to giving Aava another visit. She had insisted she was fine, that she didn't have the same thing Freya or the Dowers had, but Theo knew her. He could sense she was worried.

They had not kissed in several days, as Lyrra did not want to spread her germs to him, but she allowed him to hold her hand as they walked to the clinic. This time, they luckily did not find Dennis Reen lounging on Main Street.

They crossed over to Aava's street, where they found a short line formed outside the mage's hut. Maybe the illness was spreading faster than he had known. It probably wouldn't be long before he had it himself.

Cilia Nells stood at the front of the line, standing tall with her brown hair hanging past her shoulders. Behind her was Barbara Vere with her son Lukas, and behind them was Ann Marie Toish. Theo and Lyrra took their place behind her.

Theo recognized Ann Marie from bartending whenever he visited the pub with Al, but neither he nor Lyrra felt they knew the young woman well enough to strike up a conversation. Theo couldn't help but notice that he and Ann Marie were the only people in the line not shielding their mouths to cough every few minutes.

It took less time than Theo would've expected to work through the line. In less than twenty minutes, he and Lyrra were being ushered through the entryway into the clinic.

Aava blinked her long lashes and tucked a stray strand of hair behind her ear. "I'm sorry to see you back," she said to Lyrra with a sympathetic frown. "The tea hasn't been working?"

"It's working a little, but not much," Lyrra said. "It temporarily relieves my sore throat, but it doesn't stop the cough, so my throat just gets sore all over again."

Aava nodded, and Theo would've sworn she looked upset, though her expression only betrayed her a moment or two before she was looking chipper as ever.

"I see. Well, I'm glad you're back, then. I have something else for you to try. It's something new I've concocted called the miria potion."

"What is it?" Theo asked.

Aava answered as she shuffled to the back wall of the clinic to retrieve a vial of the potion. "It was specially crafted to combat the symptoms Lyrra is exhibiting. Half a spoonful with each meal should do the trick, until the vial runs out." She returned to where they stood with a corked bottle as tall as her index finger but twice as thick, filled with an attractive lavender liquid. "If your cough persists after finishing the bottle, come back and I can issue a refill." She said it with a smile.

"Thank you," Lyrra said, taking the vial. She slipped it into a pocket in her jeans and moved toward the door. She turned to face Theo, who had remained still. Her look seemed to ask if he was coming.

"I'll join you in a second," he said, not breaking away from Aava's face. The mage looked confused and slightly concerned.

But Lyrra didn't accept this. "No," she said sternly. "Whatever you want to say, you can do it in front of me. I'm not a little girl." She waited by the door.

Theo had a lump in his throat. He had not wanted Lyrra to be present, but he had to ask. "Is she sick with whatever Freya had?"

He caught Aava's smile wavering, but she recovered quickly.

She said, hesitantly, "Your wife shares several symptoms with what afflicted Freya."

"That doesn't sound like 'yes,' but it doesn't sound like 'no,'" Theo said, furrowing his brow. He wanted her to stop dancing around it and spit out the truth.

Aava blinked her bright yellow eyes. "A lot of people are showing the same signs of disease," she said, her voice meek. "That is true. I am sure you've heard your fellow townspeople walking around coughing."

He recalled Freya's harsh, throat-tearing coughs that night underneath the yunesca tree. He could still hear her saying, *"Excuse me. I've been sick the past few days."*

"I cannot say definitively whether it is the same illness that Freya or the Dower children had," Aava said. "It shares too many similarities with a common cough, and any other conclusive tests could not be done on a live subject. I apologize. But

I do believe the miria potion will cure you of your ailments."
She said this while looking at Lyrra, who still stood stone-faced
by the doorway.

Theo didn't know what else to say. Perhaps there wasn't
anything else to say. It was barely a discussion, let alone an
argument. He had no counterpoints, and he was no white mage.
He had to take Aava's word for it.

"Okay," he said. He walked past Lyrra and opened the
door, feeling the warmth of the sun splash against his cheeks.
"Thank you," he said, not looking back. He heard Lyrra thank
Aava again before shutting the door and slipping her hand into
his.

"I'm gonna be fine," she assured him. He glanced to his left
and saw she was grinning.

"What?" he asked. He was apparently in a much dourer
mood than her.

"I think you're still jealous," she said.

"Jealous?"

"Yeah," she chuckled. "You're jealous that I get to drink
this tasty purple junk and you don't."

He laughed and planted a kiss on her cheek. It was cold.

"You're right," he said. "I'm jealous."

\- -

The tracking had gone swimmingly for a while, but as they
veered toward the cliffside overlooking the ocean, eventually
the tracks tapered off. Both men searched high and low for any
sign of where the mirial might have gone, or where it might
have burrowed into the ground, but there was nothing. Just the

sounds of leaves rustling and waves lapping on the sandy shores below.

"Damn," Ryckert cursed to himself. Michio stared out at the sea with his hands in his pockets, humming his song. As he turned around, Ryckert asked him, "Why do you hum?"

Michio gave him a puzzling look and stopped humming.

"Why do you hum if you can't hear it?" Ryckert asked. He meant no offense by the question; he genuinely did not understand.

~ *vibrations feel good in my throat* ~

It was a simple enough explanation.

"What's the song called?"

Michio shrugged. ~ *it's something my mom used to sing when I was a kid. she would sing and press my hand to her throat so I could feel the vibrations. she said it always made me giggle. just some song she made up.* ~

Ryckert chuckled. He had grown so jaded toward the mage, it was hard to imagine him as a child, and he realized Michio was practically still a kid. He couldn't be any older than seventeen or eighteen, if that. Looking at him made Ryckert feel like forty-three was ancient.

He remembered Fenn, who had been seven years his junior, always gave him a hard time about his age. "You're halfway to the grave already," he would tease as they lay in bed together, claiming he could already spot gray hairs on Ryckert's chest.

~ *should we keep lookin or head back* ~

"Keep looking, for now," Ryckert replied. It was only mid-afternoon; plenty of time left in the day before the sun would set. Though they would be wise not to dawdle too long and get caught in the dark of the wood.

They turned around and continued on, deeper into the forest, away from the cliffside. Perhaps they could still track down a mirial nest and use Michio's Fire to burn it to a crisp. Though as time wore on, Ryckert grew less confident in their efforts.

But he had to admit he was becoming more accustomed to spending time around the boy. Their trek through the forest had not been entirely unpleasant. They had shared a laugh when Michio got his foot stuck in a particularly thick patch of mud that had snuck up on him, and Ryckert had been willing to share the bag of jerky he had brought along to keep up his energy.

Ryckert briefly wondered why Aava and Michio had broken up back at their school, and he almost found himself asking before deciding it would only create tension. If not between the two of them, then between Michio and Aava upon their return.

If it was history, better to let it remain history.

So as they walked, he asked something else. Something that hearkened back to the good times they had shared together in the pub, before everything got complicated.

"Still gonna go to Brigher after Balam?"

Michio didn't write anything. He only shrugged.

So much for starting conversation.

Ryckert's thoughts were interrupted by a discreet rustling. Ten feet ahead, the ivy-green leaves of a tree were definitely bobbing up and down.

Something was in the tree.

Ryckert stepped carefully to his left, making as little noise as possible while motioning for Michio to keep quiet and follow his lead. If they were lucky, they could circumvent whatever beast was waiting ahead and be on their way.

He quietly edged further and further away from the tree, but the creature was on the move. A tree branch dipped down then flung upward, followed a split second later by a branch dipping down on a different tree.

It happened again, then again, growing closer to the two of them. It knew they were there. No use keeping quiet now.

Ryckert unsheathed his dagger. It was seven inches long, with a serrated edge. Even though the tip was somewhat dulled by its age, it could still do some serious damage.

He took off in a straight path, unconcerned about whether Michio was following, but the creature was agile. It had to be only a few feet behind him now. And then it was above. Then ahead. Ryckert veered right, but the beast was eyeing him closely and adapted its path to match. Once again, it was above. Then ahead.

And then it must have landed on a branch too frail to support its bulky body, because it crashed to the ground and landed with a *splat* on top of a soft, rotten log.

"Fuck," Ryckert muttered. Michio abstractly vocalized his disgust.

The thing was not pretty.

It had a thick body, standing on hind legs but with its back hunched over so that it could lean on its knuckles as it walked. Its head was a vibrant yellow that contrasted with the greenery surrounding it. The head was big and oval-shaped, with a grotesque mouth hanging open to expose sharp, browned teeth and a long, wet tongue. It appeared to have eye sockets, but there were no eyeballs. Just hollowed-out blackness.

Ryckert had never faced such a monster himself, but he knew that it was a hynterling. And despite its deformities and distinctly un-humanlike appearance, Ryckert could resolutely tell that it was frowning.

The hynterling leapt forward with a clawed hand outstretched. Its nails brushed Ryckert's side, but he hastily ducked out of the way. It lurched past Michio and smacked face-first into a broad tree trunk, emitting an angry yowl as it stumbled backward, clutching at its scrunched face.

Looking at the beast, Ryckert was growing less sure that his dagger would accomplish what he needed it to. He'd anticipated hunting much smaller game. He could only hope Michio was as skilled as Aava claimed he was.

The hynterling propelled itself upward and grasped a branch, swung forward, then let go, slamming into Ryckert's chest. He rocketed backward and his fall was thankfully broken by a bush rather than a tree or rock.

Michio was finally knocked out of his astonishment and began gesturing with his hands, preparing a spell. A fireball shot through the air toward the hynterling, but it jumped up and held onto a branch, allowing the danger to pass before dropping down and letting out a vicious, wet roar.

Ryckert stood shakily and realized he had let go of his dagger. It lay on the ground a couple feet away, behind the hynterling. It stood before him, gnashing its teeth and licking its lips.

"Do something!" Ryckert yelped at Michio. He dove to the left, narrowly avoiding a fireball, and rolled under the monster's arm as it swung. He grabbed the hilt of the dagger and rose to face the hynterling.

It screamed in rage as its chest was lit up by Michio's magic. Its eyeholes were beginning to ooze a faint orange liquid that cascaded down its leathery face, dripping onto the blades of grass at its feet. Ryckert couldn't determine if it was blood, acid, or something else, but it reminded him of the mirial's green goo—and he knew he didn't want to come into contact with it.

The hynterling lunged toward him again, but this time he was ready for its speed. He ducked, edged to the right, and slashed the creature's arm as it swung. It screeched, stumbling around stupidly, bumping into trees and tripping over fallen branches. Ryckert hadn't succeeded in severing its arm, but it was sliced just above the elbow, hanging on by what couldn't be more than an inch of flesh and sinew.

Michio saw this as an opportunity. With the flick of his wrist, an invisible forced tugged on the beast's dangling arm and it separated from the body, flung off into the underbrush. The monster screamed again as orange liquid spurted from its stump.

Ryckert and Michio both instinctively ducked as the hynterling leapt into motion, but it proved unnecessary as the creature had shot upward and grabbed a branch, pulling itself into the treetops. Ryckert rose and scanned the leaves, following its erratic movements.

It was injured. It wasn't going far. He figured they might as well finish it off, rid the Cerene Forest of one more pest.

He walked ahead, until he was standing below the spot where the hynterling's movements had stopped. Ryckert kept his gaze locked onto the spot, dagger at the ready, anticipating the beast's next move.

Except he hadn't anticipated the thing dropping down directly on top of him. It wrapped its remaining sticky claw around his neck as it wrestled him to the ground.

The monster pinned him, smashing his face against the dirt, tightening its grip around his throat. He gasped for air and clamped his eyes shut. The hynterling grunted and dragged its tongue against his nape. Ryckert opened his eyes and saw a puddle of the orange liquid forming next to his head as it dripped from the hynterling's open wound.

A hole then appeared in the center of the hynterling's chest, granting Ryckert a view straight through to the forest on the other side. It was a perfect circle, no uneven or rough edges. Orange blood fell like a waterfall from the top of the new hole, raining down on Ryckert's chest. Thankfully, he felt no pain or discomfort, aside from general revulsion.

Another yell emitted from the hynterling as its grip loosened, which was enough of an opening for Ryckert. He pushed himself up and knocked the monster onto its back. Before it could stand, Ryckert jumped on its chest and swiped the dagger wildly through the air at the hynterling's lashing tongue, chopping it into several pieces that landed with wet thuds on the dead leaves of the forest floor.

The orange liquid streamed from the hynterling's eyeholes with great force, like water from a faucet, splashing into the grass. It bit at Ryckert, flopping its stub of a tongue inside its hideous mouth. He went in for another attack, but he got too close and moved too slowly. The creature landed a bite on his right arm, its teeth sinking into him with a wet ripping sound as it tore away a small piece of flesh.

Ryckert let out a yelp and stabbed his dagger through the hynterling's mouth, through the back of its head, staking it to the ground. It ceased thrashing.

He waited a full minute to make sure the monster was actually dead before removing his dagger. He stood and took a couple shaky steps backward, grasping a handful of leaves he used to wipe away the blood on his blade. He sheathed it and faced Michio.

"Good work," he told the mage. "Not sure what the hell you did, but it was good." He had never seen anything like that hole Michio had created in the hynterling's torso. It was incredible.

But his arm was bleeding. Not profusely, but more than he believed an arm should bleed. He slumped down against a tree trunk and closed his eyes until there was a tap on his shoulder. He opened them and Michio standing there, holding up his trusty notepad.

~ you need aava ~

Ryckert tilted his head back against the rough bark and let out a sigh, then a laugh. Through a break in the trees, juxtaposed against the plain blue sky, he could see gray smoke rising. It was probably Walton Vere, smoking some of his meats at the diner.

"Yep," Ryckert then said with a small nod. "Yep, I do."

He hoisted himself off the ground, staggering to his feet, and as the two retraced their footsteps back to Balam, Ryckert found himself humming Michio's tune. It was a pretty melody.

- -

"Oh, dear…"

That was all Aava said when she opened her front door after the sun had set and discovered Ryckert on the other side, dripping blood from his arm. Michio stood by, hands in his pockets, tapping his foot on the ground. She couldn't say she was entirely surprised by the tableau.

"It's a good thing I sent Michio with you," she said, urging them inside.

"Yeah, yeah," Ryckert grumbled.

She sat him down on the chair usually reserved for herself and took a closer look at the wound on his arm. Something nasty had taken a bite out of him. The bleeding had slowed, but the hole was dirty and probably stung. It would take more to heal this than the simple cut he'd sustained on his leg before, but she could handle it.

"Hold still," she instructed, hovering her right hand over the bite. Ryckert's response was a huff.

One by one, she closed her fingers into a fist, then unfurled them again. She then lowered the three middle fingers so that they were horizontal, parallel to the floor, leaving her pinky and thumb extended. A soft white glow emanated from the three fingertips and there was a light burning sensation on the back of her hand, where she saw the Ustrel symbol for *Cure* begin to etch itself into her skin.

Ryckert yowled in pain as the flesh began to reconstruct itself. She hadn't told him it would hurt; sometimes the anticipation was worse than the actual pain, she had learned. But she was sure his arm was throbbing madly while the tiny chunk of flesh grew back and the hole sewed itself shut.

"Just a few more seconds," she whispered, concentrating on her hand. The symbol was glowing a bright white, illuminating her tan skin, and she slowly began to lift the three fingers back to their original position. Once all five were upright, the glow from the symbol dissipated and both Ryckert's pain and her own subsided.

As she moved her hand away, Ryckert examined his arm and grunted in approval.

"Sorry," she said to him. "I know it hurts a little."

"Nothin' I ain't used to," said the rocyan. "Been banged up and healed plenty of times."

Michio was absentmindedly walking around the clinic, checking out the jars of assorted ingredients resting on the back counter, while Ryckert and Aava conversed.

"This was from a mirial?" she asked. "You found a nest?"

"Nope. This was from a hynterling," he said, not bothering to explain to her what in the world a hynterling was. She hadn't exactly kept up with her bestiary in school, apart from learning the most common animal attacks and the best treatments for them. *Hynterling* was definitely not part of her vocabulary, but it was beside the point. They had not found the source of the mirials.

"That's unfortunate," she said. She felt dumb, but she had nothing else to contribute.

"Yep. Followed the trail as far as we could, but it ended at the edge of the forest, by a cliff. Tried to follow it back, deeper into the wood, but couldn't pick up anything. Not sure where it came from."

"Are you going to search again?"

"Don't know," Ryckert shrugged. "Trail today didn't pan out, and we've got nothin' else to go on besides 'the forest.' And that forest is pretty damn big."

She nodded. They would just have to hope for no more attacks, but that didn't seem likely if more people died.

The miria potion has to work.

It was a sentence she had been repeating to herself over and over all day, especially after Theo Saen had bluntly asked her about his wife's condition. It had been difficult to convince herself to acquiesce to Mr. Reede's wishes, and in the end, she hoped she had reached a good compromise with her answer for the Saens.

"Kid saved my ass," Ryckert said, pointing a thumb back at Michio, who was peering into a jar filled to the brim with blue and red flower petals. "His magic's good. You were right."

"I know," she smiled.

"Thank you." They both watched Michio for a moment before Ryckert said, "Gonna head home. Been a long day."

"I can only imagine."

"See you again soon," he said, resting a hand on her shoulder. He gave it a light squeeze. Coming from him, rather than Mr. Reede, it was much more welcome. Considerably friendlier. Somewhat brotherly, she had to confess.

"See you," she said as he departed.

And then she was alone with Michio.

Alone with Michio for the first time in…well, she didn't even know how long. A long time. She breathed in deep and realized her heart was racing. Her chest swelled.

Michio turned around and blinked in surprise at Ryckert's absence.

"Went home," she explained. As he walked toward her, she said, "Thank you for helping today. I appreciate it."

He nodded and smiled. It brought her back to her days in Allinor, and all at once she was swept up in the crushing loneliness she had felt ever since arriving in Balam. But as she looked into Michio's eyes, it felt less smothering. It felt more manageable.

Don't be an idiot, she told herself.

But she kind of wanted to be an idiot. And why not be an idiot for the night? She had expended all her brainpower over the past few days, trying to cure the town of whatever this illness was. She deserved to relax. She had earned the right to shut her brain off for one single night. It wouldn't hurt to be an idiot right now. In fact, it would probably do a lot less than hurt. It would probably feel very, very good.

"My offer still stands," she said, staring into his eyes as he stared into hers. "You can still stay here, if you want."

Michio shook his head, but slowly. She wondered if he was telling himself the same thing she was: *don't be an idiot.*

Everything in Balam had been so unfamiliar and so bad, she craved a piece of her old life. And what were the chances that a piece would happen to fall right into her lap? Of all the towns he could have gone to, and all the towns she could have been assigned to, what were the chances they ended up in the same one?

Michio stopped shaking his head and was looking straight ahead at her. She slipped her hands through his arms and placed them on his lower back, pulling his waist toward hers. His mouth dropped open slightly.

They had broken up for a reason, but this wasn't getting back together, not really. This was one lonely person connecting with another lonely person. Just two young, lonely people being idiots for a night. And that was fine.

Aava pulled him closer and put her lips on his. They were salty and a little rough, but she didn't mind. She had always preferred the softness of a girl's lips, but the comfort and familiarity made up for it and enveloped her in a warmth that melted her.

She pulled away and looked at him, searching for a reaction. There was none for several seconds, but then a grin broke out across his face. He reached out and touched hers, and she shivered as the fabric of his glove ran down her cheek to her neck, where he caressed her with his thumb as they drank deep from each other.

Their mouths separated again, but only long enough for her to drag him through the hall to her bedroom.

CHAPTER XI

CIRCLES

The next day, two people died.

The first was Vanessa Dower. Speculation circulated throughout town that she passed away due to a broken heart, but her husband solemnly confirmed that she in fact had been afflicted with the same sickness as their sons.

Bromley Dower now remained locked away in his home while others tended to his wife's body, performing an autopsy and casting Preservation before the funeral service. It would now be a joint service for his sons and wife. Nobody expected him to possess the energy or willpower to plan the service, and he indeed did not have it in him. Instead, Barbara Vere worked even harder than usual to make absolutely sure everything was in order. The funeral would be the next day, so she did not have a lot of time to prepare, but she was confident in her own abilities to get the work done in spite of her incessant coughing.

Bromley showed no signs of illness.

The second person to pass was Tarr Sheere. It was later in the day, after he had eaten his lunch out back at the general store, which he owned. He enjoyed eating outside, and years before had set up a small table with a few chairs for employees to sit at whenever they took a break. He had finished his meal and was slurping down a cold glass of water when he felt his throat begin to constrict and he collapsed on the ground. He was found thirty minutes later by his daughter Harley.

This second death hit Aava hard when she heard about it, as Tarr Sheere had been the first patient she'd seen with the illness. At first she had only prescribed tea, but she had hunted him down and given him the miria potion once it was brewed.

Obviously, it had not worked.

Four people had now died on her watch, and she was still no closer to combatting the illness slowly spreading through Balam.

That afternoon, she longed for Michio. He had gone back to his campsite early that morning—not before being dragged back into bed by Aava, though he was far from unwilling—and she felt that his presence would have soothed her.

At Allinor, he had always been good at keeping her relaxed during exam weeks. His companionship was reassuring, and simply being nearby seemed to put her at ease. She would sit awake in bed for hours on end, deep into the night, reading her textbooks and practicing her gestures until every minutiae was perfect, and Michio would be by her side with a hand resting at her back or on her thigh while he studied his own texts or read novels, keeping his hand there as he fell asleep. When Aava would finally finish, she'd smile at the sight of him there, tucked under her sheets, and she would spoon him, wrapping her arm around and placing it on his belly.

She wanted that now. She wanted his hand on her back, silently telling her she would be alright. She was going to be fine. She would ace it.

Her examinations of Vanessa Dower and Tarr Sheere's bodies revealed no new information. Exactly the same as Freya Jeyardin and the Dower boys. Frustration made her insides boil, made her skin vibrate. She was going in circles, wasting time.

To calm down and re-center herself, she wrote another letter to Svend. She had not yet received a single reply from her brother (which was another source of irritation for her), but she knew the act of writing her feelings down would help, even if they were never validated and her questions were never answered.

>*Dear Svend,*
>
>   *I'm writing to you again, though I expect you won't answer. I do not know if you are ignoring me or simply busy with your studies, though knowing you, I would be surprised if it were the latter.*
>
>   *Things have worsened in Balam since I last wrote. The potion I previously mentioned has had little to no effect—two patients I gave the potion to died today, a few hours apart. The town is in a panic, and quite frankly, so am I.*
>
>   *As I mentioned before, I was hoping you could ask Professor Eies if he had any theories, as the illness appears to have similar qualities as the sickness I had to battle with my mentor (Karia Leime, a brilliant woman and a good friend of Professor Eies) in Bral Han. The two of them had written back and forth and concocted a remedy together, and since you have easier access to Eies than either of us has to Leime, I figured it would be fastest. But if you are not going to*

help or write back at all, perhaps I will need to arrange a trip to Bral Han or Allinor, whichever can be put together more hastily. If I end up at Allinor, please ready yourself for a wallop on the head upon my return.

I must admit that I am feeling rather down about this whole situation. I have never felt so lost at sea, a feeling which is exemplified by the sounds of the ocean waves that envelop you in almost every inch of this town. I am running out of ideas. My options are dwindling, and all that will happen is more people will die. If I can't do my job properly, then what were all those years of studying and training for? What have I accomplished if my skills do not translate to real life experience? These are no longer theoreticals; these are real lives. Real people are getting sick and dying, turning to me for hope and help, and I have exhausted my supply of both.

I will continue searching for a cure until there is nobody left to cure or I myself die from the disease, whichever comes first. Though I hope neither of those come to pass.

I'm rambling now, I think. I'm just angry at myself and also angry at you. I thought I could rely on you, if not for help then at least for moral support, but you are nowhere to be found. I'm not sure what happened to my brother, but I miss him.

I suppose that's all there is to say for now. Please write me back, if only so that I know you are there.

Love, Aava

P.S. Michio says hello.

She looked over the letter and heaved a weary sigh. As she reread it, every line seemed foolish, which in turn made her feel foolish for second-guessing herself about everything, including something as insignificant as a letter to her brother. At this point, it might be faster to directly contact one of her old mentors, either Karia or Fahleran. The problem was she did not know their current addresses, which is why she had tried to go through him. She folded up the stiff paper and stuffed it into an envelope, sealed it, wrote Svend's address, and placed it in the mailbox outside the clinic.

As she did, she was once again filled with that sense of going in circles. She yanked the envelope out of the mailbox and ripped it in three pieces, then ripped each of those pieces, and over and over until the letter was nothing more than useless shreds of white pocked with black ink.

She went back inside, slamming the door behind her. She marched straight to the countertop in the back of the clinic and reached for the revised miria potion recipe that she had written.

Where did I go wrong?

Aava scanned the list of ingredients, weighing each one in her mind, determining whether any amounts should be increased or decreased. Or removed altogether, for that matter.

What if none of this is right at all?

It was something she had to seriously consider now. Freya had left something behind, a place to get started, but what if she had been wrong all along? Perhaps nothing written on that sheet of paper in Aava's smooth, assertive handwriting was any help whatsoever.

Part of her wanted to rip it up like the letter to Svend.

Before she could, there was a knock at her door. The suddenness of it made her jump, and when she realized what the sound was and what it meant, she wanted to scream in frustration.

Who is it now? she asked herself, trudging to the door and swinging it open.

It was Theo.

- -

Rufus Reede was panicking. As the self-appointed mayoresque figure in Balam, he was failing his constituents.

He was holed up in his study, leafing through pages upon pages of texts that lined his shelves, searching desperately for any tidbit of information that would shed light on their dire situation.

His meeting with Aava about discretion had proven fruitless, with new deaths seemingly every passing day. The town was in turmoil, no matter how he'd tried to curb it.

Kim Reen, ever so helpful, came to him once an hour asking if there was anything she could do for him. He usually declined, but every couple hours he'd request a fresh cup of tea. Ever since his childhood, tea had always improved his thinking skills. Got the brain pumping.

The last mug she'd brought him was now lukewarm, but he sipped it with fervor as he scanned the pages of a textbook entitled *The Dire Straits* written by a jeornish historian named Gregaria Vieran. It catalogued the worst disasters in Atluan history—from weather phenomena to massacres to disease epidemics. The latter was what interested Rufus the most, but so far, he had not uncovered anything like what Balam was experiencing.

There was one somewhat similar case documented three-hundred years prior in central Atlua, in the town of Solheim.

It involved the townspeople discovering a herd of keyerans secluded in the forest. Keyerans were an ancient species, thought to be long dead, though they were known to live for several hundred years. Their bodies were huge and slug-like, and typically they burrowed underground and were found down south in Gillus, but pockets of them had migrated to Atlua.

The citizens of Solheim took this unexpected discovery as a sign of prosperity from the gods and had slain the keyerans, distributing the meat throughout the village. What they hadn't known was the toxicity of a keyeran's blood, and the magnificent feast poisoned and killed the entire village. Solheim had not been occupied since, fallen into disrepair, with the surrounding forest decaying from the lingering effects of the poison leaked from the keyeran corpses.

Rufus slammed the book shut with frustration and hopelessness. There were no dead keyerans in Balam, no one had eaten any strange, tainted meat, and nobody had any solutions. Not their mage, not him, not anyone.

Feeling demoralized, he returned the book to its place on his shelf (his mother and father had accrued an impressive collection of novels and textbooks when they were alive), and ran his finger along dusty, leather-bound spines as he sought out another text.

What he landed on was another book written by Gregaria Vieran called *The Dark Ages*. Rufus would not guess that Vieran had been the most cheerful man, but the title seemed fitting.

The book detailed a span of years, long ago, when death and chaos had followed the jeornish who fled Atlua during the Kyring War. Their resettlement in Herrilock had been a struggle for many reasons, one of which was the introduction of foreign diseases into their systems.

Perhaps he would find something there. Did that black mage at the inn say he was visiting from somewhere in Herrilock? He genuinely couldn't recall.

He skimmed the table of contents, turned to chapter four, and began reading.

- -

Aava Yren did not look the slightest bit pleased to see him. And no wonder, given how the day had turned out. He could relate.

Theo had awoken to Lyrra's constant coughing once again. He'd brewed the tea Aava had given them as well as doled out the miria potion, but after the news of Vanessa and Tarr (he made a mental note to go see Harley), he was growing even more panicked. Something needed to be done, though he had no idea what.

"Hello, Mr. Saen," Aava greeted him as they stood in the clinic's entryway.

"Just 'Theo' is fine," he told her. The stress was pounding into his chest with each heartbeat.

"Okay," she said, not without an irritable note. "What can I help you with today?"

"I heard about Vanessa and Tarr," he said, and immediately regretted the way he had started the conversation. Reminding her of them was not going to improve matters.

"Yes," Aava said, keeping her voice low and calm. Perhaps she was cooling down. "What happened to them was tragic."

Theo nodded his agreement, then said bluntly, "Lyrra isn't getting any better."

Aava closed her eyes and sighed before ushering him inside, closing the door with a soft click. She observed him as he stepped forward, toward the examination table. He turned to face her and found the young woman standing by the door with her arms crossed.

They each waited for the other to speak.

"So..." Theo mumbled. When Aava did not respond, he said, "...is there anything you can do?"

"How exactly is her condition worsening?"

Theo shrugged. "I mean, it's all the same stuff as before. Terrible cough, her body feels weak—it's all just amplified. She's barely getting out of bed now. And a big red blotch is starting to form on her stomach. What is that?"

"I don't know what that is," Aava said, and Theo was struck by her honesty.

"That's not exactly reassuring," he said.

"I know. I know," she said, lowering her voice the second time. "I'm sorry. This has been rough. I'm trying, I really am. Right before you came, I was going over the recipe for the potion, trying to think of what to change to boost its effects. I'm really trying my best here. It's just taking more time than I'd prefer."

And people are dying, he thought but didn't say.

"I hope to have something new soon," she told him. "Ideally, later today. But if not, then hopefully tomorrow. You can come back then or I can go fetch you, but right now, I don't have anything."

Theo stood there staring at the mage for a moment before what she was saying sunk in.

"So you...you don't have anything? Nothing to treat this with?"

"No. The potion in its current form seems to have staved off the illness for a couple days more, but it is not a cure, as you have seen."

He blinked.

"You've got nothing."

"No," she said, exasperation leaking into her voice again.

"I'm supposed to go back to my wife with *nothing*? My wife, who's withering away, lying in bed reading some book for the hundredth and possibly last time? You're saying there's *nothing* I can do for her?"

"Please do not yell," Aava said.

Theo hadn't realized he was raising his voice, and his cheeks flushed with embarrassment.

"Sorry," he murmured, but his words were overpowered by Aava's.

She said, "That's the situation right now, yes. I am deeply sorry that I can't do more, but the fact of the matter is this disease is nothing I've ever seen in all my years of study, and it's taking time to find an antidote. When *I* have it, *you* will have it. I can't get it to you before I have it."

"And in the meantime, Lyrra might die. Barbara Vere might die. Countless other people might die."

"Yes, Theo," she said, and it was almost a scream. "And sitting here discussing it with you will only prolong the process. I'm only one person. I am doing what I can."

He stormed past her and out the door, back into the sunlight of that warm spring day.

He felt like an ass for how the conversation had escalated, but his emotions had gotten the better of him. They always did when it came to Lyrra. She was the most important thing in his life, and every day he was forced to watch her slip further and further away.

He walked back home in resolute silence with his hands dug deep into his pockets, eyes locked on the ground.

His thoughts involuntarily drifted to his mother. He remembered going to church with her as a child; the building where services were held in Padstow was old and built out of weak, white wood. His father would go on to cut the lumber used to construct the new church, but that would not be for many years.

It was a fifteen-minute walk from their home, and Theo would accompany his mother and sister every week. Theo wasn't particularly interested in what the priest had to say, but he enjoyed spending time with his mother and knew it made her happy to have him with her at church. His father was never one for religion. His tranquility was instead found in his secret blue-flowered patch.

As they walked, Theo and Gwendolyn's mother would lay out all of the tasks they needed to accomplish that day, as well as a few that should get done throughout the week. It was their time to plan together, walking down the dirt roads of Padstow, each child holding one of their mother's hands. Theo would continue to hold his mother's hand throughout the service. He distinctly remembered being surprised by the sight of a few jeornish townsfolk at the services every week, but in retrospect he realized that Padstow had no Elder for them to turn to. The Tarasian Church had been the only religious presence in town. He was unsure if that had changed in the intervening years.

As a child, Theo had been fascinated by the idea of death. It sounded glorious. Eternal life in the After with everyone you had ever loved. No worries, just happiness forever and ever.

One day, after the first service in which young Theo learned about the afterlife promised by the ancient priest at the pulpit, he told his mother he couldn't wait to die.

She couldn't stop herself from laughing. "Why is that?" she had asked him.

"Because it sounds so great in the After!" he cheered in his high-pitched voice as he was laughed at by his mother and Gwen. Of course, he hadn't meant that he wanted to *die*, only that he was looking forward to the afterlife. It sounded like an appealing place to live.

After that service, Theo became much more enthralled by the priest's sermon each week. He wanted to make sure he knew exactly what needed to be done to ensure his entry into the After. He clung to every word.

But that changed after Gwen's death.

After Gwen's death, there was a marked change in his mother's demeanor, as anybody would expect when a parent loses a child. Theo witnessed it with Vanessa Dower, but his first experience had been with his own mother.

At first she had remained stoic, posing for her son to give him strength, but she soon broke down. She didn't last the month. After that, she spent a lot of time in her bedroom crying. Whenever Theo's father spoke with her, even about small things like what he should buy for dinner, she would snap and scream at him. Tensions were high in the household.

Her behavior shook Theo. He was ten years old at the time, so he thought he knew everything there was to know about the world, but he couldn't make sense of his mother's behavior. He felt incredible anger toward his father, as well as unending sadness about his sister's absence. But he had held on to the belief that she was in the After now, and that she was happy, and they would be reunited someday. Why was his mother this upset?

It made him think that maybe there was no afterlife at all. That was why his mother was so upset, because Gwen was gone for good and that was that. The thought gave him chills, and he tried to push it away, but it crept into his mind late at night while he tried to sleep. It was there when he was at school, taking his tests. It was always there. Gwen was dead. Gone.

And then a year later, so was his mother. Back then he had thought she had gotten sick and passed away, but as he grew older it became clear that she had killed herself, and it made him even angrier with his father. When Theo tried to confront the man about his mother's death five years later, when he was sixteen, the resentment had bubbled up and the argument came to blows. If his weak, cowardly father wasn't going to admit how his mother died, he would beat the truth out of him.

It was easy to shun his father after that. It was even easier when he moved to Bral Han for school. They hardly talked, even when his father grew ill and close to death. Theo told himself he didn't care, and it was mostly the truth. Near the end of his life, his father had sent a letter to Theo's home in Balam. It remained unopened in his bedside table drawer in the bedroom.

At home, Theo found Lyrra propped up in their bed, reading *Lyrical Tide*. When he had left to visit Aava, his wife was asleep again, distraught over the news of her friend's death. He was glad to see her awake now and not looking too bad, though he noticed her eyes were red and puffy.

"Hey," he said, entering the room. Lyrra returned the hello as he sat down on his side of the bed, folding the sheets back over his lap.

"Where'd you go?" she asked, dog-earing the page and closing her book. By now, so many years and readings later, nearly every page had the slight crease of a previously-folded corner.

He considered spilling the truth, telling her that he had gone to the clinic in hopes of obtaining new, stronger medicine, and had failed. But there was no point.

"Just went out," he shrugged. "Took a walk. Crossed the bridge, got some fresh air."

"Visiting Al?"

"Nah," he said.

It felt scummy, lying to her, but he knew the truth wouldn't do any good.

"Do you want some more tea?" he asked.

"Sure," Lyrra said with a smile. "That sounds nice. Thank you."

She leaned toward him and pressed her lips to his cheek. She giggled at the bristle of his stubble. With the past few days of weariness and stress, he had grown lazy and eschewed shaving.

"I'll get it started." He kissed her back. "Love you," he told her. The words had more weight to them now than before. Each time he said it felt more important than the last. More urgent.

He moved to the doorway, but stopped and turned back. Lyrra had already opened her book again and unfolded the top corner of the page.

"How's the book this time around?" he asked.

She flashed another smile. Her eyes were puffy, her cheeks looked hollowed-out, and her skin had the sheen of a thin layer of sweat, but that smile made her look radiant every time. No matter the circumstance.

"Good as ever," she said.

He smiled as well, though he knew he could never reciprocate the warmth of hers.

"Good," he said.

CHAPTER XII

ON THE BEACH

Ryckert invited Aava and Michio over for another meal, but he was getting a late start preparing their lunch. He originally wanted to grill some fish, but the few he caught had the strange green scaling and he recalled how sick he'd gotten last time he ate them, embarrassingly throwing up in Aava's clinic. So he opted to buy a couple cuts of juicy vissian meat from the butcher to make kabobs, and now he was running late.

With only forty minutes until his guests' arrival, he got his beans heating up in water on the stove with a pinch of salt and some spice mix he'd dreamed up years ago that he had grown quite fond of. While waiting for the water to boil, he cut the white slab of meat into bite-sized chunks, tossing each piece into a marinade that was the closest thing to a specialty Ryckert had; it was often the spotlight of his dishes, a recipe he devised while living with Fenn, who had been its biggest fan.

"What do you put in this?" Fenn would ask every time after taking his first bite, since Ryckert never allowed him in the kitchen while cooking.

"Can't say," Ryckert would always reply. "If you knew how to make it yourself, you wouldn't need me around anymore."

"Then I'll keep you around, for now," Fenn would joke.

Truthfully, the marinade wasn't anything special. In fact, Ryckert had merely adapted an old recipe he had learned growing up in Uruh. It was a classic Caer clan recipe, dating back many generations, and was used frequently at community events and within his own home. All he had done was take that recipe and added yori shavings and honey, while removing the pepper.

The bean water was bubbling as he finished tossing the meat in the sticky amber-colored marinade, so he removed the pot from the heat and covered it to let the beans soak for an hour. At this rate, the meal wouldn't be ready by the time Aava and Michio showed up.

While the beans and the meat both absorbed their respective liquids, Ryckert began to chop lettuce for a salad.

Cooking had never been his forte, except for the bare essentials every rocyan hunter learned. He had only taken up the hobby after meeting Fenn and being introduced to the chef at his inn.

The chef was a jeornish woman named Hanna whom Fenn had met while on vacation in Gillus. He had stayed at an inn where she was working, and he was so impressed by her food, he somehow convinced her to pack up and move to Atlua to work for him in Trael. Ryckert never heard the full story of how Fenn had persuaded the woman to do so, but he had been swayed by the man's undeniable charm countless times, so it wasn't hard to imagine.

But Ryckert had been impressed by Hanna's expertise too, and one day when he mentioned to Fenn that he wished he knew how to cook as well as her, Fenn suggested, "Why not ask her to teach you?"

It seemed silly in the moment, but Ryckert eventually asked her for a handful of lessons, and she had giddily agreed.

They met several times, and while Ryckert was nowhere near as skilled as her, he learned a great deal and felt like a competent chef by the end of their time together. He soon became the primary cook in the household, much to Fenn's delight.

The lettuce had now been dealt with and Ryckert was working on the red onion when there came a knock at his door. He glanced at the clock hanging above the sink and saw it was still twenty minutes until the time the trio had settled on. If it were anybody else, he would have been annoyed (and possibly still would be, if it was Michio standing in his doorway rather than Aava).

Luckily, when he opened his door he found Aava standing there, with a sheepish smile on her face.

"Sorry I'm early," she said. "I hope it's not a bother. I was just getting sort of anxious and bored at home and thought you might like some company."

"Not a problem at all," Ryckert said. "Glad to see you."

Aava sniffed as she took a seat at the table. "So what is it we're having today?" she asked.

"Vissian kabobs, white beans, and a salad," Ryckert said. "Kabob meat's marinating right now. Marinade's what I'm famous for."

The mage laughed at this. "Ryckert Ji'ca is famous for his marinade?" she asked incredulously.

He chuckled with her and nodded.

"I can't wait to try it, then."

She offered another smile, but it was strained and her eyebrows sloped downward. Nearly a frown.

"You alright?"

Aava looked at him innocently. "Why do you ask?"

"Seems like something's troublin' you, is all. Didn't mean to pry." He returned to the onion he had been slicing.

"No, you're not," she said. "I'm…yeah, I guess *alright* is a good word for it. Maybe less than alright. I don't know."

"Can listen if you need someone to listen."

She was silent for a moment. Ryckert's back was to her while he chopped, so he couldn't see what emotions might be running across her face while considering venting to him.

"It's this disease," she said.

It was extremely obvious to Ryckert that that would be the cause of her distress (*What else would it be?* he thought), but he remained quiet and allowed her to speak uninterrupted.

"I really don't know what it is. I don't have a clue. And it's driving me crazy. People are dying because I can't figure out what it is. A man lost his entire family, and I'm not any closer to stopping it."

"Ain't your fault," he said.

"I know it's not my fault," she snapped, "but that doesn't stop me from feeling guilty. Everyone here relies on me to help them get better when they're sick, and if I can't do that, then what good am I to anyone? Whoever it was that decided I should be the one to replace Freya made the wrong choice, because obviously I can't do it. I've really screwed everything up."

Ryckert wanted to tell her she was wrong, that she hadn't screwed anything up, but he refrained. The last thing she needed or wanted right now was pity. He recognized that.

"I haven't done anything to help these people except to tell them *yes you're very sick* and frighten them even more than they already were. And I cast a few Preservation and Cessation spells, but what are those worth, really?"

"Helped me a few times when I've gotten my ass busted," he pointed out, looking over his shoulder at her with a grin.

"That's true, I guess," she said, and Ryckert was glad to see it had made her smile. "You've gotten yourself into a fair amount of scraps since I got here."

"Can't help myself."

"But besides that, all I've done is offer people solutions that either stalled or did nothing. These people have contracted some fatal illness and I gave them *tea* for it. Tea that doesn't even taste that good!"

Ryckert guffawed at this, and Aava couldn't help but join him. After their laughter died down, they both were silent for almost a minute. Ryckert assumed she was finished, and went to speak.

"Way I see it," he started, "you've been doin' your best. Doin' what you could."

"But it hasn't been enough," Aava said.

"I know," he said, hoping it didn't sound harsh. "Trust me. Been feelin' the same way since before you got here. I'm the bonehead who assumed this was murder wasted both our time tryin' to make those puzzle pieces fit together. Hell, if I had kept my mouth shut and minded my own business, you mighta never gotten stuck on that poison track for so long. My apologies for that."

"There's no need to apologize. You were trying to help. You've been immensely helpful ever since I got here." She sighed. "Honestly, you're probably the only person in this entire town who has any faith in me."

"Can't be true."

"It is," she insisted. "I even got berated by someone yesterday because I didn't have anything for his sick wife. You should've seen the devastation on his face when he left the clinic. Everybody is losing hope, including me."

The air was still.

Ryckert was at a loss for what to say; none of the words in his head were coming together to form any inspirational or even simply reassuring sentences. He stopped dicing and faced Aava. Her elbows rested on the uneven table with her head in her hands, pushing up her cheeks. It stretched the bottom half of her face upward into a goofy, unintentional grin. Ryckert laughed at her.

"What?" she asked through the tiny opening of her stretched mouth.

"You just look stupid," he said.

She lifted her head and dropped her jaw, as if offended, but then laughed too. "How rude," she scoffed.

He smirked and sat across from her. There was nothing he could say that would make things right or better; he knew that. He'd been there before. He was there right now. All he could do was be a friend to her. After losing Fenn and being on his own for so many years, it felt good to have the opportunity to be a friend to somebody.

"Wanna help me chop these vegetables?" he asked. "Still got a tomato and some cucumbers. I'm runnin' really far behind."

"You're the one who decided on the time. You knew when we were coming. How'd you mess that up?" she chuckled.

"Don't know," he said, standing. "Just help me, why don't you?"

She stood and brushed off her pants then wiped at her eye. Ryckert hadn't noticed any tears, but maybe his vision wasn't quite as keen as he thought.

"Fine," she conceded with a smile, not strained at all this time. "I'll help."

\- -

As Aava expected, given his past behavior, Michio was late to Ryckert's luncheon. It gave the rocyan more time to prepare his beans, which she could tell he appreciated, but she was somewhat irritated by her friend's tardiness. When he finally showed up, though, she brushed aside her exasperation and told herself she was just on edge after everything that had transpired. Arriving ten minutes late to an event wasn't a huge deal, really.

Her greeting was amicable enough, and Michio returned a wave while Ryckert plated the food, scooping the fresh, crisp salad into three bowls and distributing one kabob and a pile of beans onto three plates. There were two more kabobs per person waiting on the countertop, if they were still hungry.

Michio placed his notepad on the table for easy access during the meal. He speared pieces of lettuce and cucumber with his fork and ravenously shoved them into his mouth.

"Might choke if you don't slow down," Ryckert said. Michio's reply was a smirk.

Aava started with the salad as well, but before she could finish the bowl, her nostrils were filled with the intoxicating aroma of the vissian meat on her plate. The white meat had an orange sheen, and the glaze dripped down onto her plate, mixing with the beans. It smelled sweet and smoky at the same time, and it made her mouth water. She had to abandon the salad, despite how much she usually enjoyed her share of greens.

The first bite must have slapped a noteworthy look on her face, because Ryckert laughed and Michio grinned as they watched her chew. The meat was crispy on the outside and exceptionally juicy on the inside, with the marinade giving it a sweet, syrupy flavor that somehow complemented the meat's muscular texture rather than contradicted it.

"Like it?"

"It's amazing," she said after swallowing. "I've never had vissian cooked like this before."

"Ain't as tough, right? That's the work of the marinade. Usually like to let it soak overnight, but it was a sorta last-minute decision."

"If marinating longer makes this taste even better, then I can't even imagine," she said before sliding another piece of meat off the skewer and popping it into her mouth. There was no doubt in her mind that she would be eating seconds and possibly thirds.

Michio had eaten all of his salad and needed to see what the fuss was about. He dropped his fork into his bowl with a clang and picked up his skewer, clamping his teeth down on the first piece of meat and sliding it off the sharpened stick. His eyes lit up as he chewed and nodded his approval at Ryckert.

~ *Pretty delicious. Thank you for cooking it and inviting me over.* ~

"Not a problem. Wanted to do it. Had to thank you both for helpin' me the other day. Without y'all's magic, I woulda been in a pretty bad spot. So thanks."

The beans did not have that same unbelievable quality to them as the meat, but they were good in their own right. It was a nice, filling meal, which Aava was appreciative of after such a grueling few days. She and Michio both got up to grab a second kabob at the same time, and Aava brought one over for Ryckert as well.

It was surreal, sitting there in some hut on the beach with a grizzled rocyan and her ex-boyfriend. It was more like a dream than reality, and she still couldn't believe the three of them had ended up together in this small village on the coast.

Conversation was light, which was another thing Aava appreciated. She had embarrassingly gushed to Ryckert about all her insecurities, and despite the closeness she once shared with Michio, she did not want him to know how vulnerable she was currently feeling. It felt safer, more natural, to have shared her thoughts with Ryckert. She was glad he showed discretion by not bringing up that delicate topic again in front of Michio. She didn't want him to think—or *know*, rather—that she had only slept with him the other night because she was feeling so anxious and scared. Even Michio Loz had feelings, and they might be hurt if he found out she was using him, as fun as that night had been.

Instead, they talked about the typical things people talked about when getting to know each other: where they grew up, their favorite places they've visited, what their parents did for a living. Stuff that usually was not too interesting to Aava, but she found Ryckert's past fascinating.

She had never been friends with a rocyan before—growing up in a mainly jeornish town, and then attending a mage academy, the opportunity had never arisen—so she was intrigued by the customs of rocyan clans, not to mention his captivating history as a mercenary.

Ryckert told them about his childhood in Uruh, a village surrounded by forest in south-central Atlua. There, he was taught the basic living skills for a young male rocyan, which mainly involved how to proficiently use weapons and hunt animals. He regaled an especially exciting tale about his first solo hunt, tracking down a wild ziolo, which had Aava on the edge of her seat. He mentioned that his father—his *ra*—had passed away when Ryckert was still in his teens, but did not go into much detail, and neither she nor Michio pressed him. They listened as he spoke of his journey out of Uruh, away from the Caer clan, out into the wider world to make it on his own, scraping by with hunting jobs from butchers in whichever town he happened to be staying in at the time. Aava couldn't imagine living on her own at the age of thirteen like Ryckert had. She was nervous enough doing so now, as an eighteen-year-old.

"I could never have done that," she told him. Michio nodded in agreement. "I didn't even know how to do laundry for myself when I was thirteen. I was hopeless!"

"Weren't so bad," Ryckert shrugged. "Got by. Pay was shit, and by the time I paid for a room at the inn I could only afford to eat scraps, but I got by, all the same. Was a lean two years, though."

"What happened after two years?"

"That's when I realized the type of money I could be making. I was fifteen, feelin' stronger and more confident, like every cocky teenager. Was checkin' a noticeboard in some town and saw someone in need of help. Monster in need of some killin'. Reward was hefty, and I was arrogant, so I accepted the job."

Aava was the one to ask questions, since she knew Michio didn't like to interrupt stories. He felt that writing out his questions or responses broke up the storyteller's flow. She asked, "What was it?"

"Ever heard of an anklior?"

Aava nodded and Michio's eyes widened. "No way," Aava gasped, totally enthralled.

An anklior was a creature she had read about in school. Ankliors primarily lived in marshes, floating just beneath the water. The ridges on their backs poked up through the water's surface, which could potentially warn a person of their presence if not for how well the animal's skin blended with the murky blue of the water. Full-grown ankliors were roughly ten feet long with slimy, blue skin and four gangly limbs that they used to propel themselves through the water. Their mouths were filled with rows of tiny, serrated teeth that dug into flesh and could cleanly tear skin right off the muscle. They were not to be trifled with.

"Yup," said Ryckert. "Guy who posted the notice lived on the outskirts of town, and one of his dogs was killed by an anklior that decided to explore the marsh a bit and found its way to his cabin. Saw the whole thing, but couldn't do nothin' to save his pet. Worried the beast might come back and get him or his other dog."

"I can't believe you agreed to kill it," Aava said, sitting back in her chair. She had finished her third kabob, and she was absolutely stuffed. She swore she wouldn't be able to eat for another week.

"Weren't easy, I can tell you that much. More'n a bitch to find in the first place, and once I did, the bastard didn't go down quick. Certainly got some scrapes and bruises that day. That thing's belly is where this went," he said, pointing to his left ear, which had a chunk missing. "Lucky it didn't take a bigger piece. But the man was grateful. Name was Jin, just like my ra. That's why the notice caught my eye in the first place. Paid what he promised and cooked me a hearty supper, too."

"And then what?" Aava asked. She had no idea what time it was, and she didn't care. She didn't want the story to end. Though once she had the thought, she began to feel guilty about not being at the clinic. She needed to leave soon.

"Then I started doin' monster killings in addition to normal hunts for butcher shops. Pay was a lot better. Eventually led into other mercenary work, and I found I'd stumbled into a career."

"It sounds like your father prepared you well for it."

"Did," Ryckert nodded. "Was a hard man, but he taught me well."

Aava was about to request one more story (*And then I'll go*, she promised herself), but before she could, their attention was caught by men yelling outside. She saw Ryckert's ears flick in the direction of the noise. Michio looked puzzled by the long pause in conversation.

She could tell they were voices, but she couldn't make out specific words. "Can you hear what they're saying?" she asked.

Ryckert nodded and pushed his chair from the table, rising and going to the door with haste. "Somethin's headin' toward the beach," he said, heading outside.

Michio shot Aava a confused look. She said to him, "Something is coming."

~ what? ~ he scribbled down messily.

"I don't know," she answered, though she had a pretty good suspicion. Her stomach sank and she felt like she was about to throw up, though she couldn't tell it if was because she had eaten too much or because of the bubbling anxiety.

The two mages joined their friend outside.

- -

Ryckert had a guess as to the cause of the commotion, and it was confirmed mere moments after stepping outside. He ran from his front porch to get a better view of the cliffside staircase and saw familiar figures racing haphazardly down the steps.

It was two mirials, both somewhat large, like the first one Harold Hoskings had killed in the cemetery by himself. They were fumbling down the stairs, one behind the other, and the mirial in the back was leaving a trail of green blood splattered on the stone. One of its middle legs had been torn off and the stump was spurting the sickly-looking liquid.

At the top of the steps were three people who shouted at Ryckert once they caught sight of him. He recognized one as Bernard Tilling and another was Walton Vere, but the woman was unfamiliar.

"Stop them!" Bernard roared as he began his descent.

The other two remained stationary, and Ryckert noticed Walton was clutching his left shoulder, his hand streaked red with blood. The woman's shirt was ripped at the torso, and Ryckert was sure if he got a closer look he would find a nasty gash on her stomach.

Aava and Michio emerged from the cabin and rushed onto the sandy beach by Ryckert's side. Before Aava could ask what was happening, Ryckert said to her, "They're in bad shape up there. Once the mirials are on the beach, Michio and I will distract 'em. You get up there and heal those two."

"Right," Aava nodded.

"Once they're safe, might not hurt to come back down and give us a hand," Ryckert said.

Another nod. And then they were off.

Ryckert and Michio ran directly toward the mirials, which were almost to the beach, while Aava ran forward but curved right to avoid the creatures.

They were thirty feet away when the first mirial crashed onto the beach, its feet digging into the ground and spraying sand. Ryckert blocked his eyes and lurched forward, not realizing until that precise moment he had not brought a weapon outside.

His only thought was: *Fuck.*

He crashed into the mirial, wrapping his arms around the abdomen and wrestling it to the ground. It writhed and screamed, its tiny mouth filling with sand as Ryckert pushed its head down. Its back legs kicked wildly. Feeling inspired, Ryckert let go of the mirial's head and grasped one of its flailing legs instead, then yanked. There was satisfaction as he felt and heard the joints strain and start to tear.

Removing his weight from the mirial's front half proved to be a mistake. The creature used one of its freed front legs to push itself upward, knocking Ryckert off before any lasting damage was done to its leg.

Ryckert leapt to his feet and brushed the sand from his face, letting out a low growl. To his right, he now saw Michio dodging attacks from the wounded mirial, which squirted blood with every movement.

Bernard, looking quite disheveled and bruised himself, reached the bottom of the staircase and lunged toward Ryckert's mirial with a large blade in hand. He sliced downward, jamming the blade into the mirial's back before being kicked away by one of its meaty back feet. The insect screeched in agony and flailed side to side, shaking the blade loose. It flung in the air toward the water.

Bernard yelled a command that Ryckert didn't catch. The rocyan darted to his left, toward the discarded sword, but was cut off by the mirial. It skittered forward, standing between him and the blade, and let out a vicious hiss. Green blood and black pus oozed from its back, streaming down the dark green carapace. The green shell reminded Ryckert of something, but he couldn't place it.

He skidded to a halt but lost balance and tumbled forward in the sand, rolling stupidly on the ground before coming to a stop a few feet from the beast. The mirial shrieked as it raised a claw and brought it down on Ryckert's left arm, clamping shut, tearing through fur and flesh.

Ryckert screamed in pain, then glanced upward to find the mirial raising its other claw to strike. A second later, the mirial's upraised arm was separated from the rest of its body and lay motionless in the sand.

The mirial screamed and let go of Ryckert as it backed away, right into Bernard, who stood behind it with his sword in hand.

"Ryckert!"

He looked toward the sound of Aava's voice and saw her kicking up sand as she raced toward him.

"Stay back!" he roared, struggling to stand.

But of course she didn't listen. He wanted to keep her as far from the mirials as possible, but he should have known she wouldn't care about the danger. She was braver than that.

He had only gotten to his knees by the time Aava reached him. "Is anything else hurt?" she asked, circling around to his left arm.

"No," he grunted. The pain was fiery and immense. There was a rush of warm blood running down his arm, staining his fur.

He stared down at the grains of sand while Aava performed her white magic and could feel it reconstructing the torn muscle, sewing his skin back together. The fur that had been clipped off would need to regrow on its own.

"That all?" she wanted to confirm.

He nodded.

And with that she was up, heading toward Michio. Ryckert saw the young mage had been knocked on the ground, his left leg bleeding profusely, ironically matching his foe. Michio performed an elaborate gesture with his hands, and for a few moments nothing seemed to be happening, but then the mirial's two front arms exploded in a shower of blood and pus that rained down on the beach and onto Michio. Aava let out an alarmed cry and stopped in her tracks.

Bernard was handling himself fairly well in Ryckert's absence. He did not look to be injured, and the mirial was stumbling back and forth with its other claw severed.

As Ryckert stood, he saw Michio was now on his feet as well, his leg looking good as new thanks to Aava. She turned her attention to Bernard and Ryckert.

The rocyan ran forward for an attack in spite of being weaponless. He mentally chastised himself for his own error, not thinking to even grab a dagger before going outside. He had known the shouts were because of mirials—what else would cause such a fuss?—so he was ashamed of his own recklessness.

The mirial was visibly angry. It lacked its two most useful weapons, so it and Ryckert were equal in that regard, and it wanted revenge. It bent its four remaining legs and propelled forward, but its trajectory was interrupted and it crashed midair into nothingness, though Ryckert caught sight of a faint blue glow as the mirial crumpled into a heap on the beach.

Ryckert shot a glance toward Aava and saw her arms raised, and he knew she had cast some sort of Shield magic.

He moved forward, a chill tingling down his spine as he passed through Aava's Shield, and knelt beside the sputtering mirial. It was alive, but barely. He grasped the creature's head in his hand, digging his claws into its skull, shuddering at the sensation of its feelers sliding between his fingers and the mirial's six eyes blinking against his palm. Bernard stood nearby and watched as Ryckert forcefully separated the mirial's head from its body, which instantly went limp.

Michio's target was hardly moving, having lost a considerable amount of blood from its three discarded limbs.

Finish it off, Ryckert wanted to yell but could only manage to think, flooded with exhaustion.

But it was as if Michio could hear him anyway. He lifted his gloved hands and swung them in a circle, criss-crossing his fingers too quickly for Ryckert to comprehend. The mirial's body began to pour blood from unseen holes before completely falling apart, its head tumbling to the ground as its torso separated from its last three legs, a few eyes popping out of their sockets. It was unlike anything Ryckert had ever seen, and it was a grotesque showcase, but it got the job done.

"Mighta been better if you'd done that from the get-go," Bernard called out.

Ryckert managed a chuckle while Aava silently mended Michio's minor wounds. After doing so, she returned to Bernard and asked if he had any. As she healed Bernard's scrapes, Ryckert collapsed in the sand, his breathing heavy. His stomach felt like it was carrying a pile of rocks. It was never a good idea to eat a full meal before a fight.

"I need a fuckin' nap," he groaned.

- -

In most cases, Theo would not have left Lyrra on her own in her current condition, but Al's house was just across the stream from his own and the man had promised to make the Saens a casserole. Theo was grateful for the chance to relax and not worry about preparing a meal, especially since Lyrra's appetite was so unpredictable as of late.

Al greeted Theo at the front door with a wide grin and invited him in. Al's decoration was sparse; he had the expected furniture like a kitchen table and a sofa, but there were no frills. No paintings hanging up, no plants tucked away in corners. The kitchen table didn't even sport placemats. It was a simple life that Alfred Opping led.

"How's Lyrra?" Al asked as he walked back to the kitchen.

"Not great," Theo confessed. "Still as sick as she has been."

"Shit. I'm sorry."

Theo shrugged. As a reflex, he had almost said "It's alright," but it wasn't. He asked, "What's this casserole you promised us?"

"Ahh," Al smiled, grabbing a deep, wide baking dish from the countertop. "It's my specialty. The one you love so much."

On the top of the dish was a layer of crisp, golden breadcrumbs baked on a bed of cheese and noodles. There was also cream of mushroom and various vegetables mixed in. Theo had eaten the casserole several times before, whenever Al felt fancy and wanted to cook. The man was a pretty decent chef when he wanted to be.

"Thanks," Theo said as Al placed the dish on the table. "I'm already starting to salivate. You can probably hear my stomach rumbling, too. Really, man, thank you."

"Not a problem," Al said, giving him a pat on the back. "Happy to do it. Hey, you hear what happened?"

Theo shook his head. He had heard people shouting outside while in bed with Lyrra, but he did not investigate. He chose to stay indoors and keep his wife safe, if it came to that. After a while, the hubbub had died down, and he had forgotten about it until now.

"More monsters showed up. That mage's Preservation spell wore off early, I guess, and they found Vanessa and Tarr's bodies."

Just the mention of Tarr Sheere's name made Theo shudder. *Poor Harley and Cid,* he thought.

Al went on. "Bernard and Walton and Kim tried their best to kill the things—even managed to rip one's leg off—but the damn things got away and were running all through town. People screamin' and running back into their houses while those three chased them. It was wild."

"Who told you all this?"

"I *saw* it! I was leaving the diner, and when I walked outside I saw the monsters—there were two of 'em—racing through town, crossing Main Street. They went down to the beach. Luckily that rocyan and the white mage were down there. So was some other guy, a mage that I haven't seen around before—friend of the girl, I guess—and all of them kicked those things' asses. It was impressive as hell. Bernard ran down there and helped too. He and the rocyan make a good team."

"Ryckert," Theo said. When Al looked as if he had no idea what he was saying, he clarified, "The rocyan's name is Ryckert."

"Oh, right. Yeah. Well, he and Bernard were tag-teaming one of those ugly bastards while the black mage blasted the shit outta the other one."

"Damn," Theo muttered, thankful that he had stayed inside with Lyrra, away from the creatures. But he couldn't stop his mind from wandering to thoughts of Lyrra's body being shredded by those beasts, whatever they were. He felt like he was sinking into the floor.

"—out of here," Al finished.

Theo blinked. "Sorry," he said, "my mind was somewhere else."

"I said that's why I'm getting out of here," Al repeated.

"What do you mean?"

Al took a seat at the table, in front of the casserole dish. Steam rose to the ceiling, but suddenly Theo wasn't very hungry.

"What do you mean what do I mean? The town's going to shit right now, man. Everyone is getting sick and crazy monsters are attacking us every few days. It's a miracle I haven't gotten sick already. Actually, it's a miracle that *you* haven't gotten sick, being around Lyrra. I wanna get out of here before my luck changes."

"Freya said it's not contagious," Theo said, "but...you're leaving Balam?" Theo imagined returning to school to work with Serys and not having Al as a filter between the two.

"Not *leaving*-leaving. It's temporary. Until things blow over and everything's back to normal. But yeah, for now, I'm leaving."

"Where are you going?"

"Bral Han's always been pretty good to me," Al said with a toothy grin. "But if I get sick of big city living, maybe Brigher. I'm not sure yet."

Theo nodded. It was an attractive prospect to him as well, but he would never abandon Lyrra and she was too sick to go anywhere. He clung to the hope that she would recover soon.

"So this was a parting gift," Theo said, gesturing toward the casserole.

"I guess so. Didn't really think of it like that, but yeah."

Theo held his arms out for a hug. Al rose and they embraced.

"Don't be gone too long," Theo said.

"I hope I won't have to be."

"You can't leave me here with Serys all by myself."

Al laughed as they parted. "I wouldn't dream of it. I'll be back by the semester, if there's even a town to come back to."

Theo opened his mouth to say something, but he was at a loss.

"Sorry," said Al. "That wasn't funny."

He moved in for another hug, and Theo felt his own body shudder. He wanted to cry. It felt like he was going to burst from the stress. With everything going on, all the issues piling up on top of each other, now he had to face them all with his best friend gone.

As Al moved away, he said, "It won't be long. That white mage seems smart. I bet she'll figure something out pretty soon."

I hope so, Theo thought.

"Anyway," Al said, picking up the dish, "get this home and enjoy it before it's cold. You know how much better it is when it's fresh." He handed the dish to Theo.

Theo thanked his friend again and left. He walked down the cobbled pathway from Al's home to the short bridge connecting both sides of the stream and crossed, then took the northbound path up to his own home. He called to Lyrra as he entered, telling her he had lunch. But he knew she would not be able to get out of bed. He cut out some of the casserole and piled it onto a plate, then carried it into the bedroom to her. She thanked him and began to eat.

- -

Aava was worn out after using so much magic during the battle, so she was relieved when Ryckert, Bernard, and Walton offered to clean up the mess on the beach.

She and Michio bade their friend farewell, then ascended the steps to the main level of Balam. Something was weighing on Aava's mind, threatening to push her to the ground with each step she took. As the two reached the top, her clinic in sight off in the distance, Aava turned to confront Michio.

"We need to discuss something," she said, staying calm.

Michio's eyes looked to the ground in shame. It was obvious he knew what she meant. He had been found out.

"Let's go to my house," she said. It would be too difficult trying to hold a conversation with him while they walked, and this was a delicate matter anyway. Best to keep it private.

The walk to the clinic was short, but felt longer with the silent tension between them. When they arrived, Aava kept the CLOSED sign on the front door and locked it as Michio leaned against the examination table.

"You weren't using black magic," she said. No point in tiptoeing around the subject. Her brother was studying the craft, and being jeornish, she had been around magic all her life. It was easy to recognize black magic, and what Michio had done was no black magic spell she had ever heard of.

Michio shook his head. She was impressed that he wasn't denying it. That made things easier, in a way.

"That was red magic, wasn't it?"

There were several moments of hesitation, but eventually Michio gave a curt nod.

Her heart sank. She had been hoping, deep down, that it wasn't true. She knew it was, but she had hoped Michio wasn't that stupid.

"That's…" she didn't know what to say. Red magic, also commonly referred to as blood magic, had been outlawed by the jeornish for decades. It was considered a barbaric and unholy magic. It had been deemed unsafe due to how some spells could alter a person's perception of the world, blurring their understanding of reality, forcing them to behave in certain ways against their will.

Michio dug into his pocket and took out his notepad. When he held it up for her to read, he had only written one word.

~ *sorry* ~

The word meant nothing. It changed nothing. "Sorry" never took back anything that anybody did or said, and his reaction frustrated her.

He placed the notepad on the table behind him and slowly pulled off his gloves. As he did so, it dawned on Aava that she had not seen his hands at all since he had shown up in Balam. As he exposed his skin, it was clear why that was the case. She let out a harsh gasp.

Michio's hands, front and back, were riddled with scars. They were the same type of markings that every mage suffered when casting magic, the Ustrel symbols for each spell, but the symbols were etched much deeper into Michio's skin, to the point where the freshest markings—surely from their bout with the mirials less than two hours ago—were bleeding, staining his hands red. Aava couldn't tell how old the rest of the markings were, but when a white mage cast a spell, the symbol generally remained visible for only an hour or two, depending on how complicated the spell was. With red magic, the symbols scarred. They never went away.

And Michio's hands were completely covered.

Aava saw his hands were shaking, either from pain or nervousness. "Go wash up," she said, waving toward the sink.

As he did so, Aava tried to compose herself and figure out what to say, if there even was anything to say. Michio had broken the law and was dabbling in an unholy form of magic. She wasn't sure if she could forgive that.

When he returned, he scribbled another note on his pad.

~ *they found out at allinor. that's why I was kicked out* ~

"What are you thinking?" she demanded to know. "How did this even start?"

He sighed and began to write. It took a while, and his messy scrawl filled up almost three entire pages.

~ it started as an experiment with Kleus. he wanted to know what it was like and how hard it was and I wanted to know too so I agreed to try it with him. tracked down some old books about it in a library when we visited Bral Han one weekend. we practiced it in our spare time at night, when people had gone to bed already. simple stuff like illusory spells at first. Kleus was able to make me think I was lost in the deserts of Gillus. I even felt hot and started to sweat. he was always better at it than me. could even morph objects. first leaves into water, but eventually living things like rats into snakes ~

Aava stopped reading for a moment to absorb what Michio was saying, disgusted by his actions. He and his friend Kleus had been "experimenting" with reality-bending magic as if it were a parlor trick.

~ but one night we got caught. there was going to be a trial and everything, figure out how to punish us. but we managed to escape and decided itd be best to go our separate ways. been hiding out ever since. please dont tell anyone at allinor ~

Aava's body went cold and she knew she did not want to hear how Michio and his accomplice had broken free. Security at Allinor wasn't as strict or powerful as the Atluan Guard, but it wasn't laughable, either. Certainly savvy enough to contain students. If those students didn't have red magic at their disposal, anyway.

"Where did Kleus go?" was all she could think to ask. She had known of Kleus, but never really interacted with him while at Allinor. He was a shady guy and always seemed to be causing some sort of trouble; he was the type of person Aava aimed to steer clear of. The type of person Michio had turned out to be, though she hadn't known.

~ *dont know didnt tell each other. he went west & I went south* ~

She looked Michio in the eye, but he quickly averted his gaze, boring into the floor. He couldn't look at her, and if she was being honest, she could hardly look at him either.

"I think you should go," she said. But he hadn't seen her lips move. When he looked back up, she repeated herself.

He nodded and snatched up his notepad, stuffing it back into his pocket. He then started to put his gloves back on, to hide the evidence of his transgressions.

Once he was looking at her again, Aava said, "I don't just mean the clinic. You should leave Balam."

He stood there, mouth hanging open slightly, a glove halfway pulled onto his left hand.

"I can't be around you, Michio. Not knowing what I know. And anyway, you'll just bring trouble to Balam if you stay. These poor people have enough to worry about as it is without having to deal with mages storming in, on the hunt for you."

Michio nodded and resumed pulling on his gloves. He picked up his pencil and twirled it between his fingers. He looked to her, his brow and mouth both downturned, waiting to see if she would say anything else. Any last reassuring words.

But she didn't.

It wasn't like she had been expecting or wanting anything more than simple companionship, but she had been let down by him before. She didn't understand why she had fooled herself into thinking she wouldn't be let down again. She wasn't upset, or even mildly sad. She just felt dumb.

Michio moved past her and left without another word written or spoken between the two of them.

As she stood there alone in the clinic, surrounded by white walls, Aava shut her eyes and took in a deep breath. She held it for a few seconds, then let it out. She blinked away the fatigue she felt in every inch of her body and mind and went to the door to remove the CLOSED sign.

CHAPTER XIII

HER RADIANT LIGHT

The incident on the beach had Ryckert worried. The mirials were still coming despite their efforts to keep them at bay, and people were getting hurt. Thankfully, Aava had been able to heal the townsfolk who had gotten in the mirials' way, but things might not go so smoothly the next time.

Ryckert awoke the next day intending to venture into the Cerene Forest to search for the mirial nest again. He had no leads, no real tracks to follow, but he had to try. What use was he if he didn't at least try?

Asking for Michio's help was an easy choice to make. The young man had proven himself a worthy ally in the battle against the mirials, as well as against the hynterling during their first expedition. Ryckert's age was showing; he couldn't deny that any longer. He needed Michio.

He couldn't decide which of those two facts irritated him more.

After a quick but filling breakfast, he got himself ready (remembering to sheath two daggers this time, so as to not have a repeat of the previous day) and began the trek to Michio's campsite. Hopefully the mage was awake already and would be ready to depart soon, despite the plan being sprung on him.

The walk through Balam was quiet. At first, Ryckert had thought it due to everyone still being asleep, but he soon realized they were more likely staying indoors out of fear or sickness. Or they were already dead. He shivered, though the sun warmed his thick fur.

The hike up the stairs strained Ryckert's leg muscles. He hadn't noticed before how sore he was. Perhaps a hunt wasn't the best idea.

Gotta be done, though.

With much effort, he reached the upper level of town. He glanced to his left and saw the inn resting on the cliff and wondered how business was going. He wondered if the managers were blindly accepting travelers' money, or warning them about the sickness that had gripped the town and advising to go elsewhere. Based on his limited interactions with the inn's managers, he couldn't entirely rule out the former scenario.

The owner of the inn where Fenn had worked was a much more dignified person than Gregory Van re Von. Her name was Lily, and Ryckert suspected she was probably still running things over in Trael. He never pegged her as the type to pack up and move. She was firmly planted in that town, and she loved it. Fenn was good friends with her, and they had often invited her over for meals.

Ryckert shook the thought of Fenn and Lily out of his head and marched onward into the patch of woods Michio was calling home. He navigated through the trees, fallen twigs and leaves crunching underfoot, until he reached the face of the cliff where Michio had set up camp.

Except nothing was there. The man's pathetic attempt at a tent was gone, as well as—much to Ryckert's surprise—his trash that had littered the ground. If not for the area of grass flattened by Michio's tent and belongings, Ryckert would have been hard-pressed to find any evidence the mage had been there at all.

Strange.

At their lunch, Michio had made no mention of leaving town. This was so sudden. But Ryckert had noticed he and Aava had been growing friendlier with each other, and they had been involved with each other before. Maybe something had sparked again and he was staying with her. If nothing else, she would at least know where he'd scurried off to.

At her doorstep, Ryckert saw that she had not yet opened for business. He guessed it was close to nine o'clock in the morning by now, so surely she was already awake. He knocked loudly.

It took a minute, but eventually Aava answered the door, still wearing her bright pink pajamas. "Hi," she said groggily. "Sorry, I was still asleep."

"Late night?"

She nodded. "Trying out new potions. Not sure I have anything good, but hopefully I'm getting closer."

Ryckert didn't know how to respond besides agreeing, so he asked, "Can I come in?"

Aava's mouth hung open for a second as she considered. "Uh, sure," she said, stepping aside.

He entered, but immediately felt embarrassed on her behalf as he realized how self-conscious and perhaps vulnerable she felt, standing there in front of him in her pajamas. He decided to make this a quick visit and get out of her hair as soon as possible.

"Just wanted to see if you knew where Michio went," he said, jumping straight to the point. "Went to his campsite just now and it's all packed up. Not a trace of him."

Her mouth hung open again, then opened and closed a couple times as if searching and failing to find the appropriate words. Finally, she said, "I...had a talk with him. I told him to leave."

This struck Ryckert. He nearly blurted something out, but refrained. If Aava had asked the mage to leave, he trusted there was a good reason for it.

"What did he do to upset you?" Ryckert asked, hoping the answer wasn't something that would make him have to hunt down their former ally.

Aava shrugged. "He didn't do anything to me, not exactly," she explained. "He...well, do you know what red magic is?"

Ryckert had heard the phrase before, but he was not well-versed in any field of magic, so he wasn't entirely aware of the differences between them all—white, black, red. And had he heard of something called blue magic before? He figured the easiest answer was a shake of the head.

"It's a special form of magic that was outlawed a long time ago. I'm not sure exactly how it works—they don't really talk about the specifics of it much in school—but it involves altering reality. Red mages can craft highly detailed and realistic illusions in order to trick people, or they can alter a person's mind to implant false memories or force them to perform an act they would not otherwise perform. Those two reasons are mainly why the practice was made illegal, but red magic has other deadly uses as well, such as manipulating the body—the way Michio killed that mirial yesterday was with red magic spells. I confronted him about it after we left your house, and he confirmed that he had been practicing the craft back at Allinor, and that was why he left the university. He got caught and was going to face trial. So he escaped and has been in hiding since."

It was a lot to take in. More than Ryckert had expected.

"How'd he even learn about this shit?" Ryckert asked. "Sounds pretty dangerous. Makes sense it was outlawed. Just surprised he was able to practice it at all, and that it ain't exploited by more mages."

"I'm not sure how widespread the practice is," Aava said. "The punishment is severe, so most just avoid it altogether. Those who experiment with it keep it as secret as they can, I suppose. But Michio found some texts about it in an old library in Bral Han."

"Why weren't they destroyed?"

"Your guess is as good as mine," she said. "Maybe the preservation of knowledge was more important than censorship. It's easy to assume that if it's outlawed, most mages wouldn't want to dabble in it and would only read the books out of curiosity, without intent to practice the magic itself."

"Easy to assume there are shitty people in the world who wanna do harm," said Ryckert with a low growl. It was unfortunate that they had lost a valuable ally, someone who could handle themselves well in a fight, but he had to admit there was some satisfaction knowing that his initial hunch about Michio had been correct.

Aava heaved a heavy sigh and plopped herself down on the examination table next to Ryckert. Her eyelids drooped and a frown was etched on her face. Ryckert felt a little guilty about congratulating himself for pegging Michio as a bad guy.

"You alright?" he asked.

She shrugged. "I dunno, I guess so," she said. "It's just frustrating. Everything keeps piling on, you know?"

He nodded. "I know. Seems like you did the right thing, though. Sometimes you gotta cut people loose. Simple as that."

"It doesn't feel simple," she said, her voice soft.

"Yeah," he said after a moment, crossing his arms. He had never been very good at consoling others, and this time was no different. He had no wisdom to impart. His life hadn't particularly been full of wisdom, and nothing his ra had taught him would be of any help here. "Had to let go of someone I had feelings for a few years ago. Hardest thing I've done."

She chuckled at this. That was a good sign. He continued.

"Loved him more than anyone else in the world, but I fucked things up between us. Did stuff I couldn't take back. Told him right away, hoped bein' honest would soften the blow, but it didn't. Dropped me pretty quick. Lettin' go of him, accepting that I couldn't be with him anymore…it took time. Lots of time." He was looking down at the floor, not wanting to make eye contact with Aava. "Might still not be totally over it. Gets easier, though. Everyone says that, but it's because it's true. It gets easier."

"I'm not even upset about losing *him*, really," she said, kicking her legs back and forth as they hung from the table. "I got over Michio a long time ago. We were never all that good of a match anyway, so I don't know what it is. This was just the final straw, I guess. With everything building up, this was just the thing that put me over the edge."

"Understandable."

She sighed again. "Thanks for talking with me. Or listening to me complain, rather. I appreciate it."

Ryckert's reply was curtailed by a frantic knock at the door. A familiar voice then came through from the other side. *"Aava? Are you in there?"*

Aava and Ryckert looked at each other. She scooted off the table and went to the door, seemingly oblivious to the fact that she was still in pajamas. She opened it and Theo Saen stood before her, wearing his pajamas as well, his hair unkempt and greasy.

"I need your help," he said, out of breath. He had to have run all the way to the clinic from his home. "Please. Please come. Fast."

- -

They rushed to the Saen household and Theo fumbled with his keys for a few seconds before remembering he hadn't bothered to lock the door, which he then yanked open, disappearing inside.

Aava looked at Ryckert uneasily before entering behind Theo. Now that they were all there, she felt uncomfortable about the rocyan coming. None of them had discussed it; he was simply present when Theo requested help, and so he ran with them.

Please, please, Aava thought to herself, praying that she would not have to deliver bad news to this man and wife today, but deep down she knew what was going to happen. A person did not look as hysterical as Theodore Saen had unless things were going terribly wrong.

She and Ryckert followed Theo's trail through the messy house into the bedroom. Clearly, Theo had not taken the time to clean for the past week. Dishes were piled in the sink, a jacket was tossed carelessly on the floor…Aava couldn't imagine what he was going through. There was no doubt Lyrra occupied most of his free time.

The bedroom, to Theo's credit, was more well-kept than the rest of the house. But everything gravitated toward Lyrra, who lay propped up in bed, her pale face sheening with sweat.

"What has happened?" Aava asked after taking a gulp.

"I don't know," Theo said hurriedly, slurring his words. "She just started hacking up blood or something. I don't know. We just need help. Please."

Aava glanced down at the blanket in Lyrra's lap and saw brown splotches matching the hue of the blood samples she'd taken from the other victims. If Lyrra was coughing up brown, Aava couldn't help thinking the woman was already too far gone.

There is nothing I can do, she thought but didn't say.

Lyrra choked back a cough while Theo, wide-eyed, looked back and forth between Aava and Ryckert. He seemed to be realizing Ryckert served no real purpose by being there, but it didn't matter.

"Please move aside," Aava said.

She took Theo's place next to Lyrra and grasped the woman's chin, gently opening her mouth. She peered inside and saw Lyrra's tongue had been stained by whatever she had regurgitated.

Next, she lifted Lyrra's shirt and was not surprised to find the large red blemish on the woman's swollen stomach, just as

Theo had described. Same as Freya. Same as the Dower boys. Same as everyone.

She gave Lyrra a weak smile and placed her left hand on Lyrra's stomach, a tingle going down her spine as she came in contact with the red mark. With her right hand, she began gesturing, and a faint white light emanated from her left hand then seeped into Lyrra.

"What're you doing?" Theo asked. His breathing had grown heavy, but his words were quieter and more deliberate now.

"Coughing up blood and skin discoloration suggests internal bleeding," Aava said. Usually if there was a spot on the skin, it would appear purple rather than red, but nothing about this illness was particularly normal, so she accepted it. "I am trying to repair any damaged organs there might be."

Lyrra's breathing slowed, calmed, and finally she was breathing normally again. As Aava removed her hand, Lyrra took a deep breath and let it out a moment later. "Thank you," she whispered.

Amazingly, Lyrra did seem to be improving. The sweating stopped as well, and Aava almost tricked herself into believing the woman might turn out okay. But then she began to cough again, spraying viscous brown liquid onto the blanket, which Aava narrowly avoided.

"What's going on?" Theo asked. "I thought you just fixed her. Why'd that happen again?" His words were gaining speed.

Aava ignored his question and commenced casting a high-level curative spell. It was a more general type of spell, something simple to seal a cut or mend a broken bone, so she didn't expect it to do a great deal in this situation, but it was better than nothing. If it could lessen Lyrra's pain even slightly, it was worthwhile. It was all she could realistically do at this juncture.

Aava had dealt with a handful of patients during her internships that were quite obviously beyond help. At a certain point, one had to accept that the sickness had conquered, and all that could be done was make sure the patient felt as little pain as possible before they passed. It was one of the harshest lessons Aava had learned, but it was the truth.

Sometimes you had to accept that you failed.

She wanted to scream at herself for losing yet another patient. Another life. She had not helped anybody. Maybe she wasn't fit to be a white mage after all.

"May I speak with you?" she asked Theo, nodding her head toward the door.

"I'll wait outside," Ryckert said, proceeding to leave the house as Theo and Aava entered the living room.

Theo crossed his arms and started pacing back and forth, not breaking eye contact with Aava. "What's the next step? What do we do now?"

"I'm afraid there is no next step," she said.

There was silence as Theo stopped moving. She cleared her throat and waited for him to ask a question, or yell at her, or throw something. She waited for the inevitable reaction.

"What does that mean?" he asked.

She sighed. She felt deeply uncomfortable—a feeling that was unavoidable in her line of work, when facing situations such as these—and she wanted to look away, to not have to see the anger and despair in the man's eyes, but she couldn't. She gave him her full attention.

"It pains me to tell you this, Mr. Saen, but I'm afraid there is nothing else I can do for Lyrra. I have cast Cu—"

"Are you fucking serious?" he sputtered. He ran his fingers through his hair and threw himself down on the sofa, his eyes fixated on the floor. "*Nothing?* There is *nothing* you can do?"

Her stomach tightened. There was nothing she could do or say to make the situation any easier for anybody. Nothing she could do to *make the patient feel more at ease.*

"I've done all I can," Aava said softly. "Unfortunately, it was not enough this time. I am so, so sorry. I truly am."

Tension crashed over them like a wave. Aava could see tears welling up in the young man's eyes. He didn't even look to be thirty years old and already he was losing his wife. It broke Aava's heart.

"I…" he muttered. She waited, but there was nothing more to the sentence.

Neither of them knew what to say.

Finally, Aava said, "I'll give you two some privacy. Please feel free to fetch me again if you need anything at all."

"Okay," Theo said. His eyes were blank. His voice was low, like his body was hollowed out.

She left.

She marched straight past Ryckert, back toward the clinic. He did not ask if Lyrra was going to be alright. They didn't say anything at all as they walked together.

\- -

Hours passed.

Aava Yren continued experimenting with potions and spells, though in her heart she felt that the disease had beaten her and the rest of the town, despite her best efforts.

Harold Hoskings finished and began reading another Balthaz He'ra novel while he waited for his daughter to come home from her girlfriend's house.

Bernard and Lisa Tilling chopped hollion steaks together.

Ann Marie Toish served drinks at the bar, thankful that attendance was low and she could relax a bit.

Kim Reen planted tomato seeds on the eastern side of the farm and pondered how she would react if her daughter were to become ill and pass away.

Bromley Dower cooked himself dinner, accidentally preparing too much food that he would never be able to finish on his own.

Harley Sheere lay in bed with Izzy Hoskings, kissing her and running a hand up her shirt across her bare back, attempting to resist ripping the shirt off but making it difficult for herself.

Rufus Reede sat at his desk, trying in vain to distract himself with history books and memoirs, wanting to think about anything besides all of his fellow townspeople perishing.

Serys White stood at the grave of Freya Jeyardin, silently mourning the loss of the woman he had loved most in the world, and regretted never telling her how much she had meant to him.

Ryckert Ji'ca went out searching for a mirial nest, as he had planned, but did not venture far into the forest before returning to the diner to eat supper.

Lyrra Saen coughed, and cried, and her condition did not improve.

- -

The rash on Lyrra's stomach worsened, turning a dark shade of crimson. It was like a smear of blood on her body. A marking.

She lay in bed with her shirt cast aside on the floor. She said it pained her when it rubbed against the rash. The cough was more severe, and Theo was hauntingly reminded of how harsh Freya's had been that night.

He held her hand tightly in his, sitting in a chair by her side. He didn't want to get in bed and shift the mattress with his weight, in case it caused her any pain or discomfort. She stared at him with wide, pleading eyes.

He wanted to say to her that he would help, that he'd make things better, but presently he didn't know how. He said the words anyway, because that was what she needed to hear, and he was her husband.

Lyrra whispered something too low to hear. He asked her to repeat herself, and with a strain she said, "Water."

Theo rushed into the kitchen to get a glass of water. He filled up the first cup he found—he was too frantic to check whether it was clean or not, but in truth, he doubted it mattered at this stage—and carried it into the bedroom in unsteady hands, splashing droplets on the floor.

It wasn't easy for Lyrra to sit up, but finally she managed and was able to drink with Theo's assistance. She lay back down with another cough and closed her eyes.

Theo's leg bounced up and down uncontrollably like a restless rabbit. He bit his lower lip, his mind racing, trying to think of what to do. He fought back tears. There had to be something else. Some solution none of them had thought of. Why hadn't Aava concocted an antidote yet? What the fuck was the problem?

Anger filled him.

Anger at Aava for not knowing how to fix his wife.

Anger at himself for not being the one to get sick instead of Lyrra.

Anger at his father for pushing him away and leading him to this shitty town in the first place.

He tried to relax. To take a step back. It wasn't his father's fault they were here; and even if it was, he and Lyrra both loved it here. They'd spent many amazing years in Balam together. It was their home. He didn't regret moving here. Yet part of him still did, because he knew that if they were somewhere else, Lyrra wouldn't be sick and everything would be okay.

"Water," she croaked, and Theo once again helped her drink.

"I'm gonna get Aava again," he told her. It was all he could think to do. Surely there was another spell Aava could cast to delay things. To ease the pain. Something. *Something.*

Lyrra lethargically shook her head. She winced with each turn. Her body was sore and every movement was an ordeal. She said a single word, too quiet to hear, but Theo knew what it was.

The word was *stay.*

So that's what he did.

Part of him still wanted to retrieve Aava, who was probably just sitting in her stupid little dome, reading a book about plants or some other nonsense that wasn't getting anybody anywhere. His thoughts were scattered—he wanted to blame Aava, even though the rational side of him knew it wasn't her fault at all. But he couldn't stop being angry. He kept imagining her sitting at home, doing nothing, not being here to help his wife. The only person that mattered to him.

Now it was impossible to hold back the tears. They streamed down his face as he watched Lyrra's. She kept her eyes closed now, coughing every thirty seconds or so. And then suddenly her eyes shot open.

No. No.

But it was happening.

Lyrra lurched forward, clasping her hands to her throat. She sputtered out more coughs, barely able to get them out, practically choking herself. High-pitched wheezes and shallow breaths. Her wide eyes glanced over at Theo, who stared blankly at her.

There was nothing.

Nothing he could do.

He wanted to scream.

He wanted to push her back down onto the pillow, grab her wrists. Tear them away from her neck. Tell her to just stop, fucking stop, this isn't funny this isn't right this isn't what's supposed to happen just stop stop fucking *stop*.

Her eyes looked desperate and she let out a small, shrill shriek.

Stop no this isn't right this isn't—

Lyrra's grip tightened. Her eyes were nearly popping out of her skull. She would be an eyeless corpse if this kept up.

Theo hesitantly reached forward to grab her shoulder, but she violently jerked away, sending herself falling onto her right side. She convulsed in the bed, still choking out harsh coughs, unable to intake any air.

Say something please stop no stop no stop—

Theo stood and took a step back, unable to do anything but watch. He couldn't touch her, he couldn't speak, he couldn't help, all he could do was watch his wife die.

She's dying, she's going to die.

His mind leapt to the image of his sister, standing at the edge of that cliff in Dusceir sixteen years earlier. The look on her face when the men turned her around to face the crowd.

The crowd that included her family. Her friends. And strangers.

All who came to watch her die.

And for what reason?

What was the point?

And Theo, ten years old with no power to stop it, just stood helplessly and watched his sister die. One of the few people he truly, deeply loved in the world, standing before him with tears streaming down her face, gazing at all the people who could save her but didn't.

In that last instance, she had opened her mouth to say something.

Her eyes had looked directly into Theo's, and he thought he knew what she was going to say. But before she could eke out the first syllable, Roderick Carlon pressed his dagger to her throat and cut. Blood spurted out, ran down her neck onto and into her shirt and then Roderick pushed her over the edge into the sea two-hundred feet below.

Watching Lyrra now, Theo felt as powerless as he did all those years ago. This was just another outside force taking away a woman he loved for no discernible reason. It was death for death's sake.

Her hands relaxed and her breathing slowed. She began to retch, as if her body were rejecting some foreign entity. She vomited a small mixture of water and blood onto the sheets. Her breathing then picked up again and she blinked wildly.

Soon it's going to be over soon this is the last part this is the last part soon she'll be gone—

He gently placed a hand on Lyrra's arm. Their eyes connected. He could barely see her through the tears. He blinked them away so he could see her when he said this. Really see her. Really mean it. There was no way he could miss this moment, because it would be the defining moment of his life.

He said, "I love you."

Lyrra's mouth moved, but no sound came out. She inhaled a deep, loud, painful breath.

This time he wouldn't let it go unsaid like he had with his sister. He and Gwen might not have had the opportunity to say it to each other there at the end, but he had seen in her face that she wanted to. Had tried to.

He said, "Goodbye."

Her breathing began to slow, as did her blinking.

She mouthed the word *bye*.

She looked at him with sunken eyes. The light in them was dimming.

The moment had come and he was not prepared.

He looked at her stomach, at the huge, red, violent splotch there, and realized her body was still. His eyes locked on hers and he could see that she was gone.

No not gone no not gone—

Theo almost had to remind himself to take a breath. He moved around the bed to the other side of the mattress and sat down, edging nearer to his wife. He delicately lifted her head and placed it in his lap. He couldn't break away from her face. Teardrops fell and stained her cheeks. With trembling fingers, he pulled her eyelids shut.

The anger had left him. It was replaced by something he couldn't quite name. His instinct was to call it grief, but it felt more powerful than that. More animalistic.

But it didn't matter what it was called. All that mattered was this moment. The last real moment he would share with her. He had lost her radiant light, and now he felt hollow, and he felt finished.

One word looped endlessly in his head: *gone*.

He needed to give Vir water. It was past her dinnertime and she was outside, probably patiently waiting in the cold, nibbling on the grass. The thought of getting out of bed was nearly inconceivable. It was too much to process. His body was too heavy.

And all at once, he was struck by the immovable fact that he would always carry this sorrow with him. It would be part of everything he said, everything he did. It would be a part of any woman he loved, and if he ever had a child, it would be a part of that child. He would see it in the glittering waves of the ocean and he would hear it in the brisk winter winds. There would be good days; he knew he would know happiness again, but this sorrow would always be within him. Because Lyrra was the first woman he truly, deeply loved, and the first woman who ever truly, deeply loved him. Completely knew him. But she was taken away, sucked from this world before she should have been. And he would always carry that sorrow with him.

He cried for a long time.

When he could finally manage, he softly placed Lyrra's head back on the mattress and scooted out of bed to feed Vir. As he stood, he noticed her copy of *Lyrical Tide* on the bedside table, with a bookmark placed three-fourths of the way to the end.

Out in the backyard, he looked up at the yunesca tree. Half of its leaves had now fallen and littered the yard. Vir was rolling in a small pile, delightedly squealing. The blue against the green grass looked weirdly beautiful.

"Hey, girl," he called. "Wanna keep me company?"

Vir rolled over and shook off a couple leaves that had stuck to her back, then sprinted over to Theo. She was getting bigger, he realized. She was up to his knee now. Just a couple weeks ago, when all this had started, she had barely been past his ankle. All the chaos in Balam had made him blind to how much his little seroko was growing.

"Want some water?" he asked, his voice breaking on the last word. Filling Vir's bowl was the most normal of activities, but it didn't feel normal anymore.

The seroko grunted in affirmation. He rubbed her head, flopping her ears back and forth. He began to cry again, and he hugged her tight.

Vir's tail wagged excitedly at first, then slowed. Theo held on for several moments before letting go. "Let's get you something to drink," he said, then grabbed her bowl and went inside.

CHAPTER XIV

QUIET

The day after was a blur.

Aava had agreed to come over in the night to cast Preservation on Lyrra's body until it could be moved elsewhere. Theo slept on the couch with Vir curled up on the floor. His arm dangled over the edge so that he could run his fingers through the animal's fur while her body heaved with steady breaths.

In the morning, there was much to be done. Rufus Reede was knocking on Theo's door not long after seven o'clock, offering condolences and explaining the next steps that needed to be taken.

Theo went with him to the cemetery, where he picked out a gravesite for Lyrra. Mr. Reede told him he had already commissioned a tombstone, and that it should be completed by the following day.

"Of course," Mr. Reede began uneasily, "it will mostly be...*symbolic*, I suppose is the word. We will have to ask our lovely white mage Aava to cast Cessation on the body, given the recent attacks on our village. You understand, right, Theodore?"

Theo nodded, but said nothing. He didn't want to think about his wife's body disappearing forever. It was too much. In the end, it was no different than burying her—either way, he would never see her again—but somehow it *was* different. He shook the thought. He would confront it later.

After choosing a spot, Mr. Reede returned to his nearby home and Theo walked back to the central part of town by himself. He stopped at the Sonata Diner to eat breakfast, where his order was taken by Missy Reen, who did not seem to be aware of what had recently transpired. She was as chipper as always, taking his order with a smile.

While he sat at a table waiting for his food and coffee, Theo realized he needed to write a letter to Lyrra's parents. His stomach churned, his brain feebly attempting to wrap itself around the prospect of how one is supposed to tell two people their daughter is dead. Worse, he knew they would not be able to come in time for the funeral. Bral Han was a few days' travel, and everyone in Balam would be anxious to get rid of Lyrra's body before any monsters showed up to claim it for themselves.

He was still trying to piece together what to write to Daere and Calyssa Fiss when Missy placed a plate in front of him. He had no appetite, but knew he needed to eat something, so all he'd ordered was a fried egg and a piece of toast. Steam drifted lazily from the egg, mixing in the air with the steam from his mug of coffee.

"Anything else I can get for ya?" Missy asked. "Awful small plate you've got there."

Theo shook his head. "This is fine. Thanks."

She smiled. "No problem, Mr. Saen." She returned to her post behind the counter.

Theo was glad not many people knew yet. It allowed him to have a subdued breakfast before the storm that would be his next few days. Or weeks. Or months. He didn't know how long things would be turbulent. But at least he had this simple, quiet meal.

It was hard to accept that he wasn't the only person affected by the disease. Several people had died already, just like Lyrra, and yet he had not felt the impact until it happened to him. While he ate, he thought of Bromley Dower, probably still asleep, alone in his bed in his empty house. At least he had Vir. Bromley had nobody.

I forgot to feed Vir.

"Fuck," he muttered, scooting awkwardly out of the booth with his meager meal still half uneaten.

"Everything alright?" Missy asked. With low attendance in the diner, his swear was impossible to miss.

"Yes, it's fine," Theo said, trying not to appear so flustered. "Just forgot to feed my seroko. Gotta get home."

"Want me to wrap that up for you?"

"No, it's fine," he said, now at the door. He pushed it open and heard Missy say goodbye behind him.

His feet were on autopilot as he navigated home. He didn't register anything he saw, anyone he passed by. His mind was focused solely on Vir, and then Lyrra's parents, and then Lyrra.

Lyrra is dead, he wrote in his head. It sounded too abrasive.

Lyrra has passed away.

It was sudden. Our white mage did all that she could do, but it wasn't enough. There is an epidemic in Balam. Nobody knows what it is.

Maybe that was too much information. They didn't need to hear about the town's woes. All they cared about was their daughter.

He had no idea what to write.

Vir was happy to see him when he returned home, but the seroko's perkiness soon subsided. He could tell she knew there was a melancholic vibe permeating the household. The door to the bedroom remained closed so that she wouldn't wander in while he was gone.

He brought Vir's bowls in from the backyard and filled them up, placing them on the kitchen floor in case she got over-eager and spilled water. Theo watched as the animal devoured her food and slopped up her drink. He sat cross-legged on the floor and stroked her back. It put him at ease, helped him momentarily forget everything that needed to be done.

After Vir was taken care of and Theo had wasted as much time as he felt he could, he sat at the kitchen table to compose his letter to Mr. and Mrs. Fiss. It had taken a great deal of effort to find a loose sheet of paper and a writing utensil in the living room and kitchen, given that he had not wanted to venture back into the bedroom just yet.

He tapped the pencil's tip on the table, searching for the right words. Nothing came to him. It was an impossible letter to write. After a while, he grew so frustrated he began to cry, and he sat there at the table sobbing while Vir propped herself up on his chair, trying to see what was wrong and how she could help.

Around ten o'clock, a while after Theo had regained his composure and managed to scribble out a few words for the letter, Aava showed up to cast another Preservation spell on Lyrra. When he acted confused by her presence, she explained that the spell's effects only last a certain amount of time before needing to be renewed. Given the spell seemed to be the only thing warding off the monsters (which she referred to as "mirials"), it was vital that she periodically return to cast it until it was time for the Cessation. Theo shuddered at the sound of the word.

He then slept until almost one o'clock in the afternoon, but nightmares plagued him and he awoke groggy and unrested.

The thought occurred to him that he wanted Lyrra close by, even if only symbolically. He shuffled out the door and returned to Mr. Reede's massive house on the farmland and rapped his knuckles on the door three times. It wasn't long before Kim Reen answered.

"Hi," she greeted him with a frown. "I'm so sorry to hear about Lyrra. Please let me know if there's anything I can do."

So Mr. Reede had told Kim. There was no doubt she would tell her daughter the moment they saw each other. Everyone would know sooner or later.

"Thank you," Theo said. "Is Mr. Reede here? I'd like to speak with him."

She ushered him inside and went to grab Mr. Reede. Encountering the man's employee reminded Theo that he had to inform the inn of Lyrra's passing. Another task added to the ever-growing list. Mr. Reede entered the room a minute later, surprised by Theo's visit.

"Theodore!" he exclaimed. "What can I assist you with?"

"I don't want that cemetery plot," Theo said, diving right in.

"What do you mean?"

"I'd prefer burying—well, I guess not *burying*, but—you know—having the gravesite in my backyard. I don't need the

342 · travis m. riddle

tombstone either, though I appreciate you setting that up. I really do. But I'd rather have something smaller, and I'd like to have it in my backyard so I can go outside and visit whenever I want."

"That would be most irregular," said Mr. Reede, cocking his eyebrows. "We bury everybody in the cemetery, as you know."

"Yes," said Theo, growing irritable. "But I would like to *not* do that. It wouldn't be a disruption to anybody. My yard is fenced off on one side, has a river on the other, and it backs up to a cliff. It wouldn't be in anyone's way. No one would even be able to see it, really."

Mr. Reede scratched his pointed chin, pondering the proposition. Though if the man denied his request, Theo was going to ignore him and do it anyway. This meeting was more a formality than anything else.

"That sounds fine, then," Mr. Reede said finally. "Sounds perfectly reasonable to me! I will stop construction of the tombstone and mark in my records that the plot you chose is now available once more."

"Thanks."

"Not a problem at all. Do not hesitate to ask if I can be of further assistance."

"I won't," said Theo, before taking his leave. He garnered one more sympathetic look from Kim as he departed.

The Cessation was to take place later that evening, so there would be no time to plan or hold a proper funeral. Naturally, Theo wanted to say his goodbyes, so when he got home, he began preparations for his own private service in the yard.

It would just be him and Vir. The other people he would have normally invited were either out of town, dead, or too annoying to be around in such a dark time. He wanted to keep things quiet for as long as possible.

The sun was beginning its descent when he felt ready to begin his service. He had lain Lyrra's body on the bed of fallen yunesca leaves, and he couldn't stop himself from smiling at how peaceful she looked. Her white hair rested on the blue leaves, with tiny pink flower petals amongst the strands, and her hands sat one atop the other on her stomach. She was plucked straight from a fairytale.

Vir was at his side, and together the two of them sat in the grass, watching over Lyrra. Theo scratched behind the seroko's ear as the wind blew, knocking more leaves loose from the yunesca tree on the cliff above, which floated lackadaisically down into the yard, dancing around Lyrra.

I didn't prepare anything to say.

It would be stupid to say anything aloud anyway, given that Vir was his only audience, but still, it felt wrong not to say a few words. It was a funeral, after all.

He moved forward, not bothering to stand, instead walking on his knees. Vir trailed behind him. He came to a stop at the edge of the leaf pile and placed a hand on top of Lyrra's.

"I'll miss you," he started.

He had intended to say more, but the words caught in his throat on their way out. Tears streaked his face, dripping off his chin, darkening the blue leaves.

You didn't deserve this, he thought, since he couldn't produce the words out loud. *You deserved much more than this. You deserved the whole world.*

He closed his eyes and wished she could say something back. Wished she would sit up, blink, and ask him just what in the hell was going on. But she wouldn't.

He tightened his grip on her hand, not wanting to let go. He felt Vir nuzzle against his back and he coughed out a sob at the seroko's touch.

And then he felt his hand rise, ever so slightly.

Lyrra was moving. Bobbing up and down. She was breathing.

He opened his eyes and saw that hers were still shut, but he wasn't imagining things—her stomach was going up and down. He let go of her cold hand and wiped away tears.

"What the hell...?" he murmured, watching. He could hear something, the faintest noise. It was like a gurgle, which then shifted into a slow, deliberate tearing sound.

And then her arms were flung aside as her stomach burst open.

Flesh was torn apart as a small insectoid creature fought through the blood and the organs and made its way out of her body. Its green carapace was slathered with brown blood and a dark ooze. It was a mirial.

Theo pushed himself backward as the creature snapped a claw at his face, emitting out a terrible screech. It scuttled toward him but he kicked it back, sending it sprawling over Lyrra's desecrated body.

Vir raced toward the monster and jumped over Lyrra, landing a solid headbutt on the mirial, sending it flying further back toward the rocky cliffside.

"Vir!" Theo called, trying to steady himself. His entire body was shaking, and he could barely support his own weight. "Get away from it!"

The seroko seemed to understand. She shot him a look and then backed away from the mirial, which was spitting out a disgusting, tar-like goo as it regained its footing. Once it had, it skittered forward again, but curved to its left, aiming its trajectory toward the river.

Theo remained still as he watched the beast crash through the fence and lunge into the water. His eyes followed the mirial floating down the river, toward the waterfall at the beach, until it was past his house and out of his line of sight.

He collapsed in the grass, catching his breath, before it dawned on him what had happened.

He sat up with a jolt and scrambled forward to Lyrra's body, which now lay nearly torn in two, her blood splattered all over the grass and the blue yunesca leaves. Pink petals spotted with red.

Theo once again held her hand and bawled quietly. He was too shaken to even make a sound. He sat there in the grass, holding Lyrra's hand, thinking about how she had deserved so much more.

CHAPTER XV

SOME MOONLIGHT

The sun had hardly set when Aava knocked on Theo's door. She waited a few minutes, allowing the man time to compose himself, but when there was no answer she knocked again. And when there was still no answer, she began to worry.

Her immediate thought was suicide. She prayed that was not the case, but she had to be ready for the possibility. She knocked again, hoping the door would swing open and the young, handsome man would be standing before her.

But Theo did not answer.

Aava stepped away, interlocking her fingers behind her back. She swayed anxiously side to side, contemplating what should be done. It was then she heard a faint noise coming from around the back of the house.

She walked around the side of the house, alongside the river, and came to the wooden fencing perpendicular to the house and river. She leaned forward, trying to peer around the building, and she could just barely make out the shape of Theo kneeled down on the ground, hunching over what appeared to be a body.

What is he doing?

She wanted to call out, but at the same time she did not want to interrupt whatever it was he was doing. The grieving process was a delicate thing, and everybody had their own way of processing emotions. But the Preservation spell she cast earlier would be wearing off soon, if it hadn't already, so measures needed to be taken to ensure the safety of the town.

So she said, "Theo!"

The man's head turned lethargically to look over his right shoulder. He leaned over a bit, to where he could spot Aava standing at his fence. She offered a meek wave before he disappeared into the house.

She returned to the front door and was greeted a moment later by Theo. His eyes looked sunken; his cheeks were red and wet.

"Sorry," he apologized. "I didn't hear you arrive."

"There is no need to apologize," she assured him.

He granted her entry, and as she walked through the living room, he asked her to wait.

"Is something the matter?" she asked, nervous. It was already an uncomfortable, depressing situation. She couldn't imagine what else he was about to stack on top of it.

"Something…happened," he said. "You might wanna get Ryckert."

"Why Ryckert?" she asked. Suddenly she noticed a tear in his shirt. "Are you hurt? Did a mirial come and attack you?"

"Yes," he said. "I mean—no, I'm not hurt, but yes, I was attacked. But it's—"

She had to interject. "I'm so deeply sorry, Theo," she said. "I should have been here sooner. I didn't think the spell would have worn off yet. Please forgive me."

How many times can you screw things up? she internally chastised herself for the error.

Theo put his hands up and waved away her apology. "No, please, it's alright," he said. "But it's…it's more complicated than that."

"But a mirial came."

"Yes. So I think you might want Ryckert here to check things out." After a beat, he said, "He's your go-to guy for all this, right? It seems like he's been the most involved in all of this, besides you."

That was true. Ryckert had certainly gotten himself tangled up in this immense mess. If Theo believed that whatever happened required Ryckert's attention, then she would listen to him. It was the least she could do.

"Should I tell him anything specific?" she asked, heading back out the front door.

"No," Theo said. "Just that he should hurry, maybe."

- -

Ryckert stood at the shoreline, gazing at the waterfall crashing into the murky ocean water.

He had been sitting outside in his chair, enjoying a glass of whiskey and some moonlight, when he had heard a splash in the direction of the waterfall, distinctly different than that of the usual water. But when he had gone over to investigate the disturbance, he had found nothing.

He didn't waste much time attempting to solve the mystery, however. There was a glass of whiskey waiting.

Ryckert returned to his chair, its legs digging deeper into the sand as he slouched down in it. He lifted the sweating glass up off the ground, where it had made its own recess in the sand. He knocked it back, relishing in the liquid's burn as it coursed down his throat. Using his sleeve, he wiped away at his furry lips.

He looked at the stretch of beach that had recently served as a battleground. He reflected on his tussle with the mirial, the way its green shell had been caked in blood and goo. It reminded him of something, but he still couldn't place his finger on what it was, exactly.

A second glass of whiskey was calling his name (though he was distressingly close to the bottom of the bottle), but as he was stood to fetch it in his cabin, he spied Aava descending the staircase onto the beach.

He met her at the bottom of the stairs. "Want a drink?" he asked. He hadn't been expecting company tonight, but it was welcome.

"I'm afraid not," said Aava. "Something has happened at Theo Saen's house."

"Is it his wife?" he asked.

"She passed last night, but that's not it. I'm not sure what happened, really. He just requested that I come get you. And he said to hurry."

It seemed he wouldn't be enjoying that second glass of whiskey after all. At least the bottle would last a little while longer.

"Lead the way," he said.

There was no conversation between the two as they marched up to the middle tier of Balam and made their way down Main Street, branching off toward the Saen household. When they arrived at the entryway, the front door was ajar, as if beckoning them inside.

"Theo?" Aava said with hesitance, edging the door open further. "We're here." There came no reply. "He must be out back," she said, entering the house.

Though Theo wasn't there, they were greeted by a plump, white seroko with a friendly squeal. Aava leaned down to pet the animal on its head, cooing softly, before proceeding. Ryckert followed her into the kitchen and out through the back door. In the yard, they found Theo bent over his wife's limp body.

Aava let out a horrified gasp and stepped back toward the door. Ryckert remained silent and kneeled beside the man, who remained motionless as teardrops slid down his face.

The body had been nearly ripped in two. It was a scene not unlike the other corpses that had been mangled by the bloodthirsty mirials. Ryckert placed a compassionate hand on Theo's shoulder and squeezed. He said nothing.

"It's not what it looks like," said Theo.

The statement was puzzling. Ryckert didn't respond, but Aava asked him what he meant.

"It's kind of what it looks like," Theo said. "A...what do you call those things? Mirials?" Ryckert nodded. Theo continued, "A mirial did this. But it didn't come from the forest or anything. It came from inside her. It burst out of her body, like it'd been growing in there, or something." He started to cry again, choking out the words between deep breaths. "It tore through that red spot in her stomach. Just tore through her like paper. While I was sitting right here beside her."

Ryckert was silent as he processed this new information. That was why he and Michio had been unable to track down the mirial's nest in the forest: there was no nest. They were incubating inside the corpses.

Aava held a hand to her mouth, her eyes bouncing around between Theo, Ryckert, and Lyrra's body. She appeared to be at a loss as well.

Finally, Ryckert was able to ask something. "What happened to it?"

"Hmm?" Theo mumbled, looking at the rocyan.

"The mirial. Where'd it go?" he asked. "If you'd killed it, I expect we'd see a corpse somewhere 'round here."

Theo pointed a thumb over his shoulder. "It jumped into the river," he said. "It seemed pretty adamant about getting into the water. It didn't really want anything to do with me."

Ryckert's eyes followed the river running on the other side of the fence, which he knew led to the waterfall near his home.

The splash.

It had been the mirial tumbling down the waterfall, crashing into the water below. But it hadn't swam back to the shore, nor had he seen it bobbing above the surface of the water. He had examined his usual fishing area, as well as peering out into the ocean. Nothing.

And then he realized what the mirials' sickly green carapace had reminded him of.

He asked Theo, "Is there anything behind the waterfall?"

The man blinked, confusion muddling his features. "What do you mean?"

"Is there a cavern or somethin' behind the waterfall on the beach?" he asked. He had never looked himself, and he had never heard anyone in town mention it. What reason would he have had to ever search behind the waterfall?

"I don't know," Theo shrugged. "What does that have to do with anything?"

Ryckert turned to Aava, who had her own scrunched-up look of befuddlement on her face.

"I think there might be somethin' back there," he said. "And I think the mirials are tryin' to get to it."

"What are you talking about?" Aava asked, still standing several feet away. She made no move to join Ryckert and Theo.

"Seems to me like the mirials are tryin' to get to the water over there. Didn't really think about it before. Like when we were tryin' to figure out who would've poisoned Freya: I was lookin' in the wrong place. Kept lookin' for a nest in the forest, searching for where they came from, not where they were goin'. Theo's mirial rode the river down the waterfall, and those two the other day came down to the beach. Hell, the tracks I followed into the forest ended at the edge of a cliff. If these things are sprouting from the bodies, then there was another one that came from the Dower boys and the ugly bastard must've scrambled off the edge and jumped right into the ocean."

"But what could they want in the ocean?" Aava asked. "What's drawing them to it?"

Ryckert stood, moving toward the door. "Like I said, don't think it's the ocean. Think there's somethin' behind the waterfall. Been catching fish near there that have grown more and more discolored. Scales are the same green as the mirials. Didn't think much of it until now, but I think somethin' back there is poisoning the fish and somehow it's spreading to the townspeople, too."

"Shit," Aava muttered.

Ryckert stared at her. Theo turned to look as well.

"What?" she asked, dropping her hand to her side.

"Just never heard you swear before," Ryckert said. "It was weird." He coughed out a chuckle. Aava did too.

"Well," she said, "what are we going to do about this? It seems like you're onto something."

"To be fair, thought I was onto something all those other times, too," Ryckert said with a grimace. "But it's worth lookin' into. If I'm wrong, all that happens is I get a little wet."

"*We* get a little wet," Aava corrected him.

"No," Ryckert shook his head. "Ain't plural. I'm goin' alone. Don't need to risk your own hide for this."

"Ryckert, excuse my language again, but don't be an ass," Aava said with a stern look, her brow furrowed. "I've been involved with this since the start, just like you. We have shared these blunders, and I want to help this town. That's why I came here in the first place. I'm going too." She added, "Plus, who was it that stopped you from bleeding out on the beach the other day?"

He grinned and gave a resigned shrug. "Guess you've got a point," he said. "Alright. Won't fight you on this. Need to get anything from the clinic?"

"No, I'm fine. Do you need to get any weapons?"

"Yeah, but we're passin' my shack anyway. I'll grab 'em on our way to the waterfall."

He started to leave when Theo piped up.

"I wanna go too."

Ryckert and Aava both turned to face the man, who now stood before his wife's body. Scattered blue leaves and pink petals had been blown on top of it by the wind.

Ryckert crossed his arms. He didn't want to say it aloud, but he saw no point in bringing a schoolteacher along on their expedition. "Why do you wanna go?" he asked. He cocked his head toward Aava and said, "She had a good reason. What's yours?"

Theo brushed dirt off his pants and said, "Those things killed my wife. She's gone. Or if it wasn't *them*, exactly, then *something* weird killed her, and I want to know what it was. I need to know. And whatever might be behind that waterfall, the answer is there."

Ryckert could see desperation in the man's green eyes. His red hair was greasy and matted. He probably hadn't bathed in a few days, preoccupied with caring for his ailing wife. Ryckert could recognize that desperation, that feeling of loss and hopelessness. Feeling like you didn't have anything to lose. He knew that if he were in Theo's place, he would want answers too. Who the hell was he to deny him that?

"Okay," said Ryckert, turning the knob and pulling open the door. "Let's go, then. Grab what you need, then we're headin' to the beach. Don't got no time to waste."

They went back into the house while Theo gave his wife one last look before following.

- -

What the hell am I doing?

It was a thought that repeated itself several times over in Theo's mind as he made his way down to the beach with Ryckert and Aava.

He had no combat experience. He had barely any experience of any sort. He severely doubted the mirials could be killed by one of his lectures. Maybe bored to death, if you asked one of his students, but that was it. All he had thought to bring was a half-empty bottle of water.

Once they reached the bottom of the staircase, their feet in the sand, Ryckert faced Theo. The rocyan looked grim.

"You sure you wanna do this?" he asked. "Ain't no shame in goin' back. Wouldn't blame you."

Theo's mind flashed to the sight of Lyrra torn open by that green, nasty bug. It sent a chill through his body, and he adamantly shook his head. "I'm sure," he said.

"Okay."

They filed into Ryckert's shack one by one, and Theo took in his surroundings while Ryckert quickly ducked back outside. He had never expected to be inside the rocyan's home. They were never friends before, so the situation hadn't seemed like a possibility.

Ryckert returned a couple seconds later with an empty glass in hand. He snatched a nearly empty bottle of whiskey from the kitchen counter and poured himself a shot. He gulped it down and asked, "Either of you wanna partake?"

Theo knew he was a lightweight. Better to not warp his senses for the trek; he was already in over his head as it was. "No thanks," he said, waving his bottle of water as if to say *I'm fine with this.* Aava declined as well.

Ryckert shrugged and poured himself one more, which he downed eagerly. He sighed with satisfaction and placed the empty glass in the sink, then disappeared into the only other room in the cabin.

He reemerged holding two weapons. In his left hand was an impressive dagger, a foot and a half long including its hilt, though most of its length consisted of the blade, which had a serrated edge and a sharpened tip.

In the other hand, he held a greatsword with a dull ruby set in its hilt. His muscles flexed as he held it aloft. Theo imagined both blades had stolen their fair share of lives.

"Gonna need to arm yourself," Ryckert said, presenting both blades to Theo. "Aava's got healing covered, and I ain't gonna let you bumble around bein' dead weight. If it comes down to a fight, you gotta fight."

Theo's stomach knotted, and he felt like he would've vomited if there was any food in his stomach to throw up. If they found themselves in the middle of a battle, he didn't anticipate seeing the other side of it. His death would be swift, that was certain. But there was no use arguing with the rocyan. He had already agreed to come on this expedition despite Ryckert's reluctance to let him join.

"I'll take the dagger, I suppose," he said, pointing.

"Good choice," Ryckert said. He lightly flipped the dagger into the air, grabbing it again by the blade, extending its hilt toward Theo. "This thing's gotten me through a number of scrapes."

"Does it have a name?" Theo asked, taking the weapon. It was heavier than he'd expected, but it was a satisfying heft. He already felt powerful, just holding it.

Ryckert scoffed at the question. "No," he said. "It's a fuckin' dagger."

Theo's cheeks flushed. "Sorry. In books, they just always name their swords and stuff."

Ryckert barked out a laugh. "There's lots of goofy shit in books, I guess," he said. "Harold Hoskings told me I should read the books about…what's his name?…Balthaz? Balthaz something. Some series about a rocyan. You ever read those?"

Theo knew what he was referring to. "Only two or three," he replied. "They're alright. Kinda cheesy. But cheesy can be fun, sometimes."

"Does Balthaz name his blades?"

Theo nodded. "I think so. I don't remember what he calls his sword, though."

"Ain't a rocyan alive that ever named his sword," Ryckert laughed. "I'm callin' bullshit on that one. Sorry, Harold."

He procured a sheath for the dagger from his bedroom, which he then handed to Theo after demonstrating how to fasten it to his belt. It was a simple enough procedure, but Theo was inexperienced and wanted to ensure he wasn't messing it up. Not when his life was potentially on the line. Ryckert then secured a sheath for his own weapon.

All the while, Aava sat at the kitchen table, patiently waiting for the two to arm themselves. She looked nervous, which made Theo nervous.

"You okay?" he asked her.

She smiled weakly and tucked her silvery white hair behind her ears. "I'm okay," she nodded. "Just ready for this all to be over."

Theo nodded too. He couldn't disagree with that.

Once Ryckert had sheathed his blade, he asked, "We all ready to go?"

Theo and Aava both affirmed and the trio headed out the door. The sand shone silver in the moonlight.

"Pretty night," said Ryckert as they trudged through the uneven sand toward the water's edge, where the waterfall crashed violently into the ocean. Nobody said anything else.

They came to a halt at the shoreline. Theo realized he was either going to have to venture onward barefoot or get his shoes soaking wet and ruined. He tried to determine which was worse.

"Well," Ryckert said, then breathed in. He let it out and sighed, "here we go."

The rocyan was first into the water, and based on his lack of reaction, Theo had assumed the temperature was fine. So it was a shock when he stepped into the water and felt how deeply, bitterly cold it was as it filled up his shoe and was absorbed by his sock. It was an intensely uncomfortable sensation, and it wasn't any better when the rest of his body was submerged up to his neckline. He swore a few times as he swam behind Ryckert, toward the waterfall.

Aava was the last to get in, and she let out a high-pitched yelp as she did so. But she made no further complaints as she followed the two.

Theo felt weighed down by the dagger on his belt. He grasped the hilt in his hand, not wanting it knocked out of its sheath underwater and lost to the ocean's depths. The absolute last thing he wanted was to be forced underwater for its retrieval.

Ryckert stopped at the base of the waterfall, paddling in place. "Let's see what's back there," he said.

"After you," Aava said, her words staccato with the chattering of her teeth. Theo mentally applauded her; he hadn't even wanted to attempt speech.

Ryckert nodded, then said, "Brace yourselves."

He swam forward, the ice-cold water cascading onto his head, and soon he was obscured by the watery curtain.

Theo was next. He took a deep breath and swam forward, almost letting out a scream as the impact of the waterfall pushed him underwater. The cold penetrated his skin, assaulting all of his senses, pounding at his brain. He surfaced with a gasp and looked around.

There was nothing. Just smooth, shiny rock that comprised the side of the cliff. He looked side to side, and Ryckert was nowhere to be found either.

He took a deep breath, then dove underwater.

With a great amount of willpower, he opened his eyes and winced at the saltwater. He instinctively tried blinking it away, which only worsened the problem. But he kept his eyes open, trailing them down the submerged cliffside. Somewhere between ten or twenty feet down—it was hard to tell just how far, exactly—he saw two legs kicking, soon disappearing beneath rock.

The side of the cliff seemed to curve inward. Theo had no idea how Ryckert had known or guessed, but he followed the rocyan's lead. He swam deeper and deeper, toward the bottom of the cliff.

His breath was already running out by the time he found himself underneath the cliff that held Balam's middle section. But once there, he looked upward and saw Ryckert ascending with haste. He did the same, cutting his arms through the freezing water and kicking his legs until he was sure they would fall off.

Theo was convinced he was going to drown, but as his lungs reached their limit, he finally burst through the surface of the water and took in a deep, relieving breath, like he had died and was being reborn.

Head above water, Theo found himself in the center of a large circular pool in a dim cavern. Ryckert stood on a smooth stone platform above eye level, holding out a hand to help him up.

Behind Ryckert was a large, pitch black opening leading to who knew where. Two thin canals, no wider than a foot each, extended from the pool and snaked through the room into the tunnel, on either edge of it. A small fish sped past Theo's left and swam down the canal, into the unknown.

"C'mon," Ryckert insisted.

Theo took the rocyan's hand and was hoisted onto dry land. He nearly slipped on the rock, but Ryckert helped him regain his balance. A moment later, the two watched as Aava's head popped up in the pool.

"Cold! Cold! Cold!" she shrieked, unable to refrain any longer, kicking her feet and paddling toward them with haste. Ryckert pulled her out of the water, laughing. "Not funny!" she said, slapping him hard on the shoulder.

"Kinda funny," Ryckert grinned, checking his sword. When he determined everything was in order, he turned to gaze out into the darkness before them.

"Whoa," Aava murmured.

"Yeah," Theo agreed.

He imagined the mirial that had burst out of his wife mere hours earlier swimming up onto the very rock where he stood now, scuttling into the looming opening before them. He could not begin to fathom what awaited inside. His first thought was a swarm of mirials, climbing the walls and over each other, squirting out their disgusting goop and chomping at the bit for a fresh meal.

"What do you think is in there?" Aava asked, voicing Theo's question.

Both of the men shrugged. Then Ryckert said, "Let's find out."

And in they went.

CHAPTER XVI

THE CAVERNS

Ryckert momentarily wished Michio had been present to cast Fire to illuminate their path, though he was now forced to wonder if that had been legitimate black magic or simply an illusion. Either way, it had burned bright, and it would've been handy.

The cavern smelled of rotten fish. They had to tread carefully, as the ground was slick with water and occasional globs of green liquid. Mirials had undoubtedly traveled these tunnels. Flanking them on either side, near the walls, were small canals wherein fish swam back and forth, some traveling deeper into the caverns and some fleeing into the ocean. Ryckert couldn't discern the color of their scales, but he would not have been surprised if they were a sickly green.

Theo reached his hand out to the wall as they walked, running his fingertips along the craggy surface. "I never knew there was a whole tunnel system under the town," he said. "I don't know if *anyone* knows. I've never heard anybody talk about it."

"Me neither," Ryckert said.

The tunnel curved to the west, toward what would be the center of town aboveground. By Ryckert's estimation, they would soon be directly underneath Main Street.

Being underground made Ryckert feel claustrophobic. It wasn't a sensation he normally experienced while in cramped spaces, but the only other time he had navigated any sort of subterranean tunnels, he had been consumed by an overwhelming sense of being crushed. Part of him was convinced that the ceiling was slowly getting lower and lower and would soon collapse on top of him. That same feeling was creeping in now.

Last time, he had been on an assignment in central Gillus and was searching through an abandoned temple (which had seemed jeornish in architecture to him, though according to history books the jeornish had never built settlements in Gillus). He, along with another man and woman, had tracked a roving troupe of bandits to the temple. They had found nothing inside, but Ryckert had spotted a hidden door in the floor which led to a widespread tunnel system underneath Gillus that connected the temple to three different towns. It had taken several hours of searching through the tunnels, but they eventually found their bandits and got the job done.

The breadth of these tunnels reminded Ryckert of that underground system back in Gillus. The ceiling towered almost ten feet above his head, and he was already taller than six feet himself. The width was enough for the three of them to walk side-by-side if they wanted to, along with an additional fourth person. Like the bandits' tunnels, this place had likely been constructed in order to transport goods, hence it being large enough to fit wagons. Ryckert wondered where it was the other end opened to, if its original creators had felt the need to bring resources in on a ship and transport them underground in secret.

But of course, that had to have been decades before, seeing as no one in Balam was making use of the tunnels nowadays, and no strangers had ever popped up unexpectedly by the waterfall. It was safe to assume nobody on either end knew of the tunnel's existence.

Ryckert only hoped they wouldn't have to walk for hours before reaching their destination, wherever it may be. He scratched anxiously at his chin.

His thoughts were interrupted by a low rumble emanating through the tunnel, almost powerful enough to make the walls vibrate. Ryckert could feel it in his feet. It had come from up ahead.

"The hell was that?" Theo sputtered. He stopped dead in his tracks and retracted his hand from the wall.

"Don't know," Ryckert confessed. He had never heard a sound like it before. It definitely wasn't a mirial.

"It might have been something from the town," Aava suggested. "Somebody's water pipes turning on, perhaps."

"Maybe," said Ryckert, though he wasn't convinced. "Just stay alert."

They pressed on.

Nobody said a word. The only noise was the slapping of their feet on the uneven stone as they walked. Ryckert appreciated the silence, which granted him an opportunity to listen ahead for any mirials. Or whatever else the cavern might hold.

They came to a fork in the path. One option was to continue straight, while the other was to veer right. Ryckert stopped to address his companions.

"Anyone got an opinion?"

Aava shook her head.

"Where are we trying to get to?" Theo asked.

"That's the question, now, ain't it?" Ryckert grinned. He pointed down the path to their right. "If my mental map's correct, that should lead us pretty much down Main Street. Maybe parallel to it, closer to the clinic. Goin' straight should lead us under the Sonata, toward the farm, and eventually the forest."

They each internally deliberated for a moment, but then Aava pointed at the ground just past Ryckert's feet. They turned to look and saw a faint trail—nearly unseen in the darkness—of a mirial's green blood leading down the path ahead of them, toward the farm.

"We're trying to uncover where the mirials are going, right?" she said. "As much as I would like to never see one again, it seems to me if we go that way, we'll run into it."

Ryckert nodded. "Good eye," he said, at the same time wondering why he hadn't spotted it himself.

Gotta retire for real after this one, he told himself, already unsure if he would be able to commit to it.

"Guess that settles that," Theo sighed.

Ryckert plainly heard a nervous quaver in the young man's voice. He could tell Theo dreaded the chance to wield his unnamed dagger. But Ryckert believed he would do fine in a fight; he never would have acquiesced and allowed Theo to come if he thought the man's presence would jeopardize the group.

So they marched forward as another rumble shook the tunnels.

- -

Aava's stomach was grumbling, and she regretted not suggesting they grab some snacks before heading out. There was no telling how long they would be down here now. Even Theo had his water, at least.

She hadn't been trained for a scenario like this. Plenty of white mages studied to be combat-ready, able to handle themselves in a battle and swiftly fire off protective and curative spells, but her area of study had been for clinical purposes. Her performance on the beach had been pure necessity, though she had to admit it had worked out fairly well in the end. Still, she felt uncertain about her skill.

The longer they walked, the sooner they would be facing another mirial. Or two. Or a dozen. Or however many had made their way into the tunnels and begun breeding with each other. There might be an entire swarm tucked away beneath Balam, biding their time until they overtook the village.

She longed for Svend's confidence. If she possessed even half of his cockiness, she would have no issue stomping through these chilled tunnels, spells blazing. He always thought he was capable of anything. The best black mage Atlua had ever seen.

The trail of mirial blood grew thicker as they proceeded, swerving from wall to wall. This seemed less like the secretions the mirials usually oozed and more like it was bleeding out, growing woozy with blood loss. She mentioned this to Ryckert and he grunted with approval. Theo remained silent.

Another fifteen minutes passed before Ryckert halted and raised a hand to stop them.

"What's—"

But Ryckert cut Theo off with a quiet *shh* and kept his hand raised. Aava narrowed her eyes, but squinting didn't help her see any better in the dark. She had managed to spot the trail of mirial blood, but whatever Ryckert had seen eluded her.

"Ready yourself," Ryckert whispered, slowly unsheathing his sword. Aava watched as Theo did the same with his dagger, his arm trembling.

She hastily waved her hands and cast Protect on her allies, granting each of them a soft green glow that eerily reminded her of the blood splattered on the ground.

Ryckert moved swiftly yet silently, raising his sword to strike. Theo lunged forward unsteadily, making much more of a racket as his shoes pattered against stone. Aava followed, keeping as quiet as she could.

The room they entered was round and closed off, a dead end. It was roughly the same size as her clinic, made even more similar by its circular shape. The two canals curved around the edges of the room, joining each other against the back wall.

As they moved ahead, the mirial came into view near the wall, with one foot dangling in the water. It didn't move as they approached.

The rocyan lowered his blade, and Theo followed suit. "Is it dead?" the latter muttered.

Ryckert nodded. "Seems so," he said, kneeling to examine the monster.

The mirial's corpse slouched against the stone wall, resting in a pool of its own blood, which had dried into a dark green crust.

"This one's small," Ryckert said as Aava joined him. Theo stood a few paces behind, fumbling to return his dagger to its sheath. "Don't stab yourself," Ryckert added.

"Ha ha," said Theo drily.

Ryckert went on. "About the same size as the one I killed in the cemetery. Must have come from the other Dower boy. This is the one that took off and leapt into the water."

"It looks like it bled out," Aava said.

"Mhm," the rocyan nodded. "Window was busted. Might've cut itself breaking out, or maybe it landed on a rock after it jumped. Either way, I'm surprised it managed to swim all the way over here and still make its way in so deep."

"Took a wrong turn, though," said Theo, finally having gotten a handle on his weapon. "Maybe it was delirious from losing so much blood, I dunno. But I'd be surprised if what they were all attracted to was an empty room."

"That's true," Ryckert said, rising. "Guess we chose the wrong way too."

Ryckert stepped past her and Theo followed, with Aava bringing up the rear. The faint green glow of her spell had not yet worn off, and it gave the tunnel a pleasant hue as they ambled silently through it.

It had been a relief to find that the blood trail had only led to one dead mirial, but her anxiety was already making a comeback, her body tense and brittle, as if with any step she might shatter like glass.

It's almost over, she assured herself.

They arrived at the fork again and Ryckert turned to their left, down the untraveled pathway. She could hear Theo sigh in front of her.

Aava smiled, thinking about the look that would plaster her brother's face when he heard about this adventure. His "prissy" sister getting down and dirty underneath the village, hunting monsters and solving mysteries. He wouldn't believe it at first. She could hardly believe it herself.

It wasn't long before they came to another branching path. Ryckert stopped at the intersection and sat on the ground.

"Let's rest a minute," he said, rubbing his head.

Aava asked, "Are you okay? Is there something I can do?"

"I'm fine," he said, waving away the proposition. Then he added, "But thank you."

She frowned, but accepted his answer. She took a step back and nearly bumped into the wall, but managed to catch herself. Not that it particularly mattered, but she wanted to avoid dirtying her clothes too much, if she could. She would not be sitting on the ground like Ryckert.

Theo had no qualms with it, however. He plopped himself down across from Ryckert and drearily held his head in his hands. The man looked exhausted, and Aava was genuinely surprised he had made it this far without breaking down, after what he'd witnessed earlier in the evening. She didn't know if it was courage or denial. Likely a mix of both.

Something was obviously wrong with Ryckert, but she didn't want to prod. She only hoped he was still prepared for whatever they faced deeper in the caverns.

She paced back and forth as another deep rumble shook the walls and burrowed deep into their bodies. They all exchanged an uneasy look.

- -

Theo was thankful it had been Ryckert who suggested taking a break. He had wanted to say something for a while, but was too self-conscious to speak his mind. He was already the outlier in the group, and he didn't want Ryckert or Aava to think him weak. To think it was a mistake bringing him.

He took full advantage of the stop (in spite of the atrocious odor assaulting his senses), especially after nearly peeing himself in the room with the mirial. When he had faced one in his backyard, he hadn't been anticipating it. Now that he was cognizant and willingly stepping into a dangerous situation with the monsters, he was terrified.

The rumble continued echoing through the tunnel as they rested. To Theo, it sounded mournful. Almost like a wail. Definitely not water pipes.

He gulped down a large sip of water and offered the bottle to his two comrades. They both accepted, and when Aava handed it back, there was only enough left for one more sip. He decided to save it for later.

"How're you holdin' up?" Ryckert asked, nodding toward him.

"I'm alright," Theo said, praying his voice hadn't wavered. He lazily ran a hand through the water, brushing past a startled fish.

It wasn't an outright lie. He was beyond scared by the prospect of facing off against a mirial in a real fight, but the expedition had taken his mind off Lyrra for the time being. Only now, while they sat here, did he think back to his wife who still lay on the bed of leaves in the backyard they once shared. Now that he knew there was no actual danger of the body being targeted by mirials, he supposed he could have a proper burial after all. Maybe a funeral could be arranged in a day or two, if Barbara Vere wasn't dead by then. He shuddered at the morbid thought.

"Hey," he said to Aava. She stopped pacing and addressed him with curiosity.

"Yes?"

"We, uh…you don't have to use Cessation on Lyrra anymore, right?" he said. "Since the mirials are leaving the bodies, not coming *to* them."

"I hadn't considered that," Aava said. "But you're right. I suppose we no longer need to uphold such precautions when it comes to the deceased." She winced at the coldness of the word. "At least the ones who have already suffered the mirials, like Lyrra. As for the others…"

Theo nodded then retreated back into his own thoughts. That was good. There was still time to write to Lyrra's parents and arrange a small, intimate ceremony. Something pretty. Something to contrast all the ugliness that had marred her final days. He was surprised to find that this news didn't lift his spirits as much as he would've expected.

No matter what, Lyrra was still gone.

He remembered the day they moved to Balam. It was a cool day, but they still dripped with sweat lugging cases into the house as they unloaded the carts they had hired.

Thankfully, the men who drove the carts had assisted Theo in moving their big furniture into the house, and with all of their boxes piled high and filling the living room, the two young newlyweds had collapsed on the couch, exhausted and ready for sleep despite it only being four in the afternoon.

Theo had sunk into the cushions as Lyrra rested her head in his lap, staring up at the ceiling.

"I never want to move again," she had said.

"I am going to die in this town," Theo laughed. "I forgot how terrible and tiring all of this is. No way am I going to move again after this. Let's unpack all our shit tomorrow and then never speak of this again."

"Agreed," Lyrra grinned. "What are we gonna do about dinner tonight, though?"

"Dinner?" he asked, incredulous. "You can eat?"

"I'm *starving*," she said, playfully smacking him on the chest. "Are you not? Did that not work up an appetite?"

Theo lightly whacked his hand on her belly in retaliation for the smack. "Quite the opposite," he said. "I could sleep for hours right now. For days, even. Don't wake me, I'm sure you can handle all this without me," he said, gesturing toward the crates that surrounded them.

The remark earned him an additional smack.

"Hey, hey!" he feigned hurt. "Alright, fine. We will consume food today. Obviously, cooking is out of the cards."

"Obviously."

"Not many options, though. We can go to that diner we ate at when we visited."

"I *did* like that soup…"

"Oh, the *starving* girl is only gonna get some soup?" he teased.

Another smack. "Soup can be very filling! Especially whatever it was I had there. Lots of good veggies. C'mon, let's go get some soup." She had then pushed herself up off his lap and stood, turning on her heel to face him. She pointed at the front door. "Soup! Soup!"

"I'm not getting soup," he laughed. "And really? Dinner right now? I don't know if it's even four-thirty yet!"

"So?" Lyrra asked, walking toward the door. "I'm hungry. We're grown-ups and we can eat dinner whenever we want! Let's go. Soup! Soup!"

They departed, locking the door of their new home, and held hands as they traipsed down Main Street to the Sonata Diner to buy Lyrra some soup.

Theo was displaced by another somber rumble coursing through him. It was a fitting way to be stirred from his memories.

"Guess that's our cue," said Ryckert, standing up. He held out a hand to assist Theo, who took it and was yanked upward with great force.

"Which way now?" Theo asked, gazing down their three options: forward, left, or right. All looked equally dark and ominous to him.

"Tried to pinpoint where the noise was comin' from while we sat," said Ryckert, pointing down the right-hand path. "Think it was comin' from there. That'd be my pick."

"Are we trying to find the source of that?" Theo asked. The plan sounded dubious, but he was in no position to question the rocyan.

Ryckert shrugged, lowering his hand. "Ain't got any better ideas. Do you?"

Theo shook his head and felt a growl in his stomach. He thought he wouldn't mind a bowl of Walton's soup as the trio ventured toward the unknown sound.

\- -

Ryckert still didn't have a single clue as to what could be producing the noise they continually heard while trekking through the caverns.

Another thing that came as a shock to him was how little resistance they were facing. So far, they had only stumbled upon one mirial, and it was already dead. The more he thought about it, though, it made sense; the other mirials had been killed by either him or another townsperson. He could only recall two that had escaped. Lucky break.

He listened intently as they navigated the twists and turns of the tunnel system, pausing to pay close attention to the rumbles, determining which paths they should take in order to reach the cause of the disturbances.

His ears seemed to be in better shape than the rest of his senses, which was another lucky break. Without them, they would have been aimlessly wandering for hours. This at least gave them a sense of purpose, even if it turned out to be yet another red herring, which had been abundant in this case.

A short while later, Ryckert noticed green stains on the left-hand wall. He swiped a fingertip through and found the substance to still be wet.

"Fresh," he said. "Looks like your mirial came through here not too long ago. Think we're on the right track."

"Great," Theo sighed.

Ryckert knew it was sarcasm, but he was genuinely feeling great about their hunt. After running down so many wrong paths—both literally and metaphorically—it was satisfying to feel like he had finally uncovered something. That the truth would soon stare them in the face.

Their journey lasted another half hour and involved multiple inane twists and turns that ended up winding them back toward the way they had come, descending deeper underground. With no real sense of space, surrounded on all sides by the same dusky stone and no light, it was impossible to tell how far below Balam they were. Ryckert had continued to map their route in his head, noting every turn they took, and his best guess was that they were now somewhere beneath the town square, though possibly closer to the pub.

Ryckert's tension and nausea still plagued him, but he managed to cope after their break earlier. If it came to combat, he was confident he could still hold his own. It would be a massive embarrassment if, after giving Theo such a hard time, he had to rely on the young man to save their skins.

Mirial.

It was a thought before Ryckert even registered he had heard the sound. But he could distinctly make out the scraping of the creature's claws against cold stone.

"Close to it," Ryckert whispered.

"Close to—?"

"Mirial," Ryckert answered before Theo could finish.

Ryckert edged forward in the dark and was suddenly filled with a warmth that he recognized as one of Aava's spells. The faint glow his body now emanated allowed him to see further ahead, and he was able to see the tunnel was about to funnel into a massive chamber from which there came a faint pink glow. The mirial's skittering footsteps bounced off the walls ahead.

"Dagger out," Ryckert instructed, unleashing his own blade. He grinned again at the idea of naming a sword. Such foolishness.

Still feeling the effects of Aava's Protect spell, the three crossed the threshold of the enormous chamber and were taken aback by what they discovered.

In the back of the circular chamber, directly across from the entrance, was a vast pool of dirtied water, from which hundreds—possibly thousands, Ryckert couldn't be sure—of gray, snake-like roots streaked with red slithered out of the water, latching onto the wall, and up through cracks in the ceiling. The canals which had curved through the tunnels came to a stop here, in the massive pool. Laying halfway into it was the hulking corpse of a beast Ryckert had never before laid eyes on.

It was insectoid, much like the mirials, but ten times as large and with much bulkier appendages, almost giving it the qualities of a slug, but with four thick legs that were tangled up together in front of the belly as it lay on its side, its thick head submerged in the water with its mouth dangling open. The creature's skin was a pallid pink that Ryckert could tell was once vibrant when it had been alive. From this dead creature came the pink glow that brightened the room.

The mirial that had escaped Theo's backyard was scuttling around the body, dipping its feet into the water, inspecting the mouth, trying to figure out what it was meant to do. It paid no mind to the three intruders.

"What in the fuck is that thing?" Theo whispered.

"Not a fuckin' clue," Ryckert replied.

Aava opted not to join in on their swearing this time.

Ryckert crept forward with caution, but it became apparent that the mirial was not remotely aware of them. He easily approached the monster from behind and stabbed his sword straight through the back shell, ending its life in an instant.

The mirial crumpled in a heap. Ryckert bent down and picked it up, then tossed it aside, far from the water. Green liquid was drifting from the larger animal's open mouth into the water, unmistakably similar in hue to what the mirials oozed.

Ryckert stepped closer, taking care not to sink his feet into the muddled water, and pressed a hand down on the creature's jaw. The flesh was soft, and he backed away before he accidentally burst through the flesh into its mouth.

"Those roots look familiar," Aava said, gazing up at the tendrils that hung from the ceiling and were soaking up the pool's water.

"It's the yunesca tree," Theo whispered.

The gray roots with the jagged red stripes matched the yunesca tree's trunk perfectly. Ryckert took another look at the creature's mouth, where the viscous green liquid was floating out and contaminating the water.

"Thing must've been wandering the tunnels and died," he said. "Just so happened to fall right here. Maybe it was drinking. Looks like whatever's inside it poisoned the yunesca's water supply, poisoned the roots."

Theo sat near the entryway of the room while Aava moved forward. He ran his hands through his hair, pulling at the strands. Breathing deep.

"If the tree produces pollen," Aava murmured, thinking through her theory as she spoke it aloud, "then…perhaps absorbing whatever this is affected the pollen, and people got sick when they inhaled it."

"Mirials were just searchin' for their mother," said Ryckert. "But mommy's dead."

Ryckert glanced back at Theo. He was staring straight ahead, glaring at the dead animal. Hatred burned in his eyes.

"I lived right underneath the fucking yunesca tree," he spat. "Why did only Lyrra get sick? Why didn't I get sick too? Or me instead of her?"

He rose and ran toward the beast, swinging his leg back then kicking with full force. His foot pierced the delicate flesh and broke right through, sending him careening forward until his entire leg was impaled inside the animal's stomach.

"Shit, shit," he sputtered, trying to jiggle his leg loose. When he finally extracted it, his pant leg was soaked with clear, thick juices.

Ryckert watched Theo attempting to shake the liquid off his leg, and while doing so, the rocyan noticed that a ways behind Theo, on the right-hand wall of the chamber, was a second huge opening leading to another tunnel. None of them had seen it when they first entered, too focused on the unidentified animal and the yunesca tree's pool.

"What're you looking at?" Theo asked when he noticed Ryckert staring past him. He turned to see what had caught the rocyan's eye.

It was then the low rumble they'd been hearing all night reverberated through the chamber, sending a violent ripple through the water. It had come from the opening Ryckert and Theo were gawking at.

Large *thump, thump, thumps* rang through the chamber, the lumbering sound of an enormous creature's footfalls, intertwining with the previous sound and sending a panic rippling through Ryckert with visions of a collapsing ceiling.

Ain't gonna happen, ain't gonna happen, he repeated to himself as the noises grew progressively louder.

"Ryckert…?" Aava whispered apprehensively.

He still held his sword in his hand. "Better get that dagger out," he said to Theo.

As Theo pulled the serrated dagger from its sheath, Ryckert noted that the man's hand was steady.

And then the creature came into view.

CHAPTER XVII

PINK

It was identical to the creature in the water, except its skin was lavender and a short, thick horn protruded from its forehead. It released another angry roar as it waddled toward its fallen companion.

Theo's leg was wet and cold, but he could barely feel it. His mind was latched onto a single thought: *these things killed Lyrra.*

He tightened his grip on the dagger's hilt and looked at its jagged blade. He imagined it slicing through the beast's purple flesh, tearing into the meat, the cries that it would unleash as he hacked away until it was silenced.

They killed Lyrra.

It was a mantra. Theo repeated it again and again in his head, justifying the fury bubbling up, ready to spew forth. He noticed his fingers turning blue, so he slightly loosened his grip. He couldn't wait to find out if this thing bled green like the mirials. He tensed his body, preparing to leap forward and strike.

"Wait," Ryckert whispered behind him, noticing the shift in posture. "Don't be hasty."

There was nothing hasty about this. They had come down into these chilly, dank, disgusting caverns to locate the source of Balam's misery and here it was, growing closer with every beleaguered step. They had come to kill these monsters. The rocyan hadn't hesitated for even a second when he stabbed his sword through the mirial's back; what was the hold-up here?

"They killed Lyrra," Theo said in response. He went to take a step forward—

"Wait," Ryckert growled sternly.

That one syllable was enough to stop Theo. He held his dagger and observed the animal's weary slog.

With every few steps, it loosed a rumbling wail that shook the walls. If this thing had been walking around underneath the village making such a racket, Theo couldn't guess as to how no one had heard it, or how there hadn't been a minor earthquake each time. They had to be much deeper in the ground than he'd realized.

Ryckert grabbed Theo by the shirt and heaved him backward as he and Aava retreated from the corpse, allowing the other creature to approach. Theo pushed Ryckert away once he regained his footing.

"What the fuck are we doing?" he whispered harshly.

"Need to calm yourself," Ryckert said, narrowing his eyes as he looked down his long, bumpy snout at Theo. "Don't think this thing's dangerous."

"What are you *talking* about? These things have killed probably half the town by now! Of course they're dangerous!" He sought Aava's support, but she didn't say a word. Ryckert nodded toward the scene playing out over Theo's shoulder.

The purple beast had finally reached the deceased pink one. It moaned again, sending a boom through the chamber, and kneeled to place its head atop the pink animal's backside.

The three watched as the creature nuzzled its companion, getting its body as close as it could. Theo thought back to that day he and Lyrra moved to Balam, sitting on the couch with her head resting in his lap. Just then the creature let out another somber roar.

They were mates.

It hadn't been roaring at them as it entered the chamber. It was crying. The sounds they had heard throughout the tunnels, leading them all the way here, had been this animal in mourning.

Theo put his dagger away.

"See now?" Ryckert asked, his voice barely audible over the animal's guttural bleating. Theo ignored him and watched the beast with awe.

He stood there, in front of Ryckert and Aava, and began to cry with the animal.

Everything that had been building up inside of him, suppressed while he went on this expedition with these two strangers, was suddenly bursting out and he felt an unbearable weight crushing him.

He thought about his mornings. How now he would wake up and look to his left and there would be nothing there. Cooking breakfast and brewing coffee for only himself. No longer calling out to ask if he should make four eggs or just three.

He thought about work. Standing in front of a classroom full of teenagers, whose family and friends had been lost to the disease, and how he could possibly bear looking them in the eye without profusely apologizing. And how when he went home afterwards, he would not have the comfort of his wife to wash away those pains or even just the stress of a regular work day.

He thought about his family. Losing his sister and mother to something so inexplicable, something so pointless, something he couldn't control, and how the same thing had happened to his wife.

He thought about his anger. How it had shaped his life, every relationship he forged and every choice he made. His anger toward his loss, the unfairness of it, had nearly driven him to kill this creature before him that had done nothing except lose who it loved most.

His hands were balled into fists and his body shivered as he mourned with the animal. His sobs were overpowered by the animal's, but he felt them both intermingling, becoming one blaring expression.

Aava placed a warm hand on his shoulder as she passed by. He immediately calmed, his breathing slow and deliberate. Tears rolled down his cheeks, but he was more in control of himself now. He closed his eyes a moment, welcoming the blackness, and when he opened them again he saw that Aava stood only a foot away from the hulking pink and purple bodies.

- -

She held out her hands, requesting trust from the beast. It lifted its head to scrutinize her as she took a tentative step toward the body.

After several moments of inching forward, taking care to keep an eye on the animal in case it became incensed, Aava placed her hands on the soft pink flesh, which still gave off a soft glow that illuminated her tan skin.

Somehow, the animal understood her intent. It stood and sluggishly backed away from its mate, each footstep sending a light quake through the ground.

Something inside Aava had told her what she needed to do. In her mind, it was the only thing that made sense.

She removed her hands from the creature. She waited a moment, her heart pounding in her chest. She kept her breathing steady, not wanting to incite panic from the massive animal that stood only a few feet away. She then began to gesture above the pink creature's body, her fingers criss-crossing languidly as she closed her eyes and focused on her spell.

As Aava's movements ceased, a flash of brilliant pink light filled the entire room.

- -

Theo wiped the tears from his eyes as the light faded. When it did, he saw that the large pink body was hovering several feet in the air. The horned animal apprehensively approached its floating mate, gazing with wonder. The pink flesh then pointilized, breaking apart into hundreds of thousands of shiny pink spheres which rotated in the air and faded away, leaving behind nothing except the pink glow.

Aava hastily backed away as the purple creature moved into the glow of its mate. It shut its eyes and basked in the light. Theo found himself crying again at the display.

The animal stood there for a full minute, until the glow dissipated, and then it opened its eyes to look at Aava. The mage stood her ground, not scared at all, but still Ryckert brought his hand to his sword on the off-chance the situation soured.

Aava and the animal locked eyes for a moment before the latter let loose a sound that was somewhere between a croak and a coo. And with that, it turned to leave the chamber the same way it had entered.

No one said anything as Theo continued to cry, continually wiping tears from his face.

- -

It took a while for Theo to compose himself again, and Aava couldn't blame him. She too had been profoundly moved by the creature's display as it soaked up the warmth and light of its fallen mate.

She felt an overwhelming sense of peace, sympathy, and—she had to confess—accomplishment. Somehow, after all she had tried and failed to do in Balam, she felt like helping this unknown creature grieve was the first thing she had truly done right. She hoped it would find peace.

She was proud.

But that still left the problem of the yunesca tree's pollen. Not everybody had succumbed to the illness, and it was true that many had already passed, but there were still some sick people walking around town at that very moment.

Aava looked to her left, into the large pool where the thick, green liquid still coalesced on the water's surface. A realization struck her.

Her lessons with Fahleran during the internship in Ebon-pass were coming in handy after all. The night the town's hunters had returned, all poisoned by vissians, had prepared her for this.

"Theo?"

He looked up, still fifteen or twenty feet away, sitting on the ground with his back against the wall. "Yeah?"

"May I have your bottle, please?"

As she approached, he gulped down the last sip of water.

He handed it to her and asked, "What're you gonna do with it?"

She answered as she returned to the pool's edge. "Getting a sample of the poison. I don't precisely know what it is, or what that animal was and how it was produced, but now that I've got a real sample of it, it should be relatively easy to craft an antidote."

As she explained this, she kneeled down and scooped as much of the green goo as she could squeeze into the bottle, making sure not to let her fingers come into contact with it. There might be no effect whatsoever, but it was better to play it safe.

"Simple as that?" said Ryckert, joining her at the side of the pool.

"Not quite *simple*, but not too difficult. I'll have to freeze the sample, in order to concentrate the poison and remove excess water, which there will obviously be a lot of. Perhaps I can acquire the help of that black mage Mhar, if he's still at the inn."

Satisfied with the amount of poison she had obtained, she lifted the glass bottle from the water and capped it.

"Then I'll need to introduce a small amount of the concentrated poison into a host—some sort of bulky animal, something sturdy—and allow its body to counteract against the poison, after which I can draw samples of the animal's blood and then from there it's a matter of brewing a potion using droplets of the blood. It's the same recipe and process that we use to craft other poison antidotes, whether it's from an animal bite or something like quillis, so I believe it should work in this case as well."

"How long's that gonna take?" Ryckert asked, staring at the green goop sliding around in the bottle.

"Not long. The entire process can take a few days, mainly spent waiting for the animal host's body to fight the poison, but I should be able to find a spell to accelerate it. The biggest hurdle might be finding a suitable animal."

Aava handed Ryckert the bottle, which he took without question. She then held her hands directly above the dirty water to cast Purify, all ten of her fingers outstretched, criss-crossing her thumbs into an *X*. She then curled the rest of the fingers then separated her hands. A symbol lightly etched itself onto the top of her left hand, next to a few Protect markings. She and Ryckert both watched as the remainder of the poison dissolved. The yunesca tree's roots were already looking more vibrant. There might still be some poison left in the tree, and some people would get sick, but she would have the remedy available and soon it would all be out of the tree's system.

"Is it dangerous?" Theo asked, still in his same spot on the ground.

"For the animal? No, not at all," Aava replied. "The amount of poison introduced to its system is minimal. It shouldn't be enough to cause a severe reaction, just enough to get the blood pumping and working against it."

Theo nodded. After a moment of consideration, he asked, "Is a seroko the sort of thing you'd be looking for?"

Aava shrugged, then nodded. "A seroko would work, yes."

"Maybe you could use Vir," he said. "She's a sturdy girl. Think you could get working on it tonight?"

"Absolutely," she said. "First thing I'll do when we get back aboveground is seek out Mhar Cown. Are you sure you'd like to volunteer Vir, Theo?" She knew he was fragile right now, and wanted to make sure he was thinking straight.

But the man nodded. "Yeah," he said. "I wanna help everyone who's sick. For Lyrra. As long as you're sure it's safe."

"I promise," Aava assured him. "I've concocted numerous antidotes in the past."

Theo stood, his pant leg stiff and darkened by wetness from the creature's stomach that had since dried. "Alright," he said. "Let's do it, then. No time to waste standing around here."

He turned and exited the chamber. Aava and Ryckert exchanged a smile.

"Good job," he said to her.

But she was modest. "It was a group effort!" she grinned.

"I didn't do nothin', and neither did he," Ryckert protested, following behind Theo. "It was all you."

"Without you, we would've never found our way down here. You may be an old man, but don't sell yourself short here."

He barked out a laugh. "Alright," he said. "Thanks."

- -

As the party weaved their way back through the shadowy tunnels, Ryckert confirmed his sense of direction had not yet begun to fail him in his old age; the mental map he'd plotted was nearly perfect (aside from one stray path, which Aava playfully chided him about), and they soon found themselves swimming through the waterfall, the ocean shimmering in the moonlight.

They dried off in front of Ryckert's home with some scrawny towels he found lying around, then proceeded into Balam to work on Aava's antidote.

It was just past midnight so most folks were already asleep, including Mhar Cown, who was thankfully still boarding at the inn. Aava had no reservations with waking the man up and explaining to him their situation while Theo went to fetch Vir.

Back at the clinic, they followed the process Aava had laid out in the caverns, with Mhar suggesting ways to speed up the procedure while Vir sniffed and inspected her new surroundings. Unfortunately, they determined that the fastest they could have an antidote ready was in two days, but it would have to do. Aava hoped she could keep people like Barbara Vere and Benedict Crogley alive until then. She didn't want to give Mr. Crogley the satisfaction of dying a horrible death like he always assumed he would.

After injecting the poison into Vir's bloodstream and monitoring her for an hour to make sure there were no unintended side effects, the trio split apart and returned to their respective homes.

There they slept, and they slept for a long time.

CHAPTER XVIII

SPRING

Theo awoke the next day after sleeping for almost ten hours. It was fast approaching two in the afternoon and his stomach was screaming at him, demanding sustenance.

He looked to his left and saw Vir curled up beside him in Lyrra's spot, still sound asleep, her breathing deep and relaxed. He smiled at her, though she had encroached on his side of the bed a little.

"Hey," he whispered.

The seroko opened one eye, then the other. She lifted her head and stared at him dully.

"Want some breakfast?"

At this, she unfurled and stretched before jumping off the bed and trotting into the kitchen. Theo followed behind and filled up her bowls, grinning as she ravenously devoured her delayed meal. For himself, he scrambled two eggs and heated up a piece of toast in the pan.

It felt good to cook. To get something done. When he finished eating, he scrambled one more egg and slid it into Vir's bowl, which she gobbled up in an instant, evoking laughter from Theo. He rinsed his plate and went out the front door.

In his mailbox was a notice from Mr. Reede, declaring that there was to be a town meeting on the farm this evening, as opposed to the town square near the yunesca tree. He deduced that Aava already informed Mr. Reede she was preparing an antidote, and that the yunesca tree had been the root of all their problems. Theo looked forward to seeing the excited, relieved looks on everyone's faces when they heard news about the cure.

But before then, there was something he needed to do.

He followed the cobbled path to Main Street, then toward Aava's clinic. He approached the door of the dome and knocked twice. While waiting, he basked in the warmth of the sun shining down. It finally felt like spring.

Aava answered, dressed nicely and appearing as if she hadn't actually stayed up into the wee hours of the morning working tirelessly to cure an entire town of a fatal disease.

She laughed at the sight of him, still wearing his pajamas. "Hello," she said. "Come in. I was just reading my mail. I'm glad to see Mr. Reede is being so proactive."

Theo followed her inside, wondering why everyone always laughed at his pajamas, but remained near the doorway. He didn't intend to stay too long. "Yeah," he agreed. "Mr. Reede's always working hard for Balam. He's kind of a kook, but you can't say he doesn't care."

She smiled, but it looked like something was bothering her.

"Everything alright?" he asked.

"Yes," she said, smiling wider. "Everything is fine. Just a peculiar letter from my brother, is all."

It seemed she did not want to elaborate, so Theo decided to drop it and instead ask what he had come to ask. "I was wondering if you would…do for me what you did for that animal yesterday," he said, taking his time to get the sentence out.

Aava blinked. "You want me to cast Cessation?"

"I think it's what I need," he said, resolute. "I think it would be best."

She nodded, then said simply, "Okay."

He sighed, relief spreading through his body. A weight was lifted. He was glad she didn't prod and ask what had changed his mind, because in truth it wasn't something he could pin down. He knew it must seem confusing, since he had explicitly told her the night before that it was no longer necessary, but after seeing how beautiful it had been…it felt like the right thing to do.

The two walked side by side through town, chatting about nothing in particular. Aava commented on how pleasant the weather was, and Theo concurred.

"I hope that chilly weather is gone for good. This is a nice change of pace."

Aava nodded, smiling, but said nothing further.

As they crossed Main Street, Theo asked her, "Are you planning on staying in Balam after you get the antidote to everyone? Or are you heading back to…?" He realized he wasn't sure what town she had hailed from.

She chuckled as he trailed off. "Back to Allinor University," she finished for him. "And I am pretty sure I'll be staying in Balam. I've come to like it here."

"Me too," Theo said. "Once you get past the weird design of it, it's a pretty nice place."

They both laughed. She said, "The set-up is pretty bizarre, isn't it?"

Soon, they reached Theo's home. Aava greeted Vir with a high-pitched voice and a pat on the head, and the seroko squealed with glee.

"She seems to be acting normal," Theo said as Aava crouched down, rubbing the animal's fuzzy head. "She's eating normally, she's not lethargic or anything. Just her usual self."

"That's definitely a good sign," Aava said, standing. "Let me know if it changes. I'll come by and check on her again tomorrow, though, if that's okay." He told her that it was.

They then entered the backyard.

Lyrra still lay atop her yunesca bed, half-covered by newly fallen blue leaves and pink flower petals, which mercifully obscured the opening in her abdomen.

Theo recalled their first date, watching the moon and the stars reflected on the water's surface at the foot of the waterfall, the taste of wine on their tongues as she kissed him.

"I love it out here," she had said that night.

And so he had given her one last night beneath the stars. He almost broke into tears again as he laid eyes on her, but he refrained.

He and Aava approached the body and kneeled beside it. Theo picked up a dry blue leaf and crushed it in his hand, scattering the small pieces as they fluttered in the wind. Aava said nothing, watching, awaiting her moment.

But there wasn't much Theo wanted to say to Lyrra. He hoped he had said everything he needed to when she was still alive. He hoped she knew how much she had meant to him. Nothing he said now would change anything, so he hoped he had been enough for her.

All he said was, "Goodbye."

And so Aava gestured above Lyrra's face, and she then slowly floated upward, leaves and petals falling from her body before being caught in the wind. They floated away lackadaisically. A light shone from within Lyrra, and then her body separated into bright, rotating spheres. Tears welled up in Theo's eyes as the form that made up his wife gradually faded into nothingness.

Rivers streamed down his cheeks, but he did not weep. He reached over and hugged Aava, taking her by surprise, but she held him tight, her silky hair brushing against his face.

"Thank you," he said.

"Of course," she whispered.

They separated and gazed down at the pile of blue and pink for a minute before returning indoors. Aava said goodbye to Vir, and Theo thanked her again before she departed.

He took a deep breath and let it out again. He looked around the room, begrudging the fact that he would need to clean it up sometime this week. Cleaning had always been his least favorite chore.

But that could be put off for one more day. He smiled at Vir and asked, "Wanna hang out in bed?"

Being unaccustomed to indoor living, the seroko didn't quite understand the word *bed* yet, but there was no doubt in Theo's mind that she would pick up on it soon enough.

"C'mon, let's go get in bed," he said, motioning toward the bedroom.

Vir eagerly followed him and jumped up onto the mattress, splaying her legs and laying flat on her potbelly at the end of the mattress.

Theo situated himself under the sheets at the head of the bed, leaning his back against the wooden headboard. He sighed and watched as Vir's drooping eyelids struggled to stay open before she gave in to sleep. The girl loved to nap.

He then looked over at Lyrra's nightstand and saw her book resting there, with a bookmark peeking out three-fourths of the way through. Theo reached over and grabbed the book and bookmark. He ran a hand over the smooth cover with the debossed text reading *Lyrical Tide: a novel by Killian Vearnas.*

He glanced over at the empty side of the bed, then back down at the book. He flipped it open to the first page and began to read.

- -

Aava left Theo's house and headed straight down to the beach, her brother's words still bouncing around her head.

She had been stunned to discover a letter from Svend in her mailbox. She didn't know why it had taken him so excruciatingly long to compose a reply, but she was glad he had finally found the time to do so.

aava,

> *sorry for not writing sooner. lots happning here. to much to explain in letter. need your help with smthing if you can.*

svend

It was short, and cryptic, and mildly concerning, but Aava was sure it wasn't a big deal. Most likely, he was simply struggling with his studies and required her guidance. The two had their fair share of late-night study sessions together back at the university. She wished there had been more of an explanation included within the letter, but that was typical Svend.

At the top of the steps, Aava paused a moment to gape at the shimmering surface of the ocean sprawling out before her. Until now, she had never spent much time on the coast. She guessed she possibly took a family trip or two in her childhood, but she couldn't recall a specific time. Her life had been spent in the wooded inlands of Atlua. Looking out at the sea, the world felt so much bigger than she ever imagined. She knew that across the water—many, many countless miles away—was the country of Gillus, but she had never really considered it before. Suddenly, she felt the desire to go out and see it for herself. Reading descriptions in textbooks was no longer enough for her. Beyond even Gillus was Herrilock. Maybe someday she would travel there, as well.

But one step at a time. She was still growing accustomed to the shores of Balam.

She smiled and closed her eyes, listening to the wind rustle the grass at her feet as the sun seeped into her skin.

That was one of the things she loved most about this place. Back at Allinor, and even in Oxhollow, they were always surrounded by so many trees, there was never a time when she could get this much sunlight. It felt so fresh, so freeing. The warmth made her feel at once cozy and powerful.

Behind and to her left, she heard a door slam shut. She turned and saw Hilli White, dressed for a shift at the inn, locking up the house then starting down the pathway to Main Street.

Hilli spotted Aava and waved with a large grin on her face. "Hello there!" she called, not breaking her stride.

Aava waved back. "Good afternoon!"

That was another aspect of Balam that felt unexpectedly nice: people were beginning to know her.

With that, she started down the stone steps to Ryckert's home. As she descended, she spied him sitting in his usual chair, watching the tide come in, just as she had been.

Ryckert was zoning out and therefore didn't notice her coming down the stairs; he only realized she was there when she called his name from a few feet away.

"Hey," he said, not getting up. "What brings you here?"

"Just wanted to see how you were doing and tell you some news," she said.

"Lemme grab you a chair," Ryckert said, rising. "Want somethin' to drink?"

"No, thank you. And a chair isn't necessary," she said, waving aside the suggestion. "I can only stay a minute. Lots to do today, as you can imagine." It was going to be long, hard work, but she was excited to complete the antidote and begin administering it to patients. Nothing in the world felt better than helping people, and it was unbelievably gratifying to finally do it.

Ryckert chuckled. "Probably more'n I can imagine, truthfully. And I'm doin' just fine, to answer your question. Tired, is all. Relaxing on the beach, like a retired man's supposed to do. Or so I hear."

"I'm jealous," she said. As good as it felt to get work done, she had to admit that more time to bask in the sunlight would be pretty spectacular.

"Don't be. Boring as shit."

They both laughed and watched the waves lap against the shore for a minute. Then Aava said, "I'll be leaving Balam soon."

Ryckert processed this a moment before responding. "How soon?" he grumbled with a low growl.

"A few days after the antidote is finished, probably. I'll administer it to those who need it, then explain the procedure to someone else—I don't know, maybe you or Mr. Reede or someone—so that they can make use of it if anyone else becomes sick after I'm gone. I expect the poison to be out of the yunesca's system soon, though. Or maybe I should say *hope* rather than *expect*."

"Where you goin' to?" Ryckert asked. She would've sworn his face contorted into a frown.

"Back to Allinor."

Ryckert nodded. "Just supposed to be a temporary gig anyway, I suppose." He slunk back into his chair, which sunk slightly deeper into the sand.

"It was," she said, "but I like it here, really. I don't find it as boring as you do," she grinned. "And that's my next bit of news: I intend to come back. Once I'm at Allinor, I'll get another white mage sent over in the meantime while I'm away."

"Ah, good," said Ryckert. "So you're sendin' me a new friend. Appreciated." His voice was still a low growl, but Aava had gotten to know him well enough to tell when he was making a joke.

"No one can replace me, and you know it," she said. "I'm going to send the most boring person I can find there. We both know you're a thrillseeker, you need that rush of excitement."

"Damn you," Ryckert grinned.

"I just need to take care of some business, then I'll be back."

The rocyan's ears perked up. "What kind of business?" he asked. "Anything I can help with?" He seemed eager to take on another job already. Retirement truly did not suit him.

But she shook her head. "No, I don't believe it's anything serious. It's just my brother. I'm not sure what's wrong, exactly, but he wrote saying that he needs my help with something. I don't expect it will take long, but I need to go back and help him however I can."

Ryckert nodded, looking out toward the ocean again.

They left it at that.

"I won't be leaving for another few days, though," she reiterated. "No need to be so down in the dumps," she teased.

"Ain't in no dumps," Ryckert grinned. "Things'll be considerably more boring without you around, though."

"Well, you're used to boring, right? You can handle it."

"Just hurry back," he said, smiling at her.

She smiled too. "I will," she promised.

- -

Ryckert had attended the town meeting that evening, smiling proudly as his friend explained to the townsfolk the process through which she was concocting the antidote that would cure their sickness. She also detailed how she, Ryckert, and Theo had discovered the source of the problem, and everybody was deeply intrigued by this turn of events, milling about and asking the trio a multitude of questions after the meeting concluded.

Once Ryckert finally succeeded in slipping away from the crowd and their endless inquiries, he made his way to the upper level of Balam and headed straight for the pub.

The place was empty, save for Ann Marie, who was planted behind the bar, awaiting customers.

"You damn near beat me here," she joked. "Couldn't get away from that meeting fast enough, huh?"

"Nope," he grunted, taking a seat in front of her. "Looks like you couldn't, either."

"Nah, but I've got a job to do," she said. "You're just drinkin'."

He grinned. "True's true."

"Whiskey?"

She didn't wait for a reply, scanning the impressive row of liquor bottles behind the bar and grabbing a glass bottle with a shiny golden label.

"This one's on me," she said, pouring a tall glass of the amber liquid. "It's the best we've got. My way of saying thanks for all you did."

"Thanks," Ryckert said, sincerely surprised and moved by her gratitude.

But Ann Marie laughed at him. "You can't thank someone for saying thanks!"

"Sorry," he apologized, then took a sip of the whiskey. It was incredibly smooth. Many steps above the shit he had back at his house. "This is great," he told her.

"I know. Don't tell Vince, by the way."

He chuckled and took another sip, then placed the glass on the wooden bar, sliding it back and forth between his hands. His long, sharp nails clinked against the glass.

"So," said Ann Marie. "Any plans tonight?"

Ryckert shrugged and thought about it. There was nothing on his plate at the moment. Nothing to occupy his time or attention.

And honestly, it didn't feel too bad. It had been a pretty stressful couple of weeks, after all.

"Nope," he answered. "Just gonna drink this whiskey, then maybe go back down to the beach. Just sit around. Relax."

"I've gotta work all night since Vince still isn't back from the Hunt," Ann Marie grumbled. "Your night sounds pretty nice."

Ryckert had to agree.

SEE WHAT GROWS

It was dark where they lived, but she gave him light.

The first time she'd seen him, she was unimpressed. He was making a big to-do, showing off, trying to demonstrate how strong he was, how beautiful, how *necessary*. A part of her was attracted to him almost immediately, but another part said—

(Wait. Let him come.)

It didn't take long.

He approached her later in the day. Now that his brothers were gone, no one left to be better than, he was softer. Not only in his sound but in his movement, in his gaze. He approached her with grace and with clarity and she wanted to reciprocate, but she waited another moment.

(Hello.)

(Hello.)

(My name is Eisbrea,) he told her.

He bowed, allowing himself a subtle glance at her face. But not subtle enough; she had noticed, much to his chagrin. Internally, he felt like a fool, and it would be many, many years before she would tell him that it was because of that moment that she'd decided to give him a chance.

They ate together that night.

She told him her name was Haibrea. She told him that she had four sisters and one brother, none of which she had seen in some time, and in fact she did not know their whereabouts. She did not tell him that her mother and father were long dead. She did not tell him that it was her own brother that had slain them.

Eisbrea listened with great interest, allowing her words and her cadence to wash over him. When they finished eating, they embarked on a short walk aboveground to seek water. She looked beautiful in the faint moonlight, but he suspected she would look beautiful no matter what.

He told her he had three brothers and no sisters, all of whom he was very close to. He told her that he had lived here all of his life and did not ever plan to leave; he was going to die here.

He said it with such gusto, she could not help but be amused by the notion. *(Why do you want to die here?)* she asked him.

(Because this is where I was born. This is my home.)

(But do you not wish to see more of the world? I have traveled but a short distance and already I have seen extraordinary sights I would never have witnessed, had I not left my home.)

But Eisbrea did not care a great deal for "extraordinary sights." What he appreciated was simply the familiar, and home was familiar. It was what he wanted, and that was that.

(If you say so,) Haibrea said. It was not an important matter. Not right now, anyway.

The two drank long into the night, and it was nearly dawn before they parted ways. Eisbrea was reluctant, but Haibrea told him she thought his brothers would be worried about him being gone for so long. He assured her she could not be farther from the truth, but that he would go back home anyway to ease her mind.

As they bade farewell, Eisbrea wanted to kiss her, but he resisted. There would be time for such things later, he hoped. Better not to sully what had been a nice night, a nice memory, if she did not actually feel the same way he did.

So he went home and told his brothers about his night. As expected, they had given little thought about where he had been, but they were excited by the prospect of him finding a mate.

He almost did not want to admit it, even to himself, but Eisbrea felt giddy. He had a good feeling about this. He hoped he would see Haibrea soon.

As he nestled into the pile of gathered autumn leaves that was his bed, needing some rest after being awake all night, he thought only of her. Her radiant pink light. He saw her in the moonlight, and he saw her next to him, and then he dreamed.

- -

When Haibrea was a child, she had lived far from where she would eventually meet Eisbrea and fall in love for the first time in her life.

She lived in a place far to the east of where she eventually wound up—still in Gillus, but nearly on the border of Herrilock. It was a place called Jule, and it was a place marked by death.

Though as a youngling, Haibrea did not know this, and so she enjoyed her years in Jule despite the uneasiness she felt at times. It was never caused by anything specific; just a general discomfort that plagued her. She wanted to ask her sisters about it, but was always too wary. Being the youngest, she did not want them to think she was afraid or immature. She wanted to appear brave, like them. Strong. Fearless.

In the end, the hate that filled Jule would seep into her brother and suffocate her entire family.

Haibrea had barely reached maturity when the day finally came. Her father had been the leader of their tribe in Jule, and her brother had wanted to change that. Feeling he would be better suited to lead the tribe, he challenged their father to a contest of strength, which had been elegantly declined.

(You cannot challenge your own father, my son,) he had been told. But her brother did not agree with the laws laid out in Jule, and so that night he took it upon himself to change things.

He murdered their father as he slept; he was old, defenseless, and never knew who or what had killed him. Their mother was horrified at the sight of her son covered in the blood of his father, and so he decided to silence her as well.

Of course, it did not take long for the news to spread about what had transpired. Jule erupted into chaos. Haibrea's brother declared himself the new leader now that his father was dead. Many in the township were afraid to oppose such a ruthless being, but some stood their ground and resisted.

That resistance resulted in more killings, more despair, more hate that consumed the entirety of Jule.

Haibrea had to leave.

She begged her sisters to join her. The sisters that remained, anyhow; her brother had killed their eldest sister the day before.

It had been the final straw. Haibrea knew she was not physically strong enough to stand up to her tyrannical brother, so she needed to leave Jule. Leave her home.

But her sisters could not go. One had already found her mate and would not leave him (and he would not be convinced leave Jule either; he was one of their brother's most trusted allies), while the other was too afraid to cross their brother.

(He will never find us,) Haibrea promised. *(We will be safe in the west. If we stay in Jule, we will never be safe. You know that. I know that you do, sister.)*

But nothing she had said was enough to shake the fear that gripped her poor sister. And so it broke her heart, but Haibrea had to leave her sisters behind and set out on her own across Gillus, in search of something new. In search of something better.

What she would find was Eisbrea.

- -

Their courtship was not a long, drawn-out process. Eisbrea continued to seek her out every day, suggesting they get some fresh air aboveground, spending as much daylight with her as possible and as much moonlight as she permitted.

After three weeks of this, he finally produced enough courage to kiss her. At first she was surprised, maybe even shocked, but she gave in without haste and melted into him. They spent that night together, and in the morning, she woke to find him still curled up, fast asleep, and she was content to merely watch him a while.

When Eisbrea told his brothers of this, they reacted accordingly. Haibrea had no one to tell, and so she kept the intoxicating news to herself. It made her stomach flutter when she thought of it. Thought of him. Thought of them. She found herself more and more wanting to see him, wanting to speak to him, wanting to do nothing more than be around him. She hoped (though, really, she already knew) that he felt the same way about her.

Two weeks later, they both knew that they would spend their lives together.

- -

At the beginning it was great, and at times it got hard, but never did they sour on each other. Theirs was a rare love.

She had even convinced him to leave his home and see some of the world with her. He had been resistant at first, as she knew he would be, but eventually he agreed. After several years of living in the same place, she had grown restless, and she was anxious to get moving again. She knew she would want to settle somewhere eventually, but for now they were young. And so why should they not explore?

They lived underneath the Carrious Plains, an enormous, barren patch of land where Eisbrea's brethren had lived for generations. He was the first in his family line to leave the Carrious Plains at all, so he was taken aback when he heard where Haibrea wanted to go.

(All the way to Atlua?) he clarified, sure he had misunderstood her. *(What in the world do you want to see in Atlua?)*

(That's the point!) she exclaimed. *(I have no idea. That's the exciting part!)* She had still not told him of the horrid events that had shaped her life in Jule and led her to him. She did not

tell him why she wanted to continue getting farther and farther away from that place.

Atlua was the kingdom to the northwest of Gillus. Eisbrea had heard of it; he had heard about how full of greenery and life it was, how full of exotic smells and sounds and creatures. It would be a long journey. Likely a difficult one, as well. Their species was naturally adept at navigating, so he and Haibrea would know which direction to go, but there was no way of knowing how many days it would take to reach Atlua. Or weeks. He shuddered at the thought of it potentially taking *years*.

But he looked at her, and he saw her beauty and felt her warmth, and so he told her, *(We will go to Atlua.)*

\- -

Luckily, their travels were not as treacherous as Eisbrea had anticipated.

In fact, those months were some of the best the two ever shared. Gillus was primarily flat, so travel was not demanding, and they got to see amazing things. Even Eisbrea had to admit it was so.

A river that neither Eisbrea nor Haibrea knew the name of ran through the kingdom, and they followed it for most of their journey up to Atlua. One night, they stopped to sleep at the foot of a gigantic stone waterwheel they had found along the river.

The gray rock was weathered and dull, but it continued to turn methodically with the river's current. There was a wooden lodge beside the impressive structure, but it was too small for either of them to fit inside. They attempted to see if anybody was living in it, if the waterwheel had a caretaker, but the area had seemingly been abandoned for some time.

Still, it was their favorite stop on the whole journey.

They slept outside, staring into the darkness but soothed by the sounds of the running water and the turning of the stone wheel.

That night was the only time Haibrea had been tempted to tell her mate of her past in Jule, but she stopped herself. She did not want to spoil the prettiest night of her life with such an ugly tale.

(I love you,) he told her, leaning up against the small lodge. She was curled against him, breathing in deep, relaxed.

(I love you too,) she said back.

Of course there was more to be said, but it could wait for another night. For now, they wanted to listen to the water. They wanted to listen to that stone wheel turn and wonder who had made it.

In the end, Haibrea would never tell Eisbrea about her brother.

- -

They spent decades together.

When they finally settled down, it was in a beautiful forest, filled with flora and fauna that Haibrea had never before dreamed of. Eisbrea, simple-minded as he was, was far less impressed, but all the same he was glad that she was happy.

(It's wonderful,) she said, embracing him. Their warmth filled each other.

(Yes,) he said. *(It is wonderful indeed.)*

They got to work building their home deep in the forest, sequestering themselves away from the rest of the world so that they could enjoy all the beauty of nature but not be bothered by the anger, the fear, the hatred of others.

They were tucked away somewhere in the greenery of Atlua, but even if they tried they could not tell you exactly where they had ended up. It was somewhere in the eastern part of the kingdom, near the ocean's edge. There was a sandy beach at the bottom of some cliffs, not far from where they slept, and in the quiet winter nights (when the bugs were all hidden away from the cold), they could hear waves lapping up on the shore, echoing through the entrance of the oceanside cave they called home.

One day, while Haibrea tended to her garden, Eisbrea came to her from somewhere off in the woods with a handful of shiny, grayish-red seeds.

(What are they?) she asked him.

(I am not sure the name,) he told her, *(but I found them washed up on the beach. I thought perhaps you might like to plant them and see what grows.)*

She kissed him tenderly and took the seeds. She then thanked him and began looking for a good place to plant her new seedlings. She found a spot at the top of the highest cliffside overlooking the beach, and she could not wait to see what sort of plant they would produce. Would they be round, full bushes filled with sweet berries? Or perhaps a great, towering tree? Time would tell.

Their home was greater than any Haibrea had ever imagined would be hers. At times, she still could not believe that she had left Jule and found Eisbrea and was living the life she wanted to live. She missed her sisters and her parents dearly, but she was truly happy here. She did not regret her life one bit.

And it was true that once, things had been dark, but he gave her light.

ABOUT THE AUTHOR

TRAVIS M. RIDDLE lives with his pooch in Austin, TX, where he studied Creative Writing at St. Edward's University. His work has been published in award-winning literary journal the Sorin Oak Review. He can be found online at www.travismriddle.com or on twitter @traviswanteat.

Made in the USA
Columbia, SC
28 May 2019